THE TOURNAMENT

ALSO BY REBECCA BARROW

And Don't Look Back
Bad Things Happen Here

THE TOURNAMENT

REBECCA BARROW

Margaret K. McElderry Books
New York   Amsterdam/Antwerp   London
Toronto   Sydney/Melbourne   New Delhi

MARGARET K. McELDERRY BOOKS
An imprint of Simon & Schuster Children's Publishing Division
1230 Avenue of the Americas, New York, New York 10020
For more than 100 years, Simon & Schuster has championed authors and the stories they create. By respecting the copyright of an author's intellectual property, you enable Simon & Schuster and the author to continue publishing exceptional books for years to come. We thank you for supporting the author's copyright by purchasing an authorized edition of this book.
No amount of this book may be reproduced or stored in any format, nor may it be uploaded to any website, database, language-learning model, or other repository, retrieval, or artificial intelligence system without express permission. All rights reserved. Inquiries may be directed to Simon & Schuster, 1230 Avenue of the Americas, New York, NY 10020 or permissions@simonandschuster.com.
This book is a work of fiction. Any references to historical events, real people, or real places are used fictitiously. Other names, characters, places, and events are products of the author's imagination, and any resemblance to actual events or places or persons, living or dead, is entirely coincidental.
Text © 2025 by Rebecca Barrow
Jacket illustration © 2025 by Justin Metz
Jacket design by Greg Stadnyk
All rights reserved, including the right of reproduction in whole or in part in any form.
MARGARET K. McELDERRY BOOKS is a trademark of Simon & Schuster, LLC.
For information about special discounts for bulk purchases, please contact Simon & Schuster Special Sales at 1-866-506-1949 or business@simonandschuster.com.
Simon & Schuster strongly believes in freedom of expression and stands against censorship in all its forms. For more information, visit BooksBelong.com.
The Simon & Schuster Speakers Bureau can bring authors to your live event. For more information or to book an event, contact the Simon & Schuster Speakers Bureau at 1-866-248-3049 or visit our website at www.simonspeakers.com.
Interior design by Irene Metaxatos
The text for this book was set in ITC Slimbach Std.
Manufactured in the United States of America
First Edition
10 9 8 7 6 5 4 3 2 1
CIP data for this book is available from the Library of Congress.
ISBN 9781665932301
ISBN 9781665932325 (ebook)

To Blair Waldorf and every great pair of shoes she wears in every single book. You would hate these girls!

THE TOURNAMENT

PART ONE

"This has been a day long in the making. Three years ago Miss Cecily Gardner and I, Liliane Bahnsen, first spoke of our dream to each other: to open a school for girls unlike any other institution already in existence. Now here we are, welcoming our very first group of students to the Gardner-Bahnsen School for Girls! We look forward to the adventure that surely awaits us all."

—**LILIANE BAHNSEN,**
cofounder of the Gardner-Bahnsen School for Girls,
Founders' Speech, September 2, 1912

1

MAX

WHEN MAX STEPS out of the car at the bottom of the school driveway, the itch that has been crawling under her skin for the past three months finally calms for a second. *Home,* she thinks, and inhales deep, like a smoker taking a delicious drag of nicotine. Back where she belongs.

The driver lifts her bags out of the trunk like they weigh nothing. They're matte black, scuffed on the corners a little. Everything Max owns is a little something or other: a little cracked, a little old, a little broken. She was embarrassed the first year she came here, even if she didn't admit it to herself, even though all the literature about the school oozed with the notion that the Gardner-Bahnsen School for Girls was *different* from most boarding schools. They took upward of ten, sometimes fifteen percent of their students on scholarship. Unspoken: *So don't worry about the girls with their two-thousand-dollar monogrammed luggage, because you won't be the only one who doesn't have it!*

Some snotty part of her brain admonishes her. *Don't act like this place* isn't *different*. After all, that was what convinced Max she needed to be here, made her fill in all the forms by herself and ace the interview and then tell her bewildered parents that all they had to do was sign the paperwork. Gardner promised difference and delivered. Gardner girls don't just take AP classes and SAT prep tests and play the elite-college-acceptance game. They do all that *and* learn to become sailors, proficient archers, swimmers with sinewy muscles. They learn how to build fires, construct shelters, survive off the land. Outsiders sometimes laugh at them, at the concept of these rich girls who could never want for anything learning how to survive with nothing. But Max has seen it close up, how those rich girls here always seem to have something else burning beneath their skin, so that they don't mind ruining their manicures digging in dirt, how they will knock each other to the ground and finish off with a foot to the chest, just to win. And then there are girls like Max, who come from not a lot at all, who want more than the empty futures stretching out before them, who come to Gardner for access and achievement and that feeling that comes after you've thrown up every single thing inside you. What they all have in common is that drive, a willingness to push themselves to the brink, all in pursuit of greatness.

Max slides her phone into the black nylon bag slung across her body as the driver slams the trunk and gets back in the car, already driving away before she even gets to her bags. *Four stars,* she thinks, a little irritated that he didn't offer to help get her bags off the gravel and onto the path at least. Then she rolls her eyes at herself. Spend enough time here, and at the eye-wateringly expensive camp she worked at all summer long, and some of those rich-bitch tendencies start to rub off. She'll give him five stars, like she always does, to prove to herself that she hasn't entirely forgotten where she comes from.

There are other cars lingering, letting other girls out, but nothing like the rush of last year. Final years, first years, and new girls get to move in a day before everybody else, so all Max can hear is the sniffles of the eleven-year-olds saying goodbye to their parents for the first time mixed with the all-knowing laughter and yells of her senior classmates.

Then one of those yells is aimed at her: "Wren! Wren, wait up!"

She looks up from her bags, her heart rate kicking up a notch. Brooke Nielsen is running over, long dark hair pushed back by sunglasses, and Max lets out a long, slow breath. It's only Brooke. Brooke, she can handle.

"You know I fucking hate when you call me that," Max says, finally hefting her bags onto the path.

"It's your name, isn't it?" Brooke says, the tease so over the top. "C'mon, *Wren Maxwell,* aren't you happy to see me?"

"Happy to see you go," Max says, but it's only Brooke, and she's no real threat to Max, never irritating enough to bring on Max's actual wrath. "Are you ready?"

Brooke grins, those perfect shiny white teeth gleaming. Max does not tell anyone else how she has a weird thing about teeth, smiles. Like, she could think a girl was the most irritating, boring bitch, but if she had the right kind of smile Max would suddenly think she was so hot. Brooke does *not* need to be told that she's hot; she's conceited enough as it is.

"Ready for our last year at this fucking place?" Brooke says.

"Jesus *Christ*, yeah."

"I was talking about the Cup," Max says, and Brooke groans.

"Already with that shit? We *just* got here." She takes the handle of one of Max's cases and starts rolling it along the path. Max doesn't have to ask where Brooke's bags are—already magicked up to her room, by some person invisible to Brooke and girls like her.

"Yeah, for our last year, which means it's time to find out which one of us will be the Tierney Cup champ."

"If I say it'll be you, will you shut the fuck up about it?"

"You're going to miss all this when we're gone," Max says, and then kicks at the back of Brooke's leg. "You'll miss *me*, at least."

"Please," Brooke says. "I can't wait until I don't have to hear about the Cup ever again, *or* see your bitchy little face every day." Then she laughs. "Instead I will just be seeing the various bitchy little faces of whatever new bitches I end up at college with."

"Say bitch again," Max says, and then they're walking in silence, concentrating on steering their way along the path that loops around the imposing school entrance and up to the dorms. Whenever she talks like that—plays along with her friends who talk about how much they can't wait to get to college—she feels bad for lying. But it's the kind of lie you have to tell to survive here, because even though they all agree that Gardner really *is* different, and even though they all defend their school to those outsiders who criticize it, it's still a little too much to admit that you love it. Too much for Max to admit that sometimes, she wishes she never had to leave this place.

Max loves the brick buildings that house their classrooms, the assembly hall with its rows of benches, the dining hall and its vaulted ceilings. She loves the dorms, how they hum with a particular kind of energy, how they go so quiet around exam time and then explode after. She loves the Washington air and the trees that cover so much of the 130-acre grounds, the ocean on one side of them and forest on the other. She loves the rabbits that plague the campus, fairy-tale charming until they're not, until they're targets for hunting practice. She loves that when they go into town, the locals always look at them in that certain way, as if they're different. She loves that she is so far away from home that the place almost ceases to exist to her.

When they reach the dorm blocks, they go straight for the last building in the U shape that frames the grassy courtyard where they lie out in hot weather. OXFORD is spelled out in white metal letters over the entrance, and a girl sitting on the steps stands as she sees them. "About fucking time," she says, launching herself first at Brooke, then at Max, dropping air kisses on their cheeks. "Safiya is already driving me insane."

"Hi, Isobel," Max says. "I'm not even going to ask how your summer was."

"Good, because it was terrible." Her accent has that lilt that Max has learned Isobel gets from spending time at the Delphy family's château in France. "You're so lucky you didn't have to spend the whole break with your parents."

Max smiles, the careful, practiced smile she reserves for these moments. Oh, so lucky to spend months running around after a bunch of spoiled brats who squealed if a fleck of dirt got on them and spoke to Max like she was their personal maid, instead of at the ancestral pile with zero responsibilities. "Yeah, camp was a blast. So fun! Totally not jealous of you at all!"

Isobel laughs, because nothing bothers her, but Brooke frowns. "Wait," she says, reaching over and tugging on one of Max's braids. "You didn't go to Nora's for the summer?"

Max winces—her braids are so fresh that they still hurt, her scalp throbbing dully. She brushes Brooke's hand away and shrugs. "No, I told you. I need to fill out my résumé a little more. Camp counselor looks good on college apps."

Brooke raises her eyebrows. "Oh, look at you, you little diligent student."

"Can we go up?" Isobel says, the slightest whine in her voice. "I want to finish unpacking before dinner."

Max is grateful for the out, not wanting Brooke to probe any further and figure out that camp is not the only reason Max didn't go to Nora's for the break. She realizes she's rubbing the charm on her necklace a moment too late, when Brooke has already looked back and noticed, too.

But Max doesn't give her time to say anything, instead grabbing her bags and dragging them up the steps. "Come on. I don't want to miss dinner, either."

2

NORA

NORA SITS ON the edge of her new bed, in her new room, in their new dorm. If she kicks her leg out, it touches nothing but air. Not like the last six years, where she could kick Max's bed from her own.

She looks around, taking in exactly how much more space there is when it's just one person. One desk, one closet, one bed. It's a privilege, of course; only final year girls get their own rooms, like a reward for putting in the work of sharing the space through all those earlier years. Before, Nora had been looking forward to this moment, the way all her friends had, too—Brooke saying she couldn't wait to not have Isobel's coat collection taking up most of the closet, Safiya saying she looked forward to going to sleep without her roommate, Vina Kashian, reciting Latin out loud. Max pinching her side and saying she was most excited about getting to decorate *her* way, not Nora's.

Now it feels wrong. Too empty, too alone.

Nora isn't stupid. She knows it's not about the room but about everything else. What happened at the end of last school year, before summer, the first summer she and Max had spent apart since they met at move-in six years ago. Sitting on the edge of another bed in a different room, no light but the string of pink bulbs that wrapped around her headboard and up to the curtain rod, spilling her stupid idiot feelings with all the confidence of a stupid idiot. *I don't want to just be your friend, Max. I feel something else. You feel it, too. I know. I know it. Max, I'm in love with—*

The door flies open and Nora jumps up, pressing a hand to her chest. "Jesus Christ," she says. "You scared the shit out of me."

"Language, please," her mom says. "Is that really what I'm paying all this money for them to teach you?"

She's smiling when she says it, so Nora knows it's nothing more than teasing, but she can't bring herself to play along, play the good little Nora part her mom expects. There's too much wrong with her to do it. And besides, she hasn't been that Nora for a long time, the prissy little insecure baby who had no idea who or what she was. Gardner toughened her up. Max toughened her up.

The problem is that maybe Max broke her again, too.

"Don't slam the door open and I won't have to say *shit*," Nora tells her mother, and then sits on the bed again.

Her mom tuts. "You're wrinkling the bedding—"

"It's a bed, Mom, people generally mess them up."

"Oh, aren't we smart today."

Nora rolls her eyes. "Mom, please."

"Nora—" Her mom stops short, and her fingers twist the eternity ring on her left hand around and around, the stones cool against her warm brown skin.

Nora watches her mom's action and wonders what there is to say to break the silence. All summer long it was like this, every little thing her mom did irritating her, every word Nora said to her mom seemingly the wrong thing. Once upon a time Nora would have run to her mom and recounted every last word of that fight she and Max had ended the year on, sobbing into her lap.

That was old Nora, though. Pre-Gardner Nora, and now she doesn't want to tell her mom anything, didn't even want her to come up to the dorm but lost that battle.

"Thank you for helping with my bags," Nora says now, and the cue is audible: *Now you can leave. Bye!*

There's a second where her mom's face crumples and it looks like she might be the one to burst into tears, but then it passes and she's back to the pristine demeanor that keeps her clients from ever having to make it to a courtroom, the formidable Alicia McQueen. "I can barely believe it," she says. "It feels like just yesterday we were bringing you here for the first time, and now it's your last year."

"I know," Nora says, and then, as a gesture of kindness, she stands and leans in, wrapping her arms around her mother's waist. "It won't be too long before I'm home again."

They stay like that for a minute, Nora tucked where she always fit on her mother, the tickle of her mom's always perfectly pressed dark hair against her cheek. The more time they spend apart, the more Nora sees the differences between them: her mom's skin deep brown and luminous, Nora's lighter and cool. Her mom's hair dyed to her natural dark, hiding any hint of gray, Nora's an ashy blond, inherited from her grandmother on her dad's side. Her mom wanting to pull Nora close, while Nora pushes her further and further away. Except in her weakest moments, like this. Those same moments in which she wonders about giving up on this place and running back home where she wouldn't have to deal with the fallout of her actions, where she could retreat into the cocoon of home and the old friends she always hated, who always hated her even though they pretended not to, the school they all go to that doesn't challenge anyone at all, not in any real way.

Nora lets herself sink a second longer, inhaling her mom's perfume, and then she puts an end to all of it. Straightens up, steel in her spine, resolve in her bones. "Thanks for helping," she says again. "I should start unpacking."

Her mom takes the cue this time and leaves, although she calls back to Nora along the corridor as she goes—"I'll text once I've landed" and "Make sure that coat gets to the dry cleaners" and "Tell Max I'm sorry I missed her."

Nora glances both ways along the corridor as her mom finally disappears from view, wondering if Max heard that. Is she already here, in her room, keeping hidden from Nora? Is she somewhere else on campus, putting off the inevitable? Is she still on the bus?

She steps back into her room and closes the door, the noise of other girls moving in suddenly quieted. It used to be that Nora knew where Max was, always, because usually she was right by her side—stealing blueberry muffins from the dining hall, writing papers in that fourth-floor window seat in the library, shooting at the archery range long after everyone else had left. Sleeping in their twin beds, breaths synced up and everything.

She leans against the door, forehead pressing against the wood, and closes her eyes. In the dark her fingers go to her necklace, sliding the pearl-and-gold *N* back and forth along the chain. "It's going to be okay," she whispers to herself, and then feels her lip curl into a snarl, teeth gritted. Oh, so fucking *sad* and *pathetic*. When did she become—revert to—the kind of girl who whispers positive little platitudes to herself? No, it is not going to be *okay*: this year is going to be the best, like every year is, because she is one of the best girls at the best school and she can take a beating. That's all it is, this shit between her and Max, a beating she needs to get over.

Before she can change her mind she flings the door wide open again, the universal signal to let others know they can come in. The door opposite opens, and there's Safiya, and they laugh at the same moment, each taken a little by surprise. Nora speaks first, pointing somewhere behind Safiya's shoulder. "Shut up," she says. "You're in there?"

"Can't get away from you if I tried, I guess," Safiya says, and then she crosses the tiny distance between their rooms and throws her bony arms around Nora's neck. "How was summer?"

"Boring as shit," Nora says as they release each other. "Yours?"

"My parents hired a college prep advisor for me," Safiya

says. "Very smart, very driven, and *very* hot. But she was in the city, which *so* sadly meant I had to leave the Hamptons and my darling parents to go back and you know, *prep* and shit."

"How horrible for you," Nora says. "And was she good at *prepping* you?"

"Oh, the best," Saf says, and she closes her eyes, a dreamy smile taking over her face.

Nora laughs. "Okay, back to earth, please."

"Let a girl reminisce, god." Safiya flips her shiny dark hair over her shoulder. "I'm starving. You think the dining hall's open yet? Maybe we should just go see."

Nora's already grabbing her phone. "Anything to not unpack," she says, and then they're walking and it happens too fast, not enough time or space to give Nora warning, as they turn the corner and almost crash right into her.

Max.

It's not like time slows or the moment stretches or any of that shit people say when they retell their heartbreak stories, mining them for tortured writings and lovestruck songs. It's two seconds, maybe three, as Nora and Max lock eyes. Nora has to try not to look away, show too much weakness. She doesn't want to take Max in, her braids half tied back off her face, her gray tank with no bra, her hands with bitten nails and that annoying thumb ring she insists on wearing. Nora doesn't want to take it in nor does she have to, because she's memorized every molecule of Max over the last six years.

It's two seconds, maybe three, and then Max looks past Nora and says, "Hey, Saf." And then she keeps on moving, like Nora wasn't even there, like she never even mattered at all.

Nora does not look back after her. She runs her tongue along the edge of her teeth, remembers how it feels to bite down. Fine. If this is how Max wants it, this is how it will be.

"Come on." Nora takes Safiya's hand, keeping her voice light. "We have places to be."

3

TEDDY

TEDDY'S MOTHER SWATS at her legs. "I told you to wear tights."

"It's ninety degrees. Why would I be wearing tights?" Teddy uncrosses her legs and smooths her skirt over her thighs. "Better?"

Her mother only sniffs.

Teddy tips her head back to stare at the ceiling. She blinks. Tiles that were once white, peppered with holes and a ring of rust-ish red about two inches over from where the pendant light hangs. It seems wildly out of place, a cheap, flimsy ceiling in this plush, quiet office, at this plush, quiet school. There's always something, she's learned: always a sign somewhere in these schools of the shit they'd rather keep hidden. At her last school it was the locker rooms, the damp smell of mold seeping out from behind the gunmetal lockers. At the one before that, it was the broken clock tower, hands permanently stuck at midnight. No matter how well these places present themselves, there's going to be something they can't quite hide, and Teddy always enjoys watching the way people pretend the problem doesn't exist.

Which, coincidentally, is what her parents are hoping to do right now, by sending her off to yet another boarding school.

"When Dr. Thompson asks you about Harbor—"

"I'll tell her I am deeply regretful of my actions and understand better now how my behavior impacts other people," Teddy says. "Is that okay? Is that good? You like that?"

Her mother sighs, and there's such a heaviness to it, such exhaustion, that Teddy thinks about feeling guilty. But then the feeling passes, and she resumes her normal state of irritation. It's not *her* fault she got kicked out of the last school, and the two before that. She just gets bored sometimes. She gets bored and then she gets tired, and then the trouble starts, and so she does whatever she has to to stave it all off. Sometimes that shit ends up getting her in a little trouble.

Okay, big trouble.

Her mother has pulled out a compact and is dabbing powder on her forehead, the shine disappearing with each little pat of the puff covered in deep brown powder. "I don't think you quite understand the severity of the situation you've put us all in," she says, and snaps the compact shut. "There is no *next time* this time. There is no other school that will take you when this one doesn't work out. This is *it*, Theodora."

"I get it! Best behavior," Teddy says, and she draws a cross over her heart, her long pink nails snagging on the silk of her camisole.

Her mother opens her mouth to reprimand her once more but then the door opens and a woman Teddy assumes is Dr. Thompson—the headmistress—sweeps in. "Hello, welcome!" she says as she takes her seat in the big, dark green leather chair behind the big, polished wood desk. "My apologies for keeping you waiting. Always so much going on during move-in."

"No apology necessary," Teddy's mother says, and shoots a look at Teddy like *Sit up straight*. Or maybe it says *I can't believe I ended up with you as a daughter*. Teddy has always wondered why they didn't stop after one, let themselves be satisfied with her older sister, Cassandra. Really, all of *this* is their fault for forcing Teddy into this world. She never asked to be alive.

Dr. Thompson jiggles the mouse and nods at something on the screen of her computer before looking at Teddy. "You must be Theodora." She holds her hands out wide. "Welcome to the Gardner-Bahnsen School for Girls. It's always such a pleasure to welcome another generation back to the school."

If this were her first time on the carousel, Teddy would say that this woman doesn't look like what she imagined a headmistress at an expensive boarding school to look like. This is school number four, though, and so she knows that actually Dr. Thompson falls right on the middle of the scale, not all military-inspired brusqueness but not new age, nurturing hippy teacher, either. She's white—duh, they're always white—and shorter than Teddy by probably seven inches, maybe more, wearing what Teddy assumes is an off-duty look of dark jeans and a long-sleeve white top with a tiny wreath of green and gold leaves embroidered on the left. *School insignia,*

Teddy already knows. Her eye catches on a black blazer hung on a hook beside a different door from the one Dr. Thompson came through. How long did this woman deliberate over her outfit today, Teddy wonders. Does she wear the same thing every move-in day? Does she look at herself in the mirror and go *yes, girl, you got it!* before she comes to the office each day? Teddy imagines the decor in her house: her prized doctorate pride of place, Ikea furniture painted *fun* and *different* colors, posters of little phrases some teacher with a side hustle sells, the kind you have to print yourself, dotted around her house in seashell-covered picture frames. *Just Be Cool. I'd Rather Be Introverting. Tomorrow Is a New Day. Keep Your Head, Heart, and Standards High.*

It's only when Teddy's mother clears her throat that Teddy realizes she's completely zoned out, and Dr. Thompson is waiting for her to say something. "Oh," Teddy says, spinning into action. "Oh, I'm so excited to be here. I'm really looking forward to getting to know everyone and making the most of the opportunity I've been given."

Dr. Thompson glances back at the screen and then at Teddy again, her neatly groomed eyebrows lifting slightly. "I should think so," she says. "If I were to put it kindly, I would say you don't have the . . . *cleanest* track record. And if I were to say it how I really think—you've abused your time at three other excellent schools and left more than a little chaos in your wake. So I hope you do know that this isn't just any old opportunity you've been given. It's a pretty big one, that a lot of people pulled a lot of strings for. You'd better keep that in mind as you make your way here."

Teddy straightens up in her seat. Maybe she didn't completely nail her appraisal of this woman. It's been a while since she had a good sparring partner. "I didn't ask anyone to pull any strings."

"Of course you didn't." Dr. Thompson lays her hands neatly on the desk. "I know you don't want to be here, but you *are* here. Because you have people who care about you, and care about your future, and don't want to see you go any further down the path it seems you're on. And because your grandmother was one of the finest students to walk these halls, we are willing to give you the chance to honor her legacy."

Legacy? *All she does is wear Chanel suits and plan dinners,* Teddy thinks. Her grandmother—her father's mother—used to be someone interesting, before she gave up her job in advertising decades ago to do what all the other women in their circle did, attending brunches and lunches and charity functions. Whenever they see her, there's always a second of hesitation before she says Teddy's name, and maybe it's that she hates the shortening of Theodora or maybe it's that she feels the exact same way as Teddy's mother: *I can't believe I ended up with you as a granddaughter.*

Teddy can sense her mother glaring at her and so she nods at Dr. Thompson. "I understand," she says, and she really does mean it. Everybody in her life seems to think that she fucks up for fun, when that couldn't be further from the truth. If Teddy could *not* fuck up, if she were physically capable of doing anything else, she would. Last night, in the hotel, she couldn't sleep and sometime around three a.m. she started to cry and then she did the thing she hates, the thing that

THE TOURNAMENT

happens when she hates herself. She started wishing. *I wish I were normal. I wish I didn't have this black hole inside me. I wish I could go to Gardner and meet some nice girls and be a nice girl and not cause trouble and not ruin anything and I could be a girl people like and I could be a better daughter and a good sister and just be anything but the person I really am.*

She has tried to explain the black hole many times, to her mother, her father, her sister, teachers, former friends, a school therapist once. *It's like it exists inside me and I'm standing on the edge of it, at the same time. This big, yawning, cavernous hole of nothing that wants to suck me in. Sometimes I'm far from the edge, sometimes I'm right there, like when you stand on a cliff looking out over the ocean, but there's no ocean underneath. It's just . . . nothing. A void. And I can't feel anything, because the black hole sucks it all away before I can even get to it, so the only chance I have is to make something bigger than the hole. So I pull the fire alarm, and I crash a car racing on the highway, and I cheat, and I steal, and I blow things up because if it's big enough, the explosion pulls me back from the edge.*

She says all that and then whoever she's said it to shakes their head like they're so sick of her bullshit, and then—here she is. Another school, another fresh start, another set of instructions to not fuck up this time, as if Teddy does it all for fun.

Her mother reaches over now and pats Teddy's knee. "I know you can be better," she says. "That's all we're asking."

Better. Best. Perfect.

Teddy fixes a rigid smile on her face. "I got it," she says. "I got it."

4

MAX

AT DINNER THERE'S this excited energy in the air—not because they're all back, but because now it's their chance to pick the tables they'll sit at for the rest of the year, taking the best ones for themselves before everyone else arrives tomorrow. *So stupid,* Max thinks, but charitably, because of course she's fucking excited, too.

The only thing putting a dampener on it is Nora, of course.

"Hurry *up*," Isobel calls back, leading their little line snaking through the tables. Isobel, then Nora, Safiya, Brooke, and Max bringing up the rear. She hadn't known what to say when Isobel had banged on her open door and told her they were all going down. Like—*Oh wait, is Nora going, too? Because if she's going, then I don't wanna go.* Of course she wasn't going to say *that*, but that meant she'd had no choice but to come out into the hall where they were all waiting, and there was

THE TOURNAMENT

Nora doing her sad little bird-with-a-broken-wing face again.

Isobel slides her tray onto the table that they all agreed last year was the absolute best spot in the room—full view of the main doors, so you could watch everyone coming in and out; far enough away from the food that you didn't have to sit with the smell of bad Brussels sprouts; close enough to the incongruous vending machine so Diet Coke was always accessible. "Victorious," she says, throwing her head back and laughing. Everything Isobel does, she does knowing that everybody is watching her, the star actress of their year.

"You put up a good fight," Max says, taking the seat across from Isobel. She looks up, catching Nora's gaze for only a second, before she looks at Safiya and says, "Saf, c'mon."

It's an interruption in their usual rhythm, a break in the pattern, Max knows, and it tips them all off-balance for a moment. She can see it ticking over in their brains: *But Max and Nora always sit together at dinner. So why would Max tell Saf to sit by her? What's going on?*

Max picks up her fork and begins stabbing at her salad. If she pretends everything is normal, then they will pretend everything is normal. That's at least one thing she's learned at Gardner: these girls with their good breeding and polished manners always let that take over when they're not sure what to do. So of course Safiya sits down beside her, and then the others sit and it's over, done.

Max shoves a forkful of arugula into her mouth and chews. This is not what she planned on. She had thought—hoped— that the summer apart would be enough. Nora could get over herself and whatever *feelings* she claimed to have, and by the time school started they would see each other again and Nora would apologize and Max would tell her to forget it and just let everything go back to normal. But then she actually saw Nora, and the look on her face told her instantly that she was wrong. So wounded, like Max had hurt her on purpose. Max was the one who should have been hurt, really. To find out your best friend isn't actually your best friend? To find out she's concocted some world in which everything you say has another meaning, and everything you do has to be examined, and to be told that actually, she's pretty sure *you* are in *love* with *her*, too? God, it was just really fucking stupid of Nora. All of it was so stupid and exactly the kind of shit that Max did not have time for. Nora was supposed to be the *one person* who knew that about Max, who understood that she had plans, and goals, and couldn't let herself be bogged down in the kind of drama their friends enjoyed. Nora was supposed to understand that Max did not have time to hear that her best friend was in love with her.

But she could have looked past all of it, if Nora had sucked it the fuck up and come back normal. That was why Max had been nervous about seeing her, although of course she would never have admitted that to anyone. But then she'd seen her in the corridor with Safiya, and it was clear to Max from the way Nora stopped and just . . . *stared,* that things were not going back to normal. Instead it seems like she wants to drag it out, and so that means things have to change. They can't sit together. They can't be Max-and-Nora anymore.

Brooke elbows Isobel. "New girl," she says, loud enough for all of them to hear, and their heads whip up from their plates, immediately searching.

Max is grateful for the distraction, and also not above curiosity. "Where?"

"Corner table," Brooke says, and they turn as one. Brooke is correct: the girl setting her stuff down at maybe the worst table, in the corner of the dining hall that the sun never quite hits, is indeed new, someone they've never seen before. Max takes in the girl's long dark hair, those seventies flicked-out bangs, the silky top with one thin strap falling off her bronzed brown shoulder. *Hot,* she thinks, and turns back to face the girls.

"Do we know anything?"

Isobel scrapes a spoon across the foil lid of the yogurt she eats at every single meal. "Hmm," she says, sucking on the spoon. "I did hear something about a legacy transfer."

"I heard she's in our year," Safiya says. "Which means something happened, because why else would you transfer senior year?"

"I heard she got kicked out of her last school for running a cheating ring," Brooke says. "Or, she cheated on her boyfriend in a sex ring. Something like that."

"Well, I heard she was in the woods with Goody Proctor," Nora says, her tone sour.

Max eyes her. Interesting, that this is the first thing she has to say for herself. "Sorry if this is *beneath* you," Max says, and she knows that Nora knows this exchange is not about the fucking new girl.

"It's just boring." Nora pushes her chair back noisily and stands up. "I'm so bored of all of this. I'm going back to my room."

She takes her tray and leaves without a look back. Brooke reaches across the table and pinches Max's arm. "Okay, what is going on with you two?"

Max watches as Nora tosses her uneaten dinner and marches out of the hall, her soft blond curls bouncing as she goes. "Nothing," Max says, shrugging. See how easy it was to say it? Nothing. Everything Nora told her last year? Nothing. Her supposed romantic feelings for Nora? Nothing.

She turns back and smiles. "She'll get over it."

5

TEDDY

IF THIS WERE her first time being the new girl at school, maybe Teddy would find the stares and the completely unsubtle whispering uncomfortable. But she knows how this goes: she's a little shiny toy for them, something to brighten the monotony of the usual back-to-school routines. They'll be assessing her, wondering what value she might bring them, coming up with their own versions of her past. Sometimes the stories are more exciting than the truth; sometimes they're so far off she can't help but laugh.

At dinner on the first night she goes down by herself, leaving her single room on the third floor of the senior dorm without waiting for the student guide who has been "assigned" to her. *Fuck that,* she thought when Dr. Thompson mentioned it in her office. *I don't need a babysitter.*

It does occur to her, briefly, as she's waiting in line for

some kind of tomato tart and roasted chicken, that perhaps ditching her guide is not the kind of thing a well-behaved, starting-over Teddy should do. But by then it's too late. So she sits by herself in the back and acts like she doesn't mind eating with a hundred eyes on her, and then when she's done eating she goes back to the dorm. Along the hall some girls have already hung little whiteboards with their names drawn on: Lauren and Sage to either side of her room, Josette and Freya across the way. She contemplates her own blank door and wonders if maybe she should do the same. She wonders if any of these girls will write her messages, if she could be friends with any of them. It's not that it's hard for her to make friends, just that it's hard to keep them, especially when they realize that by being in her orbit they're inevitably going to get in some kind of trouble.

Not this time, she reminds herself. She's going to be good this year. Find some new, different way to deal with the black hole.

So she goes into her room and spends the rest of the night unpacking, tucking her underwear into the drawers and hanging her new uniforms in the closet, before watching a movie on her laptop and passing out.

On Sunday she has to meet with Dr. Thompson's assistant to fill out paperwork and take a tour of the campus, one thing she can't get out of. It's move-in day for the rest of the school, and Teddy can hear the chaos of it wherever the assistant— Ms. Archibald—takes her. Screams outside the art building. Cheers over at the science block. Somebody crying, echoing all the way up to the top floor of the library. It's all she can focus on because everything else is boring. Like, no, she doesn't care about how old the buildings are, or how Gardner-Bahnsen prides itself on being different, or hearing the story of the two women who founded this school yet again. *It's a rich kid school for rich kids,* she thinks. She's been to many of them and no matter how different they say they are, how special, how historic, in the end they're all the same: a bunch of neurotic overachievers mixed with slackers whose parents' money makes up what their SAT scores lack, and a few scholarship kids thrown in for good measure.

On Monday she wakes up at an ungodly hour and dresses in her uniform for the first time: white polo, dark green plaid pleated skirt, gray cardigan with that Gardner insignia on the left chest shoved into her bag because it's still too hot. She's just sliding her feet into her new black satin ballet flats when there's a knock at the door. Teddy takes a deep breath. Really, two days is as long as she could get away with ignoring every other girl on this floor.

So she pastes a smile on her face and opens the door to a white girl with perfect red hair. "Hi," the girl says before Teddy can even open her mouth. "You're Theodora, right? I'm Freya. We're going down to assembly now if you wanna walk with us."

It's only then that Teddy notices the other two girls hovering somewhere behind the redhead. "Sure," Teddy says, the word leaving her mouth before she's actually decided. "Let me just get my bag."

The hall where assembly is held is in the school's main building ("erected in 1922, designed by founder Cecily Gardner's father, Thomas Nightingale Gardner!" Ms. Archibald had trilled). Teddy takes in the old brick, odd little faces carved out of stone sitting tucked between arches. The big doors are wide open and a steady stream of girls walk through, disappearing into the cavernous insides. The younger girls look like overgrown baby animals, not quite fitting right into their own bodies, uniforms either too small or too big, too short or too long, absolutely nothing in between. The older girls look bored already, well versed in Gardner's rituals and schedules. Teddy follows the girls from her dorm and as they hop up the steps to go in, a wave of exhaustion slaps into her. *Another year, another school. Another day.* It's the idea of all the performing she's going to have to do, putting on a nice smile and trying to convince everyone here that she can be one of them, when in reality she has no interest in that at all. It's the idea of all the performing, shoving down her instincts and the desire to hold her palm over a Bunsen burner flame for a little too long, or pull a wad of gum out of her mouth and shove it into the nearest person's hair, or take off all her clothes and throw herself into the frigid water that borders the school grounds. She can feel the promise she made her mother fading deep into the background already, the promises she's made herself—not ten seconds ago, even—turning to ash. This is the *other* problem. She can say all the right things and maybe even act right for a few days but then that thing inside her that sends her clawing for survival comes screaming awake and here she is. Bored, ready to snap.

"Theodora?"

It takes Teddy half a second longer than it should to realize she is being called. She looks up and finds Freya and the other two girls whose names she doesn't yet know waiting expectantly by the doors. "I'm coming," she says, her fingers finding a loose thread on the waist of her skirt and beginning to pull at it. "Also, it's Teddy. Not Theodora."

Freya nods, her smile unchanging. "Got it," she says. "Come on, we don't want to be late."

But once they're inside, after they've walked through the corridor with black-and-white checkered tile echoing with a hundred footsteps and are about to step into the actual assembly hall, Teddy feels a tug on her arm. She whips around, about ready to bite a head off, but then she sees Ms. Archibald and tucks her teeth away. "Is something wrong?" Teddy says right away, conscious that Freya and the others have stopped to watch. "Are we late or something?"

"Oh no," Ms. Archibald says, and waves the others off. "We just need you up front, not with the other final years. Carry on, girls," she says, to Freya's back. "You, come with me."

Teddy's mouth opens but nothing comes out, and instead she lets herself be shepherded inside the hall but not to the rows in the back where Freya and what she assumes is the rest of the senior class is sitting, but to a row of chairs placed along the wall, facing into the crowd of girls. There are a handful of other girls sitting there and then Ms. Archibald says, "Here you go. Take a seat here and Dr. Thompson will call you up when it's time to be introduced!"

Teddy blinks. "Introduced?" she repeats, but the headmistress's assistant is already gone, taking her place on the low stage, leaving Teddy behind.

And because she doesn't know what else to do, she sits. *Introduced?* As in, paraded onto the stage with what she now assumes are the other transfer students, in front of the entire school?

"Fucking Gardner," she says under her breath, and folds her arms across her chest, and waits.

It's mostly a very boring, very standard welcome assembly. Dr. Thompson stands behind a lectern and tells everyone that it's going to be a great year, that they have a new dinner menu in the dining hall, and that Family Weekend is in five weeks. She drones on some more and Teddy stops listening, gazing around the assembly hall instead. There are something like two hundred girls at Gardner, and on paper it doesn't seem like a lot but in their uniformed rows, it looks to Teddy like there could be a thousand of them. She squints toward the back, half-heartedly trying to locate Freya—not like she cares, but she at least could pretend to. Her gaze moves across the row, noting Freya's red hair and then moving past her, another oblivious face, another oblivious girl—

But then she locks eyes with someone. It's only a second, the girl with braids and a tight look on her face quickly averting her gaze. Teddy smirks. Won't that be fun for her, later? After assembly, she can tell all her little friends that she made *eye contact* with the new girl, *wow!*

Teddy sighs and is about to turn back to Dr. Thompson when, for the first time since she got to this school, she sees something worthy of her attention.

Two seats down from the girl with the pinched face, there's another girl. She's chewing her bottom lip and staring at the stage under heavy lids. These soft, ashy-blond coils circle her face, turning her angelic. Cherubic. Except the length of her skirt is anything but pure, revealing a large expanse of golden brown dimpled thigh.

Teddy shifts in her seat, crossing her own legs. She only really finds fat girls hot, especially in short, short skirts. She closes her eyes and imagines this girl blowing candy-colored bubbles, her tongue flicking baby-blue gum.

She opens her eyes and watches as the girl leans over and whispers something to her neighbor, both of them trying and failing to keep grins off their faces.

Somewhere inside her Teddy feels the black hole contract just a little, a sense of balance a little closer in reach. *A girl,* she thinks. *No—not a girl. That girl. I feel like a chase.*

Up onstage Dr. Thompson clears her throat. Teddy does look back now, remembering suddenly that she's supposed to go up there, and thinking this is the moment. But instead of saying something about welcoming new students, Dr. Thompson says, "Now. It's time to talk about . . ." And she pauses, her fingers tightening on the lectern and a knowing smile on her face. "The Tierney Cup."

6

NORA

THEIR WHOLE SECTION bursts into whispers as soon as Dr. Thompson mentions the Cup.

Nora has to force herself not to look for Max, exchange the same excited glances they have every other year before this, when they got to this same part of the welcome assembly. Every year Dr. Thompson introduces the Cup again, and every year before now Nora and Max have had to sit back and listen and wait, because it wasn't their time yet. Wasn't Max's time, really—she was the one more obsessed, always talking about when they would be final years and finally she would be eligible to compete.

Now, Nora realizes, she herself won't be any kind of part of it. Even if Max makes it in, Nora won't be her cheerleader anymore.

Dr. Thompson holds her hands up, and instantly the

whispers cease. "Thank you," she says, smiling out at them like she's just as excited, like she revels in the power the Cup brings her. "For our incoming students and anyone who may need a reminder: the Tierney Cup is a tournament, reserved for those of you in your final year here at Gardner-Bahnsen. The Cup is named for one of our brightest stars, Maeve Tierney, who captained Gardner's diving team to back-to-back titles in 1947 and went on to earn three world titles and two Olympic medals, as well as become a pioneering physicist. Maeve embodied precisely what it means to be a Gardner girl, adhering to the founding principles that this school was built on: to be academically excellent, yes, but also to possess great strength, ingenuity, survival skills, and determination. The tournament both challenges students to demonstrate their own capabilities and honors the guiding values that separate our school from the rest."

At this point some girls start to applaud, and somewhere down front someone whistles. Nora only nods. She knows this speech by heart, knows each and every one of Maeve Tierney's accomplishments. She knows exactly what Dr. Thompson will say next: *Entry is restricted to final year students only. There are seven competitor positions; those of you who wish to sign up may simply write your name on the sheet outside my office. On the rare chance that only seven students sign up, they will all be entered, but as always we expect there to be more aspiring competitors than spots, so names will be drawn at random after the sign-up period is finished. You have until Thursday to sign up. Names will be drawn on Friday morning and announced during a special assembly.*

Safiya leans over as Dr. Thompson pauses, like she's letting the weight of what she's said sink in. "And then you can all start eating each other alive," Saf whispers.

Nora swats at her. "It's not that bad." Well. Not *always* that bad. There was that girl in their first year who shattered her collarbone and had to leave school to recover. But it was never *proven* that her climbing rope had been cut. And then there was that incident a few years before Nora had arrived at Gardner, when the front-runner to win had ended up almost being shot with an arrow. Key world: *almost.*

"The tournament will begin in late October. That's six weeks away," Dr. Thompson is saying now. "For those of you who will be competing, those intervening weeks are best used for training. For everybody else . . ." She holds her hands up again. "Enjoy the show! Now . . ."

Nora tunes out again. The Cup, the Cup. It has loomed so large in their lives ever since she came to Gardner. It was partly why she had even chosen Gardner out of the boarding schools her parents had picked out for her—this was not just a normal, prissy school, but one that taught girls a whole raft of other shit. Archery, sailing, open water swimming, diving, climbing, how to build a fucking fire and keep yourself alive for three days out in the wilderness. It was a world away from the school she would have gone to if she stayed home, with all the other kids she'd already gone through elementary with, who Nora had never felt comfortable around. She was always too much *something* for them—too serious, too smart, too fat. Always a second too slow in laughing at their jokes, always too uncertain and self-conscious to feel at ease during sleepovers or pool parties.

THE TOURNAMENT

Faced with the prospect of a further seven years feeling the exact same way around the exact same people, Nora had been somewhat relieved when her parents started talking about boarding school. And then she'd been sitting in her brand-new dorm room when her brand-new roommate walked in. Nora McQueen and Wren Maxwell, nestled next to each other alphabetically and now physically, for the rest of their time at Gardner. Max had shown up all by herself, no parents carrying her bags or fussing over her as she unpacked on her side and made herself at home. Nora had looked at Max with envy and wished she were the kind of girl who could do shit alone. And then, with Max's help, she had become that girl. Max didn't find her too much. They were the exact same level of serious, like the rest of their classmates, like Safiya and Isobel and the others who they made friends with early on. Back home Nora had always been the biggest girl in her dance and gymnastics classes, feeling like a giant next to her skinny little classmates flinging themselves around. At Gardner she was still bigger than most of the other girls but suddenly it didn't matter so much, because here they had to climb and swim out beyond the break and other things that asked for little delicateness and far more strength and bone-deep grit. Here she stood out for good reasons, for reasons of her own making: winning the interschool archery trophy in her third year, being part of the robotics team in fourth year, having one of her narrative nonfiction pieces accepted into a Seattle journal last year. She had written about the complications of coming out, because she knew people liked to read that sort of shit even though her real feelings on coming out were far more fraught than most people had the capacity for and she had, in reality, chosen not to formally sit her parents down and tell them she was a lesbian, because she had always known and why couldn't they always know it, then, too?

She has to work so hard to stop from turning to seek Max out. Max had proofread that piece for her and even given it praise, a half-raised brow and a single, astute comment: "They're going to eat it up." That, in Max terms, was the highest praise and Nora had pretended it didn't make her stomach flip, because that was when she was still ignoring how her feelings for Max had changed. Now, of course, they can't ignore anything anymore, and Nora wonders who will be the one cheering Max on during the Cup.

If she gets in.

Safiya leans over again. "I'm going to put my name down," she whispers.

Nora blinks. "For the Cup?" It comes out loud in her surprise, and gains her a disapproving look from Mr. Gordon, the ancient English teacher they all secretly love because of his stories about being gay in New York in the eighties. She tucks her head and lowers her voice. "You want to compete?"

"I wanna *win*," Safiya whispers ferociously, and then they both laugh, hands pressed over their mouths. "Seriously, though," Saf whispers again. "It would just look so good on my résumé, you know?"

Nora nods, even though she knows it's a bullshit reason. The Tierney Cup doesn't have much impact on college acceptances, not with how late it comes in their school career. That's part of why they like it—it's not about college apps, or scholarships, or adding yet another string to an already overloaded bow. It's about proving you, out of all the girls you've spent the last six years with, are the best. The strongest. The most willing to bare her teeth.

She tunes back in to what's happening up front. Dr. Thompson says something about welcoming new transfer students and then a line of scared faces in staticky-new uniforms tiptoe tentatively onstage. It's half a dozen younger girls and Nora is about to switch to staring at her cuticles when the last girl saunters up. It's the senior, the one they saw at dinner the other night, before Nora stormed out to go back to the dorm and eat ramen made with her contraband electric kettle.

Dr. Thompson reads out each girl's name and the corresponding frightened rabbit gives a brief wave and smile before scurrying back to the shadows. *They'll get over that soon enough,* Nora thinks. And then the senior steps forward and even from this distance Nora sees how there is absolutely no fear in her eyes. "And lastly," Dr. Thompson says, "joining our senior class, Theodora Swanson."

Nora waits for this girl to wave and smile like all the others, but instead she takes another step forward and leans over the lectern, lips close to the tiny microphone there. "Teddy," the girl says. "You can call me Teddy," and then she slides away like she's entirely liquid, unreal.

Dr. Thompson sniffs and fusses with the microphone, as if making a point. "Teddy Swanson," she says, and claps. "Wonderful! I think that officially brings us to the end of our first assembly of the year. Let's finish with the school song."

The hall fills first with the sound of shuffling feet as

everybody stands, and then the voices singing the old school song that is only ever sung three times a year: at this first assembly, at the last one, and at graduation.

Nora's mouth moves along with the words without having to think. *Honorable and true . . . for hope and glory born . . .* whatever. Instead, she wonders what Teddy Swanson's real story is—not the bullshit her friends had been talking about at dinner, or whatever other rumors are surely flying around already, or even the whispers she can hear bubbling beneath the song.

When she looks up at the stage, a jolt runs through her, because Teddy Swanson is looking right at her.

Teddy smiles.

Nora's voice falters.

Trouble.

7

MAX

MAX SWALLOWS HARD as the song comes to its end and Dr. Thompson dismisses them.

The Cup, the Cup, the Cup. It thrums in her head and she can't remember the last time she felt this electric. If she's fast, she can get to Dr. Thompson's office and be the first person to write their name on the list, and then get over to her first class of the day without getting in trouble for being late. Her hand goes to the pocket of her black trousers, which she always chooses over the pleated little skirt her friends prefer and wears cuffed, an inch of ankle showing and then her black loafers. She did wear the skirt for a little while, when she first got to Gardner and was trying to fit in, before she realized everyone already knew everything about her and there was no need to act like she was some ultrafemme fantasy girl.

"Hey!"

A pair of hands land heavily on her shoulders and Max realizes there is no pen in her pocket. She turns to find Isobel right there, her lips shiny with the gloss that replaces her usual red lipstick during term time. "What?" Max snaps, and then closes her eyes. *Relax, bitch. The sign-up sheet isn't going anywhere.*

"You're so mean to me," Isobel says, hooking her arm through Max's. "Don't you want to walk to math with me?"

Max opens her eyes and gives Isobel an actual, non-bitch smile. "You have math first period?" Max says. "Me too."

Isobel makes a face. "Of course you do. That's why we're walking together. Did you lose brain cells over the summer?" And then, like she's slick: "So how come you didn't go to Nora's for break?"

Max tries to pull her arm free from Isobel, but Isobel clings on stubbornly and steers them outside, down the steps and on the path that leads to the science building, misleading in its name. "I got a job," she says, wishing Isobel would let it drop but knowing of course she won't. "I made good money and I can put it on my applications. That's it."

"That is so *not* it," Isobel says. "You basically blanked her all weekend and at dinner on Saturday you were both being assholes."

"I know it might shock you, but Nora *can* be an asshole." There is sweat collecting at the base of her spine already and she wonders when the heat is going to drop. It's never usually this hot when they return to school and Max feels a little out of sorts. "We don't have to be nice to each other all the time."

"You're so fucking annoying." Isobel lets go of Max but stops in the middle of the path, earning a slew of irritated glances. "At least tell me whether it's the kind of fight where I should be picking sides or not."

Max rolls her eyes. "There are no sides," she says, and then, when Isobel starts to frown like she doesn't believe a word Max is saying, "Honest to god. No sides, Is." And that part is true, really. It's not like Nora did anything to the others. It's not like she can say *yeah, Nora told me she had feelings for me and then got mad when I told her I didn't feel the same so I think we should all stop talking to her*. Like, they're not *children*. This is a problem between—well, between Nora and herself, really, Max thinks. Nora's the one who broke things, and so it's up to her to put them back together. When she's had enough of sulking and sucks it up, maybe things can go back to the way they were. Ideally by Christmas, because last year the McQueens were talking about spending the holiday in Australia and Mr. McQueen had said they'd need to get Max her own surfboard, and she's gone on trips with them before but this would be the other side of the *world*, a fact Max has not stopped thinking about since then. But of course, Nora will have to get over herself first. Until then, Max has her own shit to be dealing with.

Like entering and winning the Tierney Cup.

Isobel narrows her eyes and jabs a finger in Max's direction, theatrical as always. "Fine. I'm going to believe you."

"Praise the lord," Max says, pressing her palms together. "So now can we go to class?"

She starts walking and Isobel falls in step, quickly switching topics to how she's dreading third period Ancient History but can't wait for last period Studio Art. Max pretends to listen but is really planning her next opportunity to get to the sign-up sheet. It's okay if she's not the first name, because she's going to be the only name that matters at the end. They'll engrave it on a plaque and nail it on the wall with every other winner, and in fifty years it'll still be there, girls who haven't even been born yet running their fingers across the grooves and vowing to be just like Wren Maxwell, the girl who came from nothing and became everything.

She doesn't manage to get away until lunch rolls around, and then Max books it from her physics class back across campus and into the main building, up the stairs and along the quiet corridor where Dr. Thompson's office sits. The board outside is mostly clear; by the end of the year it'll be overwhelmed with flyers for musical auditions, reminders to return library books before graduation, and a million other things. Right now, though, the Cup sign-up sheet is pinned right in the center, and Max swallows as she writes her name on the fourth line down.

"So . . . there it is," she says to herself, because she feels like she should mark the moment somehow, because it feels underwhelming in a way she wasn't expecting. Instead of thinking about that too much she looks at the names above hers. *Margaret Sim. Florence Wright. Safiya Haddad.*

Max is not surprised to see Safiya's name there. She's exactly the kind of girl to win the Cup—well bred, consistently near the top of all her classes, and completely aware of what being a Gardner girl means. She'll even be a gracious loser, Max knows, and allows herself a small smile. Not that she *wants* to beat Saf, but—fuck it, no, she does. She wants to crush Saf the way she's going to crush everyone else. Her gaze flicks over the names again. *Especially the way I'm going to crush Margaret Sim, if she makes it in.* Margaret is a vegetarian; one of the challenges involves skinning and preparing a rabbit. Max licks her lips. Yeah, she'll take them all down.

She goes down to lunch and finds the others sitting at their table, Nora on the end. Good. Max fills a plate with rice, grilled chicken, and broccoli that she only likes because it's covered in a honey-chili dressing. They eat quickly and it's better than dinner the other day: instead of ignoring everyone, Nora only ignores Max, and that makes it so much easier for Max, actually, because it makes Nora look stupid.

After lunch she has English Lit, and she keeps her mouth shut when Nora starts walking in the same direction. It's not until they're standing outside the room, waiting for Mr. Gordon to let them in, that Nora clears her throat and says, "Did you sign up?"

It's a stupid question, and Max knows she only said it as a reminder: *I know everything about you.* As if that makes what she did okay, as if them being two parts of a whole the last six years meant that Max owed her love like that.

So Max nods, once. "I signed up," she says, and Nora looks like she might say something else but then the door swings open and Mr. Gordon ushers them inside.

The tables are arranged in a semicircle, and Max takes a seat on the curve, facing one of the large windows. In winter she likes to be able to see daylight, then watch the trees beginning to turn to spring. She takes out her copy of their first assigned text, then opens her notebook and runs a finger down the first page, the neat lines as yet unblemished by her cramped scrawl. She pretends not to notice Nora taking the seat two chairs down.

Mr. Gordon glances up at the clock and closes the classroom door. There is no bell at Gardner—too pedestrian, Max always thinks. Instead everyone is just supposed to keep close track of what time it is and where they're supposed to be, and if you're running late you better actually *run*, because once a teacher closes the door, you are not getting into class. Only once has Max been shut out; she had to walk down to the library and give herself over to the librarian for her appropriate punishment, which that day was recovering books in sticky, shiny plastic. And then there was the four-page essay she had to write on the topics they had covered in class, to make up for her absence. Max has not been late since then.

When Mr. Gordon slides his little round glasses onto his face, any chatter dies down. "Good afternoon," he says, scanning the faces before him. Of course Gardner classes are small, so there are only ten students for Mr. Gordon to remember. "Well, I don't see anybody I don't already know, so I think that means we can skip the preamble. You have all been in my class before; you all know the drill." He pauses and folds his arms, wrinkling his sky-blue button-down. "But just in case, somebody give us all a quick refresh."

Max has her hand in the air first, but where at the high school back home it would have earned her eye rolls or snide comments or perhaps a scrunched-up paper ball bounced off her skull, here no one bats an eye. Mr. Gordon nods at her.

"Keep up with assigned reading, because we don't recap," she starts. "Copies of each text can be found online, or in the library if there's no digital copy. Everybody is expected to contribute in every class. And—"

The door crashes open and there, looking only the slightest bit flustered, stands the new girl. Theodora Swanson. *Teddy,* Max says snidely in her head, less because of the nickname itself and more because of the way Teddy said it this morning in assembly—like it was nothing, like she had to let them all know she's not some stuffy bitch named Theodora. It's completely different from Max and her own nickname, because hers has meaning. She'd decided halfway through the bus ride up her first year that she wasn't going to be Wren anymore. Wren was the name for a delicate daughter doll, the name given to her by a mother who thought she was going to get a sweet angel to dress up and parade around. Max had never been that, was never going to be that, so it made sense to *not* be Wren anymore. So when Nora walked into their dorm room, she'd said, "Call me Max. Everybody does." And saying it aloud somehow made it true, because by the end of her second week everybody—teachers included—knew her as Max. And it became armor, became a weapon. Max could be as cutthroat as she'd always desired, and no one would question it, and she could shut Wren inside a box and lock it up and never have to see that girl again. *What has* she *ever needed armor for,* Max thinks as she eyes Teddy.

"Sorry," Teddy says now, her voice too loud. "I got lost. It's my first day."

Mr. Gordon frowns and underneath the table, Max digs

her nails into her thigh. Getting to see someone kicked out of class on the very first day of final year? She couldn't ask for anything better.

"I can't stand lateness," Mr. Gordon says, and Max catches the eye of Josette Lewin sitting opposite her. Josette slides a finger across her throat and sticks her tongue out; Max stifles a laugh, hiding her mouth behind her hand. But then Mr. Gordon sighs and points to an empty chair. "As you are a new student, I will make a rare exception. But please note, Ms. Swanson, that in future, if you arrive to my classroom and the door is closed, you may not enter. Understood?"

"Absolutely understood," Teddy says, and a hand flutters toward her chest. *What, is she gonna fucking swear allegiance or something?* "Won't happen again."

And then she takes her seat, and Max shakes her head. It's not that she hates everyone on sight, or even every rich person she meets—she's, like, totally friends with rich girls. Brooke and Saf are loaded. Isobel's family has a castle in France. Nora's house could fit Max's parents' house probably thirty times over, and that's not including the grounds. It's more that she's defensive. This is their last year and the last thing they need is some new girl who doesn't get Gardner coming in. This is their last year, their one and only chance to compete in the Cup, and they don't need some random bitch trying to muscle in. Not least a random bitch who's getting special treatment.

Max looks at Teddy, who takes out a thin notebook and nothing else. If she and Nora were talking properly, she knows what Nora would say: *You're such a fucking hypocrite.*

THE TOURNAMENT

You always say you hate how people judge you on sight and then you do the same to everybody else. Some of us can't help where we came from, you know. As if coming from money is this awful cross to bear. Max only judges because she has to, because people do it to her first. Over the years she has gotten pretty good at approximating wealth, at least at first glance: her shoes are decent quality knockoffs; she spends more than she should on skin products because rich girls get facials; she has learned the language and the way to carry herself. But it doesn't compare to the real thing, not up close, not under scrutiny. Teddy's hair is long and silky straight, half pinned up with long bangs that catch in her eyelashes, and it moves like water when she does. Human hair, no synthetic for her. Her bag is the kind of battered that speaks of disregard for its value, because if this one gets ruined, it doesn't matter—a replacement is no trouble. She's wearing the shoes Isobel wanted last year, and pearl drop earrings. Max's fingers go to her necklace, the *M* that matches Nora's *N*. Costume jewelry, because Nora knew that Max would not accept a gift of real jewelry.

She should probably take it off, but that feels like a declaration of something that Max isn't sure she wants to make.

Not yet.

Up front Mr. Gordon picks up his copy of the book they were assigned. "British First World War literature," he says. "That's what we'll be deep in for the next few months. So, initial thoughts on this one." He taps a finger against his chin and then points directly at Teddy. "Our latecomer. What do you have to say?"

Teddy shrugs. "I—I didn't get to it yet," she says. "I only got the reading list last—"

"Stop talking," Mr. Gordon says, and there's the icy tone Max had been waiting for. "In fact, do not speak for the rest of class. Until you have properly prepared, the rest of us do not need to hear from you."

Teddy's mouth drops open. "But—"

Mr. Gordon brings his fingers together in midair, silencing her. "If there is anything I hate more than lateness, it is laziness. Do better, Ms. Swanson."

This time Max does not bother to hide her grin.

At the end of a long first day, Max is mentally worn out—there is no such thing as a gentle return at this school, no easing-back-into-it. By the time she gets back to the dorm, there is a large part of her that wants to crawl into bed and stay there until dinner. But that won't help her with the Cup, and besides, she's been itching to get back to the archery range since she stepped foot back on campus. For most Gardner girls, it's mandatory to sign up for two after-school Activities—they send out the list when you first get in, and you pick from the choices: Sailing, Riding, Swimming, Diving, Climbing, Rowing, Archery, Fencing, Athletics, Soccer, Field Hockey, and Advanced Musical Performance. Her first year Max had picked Swimming, because that was at least one thing she already knew how to do, and Archery, because she thought it seemed like the kind of skill an interesting person might possess. In final year, they only have to pick one, so that they still have access to supervision and training, but outside of that they are expected to use their new-found free time to work on things by themselves. It's both a privilege and a challenge, according to Ms. Cara, the senior class leader and houseparent. The idea, Max has gathered, is that by this time in their schooling, they should have found a lane to thrive in, and the relaxing of boundaries is supposed to test whether they can continue to achieve greatness through self-guided means, or whether they'll flail and bomb out. This year she has chosen Archery as her Activity again, because even though she is the best in their class and could go without coaching, she doesn't want to. *You can't get better if no one's telling you how you went wrong,* her logic goes. And she doesn't want to give anybody the opportunity to forget that she's the best, either.

Max changes out of her uniform and into shorts, a sports bra, and an old uniform PE shirt that she cut the sleeves off. Then she takes her bow in its case out from the closet where she's stored it and fingers the zip. Not everyone in Archery at school has their own bow. Not everyone *needs* their own bow. Max doesn't need it, but she likes it, likes how it makes her feel. How it felt to buy something good with her own money, not having to ask anything of anyone. She lets her thumb run over the nylon, concealing the power within.

She's putting her sneakers on when her phone begins to vibrate, and doesn't stop. Max closes her eyes. That usually only means one thing.

She picks up her phone. *MOM* flashes on screen. "Fuck off," she says under her breath, and she could so easily ignore it, shove her phone in her shorts pocket and carry on to the range.

She slides a finger across the screen to answer and knows, *knows,* that she is weak. "Hi."

"Wren?" her mom answers, her voice lilting upward. "Can you hear me? Hello?"

Max sits down heavily on the edge of her bed. "Yes, Mom, I can hear you."

"Okay, I was just checking," her mom says, and she sounds distant, uncertain of what to say, how to fill the space. "Well . . . how is camp going?"

Max bites the inside of her cheek. Deep breath in, slow breath out. "Camp is over," she says. "I'm at school."

"Oh, of course, of course," her mom says, as if that will make Max believe that she remembered her oldest kid's schedule, as if Max doesn't know she's far more concerned with getting the girls to cheerleading and ballet and mini-diva-dancercise or whatever the fuck else they're in. "Wow. Your last year. Are you excited?"

Max shrugs like her mom can see and doesn't say anything. Now that she's in it, she's really not sure why she didn't let the call go to voicemail. She hasn't seen her parents since last winter break, and she doesn't call home. If she didn't pick up when her mom called, it would be as if the connection didn't even exist. Fully severed. But it won't be, not really, until Max turns eighteen and that won't happen until April, so maybe that's why. She needs her mom to sign forms, still, and all that shit. Yeah. That's why she picks up.

"How are your friends? How's Nora?"

"Fine," Max says. "Everyone's fine. School's fine. I'm fine. Okay?"

The sigh crackles down the line. "I know you're fine," her mom says. "You're always perfectly fine, you always tell me that."

Max scratches at an old bug bite, a souvenir from camp. She hears what her mom isn't saying; it's not subtle, it never is. *You're doing fine up there without me and that makes me feel bad. Why do you want me to feel bad, Wren? Do you just hate me? Why do you hate me? Why don't you come home to visit me and your sisters? Your dad misses you. We all miss you.*

They don't miss her. They don't know her enough to miss her—not the person she really is, not the girl that Gardner has revealed her to be. They miss the Wren they wanted and Max has never, ever been that girl. That was the problem—that and a million other things, but for her mom, that was it. Max is sure there are a hundred different parenting books or blogs or podcasts, whatever, that tell women how to be good mothers, and that an important part of that means not letting your kid know how much of a disappointment they are. Her mom skipped that part, because Max has known her entire life that she is not the daughter her parents dreamed of. It was always there, in the way her mom looked at her, like she was a poison flower. Pretty petals giving off the stench of death. A ring of blisters if you touched it.

She's not sure why she was even born. No—that's not true. Her parents were married and had bought a starter home and the baby came next, didn't it? So that's what they did, without really thinking it through, because her parents don't really think anything through, because to do so would mean examining their unfulfilling lives and coming up short. So she was born and Max isn't sure when her mom realized she wasn't the daughter she'd wanted but she herself has been conscious of it for as long as she can remember. The same way she has been yearning for *more* for as long as she can remember. That feeling of needing better, being made for something other than the dying small town and the dead-end life within it that made her seek out Gardner. And then, after she'd applied and sat the entrance exam and gotten the full scholarship, after her bewildered parents had signed the form, the other news had come: her mom was pregnant! With *twins,* no less! And that had solidified things in Max's mind, because they didn't need her anymore, they were going to have two more daughters to fill the empty space she was leaving behind and with any luck, at least one of them would live up to their mom's expectations. So when she finally left—when she got on the bus, alone, because her parents had two babies born a month early to worry about and Max was only too happy to let them off the hook—she didn't have to feel guilty. Everything was working out. She got to leave, and they got two bright, cheerful daughters who will, Max knows, live and die in that town.

"Wren? Are you there?"

Max stares down at her feet, noticing that the lace on her left sneaker has come untied. She tucks her phone between her ear and her shoulder, holding it in place as she leans down to fix it. "I'm here," she says, finally. "But I have to go. I have Archery, and homework, and dinner . . ."

There's too much silence before her mom speaks again. "Okay," she says, a sigh. "Do you want to say hello to your sisters before you go? They're in the yard but I can go get them."

Max pictures her mom then, standing in the kitchen and staring out through the window over the sink, watching the girls running around in sparkly tutus. No, she doesn't want to say hello to them. They don't even know her. "I really have to go," Max says, standing, and she hangs up before her mom can say something stupid like *I love you, Wren.*

8

TEDDY

TEDDY IS IN the dining hall with a plate of waffles and a bowl of fruit salad she's busy picking the grapes out of when Freya slides into the seat opposite. "Heard you charmed Mr. Gordon into letting you stay in class yesterday," Freya says without any preamble. "Heard you fucked up by not doing the reading, too."

Teddy doesn't take her eyes off the grape she's trying to add to the stack she's made without everything falling down. "What, nobody has anything better to talk about than me in English class?" She says it light, like she's kidding, but actually she's a little on edge. It's not like she isn't used to being the center of attention, but usually when people gossip about her, it's because she's done something worthy of the talk. At Gardner, apparently, being a *little* behind on assigned reading qualifies as scandal. And usually she wouldn't care about being reprimanded in front of the class, but of course the angel with the blond curls happened to be in that class, too. *Nora McQueen,* Teddy reminds herself. Made a mental note of her name, and of the way she kept putting her pen to her mouth, tapping it against her full lips, eyes narrowed, while she listened to that other girl who had an answer for every question and seemed to love the sound of her own voice.

She places the final grape and watches as her tiny structure collapses. Then she looks up at Freya. "You know everybody in our class, right?"

"The thirty girls I've been going to school with for the last six years?" Freya says.

"Okay, great. Tell me about Wren Maxwell."

Freya catches one of the grapes rolling toward freedom and pops it into her mouth. "What about her?"

"Whatever," Teddy says.

"First off, she goes by Max. If you ever call her Wren to her face, she'll ignore you. Probably forever but maybe only for a few days. She's smart. Maybe the most competitive bitch I've ever met, but I like that. I hate people who just roll over and let you win. See this?" Freya pushes her shirtsleeve up to reveal a small, round scar, pink against her pale white skin. "Fencing, second year."

Teddy nods. The kind of girl who would cut you, intentionally or not. Good to know. "You hang out with her outside of class?"

Freya shrugs. "Not really. She's friends with Brooke, Isobel, Safiya—Nora, of course."

Teddy raises her eyebrows. "Nora McQueen?"

"Yeah, they're, like, inseparable. Nora might look nicer but she's equally terrible. But then, we're all terrible." Freya pushes her chair back. "I'm going to get pancakes. You want anything?"

Teddy shakes her head and watches Freya walk away. *Inseparable.* Well, yesterday they had been pretty separate, definitely not sitting together in class. And from the way Nora had frowned every time Wren—sorry, *Max*—spoke, she had not pegged them as friends. Interesting.

Freya comes back with another girl from their floor—Josette, Teddy thinks—in tow, and their talk quickly turns to the Cup. Teddy has gathered that this Tierney Cup thing is a huge fucking deal to everybody but her. All day yesterday she heard it, like an echo—*the Cup, the Cup, the Cup.* Another private school thing, is all Teddy thinks: her first boarding school really cared about valedictorian, her last was concerned with athletics and Olympic trials. Gardner students lose their shit for a little silver trophy, she guesses.

"What about you?"

Teddy looks up from her syrup-streaked empty plate. Freya and Josette are looking at her expectantly. "Me what?" Teddy says.

Josette taps neatly manicured nails on the table. "Are you going to sign up for the Cup?"

"Probably not," Teddy says, and waits for them to be shocked, to start telling her how important this is and how they can't *believe* she doesn't want to be a part of it.

But the two of them only nod in perfect sync, and Freya says, "Yeah, it's not for everybody."

Teddy's hackles rise. *Not for everybody,* as in *you can't take it*? She's about to ask when Josette stands, pulling Freya with her, and says they're going to be late for French. When Teddy glances around, she notices the dining hall is almost empty. "Oh fuck," she says, and grabs her bag, preparing to run to her first class of the day. Being late two days in a row is *not* very fresh-start of her.

On Teddy's schedule the class is called Skills. That's it, nothing more, and as she half walks, half jogs to the science building she wishes she had listened a little closer when Ms. Archibald had gone over her classes the other day. She also wishes it weren't so hot still, because she can feel sweat beginning to gather at her hairline and does *not* want to sweat this hair out.

She makes it to class with time to spare and ducks into the nearest bathroom, shoving a paper towel under the faucet and then dabbing it on the back of her neck. It's cool in the bathroom, the stone tile flooring resisting what little light shines through stained glass windows. Teddy pulls a lip gloss from her bag and swipes it over her lips, rubbing them together. It's odd to watch herself trying. Trying to be on time, trying to look presentable, trying to figure out the societal machinations of this school. A reminder that she is actually capable of doing this, sometimes.

She presses a hand against her stomach. It's just that, when she's *not* in these moments, when there's less space between her and the edge of the black hole, she forgets entirely that she can be like this. Be good enough, maybe.

Behind her a toilet flushes and out of the stall comes Nora

McQueen. There's a second where they're watching each other in the same mirror, and then Nora is washing her hands, and Teddy watches the water run over her fingers with nails painted an almost unnoticeable pearl gold. "Skills?" Nora says.

Teddy frowns. "What?" she says, but then realizes. "Oh yeah. The class."

Nora smiles but doesn't look at Teddy. "Don't worry," she says. "Dr. Kessel is cool. There really isn't any prep for class. So, you know—" Now she looks up, her eyes flashing with amusement. "Much harder to fuck up than Mr. Gordon's class."

Teddy gasps in mock outrage. "I hate you," she says.

"You don't even know me," Nora says, and slings her bag over her shoulder as she pulls the door open. "Come on. We don't want to push her."

You don't even know me, and Teddy thinks there's an unsaid *yet* hanging there between them.

She follows Nora back into the hall and then into a classroom that looks identical to the labs at her last school. A woman Teddy presumes is Dr. Kessel stands at the board at the front of the room, writing something in red marker. When she steps back, Teddy sees that it says WOUND CARE in block letters. She also sees that Dr. Kessel looks like she could be a student, black hair slicked back from her unlined face into a bun and a pair of small silver hoops that Teddy is ninety percent sure she also owns dangling from her ears. She wonders what kind of doctor this teacher is.

"Take a seat," Dr. Kessel calls out, and suddenly the chatter Teddy hadn't even noticed drops out, the room quiet except for the scraping of stools. Nora takes a seat in the back corner by the window, and Teddy weighs for a second whether choosing to sit next to her would be smart or stupid before pulling out the stool beside her. "Welcome to final year Skills. It won't be that much different from every other Skills class you've taken so far, but I thought we should start with a refresher on wound care after the break. You'll all be back into Activities, and of course training for the Cup for some of you, so I think it's important we go over this *before* anyone gets hurt. Any questions?"

Teddy thinks she should speak up, say, *Yeah, I have a question, what the fuck are we doing?* But she's learning quickly, and knows that if she even raises her hand that by lunch everyone will be looking at her like she's an idiot. So instead she stays quiet as Dr. Kessel tells them to come up and collect supplies, and that she will be coming around to check their work periodically. Then the volume rises again and Teddy uses the noise as cover, leaning across to Nora. "Hey," she says. "Um, stupid fucking question, but . . . like, what *is* this class?"

Nora shakes her head. "God, Swanson. Two days in and you have no clue. I expected more from the girl who was expelled from two other schools."

Teddy straightens. "Three," she corrects coolly.

"So the rumors *are* true," Nora says, and then she shuffles closer, gesturing for Teddy to do the same. Up close her skin is creamy smooth, and she plays with a pendant in the shape of an *N*, sliding back and forth in the space between her open collar. When she speaks, there's a gap between her front two bottom teeth. It takes all Teddy's energy to focus on what she's saying and not just the way her lips move. "Skills is basically survival skills. I don't know why they don't just call it that but whatever. So we learn first aid, how to build fires and shelters, how to identify edible plants and shit, how to catch and prepare animals—"

Teddy's stomach flips in a pleasurable way. "Prepare?" she repeats. "Like—kill them?"

Nora nods. "Kill, skin, clean. It's easier than you're probably thinking."

Of course Teddy can't say what she's really thinking: *I wonder what feeling a heartbeat stutter out under your own hand feels like. I bet it feels good.*

"Got it" is what she actually says to Nora. "And—why do we do this?"

"Don't you listen at all?" Nora says.

"Maybe if they'd sent you to explain everything to me, I would have," Teddy says.

Nora rolls her eyes, but she can't hide the flush of warmth that creeps onto her cheeks. "Whatever," she says. "This is Gardner's whole thing. When it was founded, the two women that started it—"

"Cecily Gardner and Liliane Bahnsen," Teddy says. "See, I listen."

"Oh, I'm so impressed. Well, Bahnsen was this prolific writer and activist campaigning for Black rights, and she met Gardner at a conference for women's suffrage. Gardner was this, like, incredibly wealthy white heiress to some shipping fortune or whatever, but kind of a thorn in the side of the family, I think. Anyway, she was obsessed with the idea that women had more to offer than being wives and mothers, and even being artists or academics. She had this thing about how women should be able to survive anything that might happen, and provide for themselves, and keep themselves safe. So when they started the school, it was built on learning all the traditional academics you would expect, but then also—"

"Survival skills," Teddy says.

"Right." Nora glances toward the front of the room. "Hold on, I have to get our supplies or Dr. Kessel will be mad."

Teddy forces herself not to watch as Nora goes up to the front and instead focuses on what Nora has just explained. Sure, she'd heard everyone when they'd said Gardner was *different*, but she hadn't, like, *heard*. Every school she's attended so far has said they were different in one way or another. Even the Tierney Cup—again, she's heard everyone talking about it incessantly but didn't really take in what it was. Now she's beginning to think maybe Gardner really *is* different, because never before has Teddy had a class where they kill animals. Dissecting sheep hearts? Sure, but killing the animal first, then peeling its skin and fur off? She thinks this should make her feel a little sick, that if her mother or older sister Cassandra were in her shoes, they would find some way to primly be excused from the exercise. But there is an itch in Teddy's fingers, a curious urge to know what it all feels like.

Nora returns and drops an armful of gauze, absorbent cotton, bandages, and red markers on the table. Teddy picks up a marker and raises an eyebrow, a silent question that Nora answers. "To simulate protruding wounds," she says. "You know, in case you ever happen to have a piece of something fly at you and stab you in the arm, or leg, or wherever."

"Of course," Teddy says.

"Hold your arm out," Nora says, and when Teddy complies, Nora begins to wrap gauze around her wrist. Her touch is quick and confident, her fingers cool.

Teddy watches her work. "The Cup," she says. "It's, like, a big fucking deal? Because when I first heard about it, it sounded so stupid."

Nora stops, fixing Teddy with such an intense look Teddy wouldn't be surprised to burst into flames. "The Cup is not *stupid*," Nora says. "To win the Cup—it means everything. You become a legend. Everybody knows your name, forever."

"At Gardner," Teddy says. "Not outside of here."

"Outside doesn't matter," Nora says. "There is no outside of here, when you're here. That's the point. That's what matters."

She is so serious, her eyes hard, watching Teddy as she speaks. Teddy isn't sure if this is a test but if it is, it is one she suddenly desperately wants not to fail. She nods. "So you think you're going to win?"

Nora's attention returns to the gauze around Teddy's wrist. "I'm not entering," she says with a little laugh, as if Teddy is insane for even suggesting it.

"What are you talking about? If it's such a big deal to you, how come you're not even putting your name down to get in?"

Nora opens her mouth, then closes it again as Dr. Kessel comes to their table. "Nice," she says, nodding at Nora's work. Then the teacher glances at Teddy. "You're our new transfer, correct?"

"That's me," Teddy says.

Dr. Kessel nods again. "You're in good hands with Nora. But if you need any help or want to discuss class, I hold office hours on Tuesdays and Thursdays, four till six."

"Okay," Teddy says. "I'll remember."

Dr. Kessel moves across the room and Teddy glances down at the bandage Nora has secured with a neat piece of tape. "I'm all better," she says.

"Your turn." Nora slides the gauze in her direction.

Teddy's never handled anything more than a Band-Aid. But she won't admit that to Nora. Instead she mimics Nora's movements and begins to wind the gauze around Nora's wrist. "So tell me, then."

"What?"

"Why you're not entering the Cup even though you're a freak about it."

"I'm not a *freak* about it," Nora says. "No more than anyone else here."

"So sign up, then."

"I can't."

"Why not?"

"Because . . ." She tips her head back and begins to move her hand but Teddy wraps her fingers around Nora's wrist and holds her still. When Nora's gaze finds her this time, there's a flatness in her eyes. If Teddy were nicer, this would be the point at which she says, *It's okay, you don't have to tell me if you don't want to, I'm sorry for pushing.* But she's not nice, and she waits, staring Nora down, until Nora relents. "Fine. Because I was never meant to. The Cup is Max's thing. It's all she ever wanted and I was supposed to watch from the sidelines as she won and you don't even know Max so none of this means anything to you and also, if you repeat a word of this to anybody else, know that I'm aware of several ways to grievously harm you with only the items we have in front of us."

"Are you threatening me?" Teddy says, and the delight in her voice can't be hidden.

"Shut up," Nora says. "I might hate you."

"Or you might love me," Teddy says with a flick of her hair, and she wants to make Nora laugh, be rewarded for her work.

And Nora does laugh, a raspy quick sound, before she shakes her head. "Anyway," she says, "that's why I'm not entering the Cup."

"Because of Wren Maxwell," Teddy says, "who you are supposedly best friends with, so I hear. Except you, and me, and her were all in the same English class together yesterday and you weren't sitting with her, and you didn't talk to her, and in fact every time *she* talked, you rolled your eyes."

Nora flushes again, caught off guard. "I did not—"

"And in assembly, you weren't sitting with her," Teddy continues. "And you said you were *supposed* to watch from the sidelines, past tense, and all of this makes me think maybe you and Max aren't as inseparable as everyone seems to believe."

For a moment Nora seems at a loss for words. Teddy busies herself wrapping more gauze around her wrist, until finally Nora speaks again, her voice quiet, but not as if she's ashamed of what she's saying. Like it's real, and thoughtful, and like if Teddy wants her to talk, then she's going to have to really listen. "I was in love with her," Nora says. "So

I told her, because I felt like if I didn't I would go insane and also because I thought she might love me, too, but she said she doesn't. And she said I ruined everything by turning our friendship into something it wasn't. And she said it was all in my head and she really hurt my fucking feelings but I'm not supposed to acknowledge that I even have feelings at all, I guess. So we're not inseparable anymore. We're separate. Severed."

Teddy takes a moment before she responds, tearing off a ragged piece of tape and securing the gauze around Nora's wrist just like Nora had done to her. Severed. As if Max were a limb that Nora now has to live without. Lucky, then, that they are in a class that teaches them how to cauterize such wounds.

She turns Nora's hand over before releasing it and glances up. "You said you *were* in love with her," she says. "And you *were* going to watch while she won the Cup. But none of the old rules matter anymore. Right? So how come you have to keep playing by them? How come you don't just say fuck it and write your name on that sign-up sheet?" She sits back, admiring her work. Admiring Nora. "Why can't it be you that wins?"

Nora doesn't say anything now, only runs her fingers over Teddy's handiwork as a slow smile creeps onto her face.

9

NORA

ALL THROUGH THE rest of the day Nora can feel the heat of Teddy's handprint on her arm, an invisible mark thrumming. She's not completely oblivious; she knows Teddy was flirting with her. And she knows she was reciprocating, even though she barely knows this girl, even though before school started Nora would have said she couldn't even think about another girl. But Max has made it clear she's not interested like that, and not even interested in being her friend anymore, so it doesn't really matter. And Teddy is cute. She has a look in her eyes like she might be a little wild, but she also looks at Nora like she actually sees her. Something about the idea that this girl has been paying attention to her when Nora didn't even notice kind of turns her on. Noticing her in assembly. Watching her in English class. It's not like no one has ever paid Nora attention before, but when she was younger, before she got to Gardner, it was always the wrong kind of attention. Then she got to school and shed the layers of *awkward* and *not hot* and *unwanted* she had been forced to wear her whole life, grew five inches and gained forty pounds, and discovered she liked the way she looked in short skirts. *Then* people started to pay better attention, but of course Nora didn't ever try anything with anyone because she was in stupid fucking love with a best friend who seemed to find the whole idea of it inconceivable.

And now along comes Teddy, brazen, putting ideas into Nora's head. Ideas about the two of them, and about the Cup.

In third period Spanish, Nora practices conversation with Melina Georgiou while she thinks about the Cup. She can't ignore the points Teddy made. She *isn't* Max's best friend anymore. So what does she owe her, really? *None of the old rules matter anymore. Right? So how come you have to keep playing by them? Why can't it be you that wins?*

It isn't that Max ever said Nora couldn't want to win the Cup, too. It's more that—she cared so much about it, and Nora liked to see that side of her, the moments when she dropped her armor a little and let the hopefulness out, when Nora could see evidence of the girl who'd so desperately wanted out of her shitty life in a shitty town that she got herself all the way to Gardner, with none of the advantages Nora and their other well-off friends had. So Nora kind of put herself on the sidelines, stepped back so Max could have everything she wanted. But if she's being honest, it did always grate a little, how Max so easily accepted that. Never tried to convince Nora that she could enter, too, that they could do it together, because maybe in Max's brain the sidelines were the only place Nora deserved to be.

At lunch she finds herself standing with her tray and staring at their usual table, but her feet are unwilling to take her there. She watches Safiya sling her arm around Max's neck, watches them preening as the others no doubt hype them up, and she just can't do it. She knows Max has already put her name on the sign-up sheet, and Safiya, too, just like she'd told Nora she was going to do, but she can't go over there and listen to them going on about it. As she looks on, a hot anger begins to bubble beneath her skin. How come none of them have even asked her what's going on between her and Max? Everyone knows they didn't spend summer break together like they usually do. No one has asked her why. Not even Saf, the person Nora is closest to besides Max, the one who's living right across the hall. No, they just let Max call the shots and act like it isn't weird that the two of them aren't talking and go along with the idea that, of the two of them, of *course* it will be Max that enters the Cup and probably wins.

Her last class of the day is Art History and usually she has something to say about every piece they study, but today she keeps her hand down, instead adding things up inside her head. *I am an excellent archer, just as good as Max. I ranked second in the entire school for swimming last year. I gutted a buck when I was thirteen and didn't flinch, unlike Max, who threw up and then made me promise not to ever tell anyone I saw her.* She flips to a clean page in her notebook and sketches an outline of the actual Cup itself, the silver trophy you get to hold up at the Champion's Gala, where everybody yells your name and

THE TOURNAMENT

you make a mark on Gardner history. *Why* can't *I win?*

Her legs jump under the table, as she watches and waits for the hands on the clock to reach three, and when they do she races out of her seat. She's clammy, like she just popped a fever, and a part of her wants to sit down and really think it through, give this some serious consideration before making an impulsive decision. But when has thinking things through ever worked out for her? She thought—over and over and over, in a hundred different ways—about whether she was really in love with Max, and about whether she should tell her. All her fucking lists had told her she had more to lose keeping it to herself than telling the truth, so she'd said it, and look where that had gotten her.

She takes the long way from the art block to the wing where Dr. Thompson's office is, not to give herself more time to think but because she prefers this way, stepping outside and walking the perimeter of the inner courtyard under the covered walkway, the sun blazing on the grass. It's easy to become accustomed to the beauty of campus and Nora tries to keep noticing the things she likes, reminding herself that this is the last year she'll get to spend here, so she should make the most of it.

She ducks back inside the building and takes the stairs and makes her way to the board where the sign-up sheet is. She takes a pen from her bag. Writes her name in block letters. Gives a satisfied smile and leaves.

10

MAX

WHEN MAX GOES back to the archery range on Tuesday, this time for supervised practice, she's curious who else she'll see. She is also, honestly, excited, because club practice isn't divided into year groups, meaning there will be girls all the way down to first year there, and now Max gets to be the final year they look up to. When she started school, the final years seemed so impossibly adult and fascinating—the way they dressed, pushing uniform regulations to their limits; the shorthand they all had together; the ease with which they aimed arrows at the targets, the ripple of taut muscle and the concentration on their faces.

Ms. Bell, a French teacher most known for the vertiginous heels she clicks around her classroom in, supervises Archery, and she's already waiting when Max arrives, first one there. "Max," Ms. Bell says, a warm smile on her face. "I was hoping to see you here."

"I can't let everyone else have all the fun," Max says.

"I saw your name on the sign-up sheet," Ms. Bell says. "I know we teachers are not supposed to have favorites going into the Cup, so all I'll say is if you end up competing, you'd better not let us down on the archery front."

"Oh, don't worry," Max says. "If I get in, I'm going to win. It's all or nothing. And nothing is not an option."

Ms. Bell smiles again. "Good to hear," she says, and then her gaze shifts somewhere behind Max. "Pick up the pace, everyone! We have to get through induction today!"

The archery range is away from the school buildings, on the other side of a band of trees, reached either by following the paved path from the rear of the main block and around the edge of the trees, or via the shortcut trampled into the earth by generations of students. Max stands with arms folded as she watches the others arrive, mentally noting the girls she knows and trying to remember the ones she doesn't. There's Betsy Rodriguez, a fifth year, and a fourth year whose name might be Lily or Lacy or something like that. A gaggle of lower school girls, and then Freya O'Farrell from her year, and Isobel, and then—

Max rolls her eyes. Of course the new girl would pick her turf. She's walking beside Isobel and the two of them are laughing at something, and for a split second Max floods with shame and a certainty that it's her they're laughing at. But then she shakes herself and remembers that she belongs here, that she is Gardner through and through while Teddy Swanson is only trespassing. Playing at being a Gardner girl, really.

As soon as Isobel sees Max she peels off and leaves Teddy

behind, coming to stand by Max's side as Ms. Bell claps and tells them all to listen. "Hey," Isobel says as Ms. Bell begins the same talk Max has heard six times before, running over safety rules. *Archery is fun, yes, but a bow shot at high velocity can cause grievous injuries. First years, you will learn the rules of the range before you pick up a bow, and everybody else, I expect that . . .*

Max tunes her out. "Why were you talking to the new girl?" she asks Isobel, her voice low.

"Teddy? She's harmless," Isobel replies in an equally low voice. "I really want to know why she got kicked out of all those schools. My cousin Angelina used to date a boy at St. Catherine's Prep who said—"

"Who cares what he said? She got kicked out of three schools," Max says. "She's only here because she's a legacy."

Isobel shrugs, unfazed. "Me too," she says. "You know my mom went here."

"That's different," Max says. "You're smart. You give a shit about being here. She's just here because no one else would take her."

"Exactly," Isobel says, almost gleeful. "Don't you want to know *why*?"

"I don't give a shit," Max snaps. She forgets to be quiet, and Ms. Bell glares in her direction.

"When you're quite finished," the teacher says sharply, and Max keeps her mouth shut for the rest of the talk.

After she has explained the basic safety rules and the rules of archery itself, Ms. Bell pulls the sixth and final year girls out so they can demonstrate for the first years, watching with shining eyes. "Oh wait," she says, when she notices the new girl. "It's Teddy, isn't it? You can hang back and watch, too. Unless you have experience, in which case feel free to shoot, if you feel like you're capable."

Unlikely, Max thinks. The girl who couldn't read a fucking book for class? The girl who's been kicked out of three other schools? She doesn't exactly strike Max as the joining type, or the effort type, or any kind of type other than useless rich girl, really.

But Teddy just gives a serene smile. "I might be a *little* rusty," she says. "But I'll give it a shot. No pun intended."

Ms. Bell laughs at that and Max tries not to let her irritation show on her face. She can't really explain exactly what it is about Teddy that gets under her skin. Not in a way that would make sense to her friends, at least, because all the things she *can* pick out are things that apply to most of them, too. She's rich; she's spent her entire life breathing rarefied air; she's a legacy student; she's beautiful in the effortless way rich girls are, perfect teeth, perfect skin, perfect everything. All shit Max has had to put aside, because if she hated every girl just like Teddy, then she would never have had any friends here. She wouldn't be Nora's best friend, rich and beautiful and perfect Nora.

She catches herself. Wouldn't have *been* Nora's best friend. Not anymore.

Ms. Bell hands Teddy a bow and an excited hum builds from the lower school girls as Teddy makes a few adjustments, then takes the quiver Ms. Bell offers. They use recurve bows, somewhere between the classic image most people hold in their heads of a simple wooden bow and the compound bow, more mechanical but kind of fussy. Max prefers the recurve, because the archer feels the weight of everything more. She likes to feel the tension, the relief of the release.

There are several targets set up and Teddy walks toward the closest one, stopping twenty meters back. From the moment she raises the bow, Max knows she has underestimated Teddy. Everything about her stance, the certainty with which she draws the bow back, says she knows exactly what she's doing. The first arrow flies and lands deep in the outer gold circle. Not quite perfect, but close enough that it sets Max's teeth grinding.

She does it again at thirty meters, then forty, then fifty. When she's exhausted her supply of arrows, Teddy turns back to the group and smiles, dropping into a faux-curtsy, and everybody claps. She jogs back and Ms. Bell nods, impressed. "Excellent work," she says. "I take it you were an archer at your previous school?"

Teddy plays with the end of one of the two long braids she's woven her hair into. "Hmm, not that one. The school before that, I think," she says, as if she just can't quite remember, as if it's all so unimportant. "Or maybe it was more the camp I went to in eighth grade."

"Well, you certainly picked the right Activity," Ms. Bell says, and she looks at the first years all huddled together. "What do you think, girls? Do we have a new contender for the Cup in our midst?"

"Oh please," Max says to Isobel, and it's not quite loud enough for Ms. Bell to hear this time, but the perfect volume to reach Teddy's ears, and she sees the other girl stiffen. "Sorry, but it takes more than some tricks you learned at camp to win the Cup."

Inside she's seething. Of course Teddy has to be an excellent archer, on top of everything else. *What's that old song say?* Max thinks. *The one Mrs. McQueen likes to play after dinner?* Oh yeah: young, gifted, and Black. Throw a rich in there and you've got all that Teddy Swanson, irritatingly, seems to be. All that Max wishes she were.

Max squashes the thought. Wishing is for losers and Max is *not* that. She eyes the new girl again. "Besides, she's not a Gardner girl," she says. "Anyone can see that."

Isobel is only half listening, busy tying her blond hair up. "You're being, like, a level-ten bitch today," she says, and laughs. "But you're probably right."

Max laughs, too, loud and obnoxious, pushing Teddy. *Come on. React. You know you want to.* But Teddy doesn't even glance over at them, and Max is disappointed, again, because despite all that Teddy seems to be, there's so much more that this girl isn't.

11

TEDDY

MAX'S WORDS PLAY on a loop in Teddy's mind throughout the rest of Activity. That laugh of hers, so performative, like she was begging Teddy to react. But Teddy won't give her the satisfaction—not here, not now. It would be fun, sure, but it would be fleeting. And didn't she promise her mother that she was going to do better here, make smarter choices? The long game is better. The black hole likes fleeting moments of volatility but in the same way that Teddy likes shoving crackers smeared with peanut butter into her mouth at two a.m., which is to say it satisfies in the moment but pales in comparison to something richer, denser, the thing she really wants. The good girl version of her, the one who doesn't fuck up so monumentally, the one who does what she's supposed to and actually achieves great things, exists somewhere within her. Teddy is sure of it—why else would she feel so bad so much of the time? If she were pure evil, then she wouldn't care at all about the damage she leaves in her wake. She wouldn't make those promises to her mother and really *mean* them, would she? But if she wants to be that better version of herself, she can't keep on playing by the same old rules. That girl wouldn't bite back now, for an instant hit of pleasure. That girl would go for something bigger, something that might put Max in her place, yes, but more importantly would put Teddy herself on top.

So she keeps her composure as the other girls take their turns, lined up along the range, Ms. Bell watching form and calling out corrections. She keeps her composure when Max steps up and shoots all her arrows like she was created solely to do that. She keeps her composure when her fingers itch to pick up the bow herself again and launch an arrow right at Max, because even she knows that would be a move too far, a move she couldn't come back from. And does she really want to go down in history as the insane bitch who shot a girl to death on their school archery range? Fuck no. She's not afraid of a little infamy, sure, but not the *manslaughter* kind, Jesus.

"All right, I think we'll leave it there for today," Ms. Bell says a little after four, and while the little first years swarm the older girls, chattering excitedly, Teddy slips away.

Don't have what it takes?

She pulls the elastics out of her hair as she walks back from the range, not toward the dorms but to the main building, her skin burning from an ungodly combination of blazing sun and anger. Once inside, she takes the stairs two at a time to get up to Dr. Thompson's office. There's a pencil on the floor, like it's just waiting for her, and Teddy picks it up, lifts her chin, and finds the next empty line on the sign-up sheet. She writes her name in slow, slanting script, wanting to make sure it's legible, wanting to know that there could be no mistake here, that Dr. Thompson and whoever else is in charge of the Cup knows she meant to do this.

Then she scans up the list and can't help but laugh when she sees Nora's name there. *Perfect,* she thinks. *Oh, perfect. Max is going to love this.*

Satisfied, she turns and starts back to the dorms, and enjoys the burn as it turns to a simmer, satiated by her new plan. She's coming for the Cup.

12

NORA

NORA IS SITTING at her desk when there's a knock on her door. She's contemplating ignoring it—she hates to be interrupted when she's actually in a good working groove—but then a singsong voice calls through the door. "It's me, open up!"

Nora sighs in irritation. You can't ignore Brooke, she's learned that lesson a hundred times over the years, so she gets up and opens the door for her before going back to her desk. "I'm busy, Brooke."

"We're all busy, all the time," Brooke says, but she wanders in and drapes herself across Nora's bed anyway. "Looks cute in here," she says. "I never knew you had taste."

Nora closes out of the college essay she's working on and gives Brooke a middle finger. "Before I buy anything, I like to take a moment to really think and ask myself the important questions," Nora says. "*Will Brooke like this? Would she wear this? Does she think pastels are cute or outdated?* You know everything I do is to please you."

"Ha, so funny," Brooke says, and she rolls over, looking over at the bookcase where Nora has shoved her textbooks, half their English Lit reading list, and a variety of trinkets: candles that they are strictly forbidden from burning, a gold dish with a stack of rings inside, other detritus that comes along with being Nora. "You like having your own room? I kind of miss sharing," Brooke says. "I think I just like being around people."

"You need a sick amount of attention," Nora says. "That's what it is. You're an only child and you cannot stand not being the center of everything going on at all times, and being in a single means you can't constantly be spying on someone or talking shit. Like, it's not hard to figure out."

"Oh my god." Brooke sits up. "You know what I *don't* like? Being around bitches who've been to therapy and think they can analyze me."

"I've never been to therapy," Nora says. "You're just easy to read."

She laughs, ducking as Brooke launches a velvet decorative cushion at her head. "I'll leave," Brooke says, as if it's a threat. "I'll go find someone else to talk to—"

"Okay! Do it! Then I can get back to work!"

"You're always *working*," Brooke says. "I can't even be bothered."

"Sure," Nora says. "Well, if you stay quiet for ten minutes and let me finish this section, I'll talk to you."

"Ten minutes," Brooke repeats, and holds her hands up. "I can do that."

"*Thank* you." Nora opens her essay again and goes back to the last paragraph, the same one she's rewritten five times already. She'll probably rewrite the entire essay again, too, but it's okay, she's used to it. They're all like this at Gardner—even Brooke, who loves to pretend she's a slacker, as if she hasn't just spent the past hour of Activity in the practice rooms going over arias or whatever else she does with the voice teacher. It's almost a foregone conclusion that Brooke will be at Juilliard or Oberlin next fall, studying opera. Isobel will be at Yale, or failing that, the Sorbonne. Nora isn't sure precisely where she wants to go, but Brown is high on her list, as is Columbia. Of course she knows Max wants Columbia, too, but New York is a big fucking city and she doesn't get to claim everything for herself.

She taps her thumb on the space bar and looks over at Brooke, now absorbed in checking the ends of her hair. *I signed up for the Cup,* she wants to say, to see how Brooke will react, but she also doesn't want to say it. If she tells Brooke, Brooke will tell the others, and then at dinner tonight instead of having Max ignore her because of the whole *I love you* thing, she'll be ignoring her because—

Nora squeezes her eyes shut so that when she opens them again, everything is blurry. She's doing it again. Making everything about Max, making her decision to sign up for the Cup about Max, when really all she wants is to be able to *not* think about Max. Even college, Jesus—*does* she want to go to Columbia, or is that just a leftover vestige of the before times, when Max had said that was her dream and so Nora had decided it would be her dream, too?

"We'll still be friends, right?" Nora says. "Next year, when we're out of here. We'll still talk, won't we?"

"You're getting sentimental already?" Brooke doesn't look away from her hair, fingers peeling her split ends. "Of course we'll talk, you fucking loser. We have these things called *phones*? And this thing called the *internet*? And this other thing called *flights*? Come on. This is not the Stone Age. Oh!" Her face lights up and she flips her hair back, giving Nora her full attention now. "Speaking of. I heard the new girl is in Archery with Max and Isobel and was totally acting like she's the shit in front of all the first years. Isn't that so funny? Like, they're literally eleven years old. It's not hard to impress them. I don't even know why she's here. She doesn't seem like a Gardner girl to me at all."

Nora presses her tongue against her teeth and turns back to her screen. Sometimes it's like she's on the outside looking in and getting to witness the spoiled rich cliché for the first time. Look at them—so bright, so driven, and so incapable of resisting gossip, even though of course Gardner girls don't gossip, are above such things, wouldn't dare waste their intellect speaking ill of other women. *What would the founders thinks of us now?* "Actually, I really need to finish this," she says, in a tone that makes it clear Brooke is dismissed. "I'll meet you at dinner later."

"But I'm *bored*," Brooke whines, and it sets Nora's nerves on edge. "Come on, don't tell me you're not a little curious about what the new girl's deal even is."

"Maybe if you actually talked to her, you'd find out," Nora says, and she gets up and opens the door, holding it there. "I have to work, Brooke."

"Fine," Brooke says, and she hops off the bed, her pleated skirt spinning around her thighs. "I think I'll go find Max. Remember her?"

Then she's gone, leaving Nora silent in her wake.

By the time dinner comes around Nora can't be bothered to be irritated at Brooke anymore, so she drops it and lets everyone pretend everything is normal, laughing at Saf's story about almost getting cracked in the skull by an overenthusiastic first year with a hockey stick, complaining that the Caesar dressing doesn't taste as good as it did last year. Of course nothing is normal, but tonight when Nora thinks it, she doesn't mean because Max is ignoring her, but because of what she did. Writing her name on the sign-up sheet, actually putting herself in contention—

She shivers despite the dining hall's stifling heat. There's no guarantee she'll actually end up competing in the Cup, but it could happen. Her name could be pulled and then what's to say she couldn't go all the way, win the whole thing? She really does love this school, would kill to leave a mark here. After graduation, she's going to go out into the big wide world where Gardner doesn't mean as much as it should, where people will hear she went to boarding school and immediately assume they know exactly what kind of school she went to. But the people left behind at Gardner will remember her, and who knows—in a few decades, maybe she'll have her own kid to send here, a legacy by virtue of Nora's own name.

Nora wakes up with the blankets she'd kicked off before falling asleep pulled tight around her. When she looks out the window everything outside is glistening with rain, and she dimly remembers thunder in the night. It feels like the temperature has dropped twenty degrees and when she comes back from the shower she dresses in uniform and swaps the polo shirt for a button-down and adds the V-neck sweater vest she likes. On her way to breakfast she sees everybody else has had the same idea, and campus is flooded with girls in cardigans, sweaters, knee-high socks, as if fall is now officially here and they can shed their summer skins. Even the teachers seem happier, with their little electric fans tucked back into hiding and the windows left open an inch or two for a crisp breeze to come inside. Suddenly Nora can't stop thinking about campus lit up with the oranges and reds of changing leaves, the new knee-high boots sitting in the bottom of her closet, and the shock of swimming in the ocean in December. Yesterday in Activity they stayed in the pool, but soon they'll be making the trip down to the beach once a week and testing themselves in the surf. She could have picked something else this year—in fact, had thought about taking Advanced Music Practice even though she hasn't picked up her flute in years, because then she could have another thing for her college applications. But in the end she'd stuck with swimming like she has the past three years, because she likes to be in the water, even if it sometimes scares her.

In third period Ancient History she sits between Isobel and

THE TOURNAMENT

Yara Klein, who spends far too much time doodling the name Oliver in the margins of her notes. Nora nudges Isobel as their teacher is trying to draw a crude map on the board and nods down at Yara's notebook. Under the table Isobel types on her phone and angles the screen so Nora can see. *Oliver Ridgefield-Pine, he goes to Bridle Day, total slut,* she reads, and stifles a laugh. Bridle Day is the local private school, where the better-off kids from the town they go into on the weekends go. Trust Yara to get caught up on a townie with a reputation. God, even on her worst days Nora would not be caught *dead* doodling Max's name on her notes. She takes out her own phone under the table and puts Oliver's name in the search bar, and up pops a picture of a white boy with spiked hair and an honest-to-god shell necklace, posing between two people who Nora assumes are his parents, both with shiny hair that looks as if it has been cemented in place. *Oster Co. CEO and city councilman Tucker Ridgefield-Pine attends dedication ceremony with his wife and son,* the caption reads. *Of course,* Nora thinks; everyone knows Yara has political aspirations.

They're walking to lunch and debating whether or not Mr. and Mrs. Ridgefield-Pine are wearing wigs when Max comes out of nowhere. She's wearing the school blazer and the first thing in Nora's head is that she loves when Max wears the blazer, because of the way she pushes the sleeves up, how there's something sexy about Max's forearms. But then she remembers she's mad at Max and also moving on so she really shouldn't have any opinions on Max's arms at all, and then realizes that Max is looking right at her and this is the first real eye contact they've made since move-in day.

Shit, she thinks, registering the anger in Max's eyes. *Here we go.*

"Are you kidding? Are you actually *fucking* kidding me?" Max says too loudly, so now everyone walking past knows they're fighting. "You signed up? Why the fuck would you do that?"

Nora waits a beat before responding, enough to swallow the quiver threatening to infect her voice. There is no need for her to be nervous, no need to show weakness in front of Max. The Cup does not *belong* to her, and certainly neither does Nora. Max has made that very clear. "Yes, I signed up for the Cup," Nora says evenly, a little bored sounding, perhaps. "It's open to everyone in our class, you know."

"But it's *mine.*" Max jabs a finger at her own chest. "You can't have it."

"I'm sorry you feel that way," Nora says.

Isobel shifts from foot to foot at Nora's side. "Are we really doing this here?"

Nora ignores her, staring Max down. "I know you have all these ideas in your head about what's going on, but you need to actually face reality," Nora says, and she didn't know until she started talking that this is what was going to come out of her mouth, but now she's started she might as well finish. "You can't have something just because you decided you want it. That's not how it works."

Max takes a step back, and she looks a little sick, skin taking on a sweaty sheen. "Fuck off," she says, and then she turns and marches down the hall, out of sight.

Isobel swings around to face Nora. "What was *that*?"

"Nothing." Only the words Max had said to Nora last year, turned around and thrown back at her. Nora sitting on the edge of her bed as Max looked down on her with something close to pity in her eyes. *I know you have all these ideas in your head about what's going on, but you need to actually face reality. I don't have feelings for you. I don't love you.*

She inhales sharply, pasting a smile on her face as she shrugs in Isobel's direction. "She's been a real bitch since we got back. I guess she can't handle a little competition."

"So you're really entering the Cup?" Isobel shakes her head. "You, her, *and* Saf? Oh goody. This isn't going to be hell for the rest of us at all."

Nora lets her smile drop, sick of pretending for the sake of these friends who only care about themselves. "Yeah, it's about to be hell," she says, walking away. "And I'm the devil."

13

TEDDY

TEDDY WATCHES NORA stalk away and then she turns her attention back to the girl left behind. Isobel, this one's name is—at least, she thinks. It's not like there are a lot of girls to keep up with, their entire class hovering around thirty, but Teddy has always been bad with the names of people she doesn't care about. Isobel just stands there for a moment, her face screwed up like she's trying to figure out what made Nora snap, and Teddy presses herself closer to the wall. *Is it that hard to understand, Isobel? A war is about to break out,* Teddy thinks. Nora on one side, Max on the other. *Who are you going to fight for, Isobel?* As Teddy looks on, a girl with a ponytail so tight it looks painful approaches Isobel and her face completely changes, the moment over for her. She and the girl whose name Teddy does not yet know head off in the direction of the dining hall and Teddy considers following them but decides against it. She wonders if she should go after Nora, but decides against that, too. They have class together after lunch, with Max, too; she'll see everything she needs to then—

"Shit. *Shit*," she says, causing a first year walking by to glance over at her, all shocked. Teddy was never that kind of kid—that was more Cassandra, her older-by-ten-years sister, the one who put on such a prude act in front of any adult, looking for praise.

Teddy pushes off the wall as she tries to remember which direction the library is in. Cass would never have forgotten to finish the last few chapters of the reading ahead of class. Cass would certainly never have fucked up by not doing the reading in the first place. She was always better at that side of things. Made sure she didn't get in trouble at school, portrayed the ideal preppy rich girl with perfect morals and a bright future ahead of her. Of course she partied behind closed doors, of course she was an absolute menace at the right club with the right friends and the right mix of drinks and pills in her system, but their parents never knew that. Even Teddy only knew because of her spying tendencies, and because she knew the passcode to Cass's phone. To everybody else that mattered—headmistresses and college interviewers and internship bosses—Cass was perfect. Teddy used to look up to her, wanted to be exactly like her big sister, who played every role so well and had so much *fun* doing it. But Teddy could never quite get it right. When she started getting in trouble at school, it was only small things at first, but that almost made it worse. Why couldn't she stop showing up late to class? Why couldn't she wear her uniform properly until the day was done? Questions she used to ask herself every time she ended up in another detention, except she already knew the answer, she just didn't want to accept it. But then she wanted to ask Cass the same questions, figure out what it was that made her sister capable of doing all the things that Teddy couldn't? *But don't you feel like if you keep that top button closed, you're going to have to peel your skin off? Don't you feel that force pushing you away from the classroom because you know once you go in you're trapped?*

She only asked Cass once, and by then she knew she wouldn't get the answers she wanted, because by then Cass had become a different person entirely. Or maybe it was that the wild, rule-breaking, teenage version of Cass had been the act all along, and the good girl the real version of her, because one day Teddy looked up to find Cass married to a banker and popping out babies to put in the nanny's arms while she went back to the law firm. When they had talked, it had been their parents' anniversary, and Cass had looked irritated as she finished putting her jewelry on to go to the party downstairs. "What the fuck do you mean, you want to peel your skin off?" she'd said, and then come up to Teddy, gripping her chin and peering into Teddy's eyes. "What are you on?"

"Nothing! Nothing," Teddy said, and realized she was on her own.

She remembers the way to the library and that quiet fourth floor she'd been brought to on her little tour. She takes out her book and finds where she left off—maybe fifty, sixty pages left. She can do that. She'll read it, and she already has her thoughts lined up, ready to raise her hand when Mr. Gordon asks about the symbolism of the graveyard, and to start in on the homoerotic nature of the friendships between the men in the book. It's not that she can't do well at school; it's just that she finds it hard to keep it up, once she gets bored or the topic changes or she loses whatever reason she had for putting effort in in the first place.

Of course she knows her reasons this time: she wants to impress Nora and show her that she is actually smart and not a fuckup. She wants to show Max, too, because obviously that girl thinks she's better than Teddy and it's really going to be a lot of fun showing her how wrong she is. And she highly suspects that mediocre grades and poor attendance will not look good for a girl competing in the Cup, which she really, really, suddenly but not suddenly at all, wants.

And there is a part of her that remembers, again, the promise she made to her mother. *It all comes together,* Teddy thinks: she can be good, be better, because now there is the Cup and not only the potential of a contest where she will get her hands bloody, but a greater war that she can be part of. So let that be the chaos keeping her from the edge; let the competition feed the black hole inside her.

She glances outside, wind whipping through the trees. And if the prize she's thinking of is not some shitty trophy but a girl named Nora, then that's okay. All the more reason to win.

14

MAX

MAX IS PACING the length of Brooke's room, three strides past the bed to the closet, three strides back. "You should have seen her in class after," she says. "Like, just sitting there like butter wouldn't melt, like she's just the nicest, smartest, best girl in class, as if she isn't actively trying to bring me down."

Isobel and Brooke exchange a look that Max pretends not to see. "I just don't get it, exactly," Isobel says. "Why is her signing up making you *this* mad? Saf did it, too. You're not pissed at her."

"Saf isn't my best friend," Max snaps.

"And what, Nora is?" Brooke raises her eyebrows. "Not with the way you two have been acting since we got back."

"Since *before* then," Isobel interrupts. "I mean, you went to *camp* instead of going to her house this summer. You can't even look at each other properly."

THE TOURNAMENT

"That has nothing to do with this," Max says, although of course she's lying, because of *course* this has everything to do with what's going on between her and Nora. Nora made that perfectly clear when she threw Max's words back in her face. But that's not how Max meant it. Typical Nora, taking someone else's words and twisting them to give a meaning that was never intended. *What else was I supposed to say to her? How else was I supposed to put it? Your friend turns around and says not only that she's in love with you but that she thinks you are in love with her, too, and what, you're not allowed to say the truth? I was supposed to be in love with her because she had decided that was real and that was how things had to go?* She really had tried to say it as gently as she could, while making sure the point was clear and couldn't be interpreted any way Max didn't mean. "I don't have feelings for you. I don't love you." It was the only way to say it, Jesus. And she does—did?—love Nora, as a best friend, maybe even like a sister, but she couldn't say that, because it would have muddied the waters. Made things unclear where Max needed them to be absolutely crystalline.

And now, as if it wasn't bad enough that Nora had chosen to keep things weird and stew in her hurt feelings, like she was the only one hurt by all of this—now she's taking things too far. The Cup has been Max's dream for as long as she and Nora have known each other. And because Max doesn't want her, now Nora has decided to take the thing Max *does* want. So fucking petulant.

She stops pacing and looks at Isobel, sitting cross-legged on the desk chair, and Brooke slouching on the edge of the bed.

When it all went down last year, Max hadn't told any of their friends about it. She knew Nora wouldn't, and she knew if she did, it would become a much bigger thing. And she isn't heartless—she knew Nora was hurting, even if she was mad at her, too. She didn't want to make it worse by letting everyone else know that Nora tried to make a move on her and Max shot her down. Like, come on, she isn't *that* kind of bitch. Or she hadn't been, before. But if Nora wants to go there, if she wants to cross that line—and that's exactly what she's doing, going after the Cup purely to spite her, to pay her back for daring to not want her—then why should Max keep protecting her?

"What?" Isobel asks, sitting up a little straighter. "Oh my god, will you just tell us? I don't have time to be walking on eggshells around you two for the rest of the year. And actually, I just don't fucking want to. So, out with it."

Max twists the ring on her left thumb around, like she's stalling for time. "Okay, but don't be weird about it," she says, but only because she feels like she has to, has to make an overture toward being respectful, still. A good friend, still, who of course does not want to create gossip and does not want this secret to spread to, oh, the entire class. She holds her hands out, palms turned up to the sky. "Last year, right before school finished—" She pauses and swallows. Is she really doing this?

But Brooke and Isobel are watching her, waiting, rapt, and of course she's doing this. "Nora told me she had feelings for me," Max says, finally. "And I don't share those feelings, so I told her that, and so I thought spending summer together like always would not be the smart thing to do, and I thought if we had that time apart we could both, like, process things, and when we came back to school everything could go back to normal. But Nora seems incapable of moving on and also like it's all my fault for being a raging bitch just because I don't like her like that, and now as some form of revenge or whatever the fuck else, she's going after the Cup because she knows how much it means to me." She exhales heavily, a gusty sigh like a small reflection of the wind outside the window. "So, that's it."

There is a long silence before Brooke speaks. "Oh," she says.

"*Oh*," Isobel says. "Okay. That makes—" She laughs. "I was going to say that makes sense but it doesn't. I mean. I *guess* it makes sense in that I understand the weirdness now but . . ."

"She's into you?" Brooke says. "She's never said a *word* to me."

"Why would she?" Isobel says. "That's a . . . *delicate* situation to be in. Right? Like, if I woke up one day and realized I had feelings for you, am I going to run and tell Saf? What if it makes the entire dynamic for all of us weird? What if I tell *you* and *you* make it weird?"

"I didn't make it weird," Max interrupts, a little indignant. "I tried very hard to *not* make it weird. I gave her the whole summer to deal with this—"

"Summer isn't that long," Isobel says, and then, "I feel a little bad talking about this."

"I don't," Brooke says, shrugging. "It's just information. I'm not going to run down to Nora's room and be like *Oh my god I heard what happened, are you okay, do you need anything, do you wanna cry?* But now we know, maybe we can all just . . . let it be out there, and clear the air, and have things go back to the way they should be."

"That's what I wanted! That's *all* I wanted," Max says. "But Nora's been a bitch to me ever since we got back, and now she's doing this."

Isobel makes a face. "Again, Saf's entering, too," she says, and holds up her hand as Max opens her mouth to rebut her. "Yeah, yeah, Saf's not doing it to get back at you, whatever. Is it not possible that Nora also isn't doing it to get back at you? Maybe she just wants to enter, the way half our class does, the way people want to every year?"

Max looks away. Remembers the glitter of Nora's eyes, how pleased with herself she'd been reciting Max's words. Like she'd been holding on for just the right moment. "No," she says. "I know what she's doing."

There's another long moment of silence and then Brooke tears open a granola bar with her teeth. "It's just sign-ups," she says, and takes a bite, continuing to talk as she chews. Beautiful girls can get away with anything. "Maybe only one of you will make it. Maybe neither of you will."

15

NORA

NORA SLIDES HER tray along, picking up a chocolate-frosted brownie and one of the tiny apple juices that are intended for the lower school to go along with the risotto she chose from the hot food selection. The sound of the dining hall is already giving her a headache. *Only two more days and then the weekend,* she thinks. But before the weekend comes Friday and the special assembly, where her name might be pulled and she'll find out if she's going to compete. Find out if Max is going to compete.

She leaves the line and turns to find her friends, seated at their usual table. Max isn't there, and Nora expects to feel relief but it doesn't come. She knows Max is mad. Even if she doesn't have to sit through dinner tonight with Max glaring at her, she'll get it tomorrow at breakfast, or lunch, or when they pass each other on the way to the bathroom.

Isobel spots her and waves. And Nora tells herself to move,

walk over there and sit down like she has so many times before, but she can't do it. She's so tired already, three days into the school year, and this is not how she'd wanted her last year to start off.

She turns, scanning the dining hall. There, in the back corner. Teddy sits by herself, head nodding like she's listening to music, a fork dangling lazily from her fingers. Without thinking too much Nora walks over there, leaving her friends in the distance. She approaches, then stops, then drops her tray on the table and Teddy jumps, a hand going to her chest. When she sees it's Nora, she takes her headphones out. "Hello."

"Can I sit here?"

Teddy smiles, so brilliant, glowing like the sun itself. "Sure," she says.

So Nora pulls out a chair and sits, and picks up her spoon to take a bite of risotto. But then she puts it down and leans over. "I did it," she tells Teddy. "I signed up."

"Oh, I know," Teddy says, resting her chin in her hand. "I caught that little scene between you and Max." She sighs and blinks big, dark eyes. "God, she's kind of a cunt, right?"

The laugh that comes out of Nora surprises her, but it's true. That used to be what Nora liked about her. She just let her guard slip and forgot that being friends with someone like Max eventually means one day you are the one she's going to be a cunt to.

"I signed up, too," Teddy says.

This is less surprising to Nora, but she still asks the question. "Why? I thought you were all antiestablishment, fuck this school, blah blah blah."

THE TOURNAMENT

"I heard it's a real honor to win," Teddy says. "And I'm trying this thing where I'm, like, better? So I thought, why not try this other thing, too. Maybe I could be a Gardner girl in due course."

Teddy says *Gardner girl* in a lilting tone, like she's making fun of Nora. Or maybe she's making fun of everyone, or the school in general. It doesn't matter. Nora likes the teasing, because of course she does, because she's seventeen and likes when hot girls pay attention to her. "We'll make something out of you yet," Nora says, and then, "What are you reading?"

Teddy glances down at her phone and then back at Nora. "Don't laugh at me," she says. "I found this journal article about the book we're reading next. It seemed interesting so I thought I would just skim it so I can . . . shut up, I said *don't* laugh."

"You're doing extra work," Nora says, her voice a hushed, dramatic whisper. "You're *voluntarily* doing work that *wasn't* assigned, so you can get ahead and *impress* Mr. Gordon. My, my, my." She leans back, taking Teddy in. "Maybe we really *will* make something of you."

Teddy uses her fork to gesture somewhere behind Nora. "Aren't your friends going to tar and feather you, for sitting with the enemy?"

"I'm allowed to have free will," Nora says. "And you're not the enemy."

"They don't know that. Besides, I'm sure they've been talking about me. Wondering what I did at all those schools. I'm right, aren't I? Oh, I'm so right."

"They don't even know you."

Teddy tilts her head to the side. "You don't even know me."

"I know more than they do," Nora says. "Anyway, isn't this how friendships start? You get to know the other person?"

"Friendship?" Teddy says, curling her tongue behind her teeth.

"Or whatever," Nora says, and her heart pounds, because she's flirting and it's *fun* and yes, there is a part of her that feels guilty because isn't Max the one she's supposed to want? Isn't she still *in love* with Max?

But Max made it clear she doesn't want her and what's that stupid shit everyone says about getting under someone new?

Nora looks at Teddy. Takes her in, all of her, those dark eyes again and lips shiny with gloss and perfect hair, sure. But also the way those eyes never seem to settle, her gaze constantly flitting around like she's looking for something. The ragged cuticles on her thumbs.

"Or whatever," Teddy says, and under the table her shoe brushes against Nora's calf and it takes everything Nora has not to react. "Sure."

16

MAX

WHEN THEY FILE into assembly on Friday, Max pretends not to see Nora walking side by side with Teddy, the same way she ignored it when she walked into the dining hall the other night and found Nora had abandoned them for the new girl. The same way she ignored it all day yesterday, seeing Nora eat breakfast with that girl, and walking across the lawn, and sitting at that same table together at dinner. Heads bent together, one dark and sleek, one blond and curly, both shaking as though whatever they were looking at or listening to or talking about was just so fucking funny. She'd wanted to go over there and grab Nora by the arm and ask what the fuck she was thinking, but she couldn't. She's not Nora's protector anymore; if she wants to make stupid decisions and be a brat to all of her actual friends, then so be it. She can bear the responsibility for those decisions when the shit hits the fan, which it inevitably will. *Teddy Swanson has been expelled from multiple schools and that shit had to be bad for her parents to not even be able to buy her way out of it,* Max thinks. Sooner or later, this girl is going to get in serious trouble at Gardner, and Nora will probably go down with her. If that's what she wants—fine. In the meantime, Max has bigger shit to focus on.

She sits on the bench between Brooke and Safiya, staring ahead at the stage where Dr. Thompson is shuffling papers at the lectern. The headmistress gives no indication of what she's about to say, whose names she's about to read. Which, of course she doesn't—what does Max expect, that Dr. Thompson might see her in the mass of girls and wink? Get a grip.

The hall buzzes with whispers, an electricity humming. Last year Max felt like she was vibrating out of her skin with adrenaline, waiting for names to be called, knowing that the next time it happened, it would be her turn. Now it's actually here, she feels calmer than expected. Steady. Whatever Dr. Thompson says is what will be. Max checked the sign-up sheet yesterday evening: in total ten people had put their names down. *Including Nora, and that idiot Teddy,* Max thinks, *because of course Teddy signed up, even though she's not a Gardner girl and she has no real sense of the meaning behind the Cup and no connection to any of it. Sure!*

Ten girls signed up means only three of them won't make it in. So all Max has to do is *not* be one of those three names not called. Of course she knows it's already happened—the names have already been drawn this morning, and all Dr. Thompson is going to do now is read out a fate already decided. So it's too late for bargains with the universe or any bullshit like that.

THE TOURNAMENT

Brooke jabs a sharp nail into Max's knee. "Good luck," she whispers, before reaching over and doing the same to Safiya. "You got this."

Onstage Dr. Thompson holds a hand up and everybody quiets instantly. "Good morning," she says with a smile. Today she's wearing a carefully tailored suit, the shoulders sharply defined. It has always seemed obvious to Max that Dr. Thompson dresses as if she thinks she needs to mark herself out from the students—that she's so petite, with such a youthful face, that if she doesn't encase herself in suits and tweed blazers and wrap dresses with heels then people will think she's just another Gardner girl milling in the halls. Maybe that was true back when Dr. Thompson first started working here, but even from this distance Max can see the lines etched between her eyebrows, around her mouth. "As we all know what this special assembly is in service of, I won't waste too much time. But first I would like to take a moment to commend those final year students who entered this stage of the Tierney Cup. It takes a lot of bravery and mettle to even write your name on that sign-up sheet, and before I announce who will be competing, I want everyone to hear those names. For our sixth years—next year you'll be the ones weighing up your choice and deciding whether to commit yourselves to this opportunity. I hope you recognize the character exuded by each and every one of these girls and allow their examples to guide you through your remaining time here. For our lower school students and others who have joined us for the first time this year, I hope you too can see how these students demonstrate the values of Gardner-Bahnsen and I hope you'll commit yourselves to supporting the competitors and the school as a whole throughout the tournament. So, our students who took the courageous step of writing down their names—Margaret Sim. Safiya Haddad. Wren Maxwell. Jordan Riggs. Manuela Vega. Nora McQueen. Abigail Brody. Rita Perry-Jones. Theodora Swanson. Florence Wright."

She pauses and everybody in the hall dutifully claps. Max's hands make little noise, her palms too sweaty. She rubs them against her thighs, her trousers absorbing the nerves she does not want to admit are there. *Hurry up. Just tell us whose names actually got pulled and let's get on with it.*

Dr. Thompson holds a hand up again. "The names I read out now are the names of the students who will be competing in the Cup. When I call your name, please make your way up to the stage. We'll start with—Safiya Haddad!"

Brooke jumps to her feet, clapping wildly. "*Fuck* yeah!"

Max looks sideways at Safiya, who looks a little shell-shocked. "Oh . . . my god," Saf says, and then she puts her shoulders back, the surprise shifting for another, better look—pride. "Congratulations," Max says, and it sounds hollow even to her own ears. But Saf doesn't seem to hear it, or if she does she doesn't care, because she's already moving and making her way toward the stage.

"Abigail Brody!"

A cheer goes up somewhere behind Max and she swallows. Her mouth is sandpaper dry. Two down, five to go. Dr. Thompson moves through the names and each time there is a cheer, applause. *Jordan Riggs.* Applause. *Manuela Vega.* Applause. *Nora McQueen.*

Applause.

THE TOURNAMENT

Max makes herself clap but can't even look over. She's not stupid; she understands statistics. It was more likely than not that Nora would get in, but that doesn't mean Max wasn't fantasizing about her being one of the three who was *out*.

Up onstage the competitors are forming a line to the right of Dr. Thompson, and Max watches as Nora gets up there and hugs Safiya. The two of them look absolutely thrilled.

Choke, Max thinks.

"Wren Maxwell!"

It takes a second for it to register, and by the time it does Brooke has already yanked Max to her feet and is planting a sloppy kiss on her cheek. "You did it!" she's saying. "It's you, it's you, go on!"

"It's me," Max says, and then she's walking, shimmying out of their row and passing by all the girls below them until she reaches the stage. Up the steps and then joining the end of the line, right next to that traitor Nora but right now Max doesn't even care about any of that, because *she is in.* She's going to compete in the Tierney Cup and win the whole thing and go down in history and show everybody in the process that she and she alone deserves this.

Dr. Thompson clears her throat. "And last but certainly not least—Theodora Swanson!"

This time there's no cheer, but the applause still swells, and Teddy slinks out of the crowd and up to the stage, where she stands right beside Max. Her perfume is cloying, thick. "Hey, congratulations," she hears from her right, and a smug smile forms on her face. Of course Nora's congratulating her. She's too weak not to.

Max is deciding whether or not to grace Nora with a response when she hears a response from the other side. "Congratulations to *you,*" Teddy says, and it hits Max: Nora wasn't talking to her at all.

She stiffens. Let them talk behind her literal back. Let Nora roll around in the gutter, if that's what's going to make her feel better. It doesn't matter to Max, not really.

"Let's hear it for your Tierney Cup competitors!" Dr. Thompson says into the mic, a giddy note of exhilaration in her voice, and everybody down on the benches gets to their feet. The hall rumbles as girls stamp their feet. A chant of "Gard-ner, Gard-ner" goes up and Max lets it all wash over her, her nerves dissipated. She can't think about Nora, or Teddy, or any of it. She wants to enjoy this moment—the whole school cheering, lifting them up onto the precipice of greatness. It's beginning to sink in and there's no surprise in her anymore. Like a part of her always knew she would be up on this stage, having her name read out. It's the same part of her that knows she's going to win the Cup.

That she'll do whatever it takes, destroy whoever she has to, in order to get what she wants.

PART TWO

"And finally, I dedicate this win to my good friend Penelope Anderson. It's going to be a long road to recovery but I wish her all the best and hope that one day, we might be able to meet on the field again. Thank you!"

—**VICTORIA ST. JOHN,**
Tierney Cup champion, 1977

17

TEDDY

TEDDY PINCHES THE soft rabbit fur between her fingers, pulling it taught. With the knife in her right hand she nicks the fur, creating a slit too small. She swears and puts the blade back against the skin and pushes up, widening the hole a little more. When she's satisfied that it'll work, she sets the knife down and hooks two fingers of each hand into the hole. Grits her teeth and pulls, the skin tearing and sliding off the rabbit's flesh in one almost-fluid motion, only catching at the feet. She had been surprised at first, by how much strength it takes. But she's used to it by now, even if she's still trying to perfect things. She grabs the skin and tugs at one end, slipping the last little bit off the front legs, and repeats with the rear legs. "Time?"

Nora clicks the ancient-looking stopwatch, the same one they've been given at the beginning of every class for the past three weeks. "Forty-seven point three," she says.

Teddy makes a clicking noise with her tongue. "*Slower* than last time?"

"It's not all about speed," Nora tells her. "It's about accuracy, too."

Teddy nods as if she hasn't heard Nora say that a hundred times, since they walked into Skills one day three weeks ago to find dead rabbits already at their work stations. "Time to get real," Dr. Kessel had said, and everyone had gotten to work as if this was natural. Normal. Dr. Kessel had come back to their table to show Teddy exactly what she needed to do, explaining each action as she went. *We don't need the head. You could cut it off with a cleaver, if you had one. For our purposes, we only work with a small knife—what you might have on you in a real situation. In that case, you can twist the head until it almost comes off by itself, and then cut that last piece so it comes free. See?*

Teddy spins the knife on the tabletop. This is the most she's cared about school ever, which is funny because it's *barely* even school, really. The Tierney Cup cares a little about academics, sure, but much more about how quickly and cleanly you can butcher a rabbit; how accurately you can hunt it; how solidly you can survive a night in the wild. That's the last event, and the one Teddy is looking forward to the most. In the five weeks since she's been at Gardner, Teddy has learned how to start a fire, how to stitch a wound using only the supplies in one of those shitty emergency sewing kits, and that rabbit tastes better freshly killed and cooked in a tiny pan over a campfire than any of the ways she's had it prepared at restaurants. Of course she's also learned that her French teacher loves to talk about herself, and that Thursday pizza night is

THE TOURNAMENT

the best dinner night, and that surprisingly, First World War literature isn't the most boring topic she's had to study. But the actual schoolwork feels so much easier to her now that it's not the only thing people are expecting of her. Besides, it was made very clear to her that in order to compete in the Cup, she had to keep her grades up. If she ever forgets, Nora is quick enough to remind her.

Nora, Nora, Nora.

Teddy watches her now as she frowns and notes the time down. Nora says this—this thing between them, which is not quite a relationship but not *not* one—isn't a rebound or some attempt to make Max jealous. Personally, Teddy doesn't buy it, nor does she care; she is more than happy to be used if Nora is the one doing the using, and if it fucks with Max's head, well, that's a bonus. Max is just like every other head-of-the-class bitch Teddy has encountered at her other schools—the ones who want to be the best at everything, including being cool, who think the rest of the class should bend and sway to their every whim. Girls like Max think they control everything. Like how she had convinced Nora not to enter the Cup, even though Nora had every right to. Max didn't want it that way, and so, to her, it wasn't going to *be* that way. She hadn't counted on Teddy coming along, though, had she? And now all three of them are competing, and Teddy can't *wait* to crush her. She doesn't even really care that much about winning herself. The adrenaline of everything is enough, keeping the black hole at bay. If only her last school had put butchery on the curriculum instead of choir, then maybe Teddy wouldn't have flamed out there.

"Let me time you," she says, and they switch seats, and Teddy watches as Nora deftly guts the animal, her long fingers scooping out kidneys and intestines and heart. Teddy reaches under the table and draws a circle around Nora's knee with her fingertip. "Is it so sick that this really turns me on?" she says in a low voice.

Nora fights a smile. "Yes," she says, scraping away at the inside of the rib cage. "Absolutely demented."

Teddy taps Nora's skin. "So you *don't* wanna come to my room later?"

Nora stops what she's doing and looks up at Teddy. "Well, I never said *that*," she says.

At the front of the room Dr. Kessel claps her hands twice. "All right, that'll do for today. Start cleaning up," she says. "And don't forget that I will be here on Saturday from two till three for you to bring your parents by and show them what exactly it is we get up to in here."

Teddy slumps backward. She had managed not to think about Family Weekend for almost an entire hour. Of course her mother is coming this weekend, and of course her father is busy doing his usual bullshit—golfing or flying to Hong Kong or whatever—so he can't come. So of course, her mother is bringing Cassandra instead, because "your sister *loves* seeing you, and she deserves a weekend off from the children, don't you agree?" As if Teddy can't see right through her mother's excuses. The only real reason for Cass to come spend a weekend in a hotel far below her usual standards in a town whose main attraction is a yearly scarecrow contest is so she can be paraded as the perfect, number one daughter, in front of the fuckup. Except this time Teddy isn't going to be the fuckup, because this time she gets to tell them all about how she's joining in, and being a *good* student, and really becoming a Gardner girl. The problem is that she's said all of that before, because she's always had periods of managing to act like a good girl. but that's all they've ever been, short periods of time between implosions, and that is what is making Teddy nervous. Her mother and sister are going to come here and listen to her tell them all about this school and the Cup and then they're going to look at each other and shake their heads, the way they love to do. Then Cass will turn the conversation to her kids, because their mother deserves to have some descendants who aren't complete head cases, and they'll leave with the same expectations they always have—that it's only a matter of time until Teddy calls for help, or the school calls to say they're through with her.

"What are you thinking about?"

Teddy realizes Nora has been watching her this whole time, the carcass still splayed out between them. There's something special about Nora's big brown eyes and the way they seem to see inside Teddy. Or maybe she's just not used to anyone paying attention to what's going on beneath her own surface. "Family Weekend," Teddy says. "Are your parents still coming?"

Nora nods. "I think they're getting in late tomorrow," she says. "I might try to go out for dinner with them but it might not work. But it's fine, they've been here enough. They don't need a tour of campus or to see the sights in town."

"Meanwhile I will absolutely have to drag my people all over," Teddy says. "I'm just glad my grandmother didn't somehow end up part of this little visit. Then we'd never hear the end of it."

"Oh right," Nora says. 'She went here, right? What class was she?"

Teddy shrugs. "Sixty-four, sixty-five, maybe. I forget."

"She must have such fucking good stories."

"I never asked," Teddy says. "She stopped being cool way before I was born. My entire life she's just been this prim and proper society lady who doesn't like to make a fuss and doesn't like to raise her voice. She's very into respectability. Thought my mom was doing something terrible by not forcing me to get a relaxer at six years old, you know?"

Nora makes a face. "I hope I don't leave here and forget everything about myself," she says, and then she gets up and picks up the remains of the rabbit, ready to deposit it in the bucket that will go to the head caretaker, who will feed the meat to his dogs. "Oh shit," she says before she moves. "I meant to ask. My parents and I are going to Fortuna for dinner on Saturday. Maybe—"

"Ms. McQueen," Dr. Kessel interrupts, calling from across the room. "Are you planning to do something with that rabbit or just stand there?"

Nora makes another face at Teddy but Teddy is grateful for the interruption, because what was Nora going to say next, she wonders as Nora crosses the room with their rabbit in hand. *Maybe you can come to dinner with us? Maybe you and your mom and sister can come meet me and my mom and dad?* Teddy closes her eyes and sees herself swing out over the edge of the black hole. Sure, they've been hooking up for the past month or so but they're not, like, official. Teddy has never been anyone's girlfriend and isn't sure she has the desire to ever be that. Meeting Nora's parents? Sure, if she sees them in passing she'll be polite, use all that home training her mother thinks she doesn't possess and leave them with the impression that their daughter has a lovely new friend, but that's as far as anything needs to go.

She opens her eyes and sees Nora at the sinks at the edge of the room, scrubbing her hands clean. Fuck. Things have been going so good and it's her own fault, Teddy knows, for getting complacent. Of course Nora would want her to meet her parents. Nora is the kind of girl who does that, who can put on that glossy sheen of being a nice girl and actually mean it. Teddy always forgets that's the difference between her and any other girl she's ever thought has been remotely like her: they're not, deep down. They aren't at war with their own personal black hole. They take their frustrations out internally, not letting their nerves push them to pull fire alarms or burn things down. Normal girls who are broken in normal ways.

She sees Nora coming back over and steels herself. How does she let Nora down without ruining what they have going on? Because she doesn't want to stop, she just doesn't want to, like, *commit*. "Hey," she says, forcing herself to get it out quick, before she can lose her nerve. "About dinner—"

"Oh right," Nora says. "That's what I was saying. I think Fortuna is booked out, but Marigold Palace is also a pretty nice place—I mean, for our limited options. The name is truly terrible but the food is good and the wine list is nice. So if you wanted to take your mom and sister out somewhere nice, you could probably still get a table there. Score some good daughter points and all that."

"Oh." Teddy blinks, relief flooding her system. "Oh, okay. Yeah. Thanks. I'll call later."

Nora smiles, her whole face lit up. "Good," she says, and then tilts her head to the side. "And after dinner, as a thank-you for you getting good-girl points, you can come to my room and . . . well. We'll see what happens."

Teddy laughs, a burst of surprise, and Nora picks up her things and waves. "I'm going to be late," she says. "Bye!"

"Bye," Teddy echoes, and once again finds herself wondering what trouble this school is going to get her into.

18

NORA

NORA'S LEGS BURN as she kicks, propelling herself through the water of the indoor pool. It's a little indulgent, allowing herself to train in here and get used to the warmth of the water, but she's had plenty of experience swimming in the ocean just beyond Gardner and besides, the path down to the cove has been blocked off for two days while workers from the county repair the handrails. Can't risk someone putting their weight on the rope and it giving way, not when then whole school is going to be traipsing down there in a little over a week.

After a sufficient amount of lengths of the Olympic-size pool, Nora pulls herself out of the water and joins Safiya sitting on the bench running parallel to the water, catching her breath and rolling her ankles, like that will make her muscles stop aching. "Good work," Saf says, water beading in her eyelashes. "Now all you have to do is repeat that, but in the freezing cold ocean, in a wet suit, with me right ahead of you the entire time."

Nora pulls on the strap of Saf's swimsuit and snaps it hard against her skin, causing Saf to yelp. "Big talk for a girl who was afraid to put her head under the water until two years ago."

"I wasn't afraid," Saf says. "I had sinus issues."

"Sure, whatever," Nora says, and grabs her towel, wrapping it around her shoulders and shivering. She likes the pool at this time of evening, after dinner when all the lower years are in Study Session or some other form of supervised good, wholesome fun. The sky outside the tall windows is dark, turning the glass into a mirror. The only sound is the movement of the water, bodies slicing through.

Nora leans back against the wall. Family Weekend starts tomorrow, sure, but she isn't really thinking about it. Her parents have been here so many times, there's nothing new to show them. She does well in all her classes and they were so excited to hear she was competing in the Cup that they sent flowers for her room, a huge bouquet of blues and purples that she had to collect from the office and scented her room so strongly that after only a few days she had to throw them out. The only weird thing is going to be explaining Max's absence, but her mom has stopped asking about her in her weekly emails, so even that isn't a big deal. But not worrying about that means Nora has no choice but to think about the other big thing rapidly approaching: the first Cup event, only eight days away.

It's not like it hadn't felt real during the announcement assembly, when Dr. Thompson read her name. It had felt real and fucking perfect, her up there, and Teddy, and even Max. Maybe it would be easier if Max had been forced to sit this out but that's not how Nora wants it to go. Cliché bullshit, sure, but she wants to beat Max fair and square, not on some kind of technicality. If Nora had gotten in but Max hadn't, the whole thing would have felt a little hollow.

Now there is a board in the corridor outside the assembly hall, with each of their names on it, and that was when it started to feel real to Nora. When she first noticed the whispers that ripple around wherever she goes. When she started to hear girls declaring allegiances, making under-the-radar wagers on who would win each event, what scores they would get, and who would come out on top of the whole thing.

There are seven events, staggered all the way out into spring term. First: a five-mile swim in the open water, looping around the tiny wasteland island just off the coast. Second: target archery, simple enough. Then there's Identifying Elements, which everyone calls the berry test, on account of how you have to identify a whole bunch of flora and fauna, to prove you know the difference between a berry that's good to eat and one that'll kill you. The fourth and fifth events come as a pair: the Hunt, and the Preparing Prey. Go out into the fields to shoot those wild rabbits that are forever multiplying, seeing how many you can bag within the time limit; then the following day, skin, butcher, and prepare your catch. The sixth event is always the most hated, because it's boring: a half-marathon hike, just one foot in front of the other for hours. But once you get past that, you get to the event everyone wants to win: Survival. One day and one night, alone, out on that barren island, with nothing but your brain, the clothes on your back, and a knife.

Scoring is simple: ten points to the girl who comes in first in each challenge, nine to second place, and so on. The criteria for what constitutes a win varies challenge to challenge, but in the end all that matters is who has the most points. Only she can win the Cup.

A flick from Safiya brings Nora back to the moment. "What?" she says, like she didn't just space out.

"I said, I'm going to the common room when I'm dressed," Saf says. "I want to see if they have that popcorn we asked for. Want to come with me?"

She says it like it's casual, just a thought she had, but Nora knows Saf too well to believe it. It's not like she *can't* hang out with Saf, or the others—she just doesn't want to anymore. Really, Saf is the only one who's shown any kind of caring for Nora since they came back. The others just act like everything is fine, and let Max get away with treating Nora like complete shit. And they've barely spoken to her since the Cup announcement, like they've taken Max's side. Not surprising. Max has that kind of energy. That's why Nora was drawn to her in the first place; something about Max says she'll be in charge, she'll make the hard decisions, she'll lead you. All you have to do is follow. Problem is, Nora is sick of following someone who didn't hesitate to crush her. And now she has Teddy, who treats her like an actual equal. Who thinks she's smart and cool and hot and isn't afraid to actually say it, so that Nora doesn't ever have to guess what Teddy thinks. Someone who isn't ashamed to even admit the *possibility* of feelings.

"Look, this"—Nora gestures at the pool, then at herself and Saf—"is cool, but I'm not going to come crawling back to the others just to make you feel better. I'm allowed to choose to not hang out with people I don't want to hang out with. I didn't start anything, but I get to decide how to handle it. They all picked Max over me, so deal with it. You can chill with me and Teddy if you want, but they don't like her, and I'm not going to make *her* hang out with people who don't like her so we can all pretend to get along and be all fun and fine and whatever."

"Fine, Jesus," Saf says. "It's just popcorn."

"It's never just fucking anything with you, Saf. I know you," Nora says. "Don't forget it."

She whips the towel off from around her shoulders and stands, not bothering to look back at Safiya as she leaves.

19

MAX

MAX HAS RUN the same route around campus enough that she knows each step without thinking. This is useful, because it means she can do things in her head other than counting steps or wondering whether her arms are moving in the right way, like running through a checklist of all her college applications and the things she has left to do. Of course, Columbia is her first choice, like it has been for years now, but she's not the kind of girl who can only apply to one school. She considered it, of course she considered it, because how good would it feel to say "Yeah, I got in early decision" while her classmates were still waiting to hear. Or some of her classmates, at least—the ones who also couldn't afford to only apply to one school, whether that was because they also needed to rely on financial aid and keep their options open (like Vina Kashian) or because they were vapid idiots whose bad behavior couldn't be fixed by being a legacy (Teddy Swanson, obviously).

Her steps sound loudly, out of time with her ragged breathing. Campus is quiet, which is odd for a Saturday morning, but since it's Family Weekend everyone is up and out doing things, showing their parents around town, or attending various open classrooms and lectures. Max's parents have never come to see her at school. She always let Nora think it was because Max didn't want them there and never told them when the dates were, or left it too late on purpose so that they'd have no choice. She let Nora believe that and kept the shameful truth to herself, which is that she did ask her parents to come, her very first year. Yes, she was happy to be away, to be starting what felt like her real life and leaving her old self and everything that went along with that girl behind, but that was why she'd wanted them to come. She thought maybe if they could see for themselves, they would finally understand. They would know that Gardner was the best place for Max to be, and that her classmates were the kind of girls she was supposed to know, and that her new best friend was the kind of person Max would never, ever have found by staying in her hometown. Maybe they'd even see Nora's parents and understand that they'd been outplayed, outranked. *Those* were the kind of parents Max was supposed to have, the world she wanted to inhabit. And not just because of the money (although the money was nice); Nora's parents had ambition. They were both lawyers, partners in big firms, degrees from the best Ivies and HBCUs. They liked to see the world, had taken Nora to Tokyo and New Zealand and a whole bunch of

Greek islands before she was even ten years old. They mingled in the upper of echelons of Black society, had dinner parties with doctors and CEOs and artists where they discussed Du Bois, the latest Alvin Ailey repertoire, and up-and-coming Black politicians they were excited by. In Max's hometown, there were no wealthy Black families. There were no wealthy families of any variety, actually, and everyone lived the same way. Clocking in to a mind-numbingly boring job that just about covered the bills, trips to the beach in the summer, cheap hotels with tiny TVs. The same cycle of work-eat-sleep punctuated by the occasional holiday cookout and Super Bowl parties and dinner at a chain restaurant on special birthdays. And the worst of it was those people weren't miserable, not in the slightest. They *liked* their little lives. Max's parents liked the drab house and fifteen-year-old car and never going anywhere. Never even considering a better life.

So she'd wanted them to see all that, and a part of her wanted to do this one last nice thing for them—show them it was all okay, and she didn't need them, and no one needed to feel bad about it.

But then when she told her mom about it, the dismissal was instant: they couldn't come, couldn't afford the travel and the hotel and disrupting the girls' routines. Max understood, didn't she? She knew they would *really* love to be there, if things were different, didn't she?

And even if Max had been disappointed by their actions—or lack thereof—in reality, she was relieved, wasn't she? She didn't have to introduce any of her new friends to her parents and watch with barely concealed embarrassment as her parents stumbled over names and laughed too loud and just generally made fools of themselves. It was only weakness that had driven her to even ask them to come, and after that she had become hardened, a tough bitch who looked back on her younger self with a little bit of scorn, a little pity.

She loops around the far reaches of the archery range and begins the downhill cruise toward the dorms. That was all so long ago, it feels like it happened to a different girl entirely. Now Max can't even imagine her parents showing up for something like this, and she wouldn't want them to—not even in the deepest, farthest reaches of herself where she keeps all her saddest shit buried. She likes being independent, has none of the usual fears about going off to college that other kids have. She already knows how to do her own laundry and plan her own life. Today she's going to take the afternoon shuttle into town and buy herself coffee and an overpriced fancy salad and work on her applications; tonight she's going to take advantage of the empty common room to watch one of those tragic dating reality shows she likes on the big screen without anyone complaining or throwing cheese puffs at her head. What could be better?

She runs past a gaggle of first years on a guided tour with their parents. It's fun to watch the little ones change; already Max can see how they hold themselves a little straighter, shoulders back, chests up, leading the way instead of hurrying to catch up. On impulse she waves as she passes and laughs to herself as a handful of the girls wave back, the rest bursting into hushed excitement. *One day they'll be me*, she thinks, *and I'll be a memory. A name on the wall, a Cup winner they'll want to copy.*

By the time she rounds the school buildings and comes out by the dorms she's slowed to a walk, stretching her arms up over her head, rolling her neck to release the ache there. She's so busy cooling down that it takes her a minute to notice the figure hovering outside the entrance to her dorm building. She doesn't think much of it—someone's mom waiting outside for her daughter to come down from her room, probably. The woman is wearing a heavy coat better suited to winter snowstorms than the cool fall weather, and she wonders if it's this person's first time in Washington, and as she's thinking it the woman turns around and Max realizes far too late that it's not one of her classmates' moms, but her own mother. Susan Maxwell. Here. At Gardner, on Family Weekend, completely out of the blue.

Max stops walking. "Mom?"

"Wren?" Her mom's face breaks into a smile and she holds out her arms wide. "Surprise!"

Max scrubs at herself in the shower, still a little dazed. She has left her mother waiting in the main building, where she can look at the art pieces on the wall and take in the class photos stretching back decades, while Max cleans up and prepares for the visit she didn't know she was having. When she had asked her mom why she was there, with no phone call or email or anything to let Max know she was coming, especially considering Max hadn't even invited her or let her know about Family Weekend, her mom waved her off. "I realized, it's your last year here and the last chance I'll have to come to one of these things," she said, casual, as if showing up on campus weren't in any way weird. As if it weren't the first time she and Max had actually seen each other in almost a year.

Max can't figure out what other reason she has for being here, though. She's hesitant to take what her mom says at face value, but after a rapid-fire grilling she has ruled out the most obvious motivations: her mom is not sick, and neither is her dad. The twins are healthy and currently playing with their cousins while they and their dad spend the weekend at their aunt's house. All three of Max's living grandparents show no signs of dropping dead in the near future. And there's no way she's come for money, because they might be broke but they still have more money coming in than Max earned over the summer. Try as she might, Max cannot figure out any kind of angle here, which makes her think that maybe there *is* no angle, which makes her even more nervous because what— her mom has really just come to see her, because she can, because she wants to?

Max walks back to her room and dresses quickly, pulling the black work pants she likes over damp skin. She brushes some clear gel through her brows and dabs concealer under her eyes, as if that will be enough to stop her mom commenting on how tired she looks, how she should really try a little blush, how it wouldn't kill her to put on some lipstick or try lash extensions.

Her shirt sticks to her back as she makes her way from the dorms to the main building, even though it's cool outside, and she wishes she'd left the denim jacket lying on her bed but there's nothing she can do about it now. As soon as she climbs the steps she spots her mom, leaning in close to a class photo so she can read the names printed in tiny font. "Hey," Max says, and her mom turns, smiling.

"There you are," she says. "I think I've read the name of every girl in every photo here. And there are a *lot* of photos."

Max shoves her hands into her pockets. "We take a lot of pride in our alumni," she says. "We like to remember them."

"I see that." Her mom nods, gazing around, until her eyes land back on Max's face. "So. What are we going to do? A tour? I'd like to see your room. Or you could show me where you do the, uh, archery, right?"

Max tries to hide her surprise at the fact her mom even knows it's archery that she does. Max always thought their limited conversations went in one ear and out the other, to make room for all the other shit her mom has to remember about the two daughters who actually live with her, whose lives she's actually invested in. "Yeah, archery," she says. "Hey, you could even shoot a few arrows, if you want."

She means it as a joke, but her mom smiles again. "That sounds like fun," she says, and snaps her fingers. "Shall we get going?"

20

TEDDY

"**SO, YEAH.** My grades are pretty good—no, not pretty good, they *are* good, and I'm doing all my work and keeping up with everything and actually, the classes here are so much more interesting than at any of the other schools. I really like my English teacher, Mr. Gordon, but I love Dr. Kessel and Skills class. I feel like I'm learning so much more than just how to regurgitate texts and memorize things. And like I said, I'm keeping on top of everything *and* handling competing in the Cup at the same time. I have to, because if you don't keep a high enough GPA, you get disqualified. I admit, when I first heard about the Tierney Cup I thought it was just some other bullshit private school awards nonsense, but I understand it now. I understand Gardner so much better now and I get why you wanted to send me here. I don't know if I'll win the Cup but I'm, like, excited to try. I feel stupid saying it but I'll say it anyway, I guess. So . . ." Teddy takes a breath finally, nodding. "That's it, I guess."

Across the table her mother and sister sit side by side, wearing the same inscrutable expressions. They've always been like that—Cass takes after their mother, while Teddy is the spitting image of a long-dead ancestor on their father's side. Now that her sister has given in to injectables, she looks more like their mother than ever—the same unlined foreheads, the same uncanny unmoving eye area, so that whether they're smiling or frowning, absolutely nothing around the eyes gives anything away. Teddy has always liked the way her nose wrinkles when she laughs, has imagined the way her face will look when she's older, like she's actually lived a life and isn't ashamed of that fact. She does not say this to her sister, though, because she knows what Cass's response would be: "You wait until you have kids and are in your late twenties. It absolutely destroys you, Teddy. I mean, *destroys* you. When you look in the mirror and see the hell it's done to you, you'll be running to the chair to get it fixed. Are you still getting regular facials? Do they have a good aesthetician in this town?"

Teddy picks up the untouched bagel half sitting in front of her but puts it back without taking a bite. They've taken over one of the picnic benches outside the arts building—her mother had a spread shipped to the hotel, including a gold-embroidered tablecloth that now sits under the selection of pastries and fresh-baked bagels, smoked salmon and scallion cream cheese, tomatoes and burrata, and whatever else there is. Music floats out from the arts building, so their little picnic is accompanied by the string section showing off for their parents inside the building. Teddy has already shown them around the grounds, and they sat in the assembly hall while Dr. Thompson talked about the philanthropy work Gardner takes on, and she has the reservation tonight at the restaurant Nora told her about, and all that should be enough but for some reason Teddy cannot *shut up* for longer than a minute. Sitting here right now might be the longest she's been quiet since her mother and sister arrived yesterday evening.

She just wants her mother to know she *is* doing better. She's keeping that promise she made in Dr. Thompson's office and actually trying, and so far she hasn't fucked up—her teachers like her, the other girls *mostly* seem to like her, or if not that, then at least they tolerate her, and she's about to become part of a Gardner tradition. Each day Teddy wakes up and marvels a little at how she doesn't have the urge to start a fight in the dining hall. Actually, that's not it—it's that when she has those kinds of urges, she can pocket them and bring them out later, use all the frenetic energy built up inside to pull back the bow and let the arrow fly, the satisfying thud as it buries itself in the wood of the target or sometimes into the flesh of a wild rabbit. When she has the urge to set her dorm on fire, she can go to class and start a fire there, instead, and get graded on it, Dr. Kessel pleased by the height of Teddy's flames.

Teddy reaches for the champagne flute that is filled only with orange juice and downs it, itching as the silence drags on, forcing herself to keep another flood of words spooled up in her mouth. Finally, as she picks up that same bagel half and actually bites into it this time, her mother clears her throat and begins. "What about college?"

Teddy chews slowly. "What about it?" she says, speaking around her food even though she knows her mother hates it.

"What about *what*?" Cass frowns, as much as her Botox will allow. "It's *college*, Teddy. You're going to graduate this year and then—what next?"

"All that talk about everything you've been doing and not one word about how your applications are going, or even where you want to apply," her mother says. "Have you even thought about it? Because you're going to need some impressive letters of recommendation, considering your track record. And of course we'll all do our best where we have connections but you have to put the work in, too, Teddy."

Teddy swallows and feels the masticated bagel lodge somewhere in her chest. "I am putting in the work," she says. "I told you, I really have been trying, like you wanted me to. Like *I* want to now. I entered the Cup! Like, I'm really trying to be a part of this school and do well and—"

"Yes, this cup, or trophy, or tournament, whatever it is—" Her mother flutters her hands in front of her face. "I don't know that this is a good idea. I don't think you can afford to be investing your time in some school contest when you should be thinking about your future."

"A couple of months ago you didn't even think I could make it through high school," Teddy says hotly. "Remember why you even sent me here in the first place? Because nowhere else would take me?"

"There was more to it than that."

Teddy gives a quick breath of laughter. "No, I don't think there was. I think you pretty clearly told me that this was my last shot and I had better use it. Which is exactly what I'm doing! I haven't gotten into trouble here, I haven't done anything that necessitated a call to you and Dad, I haven't even been late with an assignment. Look, I admit that I thought this was going to be just another school but it's not, and I like it here, and a couple of months ago I would have said me liking any school was impossible. But I'm doing good and maybe I haven't really thought about college yet but . . . I don't know," Teddy says. "Baby steps?"

"You're not a baby," Cass says, and she runs a hand through her dark hair, pressed into silky waves for the visit. Teddy can't remember the last time she saw her sister's natural hair, or her face bare without makeup, or her clothes not perfectly pressed and steamed, even her jeans. "You know, college is a big step up for a lot of people. Even for me—I thought I knew everything because I'd already been living away from home for so long, but college is different. You think this is the real world but it's not. Mom and Dad are not going to be able to bail you out for the rest of your life, but you know where they can help you, where Alec and I can help you?"

"Oh wow, let me just think for a minute," Teddy says. "I bet it's *college!*"

Cass turns to their mother. "This is what I mean," she says, ignoring Teddy entirely now. "She has no clue what's about to hit her. And worse, she doesn't even care that she has all these people willing to help her, and advantages that I'm sure even some of the other students here could only dream of, and she turns it into a joke. I told you this place would be too easy on her. When is she going to realize she's the one in charge of her life?"

Teddy snaps a breadstick in half and flicks one piece in her sister's direction. "When did you become such an unbearable asshole?"

Cass flinches. "Are you kidding me?" She gets up, holding a hand out. "I swear to god, Teddy. I'm going to find a bathroom and when I come back, I need you to fix that attitude. I left my kids at home to come here and help you—"

"Nobody asked for your help!"

"I did." Their mother sighs and puts her head in her hands. "Cass, go find that bathroom. I'll handle your sister."

Teddy watches as Cass walks away, stomping like she used to when she was a teenager and Teddy had ruined yet another calfskin bag by getting creative with markers. Sometimes Teddy likes to needle her, only a little, and only so she can see that the Cass she used to know isn't completely gone. "She's always so dramatic," Teddy says, but when she looks at her mother she knows she has taken it too far.

"She didn't have to come with me, you know," her mom says. "She really does want to see you succeed. We all do."

Teddy is quiet for a long moment. Inside, the black hole stirs, like it is waking from a long sleep. *No, no. Can't give in. Can't lose control.*

Her phone vibrates on the bench beside her and she flips it over to read the message. From Nora: **You're a GARDNER GIRL!! and don't u forget it.** A picture of Nora's red-painted lips accompanies the text, her middle finger pressed against them. The black hole continues to swirl, but it's slow, easy. Not threatening to swallow Teddy whole this time, right now.

She squeezes her knee under the table, nails digging in.

THE TOURNAMENT

"It's not that I don't think about my future," she says slowly, keeping her voice level, looking somewhere that isn't quite her mother's eyes. "But I feel like I just got here, and things just started to work out. I really am trying my best," she says, shaking her head as a stupid sob threatens to explode. *No crying, not when you're trying to make a fucking point, idiot.* "I thought you would be—be, like, proud of me or something. I could be a doing a lot worse."

Her mother reaches over the food and waits for Teddy to offer up her hand. When Teddy does, her mother grips her fingers tight. "I know you're trying," she says. "The thing is, I can't let you operate solely on the idea that *hey, things could be worse.* Things could be worse, but they could be better, too. I didn't send you here because it was the last place that would take you. I also thought it was what you needed. I wouldn't be doing my job if I let you become complacent. I'm glad you're liking it here, but like your sister said, you'll be graduating before long. And then what? We both know that without a plan, without some kind of structure in place, everything will fall apart." She pauses. "*You* will fall apart. And we can't always pick up the pieces. It's time for you to understand that, Teddy."

Teddy nods, because she knows it's what her mother wants. Because she knows that it doesn't matter what she has to say, or how well she's doing, or how for the first time, Teddy feels like there might *be* a future for her to inevitably fuck up, which is a long way from the emptiness that used to be all she could see. To her mother, she will always be a failure; the finish line is always going to move, forever just out of reach.

She replays Nora's text in her head: *You're a GARDNER GIRL*. It was half a joke and half sincere, she knows, because that's how everybody here talks about belonging to this school: it's embarrassing to buy into it, but they do it anyway. Let themselves succumb to the propaganda because it feels good, to think you're part of something no one else can understand. And that's what this all is—her mother and her sister can't understand who she is now, or what this all means. So what else is there to do but placate them? They'll never get it, and maybe Teddy won't need them to, one day.

She looks at her mother, making actual eye contact this time, and nods. "I do understand," she says. "I don't want to fight. If I promise to behave myself at dinner, will Cass come?"

"Of course she will," her mother says, and smiles. "She loves you, you know? We both do."

Teddy knows this is where she's supposed to say that she loves them, too. But she's never quite wrapped her head around those words, for anyone. So instead she shoves another bite of bagel into her mouth and smiles as she chews, hoping that will be enough.

21

MAX

MAX WALKS HER mom around the school, in and out of different buildings, stopping whenever her mom expresses interest in some painting or photo or plaque. Max can't remember her mom ever showing interest in art—the only things she remembers hanging on the walls of her childhood home were family photographs, where all three of them looked uncomfortable, as if they were wearing the wrong skin. But today her mom spends time taking in the projects on display in the art studios, like she wants to get it. They walk past other classrooms with the doors wide open, teachers inside giving talks to parents on what kind of topics the tuition gets their kids. She doesn't intend on introducing her mom to anyone, but then Mr. Gordon spots them walking past and calls out her name, coming to the doorway. So Max has no choice but to tell him that this woman is her mom, and to Mr. Gordon's credit he doesn't make any comment on how this is the first time he's met one of Max's parents despite having taught her every year she's been at Gardner. Afterward they eat pastries in the dining hall and then, because she already suggested it and wants to see if her mom will actually do it, she walks her mom up to the archery range. To her surprise, her mom is actually willing to take a shot herself, and she listens to every word Max says with an attention like Max has never experienced from her. Her first arrow flies wide but her second lands somewhere on the target and now it's her turn to be surprised, to turn to Max with another big smile and say, "I see why you like this so much."

By the time they walk back to the dorms the sun is beginning to drop and Max is starving. The dining hall will be quiet tonight, everyone out in town with their parents, and Max thinks that once her mom is gone, maybe she'll splurge and order Chinese, which they are technically not supposed to do but the houseparents always ignore it if you slide them a spring roll. She folds her arms over her chest and rocks back on her heels as she faces her mom. "So—"

"I've had a great time today," her mom says, sudden and loud, cutting Max off. "Thank you for showing me everything."

Max shifts, unfamiliar with the thanks. "That's okay," she says. "I mean, you came all the way up here, so . . ." The end of that sentence is *so I didn't really have much of a choice*, but Max decides not to say it, because they both already know it.

"How about dinner?"

Max blinks. "What?"

THE TOURNAMENT

"Tonight," her mom says. "I know we've left things a little late but I'm sure there's somewhere in town where we could get a table. What do you think?"

What does Max think? That this day has been so weird already she almost wants to just go *Hey, yeah, sure! Let's go get dinner!* But it hasn't only been weird. Like, yeah, it felt strange to be walking her mom to the same places she goes every single day, places her mom has never before shown that much interest in. But also—she came all this way. Not because Max asked, but because she decided to, of her own free will. She hasn't asked Max for anything and she hasn't made any of her usual shitty remarks about Max's body, or her clothes, or hobbies. She hasn't made a veiled reference to the fantasy future in which Max has a husband and kids, and she hasn't even brought up the fact that Max hasn't returned home in almost a year. Max doesn't know what has prompted this good behavior and as much as she tells herself, has been telling herself all day, that there *must* be some ulterior motive behind it, maybe now she has to admit that there isn't one. Doesn't seem to be, at least, and maybe when her mom said she just wanted to see Gardner and see her daughter, that was true. Of course Max doesn't want to believe it, because she never wants to believe anything good, not when it involves her parents. She never wants to show weakness, because that's when her mom hits the hardest, when things fall apart. And it feels weak to admit that she has enjoyed the past hours spent in her mom's company. It feels weak to admit to herself that she wants to say yes to dinner, because after all, she's no longer Wren but Max, the girl who doesn't need anybody else. The girl who certainly doesn't need a mom, not the woman who never understood her, who replaced her with two perfect daughters, who doesn't even care that she doesn't go home for the holidays anymore.

It feels weak but sometimes—and Max would admit this to no one, not any of her friends, not even Nora back when things were normal with them—sometimes Max wants a mom. Everyone else around her gets to feel like that but it's like she's made it impossible for herself to ask for the same, because wasn't she the one who left? Wasn't she the one who was desperate to get out of there? But sometimes she wants to sit across a table and eat overpriced pasta with the woman who brought her into the world.

"Wren?" her mom prompts. "What do you say? Shall we get dinner?"

And Max nods, before she can get too lost in her own thoughts again. "Yeah," she says. "I think I know the place."

Marigold Palace is not the best restaurant in town, but it's good enough—better than its name implies, at least, and they were willing to seat them at seven thirty when Max called.

The hostess takes their coats and Max and her mom take a seat at their table, not tucked right back by the kitchen but close enough that Max understands why there was a table free at short notice on probably one of the busiest weekends this town sees. "This place is nice," her mom says, shaking out her napkin and laying it on her lap. "I bet you've been to a lot of nice restaurants with your friends. With Nora. That's her name, right? The one you spent last summer with?"

Max picks up the pitcher of water and pours herself a glass.

She takes a sip before answering. "I was at camp this summer," she says, trying not to feel irritated at having to remind her mom. "Remember? I was working."

"But last year," her mom says, "and before, that's who you were staying with, right?"

Max nods. "Yeah," she says, and now all she can think about is long summer days swimming in the McQueens' pool, endless snacks prepared by their chef, the guest room that she made her home for months on end and that always had a gift waiting in it when she arrived. A book on philosophy that Mrs. McQueen thought she should read, an engraved lighter from Mr. McQueen, a pair of the most perfect loafers that she still wears even now. It never felt like charity; it only ever felt like they were giving her what they thought she needed, and Max always made sure to show them she understood and appreciated the gifts, because they were the foundation, weren't they? Things she needed to keep building her new life in a new stratosphere, among people who liked to debate literary theory over dessert, who moved so easily through the world that Max was still finding her way in.

Her mom is watching her and Max sits up a little straighter, pushing her braids over one shoulder. "Yeah, I stayed with Nora. And yeah, we've been to some nice places, I guess."

Her mom nods enthusiastically. "That's good," she says. "You get to know different people at a school like that."

Max picks up the menu, scanning to see what's cheapest. "I mean, I guess."

"Who would you say is the most interesting girl at school? Or someone you've met."

Max lowers the menu so she can give her mother a quizzical look. "What?"

Her mom fills her own glass with water, talking as she pours. "I don't know," she says. "Do you have anyone who wants to go the Olympics? Or someone who might cure cancer or something?"

Max makes a noise somewhere near a laugh. "Cure cancer? Mom, we're still high school students. I think it takes a *little* more education than we have to know those sorts of things."

"I was just asking," her mom says, and she gets this wounded look, like a kicked puppy.

Luckily for Max, the server reappears. "Are we ready to order?" he asks. "Or do we need a few more minutes?"

"We're ready," Max says before her mom can open her mouth. "I'll have the mushroom risotto. And sparkling water. Thank you."

The server takes her menu and turns to her mom. "And for you?"

"Hmm, what looks good, what looks good . . ." Susan traces her finger down the page until her face lights up and she taps the menu. "Oh, the Thai duck sounds wonderful. I'll have that. And we'll get the roasted broccoli and braised cabbage, too. And a nice white, please." She peers over her menu at Max. "You like white wine, right?"

The server ignores her mom's comment, only holds his hand out to take her menu. "Excellent choices," he says, and Max knows he's thinking that he doesn't get paid enough to care whether she drinks or not.

Her mom watches him walk away, one hand tracing the rim

of her glass. "He's cute," she says absentmindedly, or in a calculated tone that's *supposed* to sound absentminded—that way she has plausible deniability, can counter Max's *Jesus, Mom, how many times do I have to say I like GIRLS, I'm GAY, I'm a LESBIAN* with a little *What, I was just noticing!*

But right as Max is opening her mouth to say it, her mom speaks again. "You know what I did find out today, when I was waiting for you? There's a girl at your school whose mother is a former prima ballerina." She lowers her voice on those last two words, a hushed reverence. "Isn't that something?"

"Oh, Gigi?" Gigi Westin-De la Cour looks exactly like the daughter of a prima ballerina, Max thinks every time she sees her. In third year she and Nora had the room right across from Gigi and Freya O'Farrell, and often they would be woken late at night by Gigi in the corridor, doing push-ups or crunches, sheen of sweat on her face, but in the morning she'd act like nothing had happened at all. "Yeah, I guess her mom is a dancer." She pauses. "Wait. How do you even know that?"

"I was looking at all those photos," her mom says. "While you were getting ready. I saw her name."

"Okay," Max says slowly. "But how did you know about Gigi's mom? She's not in any of the pictures. And it doesn't say under our photos what each of our parents do."

"Well, fine, I suppose I didn't read it," her mom says. "But it's not hard to put two and two together. She looks just like her mother."

"And you know what her mother looks like because . . . ?"

"Because I know things sometimes," her mom says defensively. "Gabrielle De la Cour is a huge name in the dance world."

Max closes her eyes and suddenly everything seems very loud: cutlery scraping on china, the obnoxious laughter from somewhere in the middle of the room, the creak of the hinges on the swinging door in and out of the kitchen. She doesn't know exactly why she's closed her eyes, except some part of her brain is saying not to look at her mom right now, because some other part of her brain is finally putting all the pieces together and coming up with the thing Max had been so stupid as to believe didn't exist: motive.

"Big in the dance world," she says, nodding, eyes still closed. "Right."

"Yes!" her mom says. "You know, I even think she runs several dance schools that are very highly regarded. If you train there, it's basically a straight shot into one of the elite ballet academies, and then a company."

Max opens her eyes. Her mom is leaning over the table, her face open and hopeful. For a moment she just looks at her mother, really taking her in. She looks older than Max remembered, and sure it's been a while since she's seen her mom in person, but it's more than that—she looks *old*, like at some point in the intervening time she slipped over the threshold, lost the youthfulness that allowed her to spend much of Max's childhood batting off compliments and saying, "No, honestly, I'm thirty-seven! I guess I just have good genes!" Now the dark purple circles beneath her eyes can't quite be covered by makeup and her skin looks dry and dull, two spots of rusty red blush hastily applied to her cheekbones. Max imagines her at the hotel, using the bright bathroom light to examine herself in the mirror, dusting the blush on her face and walking away satisfied with her work. She'd be prettier without it. If there's one thing Max could never deny about her mother, it's that she is beautiful. But her mom never seemed to see it herself, or maybe it was that she knew the way the world looked at her and decided to armor up before going to the office every day. Maybe that's why she's always on Max's case to wear more makeup, make herself more appealing—not just because Max is not the ultrafeminine daughter she longed for, but because of the way the world looks at them.

Their food arrives then, servers placing dishes in front of each of them, presenting her mom with a bottle of wine that she nods at, as if she knows the difference between a good white wine and the cheap shit she keeps stocked in the fridge at home. Max picks up her spoon and pokes at the mushrooms sitting atop the rice, bloated and gray. She wants to think that she can eat this and leave, and her mom won't bring anything else up, and the visit can end with them both pretending to have had a good time. But she knows it won't go that way.

"So." Her mom pours wine into her own glass, then reaches over and adds a small amount to Max's wineglass. "I actually have been thinking about enrolling your sisters in one of those schools."

Here it is.

Max downs the wine in a single gulp. It's sharp, not quite chilled enough. "Oh yeah?" she says flatly.

"I just think the school they're at right now isn't quite . . . I mean, it's a nice school, and the staff are great, but it's not quite rigorous enough for what the girls need. Pearl, in particular—oh, you should see her dance, she just lights up the stage. Everybody agrees that she really has promise, but I'm concerned that if I keep her where they are, she's going to learn bad habits. Better to start with a really good foundation, don't you think?"

"Oh sure," Max says.

"And Amethyst—I'm not sure she'll go all the way in ballet, but it's important to have those roots, so then if she wants to move into contemporary or maybe jazz, she'll have the technique."

"Right."

Her mom begins cutting at her duck, as if they're just having a casual conversation, as if she hasn't planned this entire thing. "I tried to enroll them at the academy but they said every place was taken and we'd have to wait until the next round of auditions, but that's all the way in spring and I just think that's far too long for the girls to stay at their current school learning the wrong things."

"So pull them out," Max says. "I mean, that's the obvious answer, no? That way they won't learn any bad habits because they won't be learning anything. And then they can audition later. It's not that big a deal. They're, like, literally babies."

"They are six years old," her mom says. "Which is absolutely the time when they should be starting out and learning that good foundation. Otherwise they're going to fall behind and every other girl who got into the right school at the right time will have an advantage over them and they'll never get into a company."

"What does it even matter? They don't know what they want yet. They don't have any idea of what a professional dancer even is."

"But one day they will," her mom says. "And when that

day comes, I don't want them looking at me and realizing I let them down, that I ruined their chances before they even knew it. It's called parenting, Wren. As a mother I have to make choices on behalf of my children to set them up for success as much as I can."

Oh, like you did for me? Max bites her tongue. No use in saying it, no use in dredging it all back up. Not when there's already enough on the table to fight about.

She pushes the bowl of rapidly congealing risotto away and folds her hands on the table. "Can we cut the shit?" she says. "Ask me whatever it is you want to ask. We both know that's the only reason you came here today. So get it over with, so we can both move on with our nights."

Her mom drops her fork, the ding it makes on the china loud and ringing. "I came here to see my daughter," she says. "I came here—"

"You came here knowing that one of my classmates is the daughter of the person who controls whether or not your *other* daughters get into some fucking ballet academy," Max says. "You came fully prepared, not to see me, but to get something for them. I knew that's what it was, I *knew* there was some reason you would show up here, because you don't do anything for me, you don't do anything that involves me unless it has some benefit for you or the girls. So ask me what it is you want to and let's stop pretending any of this"—she gestures around them, at the restaurant, the food sitting between them—"is because of me, or because you wanted to see the school after all this time, or whatever other bullshit we've both been pretending to believe in today. Okay?"

Her mom picks up her napkin, dabs at the corners of her mouth. When she speaks, her voice is level, all business. "I would like you to ask your friend to speak to her mother and pull some strings, to allow the girls to enroll at the academy now, instead of waiting. I don't think that's too much to ask of you. After all, isn't the point of going to a fancy school like that to make connections? Network with the *right* people? Now you can actually put it to use, and help your sisters."

Max drums her fingers, wishing she had the kind of long nails Brooke has, the kind that make a satisfying rat-a-tat when tapped in quick succession. "You are unbelievable," she says, and she means to keep her voice low but she just can't. Not when she's faced with the same shit her mom has been pulling for Max's entire life. Not when she's being reminded, yet *again*, that she's never been the priority and all it really took to confirm it was her taking herself off to Gardner, which allowed her parents to keep all their focus where they really wanted it, on two replacement daughters that they could do a better job of molding this time. "I've been at this school for six years now and you call me up sometimes to pretend like you care, but you don't care."

"Of course I care, Wren. I'm your mother."

Max throws her hands up. "And what kind of mother lets their kid move away to boarding school by themselves? You didn't even *drop* me *off*. I did it all by myself. I did all of this all by myself and you never fought me on any of it because you didn't want to. You didn't want me to stay, you were fine with me leaving, and I was happy to go if it meant I didn't have to see you being disappointed by my existence every day."

THE TOURNAMENT

Her mom presses a hand to her throat. "I was never disappointed, I only—"

"And it was the best thing I could have done, it will probably always be the best thing I ever did, getting out of there," Max continues. "Coming to a place that understood me and let me be myself without any restrictions, and—yeah, I know people now. I know a lot of people with a lot of money and a lot of power, and I hope that one day I'll *be* one of them. I will have money, and I will have power, and I will have the ability to influence people's lives for my own enjoyment."

"I always knew you wanted to be—"

"But I just figured out that I don't have to wait! I have power right now." Max shakes her head. "Because you know what, no. The answer is no. I'm not going to ask Gigi—who is not my *friend*, by the way, just another girl in my class—I'm not going to ask her to do a favor for me on behalf of you, because you never did anything for me. And those girls, those little girls who don't know any better yet and can't defend themselves—I'm not going to do that to them. Because they don't need to be in some uptight ballet school that you had to work their way into so that one day they might fulfill *your* dream of being a ballerina, or at the very least the perfect, delicate, feminine creature you didn't get with me. So, yeah. It's a no."

Her mom stares, her eyes darkened, and Max feels something inside her click into place. That's better. That's how her mother should look at her, that's what Max knows. "You are horrible," her mom says, and this time her voice quivers. "'Those girls,' as you put it, are your sisters. Your flesh and blood. And you won't ask a simple question in order to better their lives? You would really deprive them of something good so that you can feel big? So you can wield power over me—because, what, I'm one of the unimportant people now, one of the insignificant masses who you so desperately want to distance yourself from?"

Max pushes her chair back and stands, and of course she's aware people are looking, have been looking. This is what her mother turns her into: the kind of person who would yell in the middle of nice restaurant, ruining everyone else's night, making a spectacle of herself. "I don't *want* to distance myself," she snaps. "I've done it. I'm far, far away from you in every sense of the word and you know, in six months I'll be eighteen and you won't have to worry about anything to do with me anymore. I won't be sending any forms your way to sign without reading, because you don't even understand what they say. I won't need your approval for anything, and you know what, I won't even interfere on the girls' behalf. I figured out how much I didn't belong with you, in that house, in that town, in that *world*, and I'm sure they will, too. Or maybe they won't. Maybe they're nothing like me and everything like you, and they'll be happy with their lot in life, or happy enough to one day have their own daughters to take their own frustrations out on. Who knows. But what I do know is that we're done. We're through, and I don't want anything from you, and you don't deserve anything from me. Except—" She yanks out her wallet and takes out the only cash she ever has, a one-hundred-dollar bill in case of emergencies. She tosses it onto the table and lifts her chin. "There. That should more than cover my share. So now I don't owe you anything."

THE TOURNAMENT

She turns on her heel and strides away, whispers going back and forth in her wake. It's only when she's almost to the door that she sees her. At a table by the window, chin resting on steepled fingers as she watches Max storm out, is Teddy Swanson.

Fucking perfect, Max thinks, trying not to break her stride, shoving the door open and then she's out on the street and she wishes it were the kind of cold that slaps you in the face, a punch to the lungs, but it's not. *Perfect, perfect, she can run back to Nora and tell her all about me and they can laugh together at the stupid bitch having a trashy argument in the restaurant and Nora can tell her about my shitty parents and my shitty life and oh, it'll be so fun—*

"Hey."

Max looks over at the voice and drags her hands down her face when she sees Teddy standing there, and *god* she always looks so smug, so poised, her lipstick never smudged and her hair always doing exactly what it's supposed to and her clothes with that pristine hang that screams wealth. "Oh my *god,* what do you *want?*" Max says.

Teddy shrugs. "I don't know," she says. "Seemed like maybe you weren't okay and maybe a nice thing to do would be to come make sure you're good. But I don't know, I don't have so much experience in doing the nice thing."

Max laughs. "Right," she says sourly, sinking into a crouch. "Because you're so cool and you don't care about anything and fuck being nice, right?"

"Something like that," Teddy says.

"I'm so sick of you," Max says, and she looks up at Teddy,

who for a second looms large and terrifying. But then Max stands again and actually they're the exact same height, eye to eye on the street corner. "You could have anything you want in the entire world but you take what's mine, because you can, and none of it even matters to you."

Teddy's lips curl at the corners. "What exactly is it that I took from you?" she asks. "We don't even talk. I barely know you. How could I possibly take anything from you if I don't even know what it is you care about?"

"You know," Max says. "But it's not about me. I bet you do this all the time, every school you show up at, every place you go. You have no idea what it's like to actually work for something, or want something out of your reach. You do whatever you want and fuck everybody else. You don't even *care* about the Cup, I know. You have no idea about the history, what it really means. You shouldn't even have been allowed to put your name down but whatever, it's done now. So in a way it's good, because now I can destroy you, and everybody will be watching."

Teddy says nothing, only keeps on smiling, and Max knows she's playing into Teddy's hand but she's so worked up still that she can't help doing it. "What? What's so fucking funny?"

"You," Teddy says. "Pretending this is all about the Cup. Which, by the way, I look forward to fighting you for. But we both know this is about her, really."

Who? Max wants to ask, but even imagining herself saying it fills her with a hot shame. A protestation too far.

She wonders what Nora has already told Teddy about her. How many confidences she has broken.

"And it's just funny to me," Teddy's saying, "because I bet you never even wanted her before I came around. But you liked having her right there, didn't you? Yeah, I think that's it. I think you liked how that made *you* feel, Wren Maxwell."

"Don't—"

"Yeah, yeah, your name's Max, sure." Teddy smiles again, and her teeth gleam in the dark, not a hint of crooked anywhere. "Okay, then, Max. Since you think I took so much from you, and since it seems to really piss you off—I think I'm going to keep doing it. Who knows what it'll be next? I mean, I stole your girl. I'm going to steal your Cup. And—" She pauses, to tap theatrically at her lips. "Oh! Maybe I'll steal your place at Columbia, too. My mother has been on me to *focus* and get serious and pick a college and all that shit. Honestly, I never thought I'd make it to college but if they want me to go so badly, I guess I will. If I recall correctly, we have *quite* a few connections at Columbia. Or my parents can just buy my way in, I'm sure."

Max bites down hard on the inside of her cheek, until she tastes metal. Teddy is pushing her buttons; Max will not give her the satisfaction of responding. It wouldn't even feel good, not when what Max really wants to do is slap Teddy hard enough that her cheek matches the bright scarlet of her lipstick.

But even that wouldn't be enough. It wouldn't change the real thing in all of this, the shit that eats at Max the most. Because Teddy is right. It *kills* Max to see her with Nora, but not for the reasons Teddy claims. Teddy is everything Max wishes she could be, isn't she? Okay, maybe Teddy doesn't work as hard as Max, and she's a fuckup, but they all know none of that matters if you're the right kind of girl, from the right kind of family, with the right kind of money and connections and status. Seeing Nora with Teddy feels like watching her walk around with an upgraded version of Max, the girl Nora *should* have befriended way back at the beginning of school. Like Nora's been slumming it for the last six years and now she's free, released from her obligations to Max, a girl who could never truly fit into her life. And it seems all the more clear to Max that the friendship she and Nora had was nothing but a fluke, really—if they hadn't been put together because of their last names, would Nora have even paid attention to her? Would they have become friends at all? *She must be relieved,* Max thinks. *To finally be with the right kind of girl.*

When the silence has stretched on long enough and it's clear that Max is not going to speak, Teddy glances at the restaurant. "Well, I better get back. So glad we had this talk," she says. "See how nice it can be when we actually talk to each other?"

Max waits until Teddy is at the door, about to step inside, before she calls out to her. "You can have Nora," she says. "I never wanted her in the first place. But you'll never get the Cup. I can promise you that."

Teddy laughs, the noise pealing off into the night, and walks into the restaurant without looking back.

Max spits, blood and saliva, and leaves.

22

NORA

NORA WAVES AS the car carrying her parents winds around the entrance and off through the gates. She lets her hand drop and sighs, part relief, part exhaustion. All along the edge of the drive other girls do the exact same as her, and Nora turns to Freya O'Farrell and Sage Porter beside her. "I feel bad saying I'm glad they're gone," Nora says. "But . . ."

"I'll say it," Freya says, and the three of them begin the walk back to campus. "I'm glad my parents are gone. Oh my *god*, sometimes they're just so *annoying*."

"At least your mom didn't come with her latest dalliance," Sage says. "You would think three failed marriages would be enough for her to learn, but I guess not."

"I'm not being a bridesmaid for her again," Freya says. "I have to draw the line somewhere."

"A lesson some people need to learn," Sage says. "Nora, your parents are retro, right?"

Nora laughs. "As in, still married to each other? Oh yeah. I think they make it work by not seeing each other too much. There's always an office to run back to."

Freya nods like Nora's speaking wisdom. "Smart," she says. "So, did you meet Teddy's parents? I think I saw her with her mom."

"Meeting the parents is very official," Sage says. "But you two are, what—a couple? Hooking up? Is it official or non?"

Nora rolls her eyes. "It is what it is," she says, and, eager to move the subject along, "Did you both get the college lecture again?"

"Oh, my dad is obsessed with me going to Yale," Freya says. "He wants me to apply early and I keep telling him, it's not the same as when he went to college, and maybe I want to keep my options open, because . . ."

Nora tunes Freya out as they keep walking. She had been kind of worried, before this weekend, about what to do with her parents and Teddy. With her parents and Max, too, because she knows her mom still hasn't quite let up on the fact that Max didn't spend the summer with them, and Nora knew if they saw Max it would be impossible to stop her mom from saying hi and then they'd be in that weird space where they have to pretend to like each other for the sake of politeness, and forced niceties make Nora want to puke. But luckily her parents said they'd seen the school enough times and had planned a day of activities off campus for Saturday, and this morning there'd been the big all-school brunch in the dining hall which was so crowded and loud that Nora hadn't even seen Max, nor Teddy, so all her stressing had been for nothing. It's not like she's *embarrassed* of Teddy—god, what is there to possibly be embarrassed about? She's beautiful, and smart, and from the exact same kind of family that Nora is. She imagines that if their parents sat down together, they'd be talking nonstop about the struggles of being a Black student at an Ivy League school, or the challenge of being the first Black partner in the firm, or the worries about sending their Black daughters to predominately white private schools—never mind the fact that both of her parents went to private school themselves, grew up wealthy themselves, and that their activism only really extends as far as making sure they can be as filthy rich as their non-Black colleagues and friends.

So it's not like she thought her parents wouldn't like Teddy, it's just—maybe it would be better, this time around, to keep things separate. She let Max become too big a part of her life, only for Max to turn around and cut her off, and now there are all these memories and places outside Gardner that are ruined. Too closely intertwined with the two of them and what Nora thought they were to each other. So maybe it's better to keep what she and Teddy have, are, off to one side, and the rest of her life, out in the real world away from this place, to another side. After all, who knows where this thing with Teddy will go? There really isn't that much time before Gardner ends, for both of them, and then college, life—who the fuck knows? And who even really knows what they are now? Nora doesn't dodge those questions from her classmates because she's embarrassed or something, she just really doesn't know how to answer it. Is Teddy her girlfriend? Is that what they should call it? Is it a relationship when two people spend most of their time together and a good amount of that time with their clothes off? And actually, they don't spend a lot of time with their clothes off—that would require them to be in private, behind closed doors, but Teddy prefers to be anywhere but their rooms. So it's more—shirts tugged out of waistbands, hands seeking under clothes, underwear pushed to the side. Trying to stay quiet in the library stacks, Nora pressed up against the wall of the art supply closet, Teddy's mouth on her neck in the back of Study Session. Last week Nora had been in her room, studying with the door open, and Teddy had come in and dropped to her knees in front of Nora, her hands already doing what they're so expert in before Nora could even say *close the door* and then she couldn't say anything at all. It was all over in a minute and not too soon because then their houseparent Ms. Cara walked by, sticking her head in to tell them they were going to be watching a movie in the common room later, and Nora couldn't even answer, catching her breath, but Teddy had already moved to sit on the bed, a book open in her lap, and said they'd be there, as if nothing had happened, as if they were only innocently studying together.

And Nora likes it. She likes the way Teddy looks at her, eyes glazed, hungry. She likes how Teddy wants her, how it feels to be desired, how it feels to have everybody in their class know that Teddy and Nora are *it*, are hot, are in a world the rest of them can't even imagine. It's a world away from how she always felt with Max, because of course Max couldn't even admit to wanting Nora even a little bit, made Nora feel small for even thinking such a thing was possible, and for a while Nora had believed her. Had let herself shrink small and shamed and sad. But now she has a girl who isn't afraid to say she wants Nora, to *show* how she wants her, and Nora has remembered who she really is. That she admires herself, her body, her mind. That, actually, she has power, too.

They've reached the dorms now, and Nora waves as Freya and Sage go in, but she continues walking, over to the sports center. This time next week, the first challenge will be over, and so Nora needs to get in as much last-minute training as she can. She intends to win the first challenge—*Start as you mean to go on, right?* she thinks. See, that's the other thing—she doesn't have time to be thinking about what she and Teddy are, or what the fact that neither of them wanted to introduce the other to their parents means. The Cup is about to begin in earnest, and that's where her focus needs to be.

At dinner that night the mood is bright, everyone relieved to be off best behavior now that their parents have retreated to their own lives again. Nora carries her tray over to where Teddy is sitting, at their usual spot in the back, examining her split ends with a textbook flopped open beside her tray. "You got the mac and cheese?" Nora says as she sits down across from Teddy. "How many times do I have to tell you, it's *bad*."

"I know, but every time I really *crave* mac and cheese, I

come and find they have it out, and so I have to get it." Teddy drops the piece of hair she was staring so intently at and stares at Nora instead. "Okay. I have to ask you something."

Nora takes a bite of her grilled cheese and nods, ignoring the tiny little flicker that just caught alight inside her, the way a pinprick of anxiety always shines through whenever someone says something like *I need to tell you something.* "Shoot," she says, chewing.

"Don't get mad at me," Teddy says, and the flicker becomes a flame.

Nora swallows. "Always such a fun thing to hear," she says. "Doesn't ring any alarm bells at all."

"It's not *that* bad," Teddy says. "I just wondered, like— what's the deal with Max and her mom?"

It's not at all what Nora expected Teddy to say and she shakes her head, bemused. "What? Why would you even be asking me that?"

"I said not to get mad."

"I'm not mad," Nora says, laughing. "I just didn't expect— what, is this because her parents weren't here? I can't believe you even noticed. They never come, though. It just is what it is."

Teddy reaches over for Nora's grilled cheese and takes a bite without asking. "So you're telling me I didn't see her with her mom at dinner last night?"

Nora stills, not quite sure what to do with this information but also sure that Teddy is wrong, because there's no way Max's mom showed up at Gardner. There's just no way— she's never come here before, and neither has Max's dad, and it's never surprised Nora because Max told her all about her parents, when they first met. Max has never even invited her parents up here—Nora knows, because they used to know everything about each other. *Is that why you don't want to believe Teddy?* a part of her says. *Not because you don't believe it happened, but because you don't want it to have happened without your knowing about it?* "Bullshit," she says, ignoring her thoughts. "There's no fucking way."

"Well, she was at the restaurant last night," Teddy says with a shrug. "With a woman who looked kind of like her, and it's Family Weekend, so forgive me for jumping to a conclusion."

"They were at dinner?"

Teddy nods as she cracks open a Diet Coke. "At that place you told me about. Marigold whatever. I went there with my mom and sister and there was Max with this woman. She's, like, a little shorter than Max? Kind of has a curly bob situation? Could use a lesson on proper blush application? Sound about right?"

Nora doesn't know how to say that she has no idea what Max's mom looks like. Again—her parents never came up to school, and there was never even the suggestion that Nora might go to Max's hometown and meet them there. Nora wouldn't have wanted to, anyway. Everything Max ever told her about her parents told Nora that she was better off without them—and besides, they'd replaced her anyway, hadn't they? Max rarely mentioned her little sisters but when she did, it was clear how she felt about the whole thing: her parents never really liked her, so they popped out another two kids and focused all their attention on them instead, and Max got the message. At first Nora had thought the whole thing was kind of sad, because even if her own parents irritated the shit out of her, they were still her parents, and she knew that they loved her, that they'd always be there in an emergency, that they did all they could for her to have a good life. She couldn't imagine not being sure of that, or worse, knowing that if it came down to a choice between her and anything else, that they'd pick the anything. Even when Max got appendicitis in third year, no one came. The only flowers in Max's hospital room were the ones Nora's mom sent.

"Hello?" Teddy waves a hand right in front of Nora's face. "Anyone in there?"

Nora blinks. "Yeah," she says. "Wait. So they were just eating dinner?"

"Well. No," Teddy says. "They were, like, yelling at each other. Or actually, Max was yelling at her mom, and then she left. Maybe it was a surprise visit that didn't quite pan out?" She shrugs again. "I didn't talk to her. I just saw it happen."

Nora can't help but turn and look for Max in the dining hall. She's nowhere to be seen, though, and Nora turns back to Teddy, unsure of what to do next. If what Teddy is saying is true, it's fucking huge—why would Max's mom show up here, after five years of nothing? What were they fighting about? Did Max know her mom was coming, or was Teddy right and it was a surprise that didn't go well at all? What did Max think when she saw her mom here, what made her decide to go for dinner with her, what did her mom say that could have pushed her to make a scene in the middle of a crowded restaurant? Of course Max can be a bitch and of course she's not afraid to raise her voice but usually only when she's in control. In front of an audience of her own choosing, not a restaurant full of strangers—no, worse than that, full of her fellow Gardner students and their parents?

Nora pulls out a tube of lip gloss and smears it over her mouth, buying time. Teddy's watching her like she knows there's a thousand things racing through her head and Nora has to pick which ones to share, which ones will be right. Because she can't tell Teddy that she's overcome with the need to run off and find Max right now, so that Max can tell her everything that went down, because she's the only person who knows about Max's family. How weak would that make her look? That even after the shit Max pulled, Nora's instincts are still to take care of her, protect her? And what, like she could say all that to Teddy and *not* have Teddy think that she still has feelings for Max? Which she doesn't, of course, because Nora has Teddy now, and whatever was or wasn't between her and Max is done. And none of it matters anyway because of course Nora can't go and ask Max about any of this. Last year? Sure. Now? Well, now it's not her business, anymore. Not her problem. Whatever it is that Max's mom did or said or wanted, Nora doesn't need to know. Can't know.

But even still, she can't tell Teddy the real shit about Max's mom. That would be a violation of Max's trust. Some things, they endure. The promise Nora made to Max years ago, to keep her secrets—it endures.

So she slips the lip gloss back into her bag and picks up her spoon, stirring it through the tomato soup on her tray. "Well, whatever they were fighting about, I'm sure Max more than held her own. She's always been good at that."

Teddy arches an eyebrow. "That's it?"

"What?"

"That's all you have to say about it? You just said her parents never come here, but I saw her mom, and I saw them fighting, and what, you don't care?"

Nora tips her head to the side. "Do you want me to care? Because it kind of sounds like you want me to care."

"I don't give a shit either way," Teddy says. "I just thought you would want to know."

"Well, now I know," Nora says, and she smiles, tight. "But it's not my problem, so I don't have to care. And actually, maybe this works in my favor."

Teddy wrinkles her nose. "In what way?"

"Maybe a little freak-out from her will knock her off-balance," Nora says, and now she's not bullshitting, but voicing a real thought that just occurred to her. "You know, maybe this will throw her off her game, and just in time for the first challenge, too."

Now Teddy looks proud. "Oh, a little psychological warfare," she says. "My, my. We'll make a champion of you yet."

Nora says nothing, only smiles, preening under Teddy's adoration.

23

TEDDY

THE ATMOSPHERE IN the assembly hall is electric.

Teddy always used to think people were exaggerating, getting caught up in metaphor, when they said shit like that, but right now, in the hall and less than twenty-four hours away from the first challenge and the official beginning of the Tierney Cup, she feels it. It's like everyone is a little on fire, as if she could touch her finger to the skin of any girl in the room and feel the sting all the way up to her skull, down to her feet. Used to be the kind of energy she could only find by getting into trouble, but now it feels good to find it in something real, a contest where people are going to applaud her for playing dirty, because it's not just about winning but about showing off. Showing who can be the best and who isn't afraid to go to the limits, push beyond, in order to claim first place.

All seven competitors are up on the stage, sitting in a neat row of chairs off and back to the left of Dr. Thompson at the lectern. She leans back, trying to see down the row, where Max is sitting. Of course Teddy would like to win the whole thing, but mostly she wants to make sure that Max does *not* win. It would be best if Nora were the one to take the crown and leave Max in the dust, but Safiya in first place would do, too, or one of the others—Teddy really doesn't care about that. As long as Max is not the one who gets to raise the actual Cup over her head at the end, Teddy will be happy.

Max is sitting perfectly still, and all Teddy can really see of her is her perfect braids hanging down the back of her blazer. She clicks her tongue between her teeth and sits up straight again, trying to look like she's at least somewhat paying attention to what Dr. Thompson is saying. Something about spectators and supervision for tomorrow morning's event. *Whatever,* Teddy thinks, and tunes out again, thinking about the water, the crash of cold waves down at the beach. She's completed the actual swim only once, and the strength of the water once she made it far enough out had shocked her at first, but then she'd gotten back into the rhythm and made it back to the finish point in a respectable time. So all she has to do tomorrow is repeat that, and make sure she doesn't finish last. That's about the best she can hope for in the swim, because the only other times Teddy has been in the water in a wet suit have been in warmer climates, with a surfboard in tow, paying more attention to the instructor's string bikini top than anything else. All the other girls have spent their years at Gardner learning how to swim in the cold water off the coast, gray and intimidating. She knows she's not going to win this one but as long as she can come somewhere above the bottom, she can make up the difference in the later challenges.

She leans back again, looking the other way this time, trying to catch a glimpse of Nora from behind. Except then Nora leans back too, her gaze finding Teddy for a second, and she winks before straightening up. And it's so stupid, so silly, but also kind of sexy and Teddy has to force herself to keep from smiling as she looks ahead again. Nora, Nora, Nora. Sure, maybe Teddy had been testing her when she brought up Max and her mom and the scene at the restaurant, but she'd wanted to know what Nora would make of the whole thing, wanted to know who had her allegiance now. She had half expected Nora to say she didn't care, and whether that was the entire truth or a lie, it didn't really matter—what mattered was that she said it, which meant she wanted Teddy to *know* she didn't care, which meant she wanted to please Teddy more than she wanted to console Max. But even better, and what Teddy hadn't expected, was for Nora to see it as an opportunity to fuck with Max. Now *that* was impressive shit.

And sure, she'd lied, but only a *little* bit. The conversation Teddy had had with Max outside the restaurant, well—Nora didn't need to know about that. Not just yet, anyway. But it had been fun to watch Max squirm, even more fun than seeing her flip out in the middle of dinner. See, that was the problem with Max's bullshit: it only worked as long as she didn't display any weakness, and it takes a very strong girl to never crack. Unfortunate for her that she'd shattered right in front of Teddy; extremely fortunate for Teddy, because oh, did she love to watch a good implosion.

She tunes back in as Dr. Thompson is instructing everyone to stand, both the competitors onstage and the girls watching them in their rows. The headmistress's voice rings out, serious and clear, the weight of the tournament and its history soaking every word. Everyone in the assembly hall is quiet and still now, and Teddy feels the gravity working on her, too. "Tonight, the seventy-fifth Tierney Cup will officially begin, as our competitors take part in the Goldenrod Ceremony. In the morning, they will greet you all with their names already marked in history. Who will go on to be remembered, and who will be forgotten, will be determined over the course of the seven challenges. Now let us sing the traditional Cup song, and as we sing, keep in mind why we do this, and what each of you strive to embody as Gardner girls."

Chords ring out from Ms. Lowenstein at the piano, and then the whole room is singing, and unlike the first assembly Teddy attended where she simply mouthed along to words she didn't know, now she sings with the same clarity as every girl on the stage with her does, as everyone in the entire hall does.

> *"From the ocean to the earth*
> *Honor death, honor birth*
> *Honor all who aim to win."*

24

MAX

AS THE MOON winks in and out of view behind thick clouds, Max straightens the hood of her robe and kneels. Cold seeps into her knees but it doesn't bother her. How could it, when it's all a part of the ceremony she's been dreaming about being a part of since she was eleven?

They are far away from any buildings, at the farthest edges of school grounds, where the land drops out and the cliffs hang over the ocean below. This is all Max knows about the ceremony, even if she has been dreaming of it—it's private, secret, not written down in either the official *or* unofficial Gardner history books, unlike every other aspect of the school's history, of the Cup's history. All Max knows is that the seven competitors gather the night before the competition begins and take part in some kind of ritual. So she was only partly surprised when there was a knock at her door earlier and she opened it to see a package wrapped in brown paper, tied with string, left outside her room. Inside had been the robe she now has on—heavy, forest-green woven fabric, tiny gold and red flowers and leaves stitched along the edges, two green ribbons to tie at the throat—and a handwritten note on thick card stock, instructing her to dress in uniform and bring the robe to a meeting point at eleven p.m., well after curfew, when everyone else will be in their rooms. This was not in any of the books Max has read, and she allowed the excitement of everything to burn out the last of her lingering shame over what happened with her mom. None of that matters, now that the Cup is finally here.

She had wanted to be the first one to arrive at the meeting point but when she arrived, everyone else was already there, robes on, hoods pulled up. Two other figures—teachers—stood in black robes, masks covering their eyes: one fox, one rabbit. "Please put on your robe and join us," the fox had said, and Max thought she recognized the voice but the mask made her uncertain.

Now they are kneeling in a line, and the rabbit holds up a metal jug. "For the sacrifice of the land," she says, and the fox holds out a crystal glass, the stem long and impossibly thin, gleaming in the intermittent moonlight. The rabbit tips the jug and dark red liquid fills the glass, almost overflowing but not quite. The fox takes the crystal to the first girl in the line and Max turns, leans forward out of the line to see who is first, who is lucky. "Face forward," the rabbit snaps, and Max does as she is told, sitting back on her heels and staring straight ahead.

When the rabbit speaks again, she is calmer, more in

control. Her words are loud, enough for everyone to hear, to carry on the wind and out on to the ocean. "Our founders built this place as a refuge," she says. "As a place for education for all, in a time when many of us were shut out of institutions, due to our gender, our race, our identities. Here they made a world in which no dream was too big, and no sacrifice was too small. As times have changed, our lives have changed, and yet we carry on the traditions they began. It was Liliane Bahnsen herself who carried out the first ever Goldenrod Ceremony, and we do as she did, in her honor. Close your eyes."

Max squeezes her eyes shut. She wonders who is sitting to her left, if it is Saf, or one of the other girls. If it is Nora, or that bitch Teddy. She half expects that Teddy will ruin this ceremony by not taking it seriously, but as she sits with her eyes tightly closed, she hears no mocking laughter, no whispers of derision.

She startles as she feels the hood of her robe fall, and something being placed over her eyes. *Stay still,* she thinks, and holds her breath as the blindfold is tied behind her head. A voice rings out again and now Max doesn't know whether it is the fox or the rabbit who speaks. "When I come to you," the voice says, "I will ask you a question. Give me an answer. If I judge your answer to be true, I will place the glass at your lips, and you will drink. Is this clear?"

Max says nothing, moves no muscle, as her means of saying yes. Everybody else must do the same, she gathers, because no other voice breaks the silence, and after a moment the fox or rabbit speaks again. "Good," she says, sounding pleased. "We will begin."

Now when the speaker talks, it's so quiet that Max cannot make out the conversation. She strains to hear, wanting to know what this question is going to be, so she can have the right answer prepared. But it's no good; she hears nothing, and so she sits and waits for her turn, her feet tucked beneath her body slowly going numb.

Then suddenly a hand takes hold of her chin and tips her face upward. When the question comes, it is not from in front of her, but to her right, whispered directly into her ear. "Why do you want to win the Tierney Cup?"

Max licks her lips. *Easy.* "It's the highest honor a Gardner girl can have, and I want to earn it," she says, confident, quick.

There's a moment of silence, and Max waits for the glass to touch her lips. "No," the voice in front of her says. "Answer again, and answer honestly."

Beneath the blindfold Max's eyebrows furrow. "That is honest," she says. "I—"

"Again," the voice says. "Honesty."

Fine. "I want to make a mark on Gardner," Max says this time. "To be remembered."

This time barely a second passes before the voice barks, "No! Again!"

Max bristles. *What the fuck,* she thinks. *What do you want from me?* Those *are* her reasons, that *is* her being honest—

"Be honest with yourself," the voice near her ear says now, tone sweet and lilting. "Tell yourself the truth, not us."

And Max remembers, then, years ago now, lying in her bed in the dark, Nora in her bed across the way. How they used to talk in the night, how Max always felt safer then because she didn't have to actually see Nora's face, and Nora couldn't see her, so it was okay to say the things she usually kept hidden. It was okay to show a little weakness, because Nora couldn't see it, and even if she could hear it, she wouldn't ever tell anyone—that was the promise of darkness, wasn't it? Anything said or done under its cover faded to the back of the mind once the sun came up.

But those things never faded in her own mind. "I want to prove I'm worthy of something," she says now, voice just above a whisper. "I want to prove that I matter."

When she feels the crystal against her lips, she drinks deep with relief. The wine is bitter but she doesn't care.

"Remove your blindfolds."

Max does as instructed once again, tugging the fabric up and off her head, smoothing her braids down. She blinks a few times to acclimatize to the night again, and there's a hushed silence among the other girls, still, and she wants to turn and look but remembers the telling-off it earned her before.

The fox and the rabbit stand together now. The fox's red lips curl into a smile. "Well done," she says. "The ceremony is complete." And she takes off her mask and of course it's only Dr. Kessel, and Max feels something give way inside her as the teacher laughs and motions for them all to get up. The rabbit pulls off her mask, Ms. Bell appearing suddenly, and Max gets to her feet, stumbling a little as pins and needles rush through her legs, and all the other girls are already up and everyone is laughing now, talking loudly, the sanctity of the ceremony hidden beneath bravado.

She doesn't mean to look for Nora but she does it anyway,

and they lock eyes, and Max wonders what truth she just told, what she had to dig for in order to pass the test. Nora looks as shaken as Max feels, both of them trying to hide it, Max knows, and both doing a lackluster job. But then Teddy steps in front of Nora and the connection is broken, and Saf is grabbing Max's hand and they spin together, and the ceremony really is over, and tomorrow—tomorrow, it all begins.

PART THREE

"A question you must ask yourself: What is it about you that makes you a worthy champion of the Tierney Cup?"

—LILIANE BAHNSEN,
Letter to a Gardner Girl, 1954

25

NORA

"ON YOUR MARKS—"

Nora sinks a little, knees bent, ready to run.

"—set—"

She inhales: thin, crisp air, salt on her tongue.

"*Go!*"

The starter's gun goes off, fired by Dr. Kessel, and Nora's already away, feet pushing down hard into the packed sand that makes up the beach. Behind her she's vaguely aware of the crowd—students and teachers and ancillary staff, all down here to watch and cheer on this class of competitors—and beside her she can sense the other girls running toward the water, Abigail Brody on her left, Safiya on her right. But she tries not to focus on any of them too much, tries to keep her eyes straight ahead, as she meets the water and the slap of cold stings. *Knees up,* she thinks, *come on, you can do this—*

When the water hits her thighs she dives, body cutting a lithe path through the murky waves. Head under, everything else recedes, and her hours—actually, years—of training kick in. It's not a fast swim—they have to make it out past the break, swim to the little lump of land they call an island that sits just off the coast, loop around, and make it back to shore. All in all it's around five miles, and in the frigid ocean water there are currents to deal with, creatures snaking around, and then there is the sense of other bodies swimming in front, beside, behind her.

She doesn't think about how hard it always is to find a wet suit that both fits her large body and actually performs the way she needs it to, sealing in heat and protecting her body from the brunt of the ocean's freeze. She doesn't think about how nervous Teddy looked on their walk down, or how Max didn't acknowledge her at all, or how even Saf was reluctant to talk, headphones clamped tight over her ears. She doesn't even think about the ceremony last night, offering up her deepest secret to the teachers in their odd masks, cheeks burning with shame as she drank from the cup. She doesn't think about the dirt left on the knees of her tights, or how Teddy's wet tongue gleamed in the moonlight as she offered herself up, or how Max took the longest of all of them to make her confession.

No: all Nora thinks of is her breathing, the cut and push of her arms through the water, the repetitive *kick kick kick* of her legs. The world is muted, then not, the pattern forming as she lifts her head for air, one side of her face tilted up to the sky, and goes back under.

Getting past the break always seems the most difficult part, but after that there's nothing but miles more of work, she knows. She blocks out as much as she can and powers on, the island growing larger, slowly but surely, as she closes in. Making it around the mass might be the most dangerous part: out of sight of the crowd back on the beach, no way to quickly be spotted if you get into trouble, no way for anyone to see if someone makes trouble for you.

Nora is not playing dirty—not yet, anyway, not when she doesn't need to. She has selected swimming as one of her Activities every year, competing in interschool swim meets for the last three, and she's confident in her abilities. That doesn't mean she can afford not to push herself, though—training with Saf, they'd often been neck and neck in the pool, and Manuela Vega boasts about going to Olympic trials any chance she can get. And after all, the Cup is not about who *tries* the most—it's about who wins. Who makes it back first. Sure, everybody is going to earn points today, but Nora wants to start out big. Number one.

By the time she rounds the island and begins the stretch back to shore, she can feel the ache in every part of her body. That's when everything recedes even further. All she sees are two spots through the lenses of her goggles, alternately gray and bright, water and air. All she hears is the whoosh of her heartbeat, throbbing in her ears. She thinks of nothing but numbers: *one-two-three* strokes and then a breath, *one-two-one-two* kicks, *one* burst of energy and effort to propel her those last two miles. Moving with the waves this time, not against them, working with the water to get her back.

When the water clears a little—less silt, less sand—she

knows she's close. Another minute of stroking, and then she can see the floor beneath her, shifts position and scrabbles to get purchase, pulling her upper body out of the water. The finish line—a dark length of rope laid out on the sand—is right there, and even as her legs scream in protest Nora pushes on, breaking into a slow run that picks up speed as she leaves the ocean behind, splashing through the shallows and up the beach and across the line.

The noise that erupts around her pierces the bubble she'd built around herself, a switch flicking mute to off, and Nora flinches. There are hands on her shoulders and looking out from her rapidly fogging goggles she sees Brooke and Isobel, grinning crazily at her. Isobel's lips move but Nora can't hear her, and can't quite track what it is she's saying. Then Brooke yanks her close and speaks right into her ear: "You did it! You won!"

Nora turns, chest heaving as she tries to catch her breath. Out on the waves she sees black dots bobbing, the swim cap–covered heads of her competitors getting closer and closer to shore, but only she is already out of the water. She rips off her goggles, wanting to see it for real, and her cap comes off, too, damp curls blowing into her face. "I did it?" she says, wonderingly, quietly. And then she snaps to attention, remembering what it is she's doing here, how she needs to carry herself. *Claim it,* a voice in her head says. *Own that shit.*

She turns back to Brooke and Isobel, and this time she's calm, cool. "I did it," she says loudly. "I won."

Brooke throws her arms open, ready for Nora to dive in, but Nora is fully zoned back in now, and the adrenaline of the win is not enough to make her forget that Brooke and Isobel aren't her friends anymore, not really. "Yeah, no," she says, and pushes between them, toward everybody else, chanting her name: *"Nora! Nora! Nora!"*

It sounds like a prophecy, a sign of things to come, and she lets herself be absorbed into the crowd, laughing the entire way.

Manuela comes in second, and Nora can see the fury on her face even from her place farther down the beach, foil blanket around her shoulders, a cup of hot tea warming her hands. Max is next in, then Jordan Riggs, and then Teddy. Saf and Abigail are neck and neck as they come in to shore, but Safiya narrowly beats Abigail over the line. *Second to last?* Nora thinks, and now it's Saf's expression she's examining, but Saf keeps her emotions off her face. She must be yelling at herself internally, though, Nora thinks—all that training they did together and Saf got lost at the back of the pack? *Maybe she got in trouble, or maybe it just wasn't her day.* Either way, it doesn't really matter—after all, as much as she respects Saf, her failing helps Nora. The Cup is not a game of good sportsmanship, and there's really only one person who Nora needs to cheer for, besides herself.

"You beat me," Teddy says, her teeth chattering. "But it was close. One might even say I *let* you win."

"Oh sure," Nora says, and she passes the paper cup of tea over. "Drink this. I'm not going to be the one calling your mom to tell her you got hypothermia."

"I'm fine," Teddy says, but she sips at the tea, closing her eyes and smiling. "Okay, no dicking around—first place, bitch. You really did that."

"Didn't expect anything less," Nora says, and it might be a lie but it sounds good anyway. It's the kind of confidence that breeds winners.

With everyone back in and the pitch of the watching girls reaching something like fever, teachers begin rounding everyone up and starting them on the walk back up to school. Dr. Kessel stays behind, waiting with the competitors for Mr. Paulson, the head groundskeeper, and his second-in-command to arrive in the carts they fly around school grounds in, ready to ferry the girls back up.

When they pile in, Nora feels the exhaustion begin taking hold. She's more than ready to get out of this wet suit, take a hot shower, and then crawl into bed for the rest of the day. Except—"Shit," she says, and Saf, crammed into the same cart as Nora, Teddy, and Jordan Riggs, glances at her.

"What?" she says. "Has the thrill already worn off?"

Nora ignores the unusual acid in Saf's tone. "I just remembered the essay for French. I really wanted to do nothing for the rest of the day."

"No rest for the wicked," Jordan says, and she and Saf exchange a look and laugh.

Nora's cheeks warm, and she turns to look at Teddy, ready for some kind of rebuttal, for Teddy to say *ignore those losers* with that supercilious smile of hers. But Teddy is facing out of the cart, watching the landscape go by, and even when Nora pinches her wrist, she doesn't turn.

Fine. Fuck all of you. Nora folds her arms over her chest

and stares pointedly beyond Saf. They have no choice but to be bratty, she tells herself. They lost, and she won, and it's like she thought before: the Cup is not about supporting your competition, or any sickly sweet notions of collective success being better than individual success. She'd rather be lonely at the top than grasping for a taste of winning, like them.

They make it back to school ahead of everyone else, a chill rain starting as Mr. Paulson stops the cart in front of the sports center, and the girls hurry out of the carts and in the direction of the locker room, eager for hot showers. Nora is about to enter, hand on the door, when a pull on her shoulder stops her. She turns and there's Max, her face serious, the circles beneath her eyes even darker than usual. Silence hangs between them and Nora stays still, unsure of what to do in this moment that should feel familiar but after months feels wrong. When Max speaks, eventually, she is brief. "Congratulations," she says. "You deserved that win."

Until now Nora has not really met Max's gaze, preferring to keep her focus somewhere just above or to the left of Max's eyes, but now she faces her head-on. Max's eyes have always been Nora's favorite feature on her: big, black, expressive, so she could often tell what Max was really feeling even when she wouldn't say it. Now they are reddened from the salt water but no less clear, the sincerity right there for Nora to take in.

"Thank you," Nora says, and she can't look away now. "You did good, too. Third place, not bad."

"Not bad," Max says, a little dip of her chin. "Not good, either."

Nora nods. "You're right," she says. "Do better next time."

Max opens her mouth but doesn't say anything, and this time the silence is heavier, the weight of it palpable. "Will do," she says, and looks away so fast that Nora can't read whatever was really there, whatever it was she decided not to say.

Max pushes inside and Nora is left holding the door, wondering what the fuck they're doing.

26

MAX

MAX TURNS THE water as hot as she can bear. Maybe she can slough off the irritation at herself along with the cold and the grit of sand stuck to her skin.

She does not know why, exactly, she decided to pick today to say anything meaningful to Nora. It wasn't planned, just an urge that overtook her when she saw Nora right in front of her, and nobody else around. It's weird, still not talking to her after so long. In a different universe, they would have moved on, gotten over it all by now, and Nora would be on the sidelines cheering Max on as she took her rightful spot in the Cup, as *she* came in first place. But that isn't how it's going, and the further away they get from that initial fallout, the less it seems like things could ever go back to normal. Not now that things have escalated. Not now that Nora is competing, too. Not now that she's with Teddy.

Max turns her face up to the water and scrubs at her eyes, as if that will relieve the stinging. If she could have said what she really wanted to, it wouldn't have been *congratulations*. It would have been something more like *Did your bitch girlfriend tell you all about me and my mom, making a scene of ourselves as usual?* It would have been *Did you tell her, about my mom? All my secrets you said you'd never tell anyone else?* But of course she couldn't say any of that. And besides—it shouldn't matter, anyway. Nora can tell Teddy whatever the fuck she wants, and Max can't do anything about it, and she wouldn't even want to do anything, because that would mean she cares and she can't have anyone getting confused about that.

Shouts ring out from beyond the showers and then there's a bang, like a door slamming, and suddenly things go quiet. Max turns the water off and wrings out her braids, the last of the warmth snaking down her wrists. When she leaves the stalls, she finds the locker room empty, and when she pulls out her phone, there's a message from Brooke: **Come find us in the common room when ur done. they're putting the numbers up soon!!**

She presses her lips into a line as she towels off quickly and rushes to get her clothes on. She wants to be excited about the first points being added to the board that bears all their names. *Third place equals eight points,* she reminds herself. *Eight's not a bad number.* No, but worse than nine, and infinitely worse than ten.

All dressed and with her gear shoved into her duffel bag, Max slams the locker shut and is about to leave when she notices the shoe poking out from behind the lockers. It's silk, pink and entirely impractical, and could only belong to one person.

She rounds the lockers, and there's Teddy on the other side, sitting on the bench with one knee pulled up to her chin and the other leg stretched out. "Creep," Max says, but she makes herself sound bored, like the last thing she could possibly be is unnerved by Teddy Swanson. "Didn't you hear? They're about to put our numbers up." When Teddy doesn't respond, Max rolls her eyes. "Fine, whatever." Now she pitches her voice up a few levels, perky and pure. "Congrats, by the way! If you keep up that performance, you're *totally* going to beat me! I bet Columbia will be so impressed. I hear they love fifth-place losers."

She doesn't even wait for Teddy to ignore her this time. Just blows by and shakes her head, on her way to find the only people she actually cares about in this entire school.

27

TEDDY

TEDDY PULLS HER knees to her chest as the slam of the door recedes, as Max's words reverberate in her skull. On any other day she would have fought back, thrown her own barbs Max's way, but right now, she can't be fucking bothered. Right now, all she can focus on is the black hole and how it's bigger now than ever before.

Coming out of the water she'd waited for the feeling of accomplishment to hit. For the rush everyone talked about, the post-achievement glow, when you realized all the work had been worth it, and chemicals flooded your system and drove you to delirium. But instead, all Teddy had felt was nothing. The same thing she'd felt so many times before, and it was almost hysterically funny, now, how she had even for a *second* considered that the Cup could be the answer. As if putting rules and restrictions on her nature would solve things. As if any of the shit they were about to do, with all its constraints, could ever provide enough of a rush to shrink the black hole.

It's boring, she thinks, the realization fresh and freeing. It's *boring,* the Cup is boring to her, this school is boring, and she's been pretending that it isn't but she just can't anymore and *god,* it feels so *good* to admit it to herself!

Teddy gets up and walks over to the mirrors. The girl looking back is wan, skin dry from the salt water, lips a little cracked. *Well, that won't do,* she thinks. *Look what trying gets you.*

She goes back to her bag, ignoring her phone buzzing with a text from Nora, and takes out her makeup. A smear of concealer hides most of the shadows. A slick of cream bronzer on each cheek, up around her temples, brings back some of her lost warmth. The sticky red gloss papers over the cracks in her lips, and Teddy practices a variety of smiles in the mirror, like she's a drawing in a picture book for babies: *See Teddy smile. See Teddy grin. See Teddy laugh!*

She does laugh, now, like she's testing it out: a throaty laugh at the idea that this school is any different from the places she's been before, or that she could really change, that she ever even *wanted* to change. Lying to herself so thoroughly that she believed it, for a little while. But now she can be honest. It doesn't matter what she does: nothing ever changes. She plays by the rules, and she feels the same. She plays by the rules, and her mother is still disappointed. She plays by the rules, and the black hole still threatens to swallow her up. At least when she's behaving badly, she gets to have *fun.*

Satisfied, she smirks at her reflection, then grabs her bag and sets off toward the main building.

When she gets there and runs up the stairs, the hallway is crowded. Teddy elbows her way through, and each time she connects with someone it's like her shield strengthens. By the time she makes it to the front, where Nora and all the others are standing, she feels cool, collected. She can pretend again, for a little while. Why not? It might be fun, to see how long she can keep on convincing them all that she's one of them, a fucking *Gardner girl*, whatever that even means in the real world.

Nora's smile when she sees Teddy is big and bright, electric. "Finally," she says.

And Teddy smiles back. "Like I would miss you being crowned," she teases.

Nora flushes a little. "Shut up," she says, and then she's sliding her hand into Teddy's, their fingers laced together.

Teddy considers Nora as she turns her head, staring at Ms. Archibald coming out of the office. She has fun with Nora, doesn't she? *Yes,* she decides: making out with Nora is fun. Slipping her hands inside Nora's underwear beneath her uniform skirt is fun. Watching the way Nora squirms and sighs at her touch is fun. Teddy thinks back to that first assembly, the first time she spotted Nora. She'd thought then that Nora might have been a good enough distraction from the black hole, but that hasn't worked out.

A thought comes, insistent and loud: *Break up with her, right now. In front of this crowd, so everyone will be watching. And she'll cry, and they'll all turn on you, even her old friends who supposedly don't like her anymore, because she's one of them and you're still an outsider, really, so they'll choose her* over you and you'll become the überbitch of the entire school and then it would basically be wrong *for you to not cause more shit, because that's the role, that's the rules!*

She opens her mouth, the words ready to fall out, but then she catches sight of Max. She looks less than pleased, and Teddy remembers her outside the restaurant, how good it felt to threaten her.

Teddy looks back at Nora, closing her mouth. No; no need to cause a scene here, to end things with her. She does like Nora, and now that she's really being honest with herself about everything, she especially likes that their being together pisses Max off.

Up front Ms. Archibald puts her chalk pen to the board. There's no ceremony here, no ritual. She just writes Nora's points in careful, crisp white—the slash of a *1*, the infinite loop of the *0*—before moving on to the rest. Max came in third; that's why her face looks the way it does right now. In contrast, Nora's smile is so wide it reveals a usually hidden dimple. And Teddy is hit with another thought: that she does still want to see Max lose. She wants to see how the girl will crack at the end of it all, when she doesn't get what she wants, when somebody steals the win she believes belongs to her.

She eyes Max again. *Maybe I don't need to wait that long. Maybe it's time to really focus. Forget being a good girl, a Gardner girl. Just a little bit of chaos to satiate the black hole, just a little bit.*

Like Max can feel her stare, she looks over at Teddy, face carefully blank now.

Teddy smiles, her expression matching Nora's, and holds

it longer than is natural, until Max loses that careful control and frowns, and still Teddy keeps on smiling, until Max finally looks away.

Okay. Now *this* might be enough.

28

NORA

NORA HADN'T KNOWN how hard the weeks between challenges were going to be, but now that she's in it, it's impossible to concentrate. The glow of her first win wears off pretty fast, because after all, there are six more challenges to come, and months to go before the eventual winner will be crowned, and in between they're just supposed to, what, go to class and apply to college and act like anything else matters? In math class on Tuesday she kicks the leg of Teddy's chair and leans forward when Ms. Crestwell has her back to the class. "I just realized how much I *don't* care about understanding integrals," she whispers, and she expects Teddy to swing around in her seat, one eyebrow arched, and say something like *And it took you this long because . . . ?*

But all Teddy does is throw a half smile over her shoulder and then turn her attention back to what the teacher is writing, as if she's so invested. Nora sinks back into her chair and ignores the look she can feel Safiya giving her from across the way, like she's the world's biggest loser. It feels stupid and childish to admit but Saf treating her like shit now actually hurts, because up until the first challenge things had still been kind of okay between them, and now it's like Saf has turned on her. Not just Saf—everybody seems to be looking at her differently, and at first Nora had thought people were on her side, paying more attention to her because she's the front-runner now, her ten points putting her at the top of the table. But it only took until Monday morning for her to realize the whispers as she passed weren't hushed awe. No, winning the first challenge didn't cement an idea of her as the winner in people's minds—it just put a target on her back. She had to laugh a little at the irony. Target archery is challenge two. *Come next Saturday,* she thinks now, *maybe I'll be pulling arrows out of my own back.*

But when the day arrives, she finds herself the center of no one's attention. They're in the locker room, not as early as two weeks ago, when they had the tide to work around, but early enough that everyone seems a little dazed.

Nora sits on one of the benches, almost tucked into the corner, pretending to type on her phone. She's dressed and ready to go, but the others are still changing, and there's a charged silence in the room. Like everyone suddenly realized that they're in competition, and fraternizing with the enemy isn't going to help them gain extra points.

Before these last two weeks, Nora would have expected her and Teddy to blow off that sense of competition, because it obviously couldn't apply to them. Sure, they were competing, but Teddy wasn't really out to win, not in the way the rest of them were, and if she did, then Nora would celebrate her, the same way she knew Teddy would for her. Before the last two weeks, that's what she thought, but now?

She watches Teddy tying her hair up, her long neck on show, skin of her throat vulnerable. She can't quite put her finger on it, but Teddy seems . . . off. The same, but not. Nora can't put words to it, and so she hasn't said anything about it to Teddy, because what would she say? *Sometimes when you look at me lately, it's like you want to eat me alive?* Because that's about as close as she can get, that's what it feels like lately. Like Teddy is starving and nothing's quite satisfying enough for her. But she's not doing anything *wrong*. Nothing Nora can point to. They still spend most of their time together. They still train together, testing each other, scooping out the guts of the rabbits whose necks they snap, desire humming across their skin. Nothing has changed, and yet.

And yet.

Nora lets her gaze wander, finding Max on the other side of the room, tying and retying her laces. As much as she's spent the past couple of weeks thinking about whatever's going on with Teddy, she's also been unable to push Max out of her mind, to forget about their interaction right outside this building. The first time Max had said anything to her outside of yelling at her in months. Now sometimes Nora finds herself wondering what Max is thinking about, when they're in class together and Max has that intense frown on her face. Wonders how her applications are going, if she's still as dead set on

Columbia as she always used to be, or if she's changed her mind. Wonders what the fight with her mom back on Family Weekend was all about, if her parents even know about the Cup, if Max has *anyone* on her team.

Max straightens and for a second her eyes meet Nora's, just like after the last challenge. This time Nora looks away first, and a wave of exhaustion washes over her. God, she's so tired of all of this. Wasn't the Cup supposed to be *fun*, supposed to be the biggest honor of their lives, a moment for them to make their mark and show off everything they've spent years learning? Instead it feels heavy, maybe even a little tedious. Nora's in first place, but all it's earned her is coldness from her competitors, and she's suddenly not sure if she has the energy to keep pushing enough to win it all. She's not sure winning it all would even give her the feeling she'd always imagined the winner gets in the first place.

I wish I could go back in time, she thinks. *I wish I never told Max that I loved her and we could still be friends and I'd be—*

She stops her stupid thought. What, she wishes she could still be Max's sidekick? She wishes she could be watching and cheering her on, instead of competing herself?

Nora looks to Teddy, slicking on lip gloss in the mirror, and back to Max, now sitting with her arms folded, eyes closed. It hits her, sudden: they hate each other, but they're actually so alike it's disturbing. They both think they're the alpha, such tough bitches who'll cut down anyone who gets in their way. They're both *actually* little girls with mommy issues, constantly trying to get attention, approval, where there simply isn't any. And perhaps they even both think of Nora the exact same way, like she's some weak little thing so grateful for a scrap of their love that she'll believe anything they say, do anything they want. *Never mind what I want,* she thinks, her teeth clenched. *Never mind that I am an actual person outside of them, who doesn't exist solely for them to play with, who is an actual* threat.

The door swings open and there's Ms. Bell, cheeks glowing from the cold. "Are we ready, ladies?"

There's no chorus of responses, only a few nodding heads and then movement, everybody finishing up ponytails and braids and making sure they have their bows by their sides. Nora grabs hers and moves to the door, cutting in front of Max to be first in line behind Ms. Bell. She stands tall, ignoring how she can feel Max's glare on the back of her neck. Fuck her, and maybe fuck Teddy a little bit, too, and most of all fuck herself for that moment of weakness back there. This is *the Tierney Cup.* It is not exhausting, and it is not tedious, and when she wins—when, not if—it will all be worth it. That feeling she's imagined—it'll be so good, so sweet, and hers forever. Nora's sure of it.

29

MAX

MAX IS UP LAST.

It's different from the swim, where they all set off at once. This time, they have to take it in turns, stand by and watch each other set their arrows sailing and hope each girl that isn't you sinks it far, far away from the heart of the target.

Max is not bothered by going last. The swim was probably her weakest event, which means it's all good from here. Her nerves are steely, and she watches the others step up and take their shots with a kind of cool detachment. Abigail Brody completely chokes and wildly misfires not one but *two* of her arrows, arcing high over the target and landing in the dead grass. Nora banks a decent score, but it won't be enough to get her to first place again—maybe more like third or fourth, Max thinks. Teddy does well, too, and Max ignores the way her pulse picks up watching her shoot. *Just because she's good at this one thing doesn't mean anything.* Just because she can fire a few arrows close to the center of the target doesn't mean she's better than Max.

Her turn follows Safiya, who walks back to their observation spot looking pleased with herself and shimmies in Max's direction. Max forces herself not to smile, to keep her serious, *I'm so focused nothing you idiots do can shake me* face on as she walks up to take her position.

She inhales, bow pulled back taut, hand pressed into her jaw and arrow sitting tight below it. *This is everything you've worked for. This is what all the hours out here come down to. If you blow this, no one will ever let you forget it. If you blow this, somebody else is going to walk away with the Cup and you won't be remembered at all. You'll be just another name, just another girl who came and left, who did nothing noteworthy, who doesn't deserved to be thought about. If you fuck this up, you fuck everything.*

No pressure, then.

Max exhales and lets the arrow fly. She watches it sink right into the bull's-eye in slow motion, not hearing the cheers and claps that break out from the crowd behind her. She can't hear anything but her own breath, her own heartbeat, and the snap of the bow as she repeats the feat at thirty, forty, and fifty meters.

As soon as the last arrow lands, she lets herself relax, tuning into the noise of the observers, and then Ms. Bell through the rickety old megaphone saying, "And there we have it. Looks like Wren Maxwell takes the full ten points for this challenge!"

The fourth year in charge of the whiteboard tracking their

scores writes down Max's actual total tally and then the ten points that her win translates into. Max scans the rest of the board: Saf came in just behind her, then Nora, and Teddy, Jordan, Manuela, and Abigail round things out. She does the math quickly in her head: that means with her eight points from the swim, she has eighteen points, and with Nora's third place she gets eight points, bringing her total to the same. Tied for first.

Saf comes dancing over. "Now *that* is way more like it," she says, and for a moment Max thinks Saf is talking about her, but then she says, "Second place is obviously not as good as first, but it's better than fucking sixth."

Max narrows her eyes. "Don't get comfortable now," she says, injecting venom into her words. "There's a long way to go, and plenty more opportunities for you to choke."

"Choke on this," Saf says, and holds up both middle fingers, but then she laughs, and even though it's completely cold sounding, her eyes flat and mirthless, Max laughs, too. "Congrats, though," Saf says now. "I mean, it would have been embarrassing for you to come anywhere below first, but congrats anyway."

"Nothing less than I expected," Max says, and when Saf hugs her, she squeezes back, both of them pretending like they're so happy for the other.

It should feel good, she knows. Winning. Somehow it just feels . . . hollow. Like Saf said—like she herself thought—everyone expected this of her, so it feels like all she did was what she was supposed to. Nothing more, nothing less.

Over Saf's shoulder she sees Nora. Weird how they're now

sharing the top spot, when a few months ago Max would have laughed at the thought of Nora even competing. Not that she didn't think Nora could do it—that was never part of it, that was never why she was mad when she found out Nora had signed up. It was just that the Cup had always been Max's dream, and Nora had never shown the slightest interest in competing herself. It wasn't like Max ever said she *couldn't*, or that she thought she was the only one with a claim to it, but they had spent years being best friends, sharing a dorm room, sharing all their secrets, and Nora had never, ever talked about wanting the Cup for herself.

Well. Sharing nearly all their secrets.

Because it was only after, right, when Nora had told Max that she was in love with her and everything had fallen apart, that she suddenly decided to enter. Some kind of fucked-up revenge for Max daring to not love her back. And now here they are, deep into the competition that is turning everyone into the most self-absorbed versions of themselves, making things so that they can't even celebrate their friends' achievements, and suddenly the gap between her and Nora feels impossibly wide but there's a part of Max that still wants to throw herself into that space. Nora is the only one who knows what this really means to her. Nora is the only one whose congratulations she wants to hear. Maybe she'd fall right down into the chasm but her last message, called up from the pit, would make its way to Nora's ears: *How the fuck did things go so wrong with us?*

But then she watches as Nora and Teddy embrace and the anger comes rushing back and she remembers exactly how they got here.

"Wait, wait, we want in on this!" Brooke's voice cuts right through the noise and suddenly Max feels more arms around her shoulders, Brooke and Isobel enveloping her and Saf in an embrace way more authentic than the one that started it.

"You're crushing my lungs," Max complains, but she makes sure to grin as she says it, like she's having the best time of her life, putting on a show for anyone who might be watching.

"Quit whining," Brooke says. "Whining is for losers and you're a *winner*!"

They break apart and Isobel shoves her hands in her coat pockets. "Can we go inside now? I'm fucking freezing."

"Yeah, let's go watch them put those numbers up, baby." Brooke spins, her long dark hair flying out around her. "Number one! Number one!"

Max lifts her chin. "That's me," she says, choosing to ignore the Nora part of the equation, the same way they all ignore her as they march on by, only room for one winner in their midst.

30

TEDDY

TEDDY'S EARLY TO dinner on Monday, and Nora's still up in Mr. Gordon's classroom going over her college essay. Usually she'd just sit by herself but that's boring. She's tired of being *bored*.

So she scans the room, spotting an unmistakable red ponytail at a table in the middle. Holding her tray up high Teddy snakes her way through until she's standing in front of Freya. "Hey. Mind if I sit?"

Freya glances up, and Teddy doesn't miss the surprise there. "Oh hey," Freya says brightly, closing her textbook. "Long time, et cetera."

Teddy sets her tray down and slides into the chair opposite Freya. "I know," she says. "I guess I . . ."

She trails off. Really, what happened was she set her sights on Nora and everything else faded into the background, including the first person who'd gone out of their way to treat her like a person at Gardner. *That* was not a very Gardner girl thing to do, was it?

Freya laughs. "Relax," she says. "I'm not, like, holding a grudge or something. I'm a big girl, I get it. Although, maybe I was a little jealous." She glances around and leans in. "I always thought Nora was cute."

"You think my girlfriend's cute?" Teddy says, and she enjoys the feeling it ignites in her. A possessiveness, an ownership of Nora, the feeling that she has something everyone else wants. "Are we going to have to fight?"

Freya laughs again, holding her hands up. "No fight, no fight," she says. "I'm just saying, I would have done exactly the same as you. Anyway, you clearly didn't need my help learning how to fit in here. What are you now, third overall?"

"Joint third," Teddy says. It sounds good, until you understand that there are also two people sharing second place, and two people sharing the top spot. Not just any two people: Nora and Max, as luck would have it, right up there together. Teddy sits five points below them overall, and that's because she didn't do as well at the target archery challenge as she thought she would, for which she has no excuse. She's good with a bow, as good as Max, a fact that she has been proving since that first time in Activity what feels like forever ago now. The problem is now that she's remembered she doesn't give a shit about any of this, it's hard to keep acting like she gives a shit. Even her desire to see Max lose doesn't feel like enough motivation, lately.

"Joint third is still third," Freya says, and uses the spoon she had been swirling in her yogurt to point in the direction of Abigail Brody. "It's fucking better than last-place Abigail."

Teddy looks over. Abigail is holding court with a bunch of fifth years, as if absolutely nothing is wrong. The simple fact that she's eating dinner with girls below them, and no one from their own year, is enough to tell everybody that actually, a lot is wrong. Abigail has so far come in last place in both challenges. She has the smell of failure on her. Statistically, Teddy knows, *somebody* has to come in last, but twice? In a row? "If I were her, I don't know if I could show my face in here," Teddy says, and means it.

"I've always found Abigail to have a sort of . . . relentless self-belief," Freya says. "And that's putting it nicely."

"Delusion, in other words," Teddy says, and then her phone vibrates inside the pocket of her blazer. She grits her teeth as she takes it out to see yet another email from her sister. *Why can't she text like a normal person?* For a second she thinks about reading it, but then she swipes the notification away and shoves her phone back in her pocket. It'll just be another in a series of emails from her sister that have been coming regularly since Cass and their mother came to visit. Sometimes it's *Just checking in! Saw some boots I thought you'd love—the courier will be there on Monday!* Sometimes it's *Heard back from my connection at Princeton—off the record of course—but they'd be thrilled to have you as a sister. They only take the best and produce the best, Teddy. Doctors, lawyers, congresspeople—you get the picture. Call me and we can discuss it further.* Sometimes *For god's sake, would you call Mom back? I'm not your secretary, I'm not going to keep going between the two of you. I actually have my own life and my own kids to take care of* as if the nanny doesn't do the real work.

She could reply, but she doesn't trust herself to do it nicely, and she certainly can't be honest, because Cass doesn't ever want to know what's really going on inside Teddy's head. She didn't like it when Teddy was playing the part here—she certainly wouldn't like it now that Teddy's . . .

What? What am I? Reverting to my old ways? Giving in to the black hole? Who the fuck knows.

Teddy picks up her fork and pokes at the fish sitting limply on her plate. Then she looks at Freya, examining her face for any sign of a similar black hole yawning inside her. Her eyes are bright, vibrant, none of the sometimes haunted, sometimes wired look Teddy sees in her own reflection. But who knows—maybe Freya's just good at hiding things, better than Teddy at least.

"So, are you ready for the berry test?" Freya says it with a satirical kind of reverence, and Teddy duly gives her a smile. It's the least sexy of all the challenges, even if they try to dress it up and inject it with some theatrics. In a couple of weeks they'll all get up onstage in the assembly hall, and one by one go up and lift a silver cloche hiding some kind of flora or fauna beneath. Then they'll have fifteen seconds to correctly identify it. If they're wrong, they're out. Not exactly thrilling, but there is a kind of cutthroat pressure to it that Teddy might allow herself to enjoy.

"Oh, I just can't wait," she says, fluttering her fingers in the air like she's a performer ready for the stage. "If all else fails, I can always pop a little hemlock and exit this plane."

"Onstage self-sacrifice?" Freya says. "Now that I'd *pay* to see."

31

MAX

MAX ALMOST DROPS her glass when Brooke elbows her. "Watch it, bitch," she snaps.

"Look," Brooke says, ignoring Max's irritation. "Teddy isn't sitting with Nora."

Max follows Brooke's gaze, and she is indeed correct: there's Teddy, with her perfect ponytail and diamond studs in her ears that Max can see sparkling from all the way over here, sitting with Freya O'Farrell at a table in the middle of the dining hall, instead of at her usual spot with Nora in the back.

"Where is Nora, anyway?" Saf says.

"Huh" is all Max says, and nothing more. What does she care where Nora is, or who Teddy sits with? As long as neither of them is bothering her, they can do whatever the fuck they want.

"What do you mean, *huh*?" Brooke rips open a pepper

packet and shakes it over her food. "They always sit together, at that table. Maybe they're fighting. Oh! Maybe they broke up, and now Nora can come back to her senses and stop being a complete bitch to us."

"I still don't know what her problem is," Isobel says. She sniffs, wrinkling her perfect nose. The bump she used to have is completely gone, the work so subtle it looks as if she was born that way. "It's like she's having a nervous breakdown or something. Getting with Teddy, entering the Cup, cutting us all off?"

"That's what I've *been* saying," Brooke says. "I mean, be mad at Max, sure, but why do the rest of us have to catch heat?"

Max glares at her. What Brooke just said sounded dangerously close to acknowledging what started this whole rift, and not for the first time she wishes she'd never told Brooke and Isobel about Nora being in love with her. It all feels so stupid now, anyway, because clearly Nora can't have loved her *that* much to have moved on so fast with Teddy. "Whatever," she says. "She doesn't want to hang with us, we don't want to be around her. What does it matter? Besides, they're never going to last. Not all the way through the Cup. You can't beat your girlfriend and expect things to be fine."

Saf leans in. "Girlfriend?" she repeats. "You think they're, like, official now?"

Max barely restrains herself from rolling her eyes. Girlfriends, not girlfriends, *who the fuck cares*? God—for such intelligent and driven girls, sometimes they really do sound like every other fucking airhead at every other high school on the planet.

She pushes her chair back, abandoning her half-eaten dinner. "I have to leave," she says. "I swear to god, I can feel the brain cells *leaking* out of my *ear*."

She marches off, ignoring the way Brooke calls out, "Come on, it's a *joke*!" Maybe, but it wasn't funny to Max. Nothing is funny anymore, and it irritates her that her friends don't feel the pressure in the same way she does. Of course they don't, because Brooke and Isobel are not in the Cup, and on top of that, none of them have to worry about getting into college, let alone paying for it. Even though she knows most places don't really understand what exactly the Cup stands for, she still wants it on her applications. Something to put where everyone else will be talking about their volunteering with the organizations their parents donate to, and how they put their language skills to use doing voluntary work overseas, and how many ribbons their fucking ponies won. That's why she's pissed off. It certainly has nothing to do with Nora and Teddy fucking Swanson.

It's freezing walking back to the dorm, colder than usual this time of year. The paths are slick with rain and Max shivers as she picks up the pace, hurrying back to the senior dorm. With everyone either at dinner or Study Session, the common room is empty, and Max is already planning to stretch out on the couch in front of the big television. But as she walks through the doors, her phone buzzes, and she already knows it's her mom.

Max heads up to her room, closing the door before she answers. "Hi, Mom."

"Oh! Hi!" her mom says, and it's clear she didn't expect Max to answer. "There you are."

"Here I am," Max says, and slides down to the floor. In fairness, she has ignored the last four calls from her mom, meaning that the last time they actually spoke was Family Weekend. She just hasn't wanted to get into all that shit again. But fuck it, since she's in a shitty mood already, why not get yelled at a little more? "Sorry I missed a couple of calls. I've been really busy with school."

"Of course you have," her mom says, and she sounds bright, bubbly. There's none of the frost Max was expecting, which is odd, because Max thought she'd still be mad. She didn't help out the precious angel daughters and people who don't treat the girls with the reverence their mother requires are usually met with a chilly silence. "How's the, uh . . . what was it? Some kind of contest? Anyway, how's that going? Or is it over? I can barely keep track!"

Max rolls her eyes. The image of her mother writing down important dates or events in Max's life on the same calendar she uses to track recitals and rehearsals is hilarious. "No, it's still going, and it's fine."

"Great!" her mom says. "Great."

In the silence that follows Max clears her throat. She can't really put it off any longer; Thanksgiving break is only a few weeks away, and this presents Max with a problem. Just like she would spend summers with Nora at her house, she used to follow her home for Thanksgiving, too. But obviously that's not an option this year. And it's not like she can pick up a weeklong job with somewhere to stay thrown in, like she did with camp. She could technically stay at school over break: there are always a handful of girls who can't go back home, either because they're on financial aid like Max, or sometimes because the travel is just too far for a few days. But most of the dorms are closed, everybody moving for the week to sleep in one block where whichever teachers have drawn the short straw can easily supervise them. It would probably be easier for her to stay, but there's something about the idea of school without all the usual bodies filling it that leaves Max cold, like she'd be fully admitting to her neglected-loser-kid status if she did it. She imagines all her friends leaving, bags packed for a warm week at home, curled in front of a fire or out in a bikini in warmer climes, and having to wave goodbye as they leave her in the cold. If she had thought about it before, maybe she could have asked one of them to take her in for the week. Actually, that's a lie: she never would have asked them, because even if she calls them her closest friends, they don't know her like Nora did. She can't expect Brooke or Isobel to just pay for her plane ticket the way Mr. and Mrs. McQueen did without even asking, and the idea of explaining to them that she needs that is way too fucking depressing.

So: home it is. "You know, Thanksgiving's coming up," Max says, at the same time as her mom says, "Oh my goodness, I must tell you about Amethyst."

Max squints into the dark. "Amethyst?" she says, and her pulse ticks up a little. "Wait. She's okay, right? Did something happen?"

"Something *wonderful*," her mom gushes. "We were at rehearsals for their recital in a couple of weeks, and out of the blue another parent came over to me to give me his card. He said he's a coach at the elite gym in Tilson, and he was really impressed by Amethyst's acro routine, and that we should think about sending her there. I looked it up and it's a *really* good training facility. A ton of their girls compete at the national level and a few have even made it to Olympic trials. Can you even imagine! Amethyst, at the Olympics!"

"Oh," Max says, letting her head drop back against the door. "Is that it? I thought something bad happened."

"No, no," her mom says. "Don't be silly. Of course I went right over there the next day to see about getting her enrolled. She's only been to a few training sessions so far but everybody agrees she's showing *such* tremendous promise. Thank goodness I changed my mind about enrolling them both in that ridiculous ballet academy. I think gymnastics is going to be a much better path for Amethyst, and I'm sure Pearl will find her place in *something*, eventually."

Sorry—"*changed my mind*"? Max grabs the skin inside her elbow and pinches hard. No, definitely not dreaming. So she really *did* just hear her mother claiming that the reason the girls didn't get into that dance school is because she simply changed her mind. *Not because we had a screaming fight in the middle of a restaurant and I refused to use my connections to get them in there? Or maybe I was dreaming then! Maybe I hallucinated that entire thing!*

She closes her eyes, phone still pressed to her ear. She didn't know what else she expected, really. This is exactly how her mom operates—living in a fantasy land where anything that doesn't go her way or didn't happen the way she wanted it to can simply be recast, rewritten as her own decision, her own choice. No doubt when she returned home that weekend, she told Max's dad they'd had a lovely meal together and it was just so nice to see the school, finally. The same way Max knows her mom told everyone she knows that she was the one who found the boarding school and yes, they knew it would be hard to let Max go, but it was what was best for her education, for her future.

"Typical," she says under her breath.

"What was that?"

"Great," Max says, opening her eyes, for a moment unable to see anything but the darkness in front of her. Then things come into focus under the little bit of moonlight filtering through clouds and curtains: her unmade bed, the pile of dirty clothes she keeps meaning to take to the laundry room, the textbook still open on her desk. She's letting standards slip, she notices. Too focused on the Cup to keep things in the right order.

She pushes herself to her feet and begins moving things around, shoulder pinning her phone to her ear. "It's great. I'm happy the girls are doing good," she says, and it's only half a lie, only half an attempt to soften the landing of her next question. "So . . . like I was saying before, Thanksgiving is coming up. I was thinking about maybe coming home for the week. If that's okay." She winces. She doesn't have to check that it's okay for her to go to her own home. She should have just said it, a declarative statement: *I am coming home for Thanksgiving.*

"You?" her mom says. "Want to come home? Oh. I thought you usually went home with your friend . . ."

"Nora," Max says, when it's clear her mom won't get there on her own.

"Yes, Nora. Always so kind of her parents to have you."

"Yes, it was," Max says impatiently. "So, we're all good, then. I'm coming home, I'll buy a bus ticket—"

"Well. Hmm. The thing is, I'm not sure we're going to *be* home," her mom says. "The girls are competing in a pageant that Friday, in Arizona. So we've kind of made a trip out of it and we're going to drive down that Monday and be there all week."

"So you won't even be at home?" An opportunity presents itself to Max: an *empty house*. A whole week—okay, five or six days—that she could be alone, away from school, away from her parents. A week—five or six days—of doing nothing but ordering Chinese from that one place she used to like and watching the worst movies known to man. Uninterrupted *peace*. "That's okay. I don't mind hanging out by myself."

"The thing is," her mom says, and Max feels the fantasy shatter. "Since we're not going to be at the house, your dad told Geoffrey—you remember Geoffrey, don't you? He's having a whole bunch of extended family come up for the holiday and we said some of them could stay at our place, since we won't be there."

Max has no memory of anyone named Geoffrey, but she can easily assume exactly who this man is: one of her dad's coworkers, or high school buddies, or drinking pals, with a thick neck and high blood pressure. She pictures this man and a host of carbon copies, sitting on her family's couch, yelling at the TV turned up too loud. "Okay," she tells her mom, not even bothering to hide the frustration in her voice. What does it matter? Her mom never notices, and even if she does, as soon as the call's over she'll rewrite the whole thing in her mind. "Don't worry about it. Don't worry about me at all! I'll figure something out."

"I knew you'd understand. Hey, would you like to talk to your sisters? I'm sure one of them is around somewhere. Pearl? Pearlie girl, where are you! Mommy's coming! Your sister's on the phone . . ."

Max lets the phone drop from her ear, her mom's babbling fading away, and then she hangs up. She wonders how long it'll take for her mom to notice she's even gone.

32

NORA

NORA LEANS AGAINST the wall, in the hallway across from Dr. Thompson's office. She's supposed to be in Study Session but no one looked up when she got up and slipped out, taking all her books with her.

The board tracking the Cup points tally seems to loom large. Nora stares at her own name, the *23* written beside it. Joint second place with Safiya, now, and only one person on top: Max.

The berry test didn't go the way Nora wanted. It's always been the least exciting of the challenges, but also the sneakiest. You think it's easy to look at whatever plants and fruits and leaves they assemble on the table in front of you, and correctly identify them—you've been studying this for years, duh. It should be simple, a game of call and response: you see the item, you recall what it is, you name it out loud and move on to the next round.

But in reality, onstage with the lights shining down on them and the hall packed with students and faculty alike, it was a different game. Nora knew they weren't going to make it simple and just shove a bunch of easily distinguishable items in the mix, but she had been confident in her abilities, feeling like they weren't going to be able to trick her. She was going to take her time and make sure that she didn't say the first thing that came to mind, to actually closely examine the item and look for the smaller tells—to notice that actually, the very edges of the leaves curl up instead of lying flat, or that the flesh of the berry once split in two was not red inside but white, swapping the instant easy answer for the actual correct one. Pokeberries, not elderberries. Hemlock, not elderflower.

That was what she'd planned to do, but in the moment she'd second-guessed herself, and the clock had been ticking, the hot lights making her sweat, and she'd looked at the bark and said, "Birch—no, beech. Silver beech." But it was too late, they had to take her first answer, those were the rules, and so Nora was out in the second round, leaving her in sixth place overall.

"It's fine," Teddy said afterward. "You can afford one bad turn. You're still up near the top. Don't lose your shit over this, okay?"

Nora couldn't help hearing the note of irritation in Teddy's voice, as if Nora were being *so* overdramatic. But again: What was she supposed to say? *How dare you sound annoyed with me?* As if Teddy's only purpose were to make Nora feel good about herself, to reassure her all the time and tell her how pretty she is and how much she wants her. Maybe she wouldn't think anything of it, if it weren't for the feeling that *something* is going on with Teddy. God, she still can't quite find the words for it, can't put her finger on precisely what has changed but she feels it, somewhere deep in both her gut and her brain. Teddy has always looked at her intensely but sometimes now it's almost scary. Sometimes now when they're fooling around Teddy's fingers grip her so hard her nails cut into Nora's skin, scratches left on her body far after the fact. And when Nora talks she can see Teddy only half listening, a small smile on her lips as if whatever it is she's thinking about is so much more entertaining than Nora. But when Nora tries to catch her out, Teddy's always prepared, like her attention was fully on Nora, like it always is, *duh, of course I'm listening, what do you mean?*

Fine. If Teddy's allowed to go off into her own little world and Nora's not allowed to question it, then that means it's okay for her to do the same, right? It's okay for her to be thinking about Max more often than she should. It's okay for her to be painfully conscious of every time she and Max have to pass by each other, or end up the last two in the room before leaving class. It's okay for her to be thinking, still, about the way Max had looked at her outside the locker room, weeks ago now, those big dark eyes that Nora couldn't look away from.

Nora shifts, sliding further into the shadows. Max is in first place with twenty-six points overall. Teddy hovers closer to the bottom, currently fourth with nineteen points, just below Jordan in third with twenty points, and above Abigail and Manuela in joint last place. Abigail had—extremely surprisingly—pulled a first-place result out of the bag on the berry test, raising her

THE TOURNAMENT

overall score to something more respectable, but not enough for her to be considered a serious threat. Nora only really considers Max and Saf as her competition, and she'd thought maybe Teddy would be up there, too, with the way she'd been before the Cup started, but ever since then it's like all that drive and determination has slipped. They were supposed to beat Max together, end up in first and second place. At least, that's what Nora had imagined, and she hadn't even cared in those fantasies about which of them was first and which was second. It didn't matter, because either way, Max would not have won, and Nora would have beaten her and showed her that the Cup did not belong to her, and that was all she really wanted. Except now it seems harder and harder to remember why—not why she wants to beat Max, but why she ever thought winning the Cup and doing it would bring her the satisfaction she desires. Sometimes—right now—it just feels like there's a group of stupid little girls playing stupid little games for stupid little reasons. Max isn't talking to her, Saf has seemingly turned on her, and it's like Teddy's changing right before her eyes. Sure, the lower school girls think she's hot shit and burst into self-conscious giggles when they see her around campus and wave, and she waves back, but what the fuck does that even matter? In all her years at Gardner, Nora has never felt so alone. So lonely.

    She takes one last look at the board before she turns away, striding down the hall and around the corner—where she collides with somebody, the force of it knocking her back, shoulder bumping the wall, and her books tumble to the ground. "Shit, sorry," Nora says, a reflex, already crouching to collect her books before she even looks to see who it was she bumped into, and then she doesn't have to look, because the other person is crouched, too, and reaching for the same book as Nora, silver ring on her thumb. Max.

Their fingers only touch for a second before Nora snatches her hand back, but it's enough. She looks up at Max now, and her fingers burn where they touched, and Max is staring at her with this confused look on her face, thick eyebrows sloping together. Nora braces herself for whatever Max is going to say— *Watch where you're going, bitch* or *Needed a reminder of who's in first place?* or even just *Move.*

But Max simply collects Nora's books and hands them to her before she stands up. Her hands go to her throat, straightening the necklace there, the *M* that Nora gave her hanging from the chain. It's unconscious—habit. Nora can tell.

Nora slowly straightens, says, "Thank you" in a tone that makes it a question: "Thank you?"

Max nods once, and then she's moving, around the corner and gone before Nora can say anything else. She can't help but touch her own necklace in response, a mirror. It means nothing, probably, that Max still wears it. *It means nothing,* she tells herself as she walks away, repeating it. Reminding herself.

By the time she's back at the dorm, it has morphed, like her thank-you before: *It means . . . nothing? Right?*

33

TEDDY

THE DRIVER LOADS Nora's bag into the back of the car.

Nora brushes a curl behind her ear. "So . . . I'll text you when I land," she says. "What are you going to do until Sunday?"

"Oh, I'm sure I'll find some way to amuse myself," Teddy says. Her flight home isn't until Sunday afternoon, and she doesn't usually pine for home, but right now she can't wait to be there, just to be away from Gardner. A week without having to pretend that she actually cares about this place and these people? Can't come soon enough.

"Okay, so . . ." Nora squints into the sun, and she looks so beautiful that Teddy feels a little guilty. *Not you, sweet Nora,* she thinks. *I do still like you, I swear. It's not your fault.*

An idea hits her: it's not Nora's fault, no, it's this place and everybody else so if they could get away from here, things could be so much better. *Run away with me,* she wants to say. She could jump in the car with Nora right now and head to the airport, jet off to somewhere warm where all they need is bikinis and cigarettes—no, no. Why not take one of the many gleaming cars filling up the drive and hit the road? Rinse their credits cards until their parents finally cut them off, and then they'll steal someone else's. Check into the penthouse suite at a nice hotel under fake names, feed each other room service steak and pop champagne in the tub—no, no. They should go to Vegas, gamble away their inheritances and run naked through the fountains. No, no—

Teddy shakes her head, snapping herself out of it. The problem is that Nora wouldn't do such things. She's an actual Gardner girl, the type who likes to play cutthroat but only so far as it helps her get into college. Which is a good thing, really, after all. Nora might know how to handle a knife, but she'd never pull it on Teddy. She could be such a good influence, if Teddy would just let her. But the black hole would never, and so Teddy can't, either.

"You'll be back before you know it," Teddy says to Nora, and she puts her hand on either side of Nora's face and kisses her. "Be a good girl while you're home. Don't do anything I wouldn't do."

She laughs, and waits for Nora to laugh, too, but Nora only looks at her seriously, like she's trying to figure something out. Like she's trying to figure Teddy out.

"Go on," Teddy says, a little prickly now. She leans past Nora and opens the car door. "Text me when you land, okay?"

Nora sighs. "Sure," she says, and that's all she says before she gets in and closes the door and the car pulls away, taking her somewhere far from Teddy.

On the walk back Nora's question echoes in Teddy's head— *What are you going to do until Sunday?*—and she decides that maybe instead of watching movies in her room and killing time, she could use the time to be a good girl like Nora. Maybe get a start on that college essay she keeps telling people she's working on, or finally make a decision on which schools to apply to. Yeah, she thinks, a plan forming: she'll load up on snacks from the common room and hole up in that nook by the window on the top floor of the library, and by the time she leaves for the airport to go back to her family she'll have answers for them on any and all college questions they throw at her. She shivers and pulls her coat closed, glancing up at the gray sky. God, *I hate this time of year,* she thinks.

Of course she doesn't do any of that.

By the time dinner rolls around on Saturday evening, Teddy has written approximately three sentences of her essay, opened a spreadsheet like she might actually start tracking college details, and eaten her body weight in teeny tiny packs of teeny tiny chocolate chip cookies. The dining hall is spookily quiet, half the girls gone, the others a mix of those still waiting to leave and those staying over the break. Teddy shovels food into her mouth, realizing that not only has she not made any significant headway on college shit, but that she also still needs to pack. Back in her room she swears as she realizes half her clothes are still in the laundry room, and so she has to run down and switch the soaking mass into the dryer. By the time she finally finishes packing her suitcase it's almost one a.m., and she falls into bed to pass out.

The insistent noise of the alarm on her phone wakes her, and Teddy rolls over, burrowing deeper under the covers. *Five more minutes,* she tells herself, eyes squeezed shut, but then she sighs. *No. Get up, now.*

She rolls out of bed and over to the window, yanking the curtains back—

"Fuck. You have *got* to be *fucking* kidding me."

Teddy stares, mouth open, at the snow swirling against her window. It's coming down thick and fast, only adding to the piles of white Teddy can see in place of the courtyard, the paths, the campus greenery. Her phone buzzes on the bed and she goes back over, picks it up to see five missed calls and a voicemail from her mother, and an email from her sister. She opens that and reads. *What is the point of having a phone if you never answer it? I hope by the time you get this you'll actually be aware of the situation, but in case you're not, there is currently a snowstorm affecting travel out of Washington. I suggest you call the airline as soon as you read this. If you even bother to read it, that is.*

"Fuck," Teddy exclaims, and opens up the airline app even though she already knows what it will say: *CANCELED.*

There it is, clear as day, not delayed but straight up canceled, and judging from the way the snow is still coming down, simply getting on a later flight will not be possible.

She calls the airline anyway, just so at the very least she can report to her mother and sister that she did it, and sits on hold for forty-five minutes before being told that all flights out of the airport have been canceled for the next two days and even after that, it's going to be difficult to get anything. "Great, thanks so much for your help," she says through gritted teeth, and she hangs up and is about to crawl back under the warmth of the blankets when there's a knock on her door.

She opens it and finds Ms. Cara, their dorm parent, standing in the corridor looking stressed. "Hi, Teddy. I take it you've seen the situation?"

"The shitload of snow? Yeah, I've seen it."

Ms. Cara ignores Teddy's language and shakes her head. "It's *quite* the inconvenience. Dr. Thompson wants everyone in the dining hall in twenty minutes. Don't worry, we'll figure things out. And if we can't, then it's a good thing we're a boarding school, isn't it?" She pats Teddy's shoulder. "Get dressed and meet me downstairs in ten. I'll round up the others who are still here."

Teddy retreats back into her room and puts on the sweats she was wearing last night. The others—*I wonder who else is still here,* she thinks, pulling her never-before-worn big puffy coat out of the closet. She had said the coat was stupid and she wouldn't need it, and her mother had insisted that she knew better, so it had wound up in her luggage anyway. She will never admit to being wrong, she knows.

When she goes downstairs she rolls her eyes. There's Max, leaning on the wall across from Ms. Cara's office, a foul look on her face like always. At least there are two other girls from their year also waiting—Noelle Winters and Corey Cohen, both looking weirdly pleased with the whole situation. Teddy's never really spoken to either of them to say anything more than "Do you want that last slice of pie?" in the dining hall and "Here you go," passing back handouts in biology.

Ms. Cara pops out of the office. "All here? Good. Let's be on our way, then."

They arrive at the dining hall freezing, shoes sodden. Teddy wishes her mom had insisted on shoving some ugly winter boots into her luggage as well as the coat. She shakes off the snow and ice and follows the others to a table, scanning to see how many others have been stranded. Altogether it looks like maybe forty or fifty students are in the room.

Dr. Thompson stands and claps her hands to get silence. When everyone quiets, she gives a grim smile. "Thank you. Well, this is certainly one for the books. I know I may seem like I'm always prepared and I know everything coming, but I guess even I can't predict a freak snowstorm that gets past the meteorologists! As I'm sure most of you know, we usually have a handful of students and faculty staying on campus over break. Obviously, that number has now increased, but I don't see any reason why that should worry us too much. We still have our kitchen crew and other maintenance staff here, and with a little ingenuity I think we can all have a wonderful Thanksgiving break here together. Now that that's out of the way, let me reassure all of you students that we have been in contact with your parents and we will continue to update them as things change. I'm sure you've all spoken to them yourselves by now, but please remember there's no need to panic. This is the Gardner-Bahnsen School, after all—we pride ourselves on being able to handle unusual situations. . . ."

Teddy plays with the ends of her hair as Dr. Thompson

goes on, barely registering what the headmistress is saying. She can't stop thinking about the fact that she's going to be stuck here all week, which shouldn't really be a big deal since she lives here and spends all her time here anyway, but she had been counting on this break for, you know, a *break*. Yes, her parents and sister were going to nag her, and yes, her sister's kids were going to be annoying, and yes, she hates flying at the best of times, but at least she could have gotten away. Now she's just going to rot in her room for a week and get no space at all and Nora's going to come back and the Cup's going to resume and—

Her head snaps up, as she tunes back in to Dr. Thompson's speech. ". . . in the interest of safety. Since there are a few more than usual, we are going to be doubling up in rooms—apologies to those lower years who were looking forward to having a single for the first time, and also to our final years who will have to go back to sharing like they did for so many years! So, now that I've gotten through everything, why don't we all have some breakfast, and after that all students can go back to their rooms, pack what you need, and bring it over to York Hall. Okay! Thanks, everyone!"

Teddy turns to Ms. Cara. "Wait. Did she just say we all have to stay in the same dorms? And that we have to share?"

Ms. Cara nods. "We always have everyone move into York Hall over breaks," she says. "It's much easier to have everyone in one place, and close to everything. Think of it like a slumber party! You and a roommate, staying up late, no classes—it'll be fun!"

Noelle and Corey grab each other. "I want to share with

you!" they say in unison, and burst into peals of laughter.

Teddy bites down on the inside of her cheek. If Noelle and Corey room together, that means—

She looks at Max, the realization clear on her face, too.

Some fucking slumber party this is going to be!

34

MAX

MAX IS HALFWAY through unpacking her clothes into the skinny shared closet when the door flies open and there's Teddy, cheeks bright from cold, dragging her suitcase and its wet wheels into the room.

She closes her eyes and counts to five. Of *course* a snowstorm would ground flights, and of *course* Teddy had to be one of the girls left behind, and of *course* Max would end up forced to share a dorm room with her for five days. Why the fuck not? Anything else would just be too kind and Max doesn't get kindness, not in this world.

She opens her eyes and speaks without looking at Teddy. "I'll be done in a second," she says. "Then you can have the other half."

She hears rather than sees Teddy throw herself onto the bed on the left-hand side of the room. "It's fine, I don't need it," she says. "I never unpack on a trip. Although I wouldn't classify this as a trip, because usually that implies some kind of fun for me, and sorry, but rooming with you is more my idea of hell than fun."

Same here, Max wants to say, except she'd rather die than agree with Teddy out loud. She whips around, hands curled into loose fists at her side. "Look," she says. "The way I see it, we just have to make it through this week. I won't get in your way, and you won't get in mine. In fact, I plan to be out of this room as much as humanly possible, so all we really have to do is manage to be unconscious for eight hours every night without killing each other. Do you think you can handle that?"

Teddy rolls her eyes. "Relax, Jesus," she says. "Fine. We'll stay out of each other's way. Happy?"

"Ecstatic," Max says, then eyes the window, the snow still swirling beyond it. "Shame about the weather. I was going to suggest you use the extra time to work on your hunting skills."

"I was going to suggest you use the extra time to jerk off," Teddy says. "An orgasm a day keeps the raging bitch energy away. Or are you so uptight you can't even come?"

Max laughs, a hollow sound, hoping her cheeks haven't flushed too much. It's not that she's a prude, it's just that every single thing Teddy says pisses her off, and anyway it's perfectly normal to have a hard time actually reaching orgasm. *Not the point, don't let her see she's rattled you.* "You know how I relax? By thinking about how thoroughly I'm crushing you in the Cup. Because—" She taps a finger against her chin, furrowing her brows. "Wasn't it supposed to be the other way around? Didn't you say, what was it—oh yeah: you were going to *steal* the Cup, right? Like you *stole* my girl, even though she wasn't ever my girl, and I never said I wanted her, so really all you got was my trash. And what was the last thing? Oh! Columbia! Tell me—how's that going?"

The supercilious smirk drops off Teddy's face. "You know what? Maybe we should get started on that staying-out-of-the-way thing right now."

"Perfect idea," Max says, and Teddy stands up, storms out, and slams the door behind her.

Long fucking week, Max thinks, and then she turns back to her unpacking, folding her sweaters into the drawers until her hands are no longer shaking with anger.

The snow stops falling sometime around midday on Monday, but the freezing temperatures don't let up, and campus is suspended in a sparkling icy scene. Every day there are activities arranged—watching movies in the assembly hall, creating papier-mâché winter sculptures, learning how to bake fragile pastries with the head of the kitchen staff—but Max blows them all off, yet another privilege of being a final year. No one expects her—or any other final year girl—to take a break from college prep and catching up on reading to make stupid arts and crafts. So Max keeps herself busy, and out of the hell that is the shared dorm room, going over to the library where she reads ahead, and polishes up assignments, and takes breaks to listen to music as she stares out over the quiet campus. On Tuesday she finally gets up the nerve to actually submit her college applications, an instant queasiness bubbling up inside. On Wednesday she watches and rewatches various videos she took of herself skinning and butchering rabbits, taking notes on mistakes she catches, plotting out an exact rhythm to her movements. Once school is back in session, so is the Cup, and the next challenge is a two-day affair: the Hunt on Saturday, and Preparing Prey on Sunday. It's just as it sounds: first they must go out hunting rabbits, returning with as many kills as they can manage, and then they must skin, clean, and prepare their catch, with judging taking into consideration speed, skill, and precision.

Max is more than pleased with her current first-place ranking, but she knows she can't afford to get comfortable. Both Saf and Nora are only three points behind her, and if she gets sloppy, allows her ego to inflate too much, it won't be hard for either of them to pass her and steal the top spot.

So she watches, and practices on the air, and returns to the room only when she has to, but still she manages to see Teddy everywhere she goes. When she's in the library, Teddy's there too, suddenly appearing in the stacks right by the book Max wants. When she goes to the dining hall, there's Teddy, taking the last blueberry muffin. When Max is heading into the showers, Teddy's sauntering out, the towel wrapped around her threatening to fall and no sign of caring on Teddy's face. And then, of course, she's *there* every night snoring in the next bed, *there* as soon as Max wakes up, *there* when she's getting dressed. And if she's not there, then her shit is—she's so *messy* that it's driving Max insane, Teddy's dirty clothes dropped on the floor, her books and papers spilling off the desk on her side of the room. It's been three days but it looks as if Teddy has lived there for *weeks*, but Max bites her tongue. Telling Teddy to pick up after herself will only give Teddy more ammunition for her uptight accusations, and Max is pretty sure if Teddy says one more irritating thing they're going to have to physically fight each other.

Max takes a sip of the nonalcoholic cider that Ms. Cara had given them with a wink, as if it was such a special treat for them. The dining hall echoes with after-dinner chatter, plates empty of the better-than-expected Thanksgiving dinner put together by the kitchen staff, an extra few dozen guests apparently no issue for them. Of course before dinner they listened to Dr. Thompson and history teacher Mr. Giles talk about the true history of the holiday and the importance of not only recognizing the fact that at this very moment, they were living on stolen land, but what concrete actions Gardner students should take in the present day. Max had caught surprise on Teddy's face, like she hadn't expected anyone to even mention Native history, and she let that irritate her for a second—obviously Teddy *still* didn't really understand Gardner, obviously she hadn't read the biographies of both Cecily Gardner and Liliane Bahnsen in the library, because then she'd know what the women stood for, the alliances they had made and knowledge and support traded between them and other women activists and writers of their time, including Native women.

(She tries not to think about Safiya a few years ago, saying, "Okay, but if Cecily was so down for the cause and understood that the money and land her family owned never truly belonged to them, wouldn't the better thing to do have been *not* building a school here? A school that has had, what, a handful of Indigenous students in its entire history?")

A few seats down, two second years are playing one of those stupid clapping games, their voices raised to fever pitch, the exact right tone to set Max's nerves on edge. *If I don't get out of here soon, I'm going to kill someone,* she thinks. Her gaze skitters across the table and meets Teddy's, and Teddy raises her eyebrows, and for the first time ever Max knows they're on the same wavelength.

Then Max senses someone behind her and turns to find Noelle and Corey, bending over, voices lowered to a whisper. "Want to come back to our room and watch a movie?" Corey asks.

Before Max or Teddy can answer, Noelle grins. "We have whiskey."

Noelle winces as she swallows, passing the bottle to Max. "Shit. I don't think whiskey is my drink."

"I don't think anything's your drink," Corey says with a laugh. "Remember that time you—"

"Quiet!" Noelle launches herself at Corey, waving her hands in front of her friend's face. "Taking it to the grave, remember?"

Max tips the bottle to her lips. She doesn't wince as the whiskey goes down; she's had plenty of practice, mostly during those summers at Nora's, and more importantly, with every sip it becomes easier and easier to bear sitting in the same small room with Teddy. Not her ideal way to spend Thanksgiving, sure, but there's no use trying to fight it anymore. Easier to give in. Well. Easier, as long as Teddy keeps her mouth shut like she has been so far.

Corey leans over and grabs the bottle out of Max's hands. "Let's play a game," she starts, but Teddy shakes her head.

"If the next words out of your mouth are 'truth or dare,' don't bother," Teddy says. "That goes for 'never have I ever,' too."

"Killjoy," Noelle says.

"Maybe," Teddy says, "or maybe I've just played so many stupid games with so many stupid girls that I'm bored."

Corey frowns. Her eyes are already glassy, her cheeks red. "Wait. Are you calling us stupid?"

"As *if*," Teddy says with a smile, and Corey looks relieved, laughing a little, and then Teddy's eyes meet Max's once again. *Oh, she's the absolute stupidest girl I've ever met,* her eyes seem to say, and Max fights a smile but can't quell it completely. Well, she has a point.

"I just have a better idea," Teddy says, and she takes Noelle's laptop off the bed and starts typing. "It's called, we watch a stupid movie and take a shot every time we see a bad wig. Got it?"

"As long as we get to drink, I don't care," Noelle says.

Max steals the bottle back and takes another swig. Some trickles out of the corner of her mouth, and she wipes it away, licks it off her thumb. "Ditto," she says. If she's drunk, the rest of the day will go faster, and she'll pass out in bed, and then there will only be one more day of having to tolerate Teddy in such close quarters. Perfect.

Teddy selects some truly god-awful horror movie from the early 2000s that seems more concerned with how many topless girls it can cram in than anything else. Within twenty minutes Corey and Noelle are hammered, cackling at the predictable jumpscares, and Max has a good buzz going, enjoying the warmth, how her always-tense muscles have relaxed, liquefied a little. "Wig! Terrible wig!" Corey yells, and the bottle goes down the line: Noelle to Corey, to Max, to Teddy. She has the bottle to her mouth, head tipped back, when there's a sharp rap on the door.

They all freeze, and then Corey begins to panic. "Hide it, hide it!" she says in the world's loudest whisper, lunging over Max to rip the bottle out of Teddy's hand.

"Where's the cap?"

"Turn off the movie!"

"What does the movie matter? We're allowed to watch movies, Noelle."

Another knock, and then a lilting voice through the door: "Girls! It's Ms. Cara. I'm coming in!"

"Shit," Noelle says, and Max rolls her eyes.

"God, you really are stupid," she says, and hops to her feet, making it to the door right as Ms. Cara opens it. She leans against the doorframe and pastes a wide smile on her face. "Hi, Ms. C. What's up?"

Ms. Cara's gaze roams the room, and if it were any other faculty member, Max might be worried, but Ms. Cara is so trusting and so desperate to be liked that Max knows she'll only see what she wants to: four upstanding final years having a jolly old time watching a movie, just like the slumber party she'd described this whole week as being. "Looks like a fun party in here," Ms. Cara says, and her gaze returns to Max's face. "I just came looking for a couple of trustworthy volunteers. Some of the lower school girls want to put on a little play tonight—entertainment for the troops, that kind of thing."

"Sounds great!" Max twists to look at the others still sitting on the floor, a blanket thrown over Corey's lap where Max knows the bottle of whiskey is hiding. "Doesn't that sound like fun?"

Noelle and Corey nod automatically, little wind-up toys whose strings Max has yanked. Teddy stands up and moves to the door, hovering right behind Max, close enough that when she speaks her breath hits Max's ear. "So what do you need volunteers for?" Teddy asks. "I'm no good at remembering lines, but I make up for it with my enthusiasm."

This sends Ms. Cara into peals of laughter. "I'll bet," she says when she's calmed down. "No, no, nothing like that. I just need two of you to go over to the drama studio and raid the costume closet. Whatever you can find that seems fairy-tale appropriate. I'm not sure what the exact plot of this play is but that's half the fun, I suppose."

Two of you. Max turns again. Noelle and Corey can barely sit upright. The moment they stand up, Ms. Cara's going to know they've been drinking. God knows what shit they'd come back from the drama studio with.

She glances at Teddy. Suddenly her buzz is muted. "Okay," she says. "Me and Teddy will go."

35

TEDDY

THEY CRUNCH THROUGH the snow in silence, just the sound of their footsteps accompanying them. This is how they work best, Teddy has decided; when they talk, they fight, and usually that's fine, fun even, because Teddy gets to control when that happens, but now they've spent all week sharing a room and there's one more day to go and it's really *not* been fun. Which, by the way, is not her fault: they agreed to stay out of each other's way as much as possible, and so far Teddy's stuck to her side of the bargain, but Max? Well, she's appeared everywhere Teddy has been all week. In the library when Teddy was pretending to study, right behind her in the dining hall line, giving her that snotty look on her way into the showers right as Teddy was coming out. It's like she's *trying* to get on Teddy's nerves, trying to get a rise out of her.

THE TOURNAMENT

Her phone buzzes with a text from Nora: no words, just a picture of her hand holding a glass of something shiny and golden. Teddy stops to snap a quick picture of the frosty trees and sends it, only noticing afterward that Max's arm appears as a blur at the edge of the photo. It's fine, she thinks; Nora won't notice, and if she does, she won't be able to tell that it's Max. Not that Teddy's trying to hide anything. She thought about telling Nora about the room-sharing predicament, but only for a split second, because then she realized how Nora would react and she doesn't want to deal with that right now. Nora pretends to be so confident, so assured, but it all falls apart when it comes to Max, and her being thousands of miles away from school would only make the jealousy and paranoia worse. Might cause a little chaos, sure, but not the kind that Teddy thinks would soothe the black hole. Just the irritating kind that would leave her picking up the pieces of a mess she shouldn't even be part of, really.

Up ahead, almost to the arts building, Max turns around. "Hurry up, Swanson," she calls. "Your girlfriend can wait."

"For me? Yeah, she will," Teddy says, and even from here she can see Max roll her eyes.

"Just hurry the fuck up."

When they get inside, Teddy rubs her hands together and watches her breath appear in a cloud. "Is the heat even on?"

Max shrugs. "Doesn't feel like it. Just keep your coat on, it's fine."

She leads the way to the drama studio, a big box of a room with heavy black drapes lining all four walls. Max heads toward one of them and opens a door out of nowhere, almost like magic. "We'll just get whatever and head back," she says, waiting for Teddy to enter. "Come on."

Teddy brushes past her and enters the costume closet. Inside it's small, maybe five by eight feet, and there are rails crammed with clothing making the space even smaller, shelves stuffed with hats and plastic swords and more faux feathers than Teddy has seen in her life. "Whoa," she says. "This might have just become my favorite place at this school."

"Trust me, if you'd had to go through the trauma of a Gardner musical, you wouldn't be saying that." Max begins rifling through the hangers, her expression serious. "Here, look. These will do fine."

Teddy looks at the shapeless brown sacks Max is pulling off the rails and then at Max. "You're joking, right? Ms. Cara said *fairy-tale*."

"These are fairy-tale," Max says. "I think they were, like, mice in *Cinderella* or something."

"Those are not mouse costumes," Teddy says. "And even if they were, we're not taking them. We need dresses, maybe some fairy wings or something, some cute shoes—" She starts searching through the opposite rail. "I know you're, like, absolutely devoid of joy and you don't care about anyone else's feelings, but it won't kill you to do something nice for once."

"Oh yeah, because you're such an angel," Max says. "It's a stupid made-up play. They're only doing it to suck up to the teachers."

Teddy clicks her tongue. "So cynical," she says. "Not everybody has political machinations. Besides, they're literally thirteen."

"And? Thirteen at Gardner is not the same as thirteen everywhere else."

"Because Gardner's *so* different from everywhere else." Teddy spots something silky and forest green. *A ball gown, maybe?* She pulls the hanger out. "Even Gardner girls can still have fun, you know."

"I never said we don't. I keep forgetting, you're not really one of us."

"Whatever, Max. I've been to four different schools and Gardner does not have the monopoly on *serious* or whatever you think it is. God, you're all so invested in this place. You know there's a whole world out there, right? You know you're going to graduate soon and the rest of the world does not give a singular *shit* about Gardner?"

Max makes a noise of disgust. "God, I can't believe they let you in the Cup. I swear to god, Maeve Tierney is rolling in her grave. At least there's no chance you're going to win."

Teddy feels the blood rushing in her veins, simmering and hot. "I wouldn't count me out just yet," Teddy snaps. "There are four challenges left."

"Based on your track record, that doesn't worry me."

"Maybe it's not me you need to be worried about." Teddy turns, fist closing on the dress in her hands. "Nora and Safiya are right behind you, aren't they? And who beat you in the swim? Who came out on top from the very beginning? That's right: Nora! So if I were you, I wouldn't be thinking about my name on the trophy just yet. There's a long way to go before any of that happens, and I think once I tell Nora what a colossal bitch you've been this week, it might add a little extra fuel to her fire."

Max whips around too, eyes wide and angry. "Sure, tell her all about me. I'm the whole reason you two are even together, anyway. You know she's only using you to make me jealous, right? You're nothing but a rebound."

She delivers this like it's so sharp, so explosive, her anger shifting to a self-satisfied, superior smile. She thinks she's telling Teddy something she doesn't already know, and it's almost enough to make Teddy laugh, but she manages to hold it in. "What," she says instead, ready to pop Max's smug little balloon, "just because once upon a time she was in love with you?"

It has the exact effect Teddy wanted, and now she does laugh, as Max blinks, the smirk wiped off her face, her mouth opening and closing a few times before she eventually speaks. "She—told you?"

Teddy lets the dress slip through her fingers, hanger clattering to the floor. "Even if she hadn't, I would have known," she says. "Jesus, anyone can figure it out. It's *so* obvious. I mean— obvious to everyone *but* you, I guess. Or at least that's what you want people to think, but you're a smart girl. I know you acted surprised when she told you, but of course you already knew. Unless you really didn't, which would make you not as smart as you so desperately want everyone to think you are."

She watches, her turn for smug satisfaction now, as Max's cheeks redden and she visibly shrinks back, pressing into the costumes behind her. "You don't know anything," Max says, finally, weakly.

"Oh," Teddy says, making her voice soft, slippery. "I know everything. I've known from the very beginning. You know,

I was the one who talked her into putting her name down for the Cup. Even after everything that went down between you two, she was happy to sit on the sidelines and let you take it for yourself. But that didn't seem fair to me, because what had you ever done for her? Except lie and tell her you weren't in love with her, too."

"I never lied." Max steps forward now, a little bravado recovered. "It's not my fault if she read into things and made up some fantasy where I had feelings for her. I never did anything to make her think that—"

Teddy cuts her off with a wicked laugh. "Except for *everything*," she says. "God, even now, you can't see it. But I do. You watch her, you know. When you think no one's looking, especially when you think *she* isn't looking, you watch her. You want her to do what you want and nothing but that. Compete in the Cup? Out of the question. Apply to Columbia? Absolutely not. And you let everybody know it, didn't you? When you saw she'd signed up, you could have gone to her in private, but you chose to cause a scene in the middle of the hallway where everyone could listen in and repeat back to their friends. It's such a performance and the sad thing is, you don't even know it." Teddy takes a step forward too, closing the space between them. "If you didn't love her, it wouldn't bother you that she loved *you*. You'd be nice to her about it, tell her it's okay, you understand, maybe a little space would be good for the friendship, because after all, you're best friends, you don't want to lose that! If you didn't love her, it wouldn't *kill* you to see her with me. And you tell yourself it's because it's *me*, right?" She stares into Max's angry eyes, noticing the way her nostrils flare, the ragged in-and-out of her breathing. "Teddy Swanson, basket case, legacy, spoiled rich girl who doesn't deserve her place at Gardner, let alone understand it. But it's really just the cherry on top that it happens to be me she's with. You'd hate any girl she picked, because it's not you. You really don't see it?"

"You don't know what the fuck you're talking about," Max says. "I. Don't. Love. Her."

Oh yeah? Teddy lifts her chin, a challenge. "Prove it," she says, and the black hole calls to her, says *do it do it do it* and that's when she kisses Max.

She tastes different from Nora—smoky, the whiskey they've both been drinking. She slips her tongue inside Max's mouth, just for a second, and Max lets her. She feels it, the way Max softens beneath her, the ice queen melted for a brief moment.

And then she pushes Teddy away. "What the fuck are you doing?"

36

MAX

"**WHAT THE FUCK** are you doing?"

Max holds Teddy at arm's length. It's silent except for both of their breathing, and not silent at all in Max's head. Why the fuck would Teddy kiss her? She's with Nora, and Max hates her, and not in that cliché the-line-is-so-thin, two-sides-of-the-same-coin way. She just straight up hates her, for all the reasons Teddy just stated: she's the worst of what a Gardner girl could be, the worst kind of spoiled rich legacy bitch who doesn't really care about anything she does, or anyone around her, anyone she hurts. Like Nora, obviously. What would Nora say if she could see them now? She'd probably have that same hurt look on her face that she did when Max told her she didn't love her.

(She doesn't, she *does not* love Nora, she is not in love with her, Jesus Christ.)

Actually—Nora would probably see this and make it all Max's fault. Must have been her going after Teddy, right? Wanting what Nora has, because she can't have Nora anymore, and after all, Nora's who she wants, isn't it?

In Nora's mind, at least. In Teddy's, too.

Max looks at Teddy, and she should be disgusted, right, should hate her still or maybe even more now, out of some old loyalty to the girl she used to call her best friend. But instead she feels a heat, the kind of heat she usually can ignore because of all the walls she's so painstakingly constructed. But for a moment there, when Teddy was kissing her, when she felt Teddy's tongue move over hers, it was like she found an entrance. A door Max forgot to lock, or a tunnel beneath the foundations, a way for her to get inside. And suddenly Max is aware of how hungry she is to be touched.

And maybe she is that cliché, after all, because she knows she's supposed to hate Teddy, but now it all just feels like fire. She could stop it now, she could keep on pushing Teddy away and wipe the kiss from her mind and go back to where everybody else is waiting for them, but then she'd be cold again. Lonely. Nora was the only person she used to let touch her: play with her hair, smear sunscreen on her back, tuck her bare feet under Max's legs as they watched a movie together on the same bed.

But now Teddy's looking at her like she wants to touch her, and Max knows there are a thousand reasons they shouldn't but she can't bring herself to voice them.

"Fuck it," Max says, and pulls Teddy back to her.

This time she's in control of the kiss, her hands on Teddy's waist, her tongue in Teddy's mouth. That's about as long as she holds on for, though, because the second Teddy breaks away and whispers in her ear, Max turns to liquid.

"Tell me when to stop," Teddy says, her breath hot on Max's ear once again, and then she's kissing Max's neck.

Pushing Max's coat off her shoulders, shrugging off her own, pulling them down to the floor.

Sliding her hand inside Max's sweatshirt, fingers warm against Max's cold hips, stomach, breasts.

Undoing the button of Max's jeans, pulling the zipper down.

Moving her hand inside Max's underwear, between her legs, finding the right spot to make Max gasp and then she puts a hand over her own mouth, equal parts ashamed and encouraged by her own noises but she doesn't want Teddy to stop, doesn't say stop or anything close to it, only takes her hand away to say, "Yes, yes, please—"

When the orgasm hits, it's delicious, intense, a rushing noise in her ear that turns into Teddy's laughter, but not the bitter kind Max usually elicits from her. It's delighted. Pleased. When Max opens her eyes, she can see how pleased Teddy is, too, a gleam in her eyes, but as Max watches, Teddy changes. She sees it, how the light leaves her eyes, how she begins to pull back from Max even as her hand is still on her.

But then Max feels it in herself, too. The sudden clarity, her breath returning to normal, remembering that they're in the fucking costume closet and someone's waiting for them to come back and Teddy has a girlfriend and that girlfriend is Nora and what the fuck have they done.

"What the fuck did I do," Teddy says, echoing Max's

thoughts, but she's not talking to Max. She pulls all the way away now, and Max is left cold without her touch, cold as the walls slam back up.

She takes another beat or two, her pulse slowing. She pushes herself up to sitting, reaches down to button her jeans, pulls her sweatshirt back into place. Now that the moment is over, she can't see anything but how ridiculous it was. How fucked up. As if things weren't fucked up enough already.

Forget about it, her brain says. Yes: they'll just forget this ever happened. What else is there? Max cannot even begin to process it and that's how it's going to have to stay, because after all, there's the Cup, and Columbia, and all the things Teddy mocks her for wanting, and Nora—

Max squeezes her eyes tight shut, like that'll make her stop thinking of her. Nora. She just let Nora's girlfriend make her come on the floor of the costume closet. That might really be unforgivable and if she thought Nora hated her before, then—

No. There won't be an after, because Nora will never know. Max decides this, and only then does she twist around to look at Teddy, still lying flat on her back. "I'm going to pretend this never happened," she says. "You should do the same."

Teddy props herself up on her elbows. "You can't tell Nora," she says, desperation flooding her words. "You can't—"

"Bitch, did you hear what I just said? I'm going to pretend this *never happened*." Max shakes her head. "How can I tell Nora about something that never happened?"

"Oh please." Teddy screws up her face. "There's no way you won't use this. I'm not stupid enough to fall for your act."

Max looks to the ceiling. Jesus, Teddy always has to be so fucking dramatic.

She gets to her feet. "Think what you want," Max says. "But trust me. The only way she's going to find out is from you."

She grabs at the first pastel thing she sees. Then she tries to ignore the way the hanger shakes in her hands. "Hurry up and find something. We have to get back."

They don't speak on the way.

Max walks fast, leaving Teddy behind. Back at the dorm, she finds Ms. Cara in the office and thrusts the costumes she's carrying at her, telling her that Teddy's right behind her. She doesn't even let Ms. Cara finish thanking her before she rushes off, back to Corey and Noelle's room. She bangs on the door and waits impatiently, and then when neither of them opens it, she goes in herself. Corey and Noelle are gone, but it's fine. She only wants the bottle, and Max opens the closet, crouches down to retrieve it from the hiding place she watched Corey extract it from earlier. She sits on the edge of one of the beds and takes a long pull, like she can scrub the inside of her mouth clean with the whiskey, like it'll wipe the memory of Teddy's tongue pressed against hers from her mind.

She screws the cap back on, not stupid enough to keep on drinking. Either that, or she's afraid of what will happen if she does, afraid of losing the ability to see boundaries again.

She covers her eyes with her hands. One more day of this. Two more nights in the same room as Teddy, and then everyone will start returning from break, and things will go back to normal, and she can go back to focusing on beating Nora the normal way. Not fucking around and fucking her girlfriend—

Max stands, hides the bottle, heads out of Corey and Noelle's room and down to the common room. There are a couple of fourth years in there, watching a black-and-white movie with French subtitles. They nod at her but other than that ignore her, and Max lets herself breathe as she makes a coffee in a mug with GARDNER-BAHNSEN printed on the front, half the letters worn away with use.

By the time they trudge back over to the assembly hall later, Max is sober. Painfully so, she thinks, as she sits through the hastily put-together play from the lower years. There isn't really any plot, just a series of scenes strung together and a few songs, but everybody claps loudly at the end and Dr. Thompson gets on stage to say this is the kind of thing that makes her *so proud* to be the headmistress.

Max claps again, robotic, and forces herself not to turn her head and look for Teddy.

She manages to avoid her—or Teddy avoids Max, whichever way around it is—for the rest of the evening. Dread builds the entire time, and when she finally gets into bed she's sick with it. It's dark outside and dark in the room, and Max tries to go to sleep, closing her eyes, headphones in like always.

But sleep doesn't come, and as the minutes tick by she can only think of the costume closet—Teddy's hands—Nora—

The door opens.

Max stiffens, forces herself to keep her eyes closed.

THE TOURNAMENT

Footsteps over the carpet. A pause, and then the creak of the other bed.

Max listens to the sound of Teddy getting ready for bed, the pressure inside her chest easing a little.

Two more nights.

37

TEDDY

TEDDY SITS ON the edge of her bed and watches Max for a minute. She'd waited it out as long as she could, hoping that Max would be asleep by the time she came back to their room and for the first time today, things went to plan.

She slips under the covers and curls into a ball on her side. There's no way she's going to sleep tonight. Her mind is racing, stuck in an endless loop of thinking about what she did, questioning why she did it, berating herself. *You stupid bitch. You ruin everything, you make a mess out of everything you do everywhere you go. Nora's going to hate you now. Why would you do something like that? With* her? *What is your fucking problem, you stupid bitch? You ruin everything.*

A tear slips out from beneath her eyelid, sliding sideways over her nose and spilling onto the sheets. She knows why she did it. It's the same reason she does anything she does:

because, for a moment, it seemed like the best option. Like if she gave in and did the bad thing, the black hole would go away. Except it never does, never has, probably never will. It will remain within her, this sucking void that only ever gives her a break when she's causing chaos outside, and so she'll keep on chasing chaos because that's all she's good at. And she'll keep on leaving damage in her wake, like she always does. Will she forget Nora's name, the way she's forced herself to forget the people she dragged down with her before, at her other schools?

Nora, Nora, Nora.

Teddy bites the inside of her cheek. As long as she never finds out, then she doesn't have to become damage. Teddy's never wanted to hurt Nora. That's been the problem for a while now, that she doesn't want to and yet knows she somehow, at some point, will. This is that point, she guesses, but it can still be okay. If Max sticks to her word, and Teddy keeps her mouth shut, too, then Nora never has to find out.

She rolls onto her back and stares up at the ceiling. *Okay, but if I'm going to do this, I have to be better.* Since the swim and the realization that the Cup—this school, this everything—is not enough, she's been letting things slide. Letting herself be a little bad, because what does anything really matter anymore? But even with that, she's tried to keep Nora out of it. Let her be the shining spot of something sweet, the only thing worth sticking around here for. And now, of course, at last, she's done the stupid terrible thing that will ruin her and Nora, too.

She presses a hand to her stomach. It's quiet and still in there, the black hole fed. For now. *Or maybe not for now. Maybe for longer,* Teddy thinks. Maybe that will be enough to satisfy it for long enough that Teddy can take a break, rest from the chaos seeking. And actually—if Nora never finds out, then she won't get hurt. If Teddy can do the right thing and keep her mouth shut, like Max told her to, then Nora won't ever know and Teddy won't have another crime to add to her list.

Yes. I can do that, she thinks. *Forget this ever happened and remember what it was like in the beginning, go back to that.* When it was good, when everything they said was charged with an undercurrent, each look and touch electric. Let herself be thrilled in that way, only. Be better, be more convincing, be the girl Nora chose.

She owes her that much, at least.

38

NORA

WHEN NORA GETS back to campus on Saturday, most of the snow is gone, campus returned to its usual, gloomy self. Feels like home, and she's glad to be back, eager for the next challenge. She's still within reaching distance of the top spot, and it was all she could think about all break, getting back to school and going up against Max in the Hunt this coming weekend. She keeps imagining Max's face when Nora comes out of the field with more kills than her, when Nora slices through flesh and bone quicker than her, when Nora finally wins it all and gets her bloody hands on the trophy.

She keeps imagining Max doing a lot of things.

When she finds Teddy in the dorms, the first thing she says is "Good break?" And she's teasing, because of course it sucked that Teddy had to stay on campus because of that stupid snowstorm, but to her surprise Teddy nods.

"Just what I needed," she says, and then she kisses Nora like she did the first time they ever kissed, her fingers beneath Nora's chin and a smile on her lips. And it feels better than things have been with them recently—when they separate, Nora searches Teddy's face for that *off*-ness that she felt before, for the insatiable hunger that had begun to scare her a little, but she doesn't find it. She just sees Teddy smiling, a little wickedness to it, and it's reassuring in the best way but also—there's a guilty feeling in the pit of her stomach, and she knows where it's coming from. Nora spent the whole week thinking about Max when the girl who *actually* wants her was right here, waiting.

"Good," Nora says to Teddy. "I'm glad you had a good time." And she resolves in that moment to stop thinking about Max at all.

What's the point, anyway? she thinks later, when classes are back in full swing and they're falling back into the rhythm of Gardner life. What, because Max spoke to her one time, and looked at her a certain way, Nora's going to allow herself to fall back into that spiral? Fuck no. They're not friends anymore, and any deluded thinking on Nora's part that maybe there was something still there is exactly that—deluded. Besides, judging from the way Max breezed past her on the way out of the dorm on Sunday, leaving a frigid chill in her wake, she's back to her usual ice queen self. Fine. If that's what she wants, then Nora can play it that way, too.

And anyway, there really isn't too much time for her to spend getting mired in thinking about all of that, because the next challenge is almost upon them. They're not allowed to go practice hunting without supervision, so instead on Wednesday Nora and Teddy go up to the range, just to get their muscles thinking the right way again. "I need to do better this time," Teddy says, before firing off three perfect arrows.

"You can, and you will," Nora says. "I think your problem is a lack of urgency."

Teddy whips around, the two long braids she always does when they're training swinging and wrapping around her neck. "Urgency?"

"It's too boring for you," Nora clarifies. "You need a pulse to make it worth it."

Teddy looks up, like she's retreating somewhere inside her mind, and smiles. "Hmm. You may have a point."

They switch places and Nora nocks an arrow, exhaling slowly. She needs to do better this time, too. Everyone will be thinking of her piss-poor performance in the berry test, and she needs to set them straight, shut them up. She's still in second place—fine, joint second, but there isn't such a big distance between her and Max that she can't overtake her, come out on top. And what she knows that no one else does is that Max still gets queasy when she has to butcher. She's learned to cover it well, sure, but she can't quash it entirely, and sometimes it makes itself known despite her best efforts— a hesitant cut here, a clumsy nick of the flesh there. Nora's butchery, on the other hand, is slick and smooth. No hesitation, iron guts.

Does this count as thinking about her? No: she's thinking about the Cup, is all. That's allowed.

"We're going to take it this time," she calls back to Teddy. "First and second place. You and me. You just watch."

They head back to the locker room, faces flushed from the chill. There are a few others in there, including Brooke and Isobel, but Nora pays no attention to them, or the way they roll their eyes and turn away when Nora laughs obnoxiously loud at something Teddy says. Whatever: no pretense of friendship with people who don't want her anymore, right?

"I still think I could shave half a second off my time," Teddy says as she peels her Gardner gym shirt over her head and throws it in her locker. "If I could use a cleaver—"

"No cleavers allowed," Nora says sternly. "You know the rules. You think when the apocalypse comes, you're going to have a cleaver in your bag?"

"When the apocalypse comes, I'm swimming out into the ocean and never coming back." Teddy pulls on the polo she was wearing earlier, then shrugs on her cardigan.

"What's the point in learning all this—" Nora stops abruptly. *What's the point in learning all this if you're just going to kill yourself when the time comes?* is what she wanted to say, but a flash of something on Teddy's cardigan caught her attention, and now she can't think of anything at all.

She reaches over and grabs Teddy's elbow. "What?" Teddy asks, but Nora ignores her, twisting the sleeve around until she finds it again.

Yes, right there by the inside seam: a wriggly-edged patch of white where it should be gray. Put there by acetone, Nora knows, because she's the one who did it. Three years ago, painting her nails in the room she used to share with Max, a careless wave of her hand that knocked the bottle of nail polish remover onto Max's cardigan.

Teddy is wearing Max's cardigan.

Nora looks up at Teddy. "This isn't yours."

"What?"

"This isn't your cardigan." She pulls at the sleeve, stretching it out so Teddy can see. "I spilled nail polish remover on it. The stain never came out, but Max never threw it away because she said it would be a waste. This is Max's cardigan," she says slowly. "So why are you wearing it?"

Teddy stares at the patch between Nora's fingers. She looks confused, her eyebrows furrowed, but is that confusion because she doesn't know how she's managed to be wearing Max's cardigan, or because she isn't sure what lie to tell Nora to explain it all away?

"I—I must have picked it up accidentally," Teddy starts, and Nora drops her arm.

"Accidentally?" Bullshit. *You don't just accidentally happen to end up wearing a piece of clothing owned by a girl you hate,* Nora thinks. Besides, everyone is fiercely protective of their shit, watching the washers down in the laundry like hawks, marking their clothes with a stitch of gold embroidery thread on the inside or a babyish name label tacked in by a housekeeper. Max especially clings to her shit—the uniform is not cheap, and anything Max replaces, she has to pay for herself, Nora knows.

"Yes, accidentally. Over break," Teddy says, and then she looks down at her feet before looking back at Nora. She deflates a little. "You know they move everybody into one dorm during breaks. And then there were more people than they had planned for, so we had to double up. So I . . . had to share a room with Max."

Nora blinks. "I'm sorry, what?"

"Honestly, it was nothing, and I didn't tell you because—"

Nora stands. "You and Max shared a *room* for the *whole* break and you didn't tell me?"

She doesn't realize she's yelling until the moment she finishes talking, when the silence echoes so loud it's impossible to ignore. Of course everyone in the locker room is staring at her now, and she can see Brooke with that irritating smirk she used to enjoy so much, Isobel leaning over to whisper something in her ear.

Nora's cheeks heat and she grabs Teddy by the elbow again, pulling her along this time. They smack through the door and then they're outside, in the cold, a fine mist of rain instantly settling over their skin. "What the *fuck*?"

Teddy pulls free of Nora's grip, rubbing her arms as she shivers. "Listen, I know! I know, okay? I get it, you're mad, I would be mad, but that's why I didn't tell you—"

"Bullshit," Nora snaps. "Please do not try to spin this like something you did to protect me."

"That's not what I meant." Teddy rocks back on her heels. "Look, it was just a situation that happened and I didn't tell you because I knew it would annoy you. Not because I was trying to *protect* you or something," she says, holding a hand up when Nora opens her mouth. "Because it was fucking annoying but I had no choice and my break was already ruined, so what would have been the point of ruining yours, too? Because it would have. You would have thought about it all week long and wondered what was going on and what was she saying and what was *I* saying, and what was *she* doing and it would have just been another way for her to get in your head. That's it, okay?"

Nora nods, a bitter little laugh escaping her lips. "Oh, that's it?"

"Yes. What the fuck else do you think? I basically only went to the room to sleep, and so did she. We avoided each other as much as humanly possible. And then I guess when I was packing all my shit back up to go back to my normal room, I grabbed her cardigan by mistake. See? An accident."

Nora folds her arms and looks away. Teddy and Max, in forced proximity, for a whole week while Nora was thousands of miles away. And what, she's supposed to believe Teddy didn't tell her because she was being . . . *nice*? *Thoughtful*? Teddy's a lot of things but not that. But what other reason would she have for not telling her? Besides, despite everything, Nora does know Max, and she knows there's no way she would have been happy with the situation either. Avoiding each other—avoiding Teddy—is definitely a move out of Max's playbook.

She sighs and looks back at Teddy. "It's just weird," she says. "I don't know, it feels weird that you didn't tell me, even if I can believe you had good intentions for not doing it. Wasn't there anyone else you could have roomed with? Would it have killed you to just let me know?"

Teddy shrugs. "There were only four of us final years left

here," she says, "and Corey and Noelle picked each other, so like . . . no, there wasn't anyone else. And okay, maybe I could have told you, but I didn't think it would do either of us any good. There was no nefarious intent or anything." She says *nefarious* like a comic book character, or a femme fatale poking fun at the private detective peppering her with questions. "But I'm sorry, anyway. I didn't mean to hurt you, or piss you off. I was trying *not* to piss you off, but I guess I fucked it up anyway."

It catches Nora a little off guard, how genuinely remorseful she sounds, how she bites at her nails like she's afraid Nora won't accept the apology. It's the first time, Nora thinks, she's seen Teddy be sorry for something. And maybe Nora just proved her point with her reaction. This is why Teddy didn't tell her: because she knew Nora would be jealous and paranoid, because she knows Nora isn't over Max, right?

Except Nora is, or she so wants to be, and she so *doesn't* want Teddy to think there's anything still between Nora and Max. She wants Teddy to know that she's the one Nora wants, the one she chose, like Teddy chose her.

It would be stupid to let Max come between them, especially when all that really happened is she and Teddy slept in the same space, just like Max and Nora had for years. It's especially stupid because Max would love to know she's causing issues between them, would be thrilled to be the one putting them off their game.

Nora watches Teddy chewing on her nails, then reaches over and pulls her arm again, gentle this time. No: she's not going to give Max that power. More importantly, she *is* going to give Teddy the power to say sorry, and have that apology accepted. "It's okay," she says quietly. "I'm not mad at you."

"You're not?"

"Not anymore," she says, and smiles, so Teddy will know it's not that serious, it's not that bad. Because it's *not* that serious, right? It's *not* that bad? It's not like Teddy lied to her. Okay, it is like that, but it was more a lie of omission than anything else.

Teddy plucks at the hem of Nora's shorts. "Good," she says, and then, "I don't know what I'm doing. I'm bad at, like, communicating, I think."

"No, you're, like, terrible at communicating, I think," Nora says, and that makes Teddy laugh, and Nora pulls her close, quickly. "Just promise me," she says, hating how weak she sounds but needing the reassurance anyway, "that you'll try harder."

"Oh, I promise."

Nora swallows. "And that you'll be honest with me from now on."

Teddy nods, once. "I will."

"And . . . that you were honest about last week," Nora says. "That there's nothing else I need to know about?"

Teddy crosses herself and then slips her hand around Nora's neck. "I swear," she says. "That's all there was."

And Teddy kisses her, and she wants to believe Teddy's telling the truth but something in that kiss feels like a lie, too.

39

TEDDY

TEDDY STRIDES INTO her room, slams the door behind her, and peels the cardigan off. It clings to her like it doesn't want to let go, won't relinquish her from its grip, a reminder of the bad she's done and the lies she has to keep on telling. But still she strips it from her body and balls it up, fires it into the trash and wishes she could incinerate it.

She throws herself on the bed, pushing the heels of her hands into her eyes until she sees fractured shapes and colors. "Fucking idiot," she says aloud. "Stupid fucking idiot, you're *wearing* her fucking *cardigan*, what the fuck is wrong with you?"

Yes, she lied her way out of it, but Nora's not stupid. Case in point: it took her half a second to catch what Teddy hasn't, the fact that she's been walking around wearing Max's cardigan. What is it, some kind of subconscious sabotage? And how has Max not noticed that she's missing it yet? Or maybe she has, and maybe she knew exactly what would happen when Nora saw it.

She opens her eyes, blurry black spots swimming in front of her. She doesn't *like* lying to Nora. She wishes there were nothing to lie about, but that would mean that she hadn't done what she did and for that to be true she'd have to be a completely different person. It's like she can't control herself, even though she knows that's a cop-out, a weak excuse. She could control herself if she tried harder. If she were better. That's why everyone has always been so frustrated and disappointed with her. They can tell she's not trying, or they don't believe when she says she is, and maybe they're right not to. Maybe, Teddy thinks, it's not so much that her mother and her sister, and teachers at her old schools, and friends whose trust she betrayed, and people whose hearts she broke—maybe it's not so much that they never believed her even when she really *was* trying, like she's always felt. But that they knew. They could see through it, through her. Because maybe even when she's trying she's really not, or she's trying for the wrong reasons, or maybe they could just see the truth of her that Teddy always turns away from. They can see what the black hole does to her, even as they don't understand the black hole itself, and they know she'll never really be better. No matter what she says or what she does, what she promises, Teddy will never actually come through.

It's only been a few days since Nora came back and here they are already, a crack in the tenuous control Teddy has over the situation. *Get it together*, she thinks. *There's, what, three weeks until winter break? Three weeks and this time I'll actually get to leave, fuck a snowstorm, whatever it takes I'm going to be out of here. I just need some space from this place and then I'll be better. And I'll come back and by then this whole thing with Max will be so far behind me that it won't even mean anything anymore, and Nora will never have to know and we can carry on and I'll be better and honest and all the things she wants from me. As long as I can give her what she wants, she'll be happy, and I won't be the girl who ruins everything again. It's fine. Easy. I can do this.*

Teddy sits up and moves to her desk, eyeing herself in the mirror. A part of her wants to march down to Max's room and pound on the door, throw the fucking cardigan in her face and ask her if this was some part of a plan to fuck Teddy over. But the rest of her says no—that's the kind of shit the black hole makes her do and she's not answering to it right now. Hasn't it had enough? Can't it stay dormant long enough for her to recover from this and let things even out with Nora, be a good girl for once? Besides, it would give Max too much satisfaction to see Teddy panicking. No: what she needs to do is let this moment pass. Nora believed her story, and that's all that matters. Sure, it wasn't quite the honesty she swore it was, but you can't change what's already happened, only what comes next. And she can be honest, from now on.

Three more weeks. Two more events. Don't tell any more lies.

Teddy watches her reflection as her lips curl up. *Easy.*

PART FOUR

"We dreamed of creating a place where young women could find themselves, find each other, and go out into the world armed with the skills to survive, and thrive. As long as that sisterhood perseveres, then my legacy is secure."

—**CECILY GARDNER,**
interview with *Harper's Magazine*, 1973

40

MAX

THEY STAND ON the edge of the fields, shoulder to shoulder.

Saf presses her fingers to her mouth, and Max stifles a smirk. She heard Saf this morning—everyone on their floor heard Saf this morning—emptying her stomach over and over. *Food poisoning,* the whispers said, but no one said the other part, the thing everyone was thinking: If Saf got food poisoning from the dining hall, wouldn't other girls be sick? Isn't it a little convenient, right before the Hunt?

If someone was going to slip her something, they'd have to have access to her food, wouldn't they? Max thinks. *Somebody close to her. And who would do such a thing? Certainly not me. Forget to warn her that the salad she asked for a bite of before finishing the whole thing was not fresh from the dining hall but had been sitting in my bedroom for three days? Well. Maybe me.*

"Girls." Dr. Thompson strolls down the line, taking a second to look in each of their faces. "You have two hours. You may only use your bow. Any prey found to have been captured or killed by methods other than bow and arrow will be voided and removed from your total, and will also earn you a five-minute penalty during tomorrow's challenge. Understood?"

"Understood," Max says in chorus with the others. Her teeth chatter a little and she knows she looks as bad as Saf, dark circles and sallow skin, but she's wired, the lack of sleep giving her a dangerous kind of nervous energy. And since Thanksgiving, she hasn't been sleeping well at all.

She can push what happened with Teddy out of her mind during the day, pretend like nothing happened just like they agreed. But at night it's a different story. Dreams about Teddy that she wakes up from in a sweat, except sometimes in the dream it's not Teddy but Nora, and sometimes it's both of them, and sometimes it's another version of herself Max is looking at and she kisses herself, touches herself. But no matter what combination of people she dreams of, she wakes up the same way, and she's almost afraid to go to sleep because she knows what she'll see and the more she dreams of it the harder it becomes to forget.

The way it felt to be touched. The truth about her and Nora. How something in her has awakened and refuses to quiet down again.

She's been ignoring Nora even more than usual. But there's a guilty sense that even as she does it—studiously looks away from her in class, brushes past her in the halls, watches to make sure they're never in the showers at the same time—the truth of what happened is radiating off her.

THE TOURNAMENT

She focuses on the field just behind Dr. Thompson. Two hours in there to shoot as many rabbits as they can. One year—back in '87, maybe '88—a girl shot a deer that she tracked through the trees. It wasn't technically against the rules, but it wasn't within them either, so she didn't gain anything extra from it. She quit the Cup in protest, saying the rules of the challenges were arbitrary and against the entire ethos of the founders. "The point is to show our survival skills," she's quoted as saying. "If I'm out in the world trying to survive on my own, what's better, a few skinny rabbits or a deer that I can actually use?" At least, that's what she's quoted as saying in the unofficial Gardner history book produced by a small group of students that same year. It was contraband back then, underground, but now it's in the library as part of Gardner's history—the example of the best kind of Gardner girls, rebellious enough to question authority, determined to put out what they considered to be the real and honest version of true history.

Max's hands itch for her bow. Two hours and as many rabbits as she can catch and she'll stay on top. That's what's really important here. Fuck the noise and the bullshit going on—she's not thinking about that today, and by the time she emerges with her spoils she'll remember that this is what matters.

Ms. Bell holds a whistle just in front of her lips. "One blow to begin," she says. "One blow to finish. Three short blows in case of emergency, on either side. Clear?"

Max thinks of the whistle shoved in the pocket of her leggings, spandex pressing it tight to her skin. She thinks about what it would take for her to blow that whistle and call the cavalry to come rescue her.

"On your marks," Ms. Bell says, and then there's the shrill insistent shriek of the whistle and they're off.

They move in silence. No crowd today, because no one wants a repeat of the '76 cup, where a second year got nailed in the shoulder by a stray arrow from a weak competitor. She recovered, but still. Can't be too careful.

Max separates from the pack as soon as she can and heads east, moving through the long grass carefully and deliberately. She patterns her movements in a zigzag, pausing for long stretches before resuming walking again. She's not a natural hunter but she's been preparing for this for the last three years, going out on the weekend hunts Ms. Bell leads, reading up on best practice. She likes the quiet focus of it.

Before long she spots her first target. She moves slowly and methodically, nocking her arrow and exhaling slowly, waiting for a lull in the wind. All the while she keeps her focus on the rabbit, its movements fast but not panicked. It cleans its face, an ease that says it has no clue its hunter is right there, watching, waiting. Max licks her dry lips. The hushing of the wind stills.

Her heart thrums.

She lets fly and watches the arrow smack straight into its home, the quick and quiet wet thud of the arrow piercing flesh. The rabbit slumps to the ground, and Max finally breathes in again, a wicked smile on her face.

One down.

◆◆◆

When the final whistle blows, Max returns to the edge of the field. She's carrying five rabbits, hanging limp in a sack slung across her back. She's done better before, but she's certainly done worse, too, and with all the girls out in the field together, competition was hot.

They stand in the same line as before and keep quiet as Dr. Thompson works her way down, checking everyone's kills and announcing them as she goes. "Abigail Brody: three. Nora McQueen: four. Jordan Riggs: six. Manuela Vega . . ."

Max bristles at being outdone by Jordan Riggs. It's fine, though: Jordan's in third place overall, fifteen points behind Max. Even taking a win in this challenge leaves her behind. She listens to Dr. Thompson call out Manuela's surprising two—*Really, Manuela? I expect better of you*, Max thinks—and then stands tall as her own haul is inspected. "Wren Maxwell: five," Dr. Thompson says, and is it Max's imagination or does the headmistress nod as if she's pleased, a hint of a smile on her stern face? "Safiya Haddad," she continues, "four. Teddy Swanson: four."

The headmistress pauses as she steps back, hands folded behind her back now. "Well done," she says, and now Max knows she's pleased. It was a clean hunt—no accidents, no fuckups. "We'll head back to campus now. Your kills will be taken by Dr. Kessel in preparation for tomorrow. The points tally will be updated this afternoon."

As soon as Dr. Thompson turns her back, the silence shatters. Max can hear the others talking around her but she keeps quiet, calculating the points in her head. Saf, Nora, and Teddy all got four kills, putting them in shared third place, which means they each get eight points. Teddy doesn't matter, Max thinks, and only a split second later registers the thought again. *Teddy doesn't matter.* She grins to herself. Yes, this is what she wanted. The Hunt clarifies. Something in the killing of another living thing puts everything into perspective, and Teddy doesn't matter—she's so far behind that eight points isn't enough to threaten Max's spot, and even Saf and Nora will still be four points behind her. *I'm going to win,* Max allows herself to think, and she's so busy in her fantasy that she doesn't notice Nora slowing ahead of her. Max walks straight into her, the smack taking her by surprise, and Nora stumbles, falling to the ground. "What the fuck," she says at the same time Max says, "Watch where you're going, bitch."

Nora looks up at her, and for a second Max thinks about holding her hand out and helping her up. It's the guilt talking. Or is it the loyalty, still so hard to shake, clinging on an unconscious level?

Max glances ahead and sees Teddy there, waiting, looking back at them with a grim expression on her face, like she's afraid of what Max might do. As if Max might choose this moment to spill everything.

She looks back down at Nora. No. The Hunt clarifies everything.

She steps right over Nora and keeps on walking.

41

NORA

SUNDAY MORNING.

They're in the Skills room, no audience. Just the seven competitors sitting alone at their bench, Dr. Kessel and Dr. Thompson at the front, Ms. Bell in the top corner of the room keeping an eye on things. They have timers on the benches which they will hit as soon as they've completed the butchering of one rabbit. Then they will take their spoils to the front, for the teachers to judge. They will be scored on speed, skill, and precision, and they may butcher as many of their kills as they wish, but only their top score will be taken. That way, even though every competitor has a different number of rabbits, it doesn't influence the scores in this challenge.

Nora knows all the rules, like she always does. She's sitting at the back of the room, her bench facing Saf's. She's trying not to make eye contact, which is easy enough because

Saf seems to be doing the exact same thing. Nora focuses on a spot to the left of Saf, keeping her gaze there and not letting it wander. If it wanders, she might look at Teddy and then the unsettling notion that Teddy is lying about something will creep in and fuck up her game. If she looks at Max then she'll be flooded with a different feeling—anger, fresh and tender to the touch, the memory of the way Max literally walked right over her yesterday unshakable. She couldn't even treat Nora like a human for half a fucking second. Nora had picked herself up, face hot with embarrassment, and seethed in Teddy's general direction. "Did you see that? Can you fucking believe her?" Only for Teddy to smile beatifically and say, "Whatever. She's probably just scared you're going to beat her." Which made absolutely no sense to Nora, not really, and there was something about the speed at which Teddy replied—as if she'd had it locked and loaded—and the lack of conviction to her words—like she would say whatever in order to shut Nora up—that made Nora wonder what the fuck was going on in either of their minds.

Dr. Kessel stands. "Is everybody ready?" She's so bright-eyed today, a bloodthirsty sort of appeal. Nora runs her fingers along the handle of the single knife laid out to her left, the fluorescent lights refracting off the blade, razor sharp and whispering to her. *Pick me up. Let's cut.* She wonders idly if this is really what Cecily Gardner and Liliane Bahnsen had in mind when they first conceived of a school. That a hundred years later a group of mostly spoiled girls would be sitting here playing with knives. That a girl like Nora would be sitting here about to play with knives but still thinking about shit like the never-ending fight with her former best friend and the relationship she's fallen into that lately doesn't feel good at all and why the girl sitting opposite her, who until a few weeks ago was one of her closest friends, now refuses to look at her.

The silence that follows Dr. Kessel's question seems to please her. "Excellent," she says. "Your time begins—now!"

Nora picks up the knife and wastes valuable seconds curling her fingers around the handle, letting the weight of it settle in and become familiar. *Easy*, she thinks, and the dead rabbit on the board in front of her offers no resistance when she makes her first cut. Blood blooming beneath the blade like a happy sacrifice.

She sinks into the movements, practiced over and over again, going swiftly from one step to the next: head removed, twisted until the neck snaps in her hands. Soft brown fur peeled off with a slick suction and pop. Move here—cut there—scoop out lungs, heart, kidneys—feel blood filling the tiny grooves of your fingerprints—flesh and gristle collecting beneath your fingernails—smell thick and metallic.

When she smacks the timer she leaves a bloody smear on the plastic, and carries her kill to the front, leaving it there with the teachers and walking back to her station. The timers ding when they're stopped and Nora tries to ignore the chorus of them as she moves on to her next rabbit, the off-kilter ringing of church bells. Ms. Bell moves throughout the room silently, noting down each time of each stopped clock. She tries to ignore but can't help herself sneaking a look every time she hears the ding, watching Abigail Brody going up to the front, the way Jordan Riggs almost trips and drops her rabbit but catches herself at the last second, the smug look on Saf's face as she saunters back. Nora carves her kill up and carries another to the front, returns to her seat, restarts the process. Hears a ding and looks to see Max going up. Hears another ding and there's Teddy on her way, too. *Focus,* her brain says, and she looks back at her work for a second before her gaze goes back to the front.

So she's watching as Max walks back to her seat and has to pass Teddy, and as she does so Teddy stretches her fingers so that they brush the back of Max's hand.

And Max jumps, like an electric shock passed through her, and turns to look at Teddy over her shoulder and when she turns back she has this nervous look on her face.

And Nora knows. She doesn't understand how and she barely understands what but she knows, she knows, everything finally *finally* clicking into place.

"You have to be fucking kidding me."

Nora doesn't mean to say it aloud but it comes out anyway, and across the way Saf finally looks at her, eyebrows furrowed together in confusion. Nora ignores her, letting her gaze flick from Max to Teddy and back again. "Are you *fucking kidding me?*" she says this time, loud enough to stop everything and everyone looks up, the same confusion as Saf on their faces as they take in what was said and who said it.

Nora stands up, kicking her chair away so hard it smacks to the floor and Teddy's looking at her like she's gone insane but then there's Max, shoulders rounded as she curls into herself, the picture of guilt, the first time Nora has ever seen her truly give in and that's how she knows she's right. That's how she knows something happened between them and that's how it all suddenly makes sense—that unsettling feeling that something was *off* with Teddy, her showing up in Max's cardigan, Teddy lying about them sharing a room—

Nora balks. They shared a *fucking* room for an entire fucking *week*—

Everyone's staring and Max can't meet her eyes and Nora knows all of it is terrible and true and she has the knife in her hand still. She has the knife in her hand and then she moves without thinking, a guttural noise of rage spilling out of her as she launches the knife out of her bloody hand and it sails through the air, clear past Max to land deep in the wall.

For a long moment there's nothing but shocked silence, everybody frozen. Until Teddy speaks—until she holds her hands up and says, "Nora, no, wait—"

Later on Nora will recount every minute, every movement, every single thing that happened in that room. But in the moment it's only chaos.

The room erupts as Nora comes around from her bench and lunges at Max, Teddy's arms in an instant around her waist trying to hold her back but Nora can't stand the feel of Teddy's hands on her so she turns, kicks at her, and Dr. Kessel's yelling "Girls, please, stop this right now!" but Nora reaches Max and she doesn't break her stride, only raises her hand and slaps Max hard across the face and then Saf throws herself between them and somewhere in the background Nora hears Abigail's high-pitched voice saying "What the fuck is wrong with her?" and she wants to turn around and scream it all out.

What's wrong with her? How about she was relegated to the background until Teddy came along and convinced her to enter the Cup, so she could beat the girl who broke her heart, who used to be her best friend in the entire world, and how about she let herself believe that Teddy wanted her but of course it was Max she really wanted! And of course Max went there, because if Nora wants to take the Cup from her, then she'll take the girl Nora wants, right? As if it wasn't enough for Max to humiliate her by pretending Nora was crazy for being in love with her, crazy for thinking Max could love her back. Well, maybe she was crazy, maybe she *is* crazy—that's the way everyone's looking at her now, and maybe they should because in this moment Nora feels like she's lost her entire fucking mind.

Teddy grabs her again and Nora spins and shoves her away, except it wasn't Teddy, it was Jordan, and now everyone is in the mess and Dr. Kessel keeps yelling and Dr. Thompson sprints out of the room and Nora makes contact with Max again, clawing at her this time saying "I hate you, I hate you," as she leaves red smears on Max's face and neck and Max isn't even putting up a fight and then in rushes a whole flood of teachers and Nora is lifted off and away—

Dr. Thompson steeples her fingers, sitting behind her desk. "I just—I cannot even *begin* to express—" She pauses and inhales loudly, her nostrils flaring.

Nora sits perfectly still in her chair on the other side of the desk. Her fingers twist together, scrubbed clean now. That was not her choice. She would have left the blood and guts if she'd had her way. But once the chaos had been quelled, Nora separated from the others and a new kind of silence ringing through the room, she hadn't had much choice in what came next. The challenge was abandoned, their rabbits still lying there on the benches where they left them, mutilated bodies and staring black eyes. She's not sure what's going to come now, except that she probably just lost her place in the Cup. That's it. Over for her, no history making, no name on a trophy.

What does it matter anyway? Max can have it. It's ruined, now. This silly game she's been playing—what does any of it matter? She could win and Max would still have beaten her, because she took the only thing Nora had that was hers and hers alone: Teddy.

She cracks her knuckles, staring straight ahead. Teddy's sitting in a chair on her left. That's all she knows, because she really can't look at her again. She can't risk looking at her, because she knows Teddy and this is the type of shit she does, isn't it? Breaking rules and ruining things and doing it all with a smile on her face. If she's smiling, Nora can't see it, because then she'll lose her mind all over again and what would that get her?

Dr. Thompson clears her throat now. She looks worn out, the crow's feet at the corners of her eyes particularly pronounced. "Your behavior today was absolutely unacceptable," she says. "Not only did you endanger yourselves, but you endangered every other girl in that room. You endangered the Tierney Cup itself. If that knife had gone a few inches in a different direction, we could be telling a very different story right now. This is absolutely against every value that this school was founded on and stands for. The Cup is meant to challenge you and allow you to demonstrate the skills and knowledge you have learned during your time here. It is not meant as a show of aggression or domination. Nora." Dr. Thompson trains her gaze on her. "Your actions were utterly inexcusable. I have no choice but to suspend you. You will remain here at school until the end of the week, but you will not attend classes. Your parents will need to arrange for you to leave campus and return home for the remainder of the semester. Until then, you will report to my office at seven a.m. daily and do exactly as you are told." She shakes her head, a sad, slow breath escaping from between her lips. It's a sigh that says, *I expected better of you, Nora*, or maybe it says, *All you spoiled rich girls are the same in the end*.

"Max, Teddy." Dr. Thompson sits back. "You will go to class, and report to Study Session immediately after, and that's all for you. No Activity, no free time, no trips into town— for the next two weeks I want you working on your grades and nothing else. And if I hear about so much as a squabble between the two of you, you may find yourselves joining Nora. Whatever it is that has gone on between the three of you, I don't want to hear another word about it. If you cannot be civil, then I expect you to simply not talk at all. At Gardner, we do not solve our disputes with physical violence or with public displays. Do I make myself clear?"

"Crystal," Teddy says quietly.

Nora pulls her left index finger so far back it feels like it might snap right in half.

"Now." Dr. Thompson runs her hands over her face. "The Cup. I'll be brief. Having discussed it with several other faculty members, the decision has been made to suspend the remainder of the challenges, effectively canceling this year's Tierney Cup."

Canceling? Nora's mouth drops open. What, just like that? It's *over*?

"You're joking, right?" Max speaks up finally. "You can't cancel the Cup. What about—"

Dr. Thompson silences Max with a single steely look. "Believe me, Ms. Maxwell, I have run through all the reasons you're about to give me in favor of *not* canceling the Cup, and I cannot in any way find that they outweigh what happened today. The Cup is not designed to risk your *lives*. Do you know how many parents I'm going to have calling me, emailing me, wanting to know what kind of school it is I'm running where students throw *weapons* at each other? It brings me absolutely no pleasure to cancel it. I look forward to the Cup every year. I understand the weight it holds, the meaning it has to our students. But I cannot let it continue when an incident like this happens. I cannot let it continue when I have no certainty that another similar incident won't happen in any of the remaining challenges."

"But it was me," Nora says. "It was—" *It was my fault* is what she wants to say, but she can't get the words out. Sure, she threw the knife, but Max lit the fire, so long ago now. And Teddy was the one pouring gasoline on it.

She clears her throat. "I did it," she says. "I made a huge mistake, I know, and I accept the punishment I've been given but everyone else shouldn't have to pay for what I did. If you cancel the Cup, everyone else loses out."

"Be that as it may," Dr. Thompson says, "the decision has already been made. And it's final. There will be no more Tierney Cup this year."

42

TEDDY

THE RAIN HITS Teddy as soon as they step outside, a harsh drumming that soaks her—all of them—to the skin within seconds.

She reaches out toward Nora, already stalking off in the direction of the dorm, where they've been told to go, to stay in their rooms until dinner. "Nora, wait," she says. "I'm sorry—"

Nora whips around. "Don't you fucking say that," she says. "You're such a liar. You're not sorry. You're never sorry! You just want me to make you feel better. You want me to believe that you're sorry so then you don't have to feel so bad about what you did. What you *both* did." She folds her arms over her chest. "I want to hear it."

Teddy swallows. "Hear what?"

"What you did," Nora says. "The truth. I know something happened between you two. I could fucking see it. You both think I'm so stupid, so naive, but I have eyes and I know you both and I want to know exactly. What. Happened."

Teddy knows if she looks at Max it will only make things worse, further enrage Nora, but she can't stop herself from glancing over to where Max stands, fat drops of rain ricocheting off her loafers. She looks guilty, not even trying to hide it anymore. "Does it matter?" Max says, so weary. "Is it really going to change anything?"

Nora opens her mouth but Teddy gets in there first. "It was Thanksgiving," she says. "I was drinking. We were both drinking. Ms. Cara wanted us to go do something for her. Get costumes for—it doesn't matter. We were in the costume closet. We were arguing, and then we kissed." She pauses. No: better to get it all out, stop pretending like anything can be hidden. "We kissed, and then we kept on going. I touched her. She didn't touch me. It was over in a few minutes. It was only then. It was a mistake we both made. It was a mistake that was not repeated. I regretted it as soon as it happened. That's all there was."

Nora's nodding, a bitter smile on her lips. "Cool," she says. "Great. Fucking awesome! So glad you regretted it! So happy it *only* happened one time! As if I believe that shit."

Max throws her hands up. "See? This is why I didn't—"

"What? Didn't tell me?" Nora rounds on Max. "Didn't *want* to tell me? What, to protect my feelings? Yeah, because that's really something you care about it, isn't it? Not hurting me. You're so transparent. You have never done anything in your life that wasn't about you. You didn't want to tell me because you didn't want to risk anything fucking up *your* life and *your* chance at winning the Cup. It had nothing to do with me or my feelings. Don't even try."

"God, you're always so fucking melodramatic," Max says. "Fine, Nora. Believe what you want. You always do."

Nora takes a step back. "Right," she says. "Right. Here we are again. This is it, isn't it? This is always the thing with you. I'm just some idiot girl who made up a fantasy where I was in love with you and you felt the same, right? No. I'm not doing this anymore. You made me think it was all me, all in my head, but I'm not going to pretend to believe that anymore. To let you make me think it was all on me when you were the one who couldn't go a day without talking to me. You were the one who liked to sleep in my bed, and wanted me to rub your back so you could fall asleep, and told me all your secrets, and cried to me about the shit you wouldn't say to anyone else, like how you wanted so badly to leave home behind but you still wished they could have pretended to care for a moment at least." She jabs at the air. "And we spent every waking minute together, every *single* day here at school, every single holiday at my house, and you loved it, you loved *me* but you couldn't actually admit it. You knew all along how I felt. Of course you did, you're smart. You understand things. You knew how I felt and you felt it as well but you couldn't say you wanted me too because then what would make you better than me? What would you have over me? Nothing." Nora spits the word and Teddy winces as if it were thrown at her, not Max, who's staring at Nora with her teeth gritted so hard Teddy can see it from here, the way her jaw juts out.

Nora pushes her rain-soaked curls back from her face. "You

liked that I loved you and you liked that you could withhold your love from me because then that made you better than me, in some way. I had more money, I had the right background, I had all the opportunities, but you could pretend not to love me and then I wouldn't have you and that's the one thing I couldn't get, right? Everything else I can buy my way into but not you. Even though you still wear the fucking necklace I got you, which—" She laughs here, the sound carrying on cold wind. "Which, by the way, is not costume, it cost thirteen hundred dollars but I couldn't tell you that because then you wouldn't take it. Because Wren Maxwell doesn't need charity, right? Even though charity is the only reason you're even able to be at Gardner. Even though you took all the shit my parents gave you, but I guess that's different. You didn't want to push them away, because you could use them. They could be good for you one day—a connection, a network. Or maybe you just liked pretending they were *your* parents, pretending like you came from them instead of the shitty parents you hate. No, wait—it's not that you hate them, it's that you're ashamed of them. Isn't it? They don't live up to your impossible standards, they're not useful to you, so you act like they don't exist and obsess over *mine* instead. And me? I guess I was something you looked forward to throwing away. One day, in the future, when you'd done Columbia and law school or whatever the fuck else and you could sit in some apartment in Manhattan paid for with your own money surrounded by new friends who never knew the real you. But I guess none of that was enough. It wasn't enough for you to humiliate me and lie to me and throw away all the years we had together. You couldn't stand to see me with somebody else, *especially* not someone like Teddy. You're so jealous of her it's pathetic, honestly, because she's everything you say that you hate but really wish that you were. A legacy, a rich girl, the kind of girl who doesn't even have to work to get what she really wants, right? And you couldn't stand to see me doing well in the Cup, so you went after the only thing you knew you could take from me. You didn't want me but you didn't want anyone else to have me. So you had to have Teddy, too. Forced your way into her world like you forced your way into mine, to be some kind of leech, stealing what will never, *ever* truly belong to you. God, it's so cliché but that's what it is, right? Couldn't let me move on or build something without you. You had to come in and destroy that, too."

Teddy's reeling a little, the force of Nora's tirade knocking her off-balance, not only what she's saying but what Teddy can hear in it. The weight of her love for Max, so evident because look at her, look at how much she still cares, look at all of it spilling out of her. Nora loved—loves—Max in a way Teddy can't even comprehend, and there's a part of her in mourning already, because maybe she could have had some of that same love one day, if she'd known what was good for her. If she'd been a different, better person. But then again, Teddy has always known who and what she is. All of this comes down to her, really.

And then Nora turns to her, and it's Teddy's turn now. "I guess you destroyed it, too," Nora says, and now she sounds flat, exhausted, like she just can't bear any of this anymore. None of the fire that Max inspired in her, and Teddy knows why. "I wish you just would have been honest. No—I wish you never even came to Gardner. But you did, and I let myself get wrapped up in your shit, and here we are. I wish you would have been honest with me but that's never been you, has it? I should have listened to all those rumors you said weren't true. I should have listened to *myself* when I thought you were lying, but I didn't want to believe that you would do that. Maybe you two are better for each other than I could ever have been for either of you. You're both so good at making your version of events the only real one, and everyone who thinks differently is just crazy. Great. So now it's all over and none of it matters. Nothing matters."

Nora turns and marches off and Teddy wants to call out again, say *Nora, please, I never meant for this to happen* but it's like she said. It's all over. Nothing matters.

She watches Nora walk away, watches Max leave, too, but Teddy stays right there in the rain until she's numb, the only feeling the black hole pulsing inside her.

43

MAX

DR. THOMPSON ANNOUNCES the Cup's cancellation in a hastily called assembly Monday morning. Max keeps her eyes forward as she feels people look at her, as she hears the whispers racing around her.

"Nora threw a *knife* at her—"

"—being punished for something we didn't even do—"

"—won't be a winner? So there just won't be anything this year? That doesn't—"

"I heard Nora's suspended—"

"—should be Max who's suspended—"

"No, it should be Teddy, she caused all this—"

"—see why the rest of us have to lose out just because those bitches had to involve us in their drama—"

"—did you say she threw a knife? No fucking way—"

"Yes fucking way, I was there."

There's no use fighting the rumor mill, Max knows. Some of what they say is true, some isn't, but it doesn't make that much difference in the end. The truth is that she fucked up and Nora found out and now the Cup is done. Game over.

Brooke leans over. "I know Nora's been a raging bitch this year, but I still don't think it's fair that she's suspended and Teddy isn't."

Max leans away. Whatever perfume Brooke's wearing is so sweetly cloying it makes Max gag. "She threw a knife at me," she says flatly. "I really don't give a fuck what happens to her."

At least, that's what she's been telling herself. That she doesn't care what happens to Nora, whether she's suspended or expelled, whether she'll come back after winter break, whether Nora hates her or not. She doesn't care, why should she care? Nora thinks she knows her but she doesn't. All that bullshit about Max being in love with her and hiding it because what, it gave her some kind of power? *How fucking self-absorbed do you have to be?* she keeps telling herself, like if she says it enough times it'll make it right, like if she believes it hard enough it'll make everything Nora said not true. Not true, not true, she doesn't love Nora, she never did, she doesn't miss her, she doesn't wish she could go back in time and undo everything that happened since last summer.

A hand goes to her necklace and she slides the charm along the chain, feeling the weight of it. Thirteen hundred dollars. She's right; if Nora had told her how much it really cost, Max would never have taken it. But she can't suddenly stop wearing it now. It's a piece of her, clinging around her neck the entire time she and Nora have been apart. Nora would probably say it's another sign of how much Max loves her.

Max stops short of thinking it: *Maybe she's right.*

The whispers don't stop. They follow Max through the halls, into class, back into the halls, in the dining hall, in the bathrooms. She's grateful, in a way, for the quiet of enforced Study Session, sitting at a table on the third floor far away from anyone else, only Teddy and whichever teacher has been assigned to supervise them that day for company. It's basically the only company she has at all—only Brooke is still talking to her. Saf is so mad about the Cup she won't even look in Max's direction, and when Isobel heard the truth of the whole situation from Max's own mouth she looked disgusted and said, "Jesus, Max, what the fuck? She's your best friend, remember?" She hasn't even spoken to her mom yet: Dr. Thompson looks embarrassed, or maybe it's just pitying, when she calls Max back in to the office on Monday afternoon to say she's been trying to reach Mrs. Maxwell but having some . . . trouble getting through. *Surprise, surprise,* Max thinks, too tired to even pretend to be hurt. "She's very busy" is all she can think to say to the headmistress. "With the twins, and . . . everything." She doesn't tell Dr. Thompson that even if she could reach her mom, it wouldn't really matter.

By Wednesday she's bored sick. She's sitting at that table in the back of the library and all her work is done—every assignment up-to-date, all her Lit reading finished, even the extra work her teachers were instructed to give her completed. She stares out the window, watching raindrops skitter down the glass. Too much time to think always leads to her replaying

Nora's angry words, reliving the expression on her face the second before the knife flew from her hand, the sound of her sobbing after the melee was finally broken up.

Max stands abruptly, earning a look from Mr. Reeves, the music teacher assigned to guard duty tonight. "I just need to get a book," she says. "From the first floor. Is that okay?"

Mr. Reeves nods and goes back to staring at his laptop. Max ignores the look she can feel Teddy giving her and heads downstairs, to the shelves that hold the small selection of books written by or about former Gardner girls. If she can't compete in the Cup, then at least she can still read about it.

It's a fragile satisfaction, but since she's not allowed to do any kind of Activity either, it's as close as she can get to feeling alive. She carries the stack back upstairs and settles in, still an hour left until they're released to go to dinner (after which they'll come right back, like the good little girls they aren't). Max has read all the books before but it doesn't matter. She flips through the biography of Maeve Tierney herself, reading about her life before Gardner, how she grew up dirt poor in a family of eight, raised by a single mother after her father died in an accident at the factory. She opens the official history of Gardner and pages through it, knowing every fact before she reads it. She checks the time—still fifteen minutes to go—and opens her favorite of them all, the unofficial Gardner history written by students just like her. There's a chapter in there on every Cup-adjacent scandal and Max finds herself idly stroking the pages, wondering where their year would fit in another book like this. Will they go down in infamy like the girl who shot the deer, or the girl who—allegedly—poisoned her rival's tea in order to win? Will someone write about the '25 Cup the same way they wrote about the '55 Cup, which had to be canceled due to reasons no one can exactly explain? *Better that than me becoming another casualty,* Max thinks. Imagine if Nora had really been trying to hit her, if that knife had landed in the right space between Max's ribs—she could have died, and then she'd be in the histories just like those early casualties of the Cup, back before they realized some of the challenges were way too deadly—

Max stills. Huh. *Old challenges.*

She flips through the unofficial history until she finds the section she wants. "Retired: The Challenges Too Scary for Headmistress," the title reads, accompanied by a comic strip of caricatures, several previous Gardner leaders dressed in clown costumes. Max smiles and runs her finger down the page, to a table listing each challenge and exactly why it was removed from the Cup.

And the idea comes to her fully formed, ready to go. It's a lightning bolt to her heart, and Max sits up straight, a new electricity sparking from her.

What has she always wanted more than anything else? To make a mark here, to prove that she means something, that she's worth something. That she matters. With the Cup canceled, and everybody in school blaming her for playing a role in that, she thought she had lost that chance forever. But now, with this idea—

If she can pull it off, no one will ever forget her name. Everyone will know exactly why Wren Maxwell mattered.

She glances down the long table, to where Teddy sits, her

eyes glazed over with boredom as she pretends to read. Okay, but in order to pull it off, she'll need to make a deal with this devil.

She scribbles on a page in her notebook, then carefully and slowly rips it out, not wanting the noise to attract Mr. Reeves's attention. She balls it up and waits one, two, three before tossing it, watching it sail through the air and bounce right off Teddy's knee. Teddy comes to, frowning down at the ball, and then looks over at Max.

Read it, Max mouths silently, and for a second she thinks Teddy's going to ignore her. But then she leans down slowly and scoops it up, unfolding it quietly, pressing it flat against her book. She reads and Max can tell the instant she understands, the way Teddy's eyes light up and she looks back over at Max. *Are you for real?* she mouths, and Max nods, then lifts her shoulders to her ears like *So? Are you in?*

For a moment Teddy doesn't move, only stares at the note again. Then she looks back over at Max and nods, once, final. *I'm in.*

Max grits her teeth. *Here we go, then.*

44

NORA

NORA PULLS HER suitcase out of the closet and then stares at the clothes hanging from the rail. Her flight home isn't until Friday but she might as well start packing, she figures. There's nothing else to do, nowhere to go—she's not even allowed in the common room. During the day she sits at a desk set up directly across from Ms. Archibald's desk, right outside Dr. Thompson's office. She is escorted anywhere else she might need to go—to the bathroom, back to her room to pick up a book she needs, down to the dining hall when it's time for lunch and dinner. She talks to nobody and nobody is allowed to talk to her. Although maybe that rule is working in her favor, because she's not sure who of her classmates would actually deign to speak to her, and she can gather the general gist of what people want to say from the snatches she hears as she's chaperoned through the halls.

"Are you sorry, at least?" That was what her mom had said on the phone, once they had spoken with Dr. Thompson and heard all about the chaos their supposedly perfect daughter had orchestrated. After her dad had yelled at her, and after her mom had told her half a dozen times how terribly disappointed they were. *Am I sorry?* Nora thought. *Sometimes yes. Sometimes no.* She's sorry that the Cup can't continue and that everyone else's hard work has been for nothing. She's sorry she's made such a mess of things that she's alone now, with no real friends to speak of and certainly no girlfriend. She's sorry that all the teachers she respected no longer respect her, years of loyalty to this school tarnished in one act. But she's not sorry that she threw that knife. Of course she hadn't really meant to, hadn't planned it, and of course if it had actually hit Max then she'd be saying something different, but it didn't. It hit the wall, and no one got hurt, and Max got the message. *Like that matters,* she thinks bitterly now, yanking a shirt off a hanger. So she slapped Max a couple of times. So she scared her with the knife. Max still wins, doesn't she? She and Teddy—they made Nora look like a fucking idiot, and maybe the worst part is that Nora can't even fully blame them. She knew something was wrong weeks ago. She knew Teddy was lying about something, but she still let Teddy convince her she was worried about nothing. Max's cardigan—Nora can't stop picturing it, imagining the two of them rolling around in the costume closet and Teddy slipping into Max's clothes instead of her own afterward. Maybe that's how it happened, or maybe it really was an accident, swiped from the floor of that room they shared all week, but it doesn't matter. She let Teddy convince her nothing was wrong and that she was imagining things, the same way she let Max convince her last year. And maybe she got it all out in the open—what they did, what she knew, all the shit she held back from telling Max before because she was too much of a coward to say it—but what has any of it gotten her? Here she is, packing to leave school, and unsure if she'll actually come back after winter break, while Max gets to stay and reap the sympathy of being Nora's victim. While Teddy gets to stay and continue her act of being a Gardner girl, when it was *her* actions that turned Nora into a monster. Not just hooking up with Max, with her—all of it. If there's one thing Nora is the most sorry about, it's that she ever believed a thing Teddy said.

"Stop," she says aloud, shaking her head. God, she has to stop running over and over and *over* the same shit, as if anything will change. She opens her laptop—officially cut off from the Wi-Fi, lest she have any enjoyment at all—and presses play on whatever ancient music she actually has downloaded, turning it up as loud as the tinny speakers will allow. Then she busies herself packing, folding clothes into her suitcase, emptying out the drawers holding her sweaters and underwear. Going home might be good.

Nora's sitting on the floor, trying to squeeze a packing cube shut, when the note slips under her door.

She pauses, head at an angle, music still playing loud. It's a plain piece of paper, something scrawled on it in thick black marker.

She reaches over and picks it up by the corner, handling it delicately as if it might explode, and scans the message:

THINK THE CUP IS OVER? THINK AGAIN. ONE FINAL CHALLENGE, ONE WINNER. COME TO THE LAUNDRY ROOM AT ONE A.M. FOR MORE.

"What the fuck is this?" Nora mutters, frowning at the note. She doesn't recognize the writing but that feels purposeful, the block capitals disguising the sender. Someone with a plan to, what, claw the Cup back from the void?

She tosses the note aside and resumes wrestling with her packing. Whoever it is, whatever plan this is, Nora wants no part of it. Hasn't everyone realized yet? There's no point in trying to change things. Shit happens the way it happens, and thinking you can make any of it different is what leads to trouble. Besides, Nora's leaving in just two days. It's all over for her.

Sometime around midnight Nora gives up pretending she might sleep.

She gets out of bed and grabs her laptop, slipping back under the covers as she presses play on the only film she has on there, some ancient musical her mom likes where a young ballerina and a washed-up actor put on an insane show and fall in love. She pretends to watch it just like she pretended to be asleep, just like she pretends not to watch the time getting closer and closer to the one a.m. meeting time. Finally she sighs and gets back out of bed, finds a sweatshirt to pull over her pajamas, and scoops the note off the floor. *Laundry room.*

It's quiet in the hall, and Nora gently pulls her door shut before creeping along and down the stairs. The laundry room is in the basement, accessed by a second set of stairs at the

THE TOURNAMENT

other end of the hall, which means passing by Ms. Cara's office and room. Nora holds her breath as she tiptoes past, then rushes toward the stairs. Halfway down she hears whispers, and then the conspicuous hushing of those whispers. She rounds the corner without saying anything and there, huddled around the bench in the middle of the room where they fold their clothes, is everyone who hates her most in the world. Jordan Riggs, Abigail Brody, Manuela Vega. Saf, sitting on one of the dryers. Teddy, tucked into the corner, and of course, at the center of all of them—Max. "Wait," Jordan Riggs says, looking Nora up and down, "*she's* in this, too?"

Jordan's looking at Max, and it's apparent to Nora that she's the mastermind behind whatever this is. "Don't worry," Nora says, staring Jordan down. "I don't know what I was thinking. I guess I lost my mind again. You all have fun with . . ." She waves her hands. "Whatever this is."

She turns to go back up the stairs, but Saf calls after her. "Nora, come on. You fucked it up for the rest of us. The least you could do is stick around and see what Max has to say, if there's a chance to get the Cup back on track."

Nora twists to look at Max. "So that's what this is? You think you can fix this?" She laughs, loud enough to earn a few glares.

"Keep your voice down," Saf says. "Jesus. Look, we get it, everyone gets it, you're mad at Max! We're mad at you! Fucking great! But maybe we can put that aside for a second because I've spent all my time at this school waiting for my turn to be in the Cup and I had a pretty good chance of winning, until you threw your little tantrum, and I don't think it's *fair* that the rest of us have to be punished for what you did. So, like I said, if there's a chance to get the Cup back on track—"

Max clears her throat. "I mean. I don't know if I would put it like *that*—"

Manuela folds her arms. "So this isn't about getting the Cup reinstated?" she says at the same time Nora says, "Oh, here we go."

"Listen," Max says as the rumblings of discontent begin to grow. "I have an idea, okay? Like I wrote in the notes—one final challenge to decide the winner. Maybe it won't be school sanctioned, maybe whoever wins won't get to claim it as an official victory, but we'll always know who it was. We can write our own history, just like those who came before us."

She holds up a book and Nora knows it instantly. She's read it just as many times as Max has. "You all know what this is, right?" Max says, and everyone—including Teddy, much to Nora's surprise—nods. "Okay. So you know playing *outside* the rules is as much as part of the Gardner philosophy as anything else. And you know what else is in this book? Old challenges that used to be part of the Cup. What I'm proposing is that we do one of these challenges. Just one, a final chance, and whoever comes out on top gets to claim the title from now until, like, the end of fucking time. Sure, it won't be official but we can make our own Cup. Don't you think it's what the founders would have wanted? Don't you think it's what Maeve would do?"

There's a silence as they take it in. Nora tries to keep her face blank, keeping her interest secret. It sounds absolutely ridiculous but at the same time, it sounds absolutely perfect.

THE TOURNAMENT

A renegade challenge for a Cup that officially ended in chaos. She hates that Max thought of this, and she hates even more that she instantly wants to do it. Of course she shouldn't, of course she should go back to her room and forget this clandestine meeting happened. She'll go back to her little desk outside Dr. Thompson's office tomorrow, and later she'll finish packing, and on Friday she'll leave and this whole mess will be behind her.

She scans the room, checking everyone else's faces to see what they're thinking. She tries not to look at Teddy but of course she does, surprising herself again by managing to keep still when Teddy looks right back at her. Except leaving won't put anything behind her, she knows. It feels far too much like running away. And if she's going to leave, she wants to do it on her own terms.

"Wait," Abigail says. "What's the challenge?"

Max lifts her chin, a defiant fire in her eyes. "A cliff dive."

There's silence for a moment, and then—

"A *cliff dive*?"

"That's suicide."

"Depends how high the cliff is."

"I never heard of a cliff diving challenge before."

"Yeah, because they took it out because it's too *dangerous*, duh."

"Or because they were too chickenshit." This, from Saf. "I mean, hold on—it could be cool."

Jordan raises her eyebrows. "What are we talking?" she says. "Like, where would this actually happen?"

Max lifts the book again. "According to this, they used to do it from the spot where the ceremony is. There's a clean drop there. It's far but—it's totally doable. They did it for ten whole years. That means at least seventy other Gardner girls did it and lived to tell the tale."

"So what happened?" Abigail asks. "Why did they take it out?"

"Some girl probably broke her neck smashing into the water," Manuela says. "Or hitting the wall on the way down."

"Wrong," Max says. "Okay, a girl did fall, but she survived. And it was only because she got vertigo standing up there on the edge. If she'd actually jumped, she would have been perfectly fine. It was the lack of control that hurt her the most."

"So you want us to throw ourselves off the cliff edge and pray that we don't get vertigo, otherwise we'll fall and crack our skulls open?" When Nora speaks, all eyes snap to her. She holds a hand out to examine her nails, as if she's so bored with Max's proposal. "Seems like a solid plan."

Max doesn't quite look at her when she responds. "I'm just trying to keep the Cup alive a little longer," she says. "Look, if no one wants to do it, then we won't do it. But think of how much work we already put into this thing. Think of all the years we each sat around dreaming, hoping, of our time to compete. Dr. Thompson and the rest, they've made their decision, and nothing we do is going to change their minds but they're not us. They're not *Gardner girls* the way we are. We can sit back and take the punishment and let ourselves become a joke, a shadow of the people we thought we were. Or we can be inspired by those who came before us and take a fucking risk. Create our own legacy."

Saf makes a clicking noise with her tongue. "Okay. I'm not

saying yes but—if we did it. How would we score it? Are we taking our existing scores into account? How do we decide who wins?"

"If we're counting our existing scores, that's not fair," Jordan says. "Max would pretty much win by default."

"Oh," Teddy says, and it's the first time she's actually spoken. She nods and when she speaks again her tone is icy, sharp. "I see how this is supposed to go—"

"Shut the fuck up," Max says, and she holds her hands out like a boxing ref calling for calm in the ring. "No. We start with a blank slate. All the old scores are gone. It's just this challenge and this challenge alone. We can judge it . . ." Her eyelids flutter as she thinks. "Okay. We'll get a group to judge. They can score us on . . . form. And how clean the dive is. And, uh—style. Put all their scores together and whoever has the highest gets to claim the crown."

Saf opens her mouth, but closes it without saying anything. Nora looks at everyone, trying to read their faces and judge who might be in and who's desperate for someone else to say no first.

A cliff dive. It *is* dangerous, probably absurd to even consider it. But then again, is it any more absurd than the Hunt? Is it any more absurd than the final challenge they were all going to take on, spending an entire day and night on the island just off the coast with nothing for survival but a knife and their own wits? And just think—even those who don't win will go down in history. They'll be remembered as the class who went rogue, who brought back an outlawed challenge to prove their worth.

Nora raps her knuckles on the cinderblock wall. "When?"

Max looks over. "What?"

"When would we do it?" she says. "I have to be out of here on Friday."

It's unsaid, her real message, but whether they like it or not, Nora and Max understand each other in a way that no one else does. Nora knows that Max hears what she's saying—she wants details, now, real information. She needs to know how it's going to go down, because she's in. She wants to do it.

"Friday morning, then," Max says. "At dawn. We'll go out in the dark, before anyone can see us. And by the time they figure it out, it'll already be done."

"What's that saying? Better to ask forgiveness than permission," Saf says. "They can punish us after, but they can't undo what we did."

Jordan steps forward. "So—are we doing this? Is that we're saying?"

One more challenge. One more chance to crush Max. *And Teddy,* Nora thinks now. Perhaps she can still come out on top of all this fucking mess. A perfect send-off as she leaves this place. "I'm in," Nora says.

It's dominoes, then. "I'm in, too," Saf says, and then Jordan's nodding, and everyone's saying yes and laughing the same delirious, excited laugh, except for—

Teddy. She kicks her feet into the dryer she's sitting on top of, cool and composed even as everyone turns to look at her.

Nora has to be the one to do it, she knows. "Well?" She stares at Teddy, and this is the first time she's spoken to her since Sunday, since she left her standing there with nothing to say for herself in the freezing rain. She's been trying her best not to play out imaginary confrontations in her head—*Are you even sorry? Did you ever love me? Did you ever even want me at all?*—and now, face-to-face, she realizes this is the only apology she might get. "Just say yes, Teddy. It's the least you could fucking do."

Teddy kicks the dryer again, a one-two thud of her feet again metal. "Fine," she says curtly. "Yes."

Nora looks from Teddy to Max. "There you go," she says. "I guess it's not quite over, yet."

Max nods, and Nora knows she heard it, what she really wanted to say: *I guess I'm not through with you yet.*

45

TEDDY

THERE'S A MOMENT when Teddy wakes up, before she remembers what happened last night, when she feels like it's just going to be another day of punishment. And then it comes back—middle of the night, laundry room. The new challenge. The way Nora had looked at her with such hate, like she was waiting for Teddy to let her down one last time.

But Teddy had said yes, yes to this insane cliff dive idea, and maybe part of it had been because of Nora and not wanting to disappoint her again, but if she's honest, a larger part of it was down to the black hole. That void inside her that won't let go, calling for more, more, *more*. If throwing herself off a cliff into the ocean won't be enough for it, then Teddy isn't sure what else there is to do, and so—*Fine*, she'd said. *Yes.*

As she gets dressed she wonders if the promise will hold in the light of day, or if the rest of them will think of it as a moment of midnight madness. She steps out into the hall, girls rushing to and from the bathroom or out to breakfast, and she knows. She can feel it: the electric air, the hum of illicit excitement.

It's happening.

All through the day she keeps her head down, playing good girl even though no one buys the act anymore. Around her notes are passed, questions asked and answered in silence. By the time lunch rolls around, it's clear the entirety of the senior class has gotten the message, and she hears snatches of further plans—how to ensure everyone makes it out of the dorm without being caught, who will be judging their dives, what the tide charts say. At the end of the day she goes to the library as usual, and finds a note already folded and placed on the seat she usually chooses. Teddy bends down, pretending to fix her tights, and opens the note. *Five a.m.,* it says. *Leave your room and go to the athletic center. Wait there for Saf. When she gets there, both of you go up to the archery range. We move in shifts. Once everyone is there, we'll go to the cliff together.*

She refolds the paper and slips it inside her shoe before straightening up. Ms. Bell is supervising today, and she's already giving Teddy a suspicious look. "Quite all right there, Teddy?"

Teddy smiles her most brilliant smile. "Great," she says, and then, "Actually, do you have a highlighter I could borrow? Mine are all dead."

Ms. Bell frowns and rummages through her bag. "Here you go," she says, producing a neon yellow marker.

"Thank you," Teddy says, already flipping through her

Spanish notes, like she's so eager to work. "I'll return it, I promise."

Ms. Bell sniffs but doesn't say anything, and Teddy doesn't risk glancing at Max. Everything she needed to know was in the note, anyway.

On the way back from dinner her phone rings. It's her mother, of course, and Teddy silences it as she walks back to the library, shivering a little in the wind. It's dark now but the day earlier was bright and clear, the temperature rising sharply, the kind of day where you have to stop and close your eyes as the sun beams down, taking in the little bit of warmth offered. It's the kind of thing she could tell her mother, if she were a different kind of daughter, if she could answer the phone and have a simple, civil conversation. But she knows if she answered, it would just be more of the same: *What did I ever do to you to make you act this way* and *You've really crossed a line this time* and *For god's sake, Theodora, you promised you'd do better.*

She returns to the library and resumes working, writing out the same phrases over and over again until they're etched in her brain, ready for next week's final. When Ms. Bell finally tells them they can leave, Teddy slides the borrowed highlighter over and smiles again. "Good night, Ms. Bell," she says, voice lilting. "See you tomorrow."

She walks out ahead of Max. Plausible deniability and all that.

The dorm is quieter now, the hum somewhere below the surface. Girls brush their teeth, argue over the TV in the common room, go in and out of each other's rooms like it's just another night. Teddy ignores them all, or they ignore her—what's the difference? She means to head right to her room, but in order to do that she has to pass by Nora's room and she can't help but slow. Stop. Press her palm against the door that she used to throw open, marching into Nora's room like it was her own, throwing herself onto Nora's bed and smelling the lingering traces of her on the sheets. She doesn't usually feel so bad for the people damaged in her wake. She's left other girls behind, left friends behind, enemies, too. Almost immediately they recede in her memory, but not this time. Even though it should be easy, because Nora's not in class with the rest of them, not wandering the halls freely like normal. She's hidden away somewhere and that should make it easier to not think about her but here Teddy is, lingering outside her fucking door like a stalker, and it's that thought that gets her moving again.

The idea of sleep feels impossible, but once she's ready for bed she gets in, lies down, closes her eyes like it'll come. She wonders what the dive itself will feel like—more falling, or flying? A moment of weightlessness in the air. Or maybe it'll move so fast she won't even get a chance to feel anything, except the crack of the water as she hits it.

That's the last thing she remembers thinking, and then suddenly her alarm is going off, a series of unbearably loud chimes disturbing the peace of the night. Teddy turns it off and sits up, wired. What time is it? Why is she awake? Oh yeah: five a.m., she remembers, thinking of the note. Time to go.

It's easy enough to slip out of the dorm, and she keeps to the shadows as she makes her way over to the athletic building. The note didn't say how long to wait, and Teddy wonders what she'll do if Saf doesn't show, wonders if any of them will back out before they even make it up to the cliff. But then Saf appears out of the shadows, too, and they nod at each other and set off without a word.

When they arrive at the meeting point, Teddy sees they were the last ones. All the competitors are there, and so is seemingly everyone else in their class, she realizes, noticing Freya waving at her from across the way. Teddy lifts her hand and waves back right as Max snaps her fingers.

"Eyes on me," Max says, and Teddy hates how smug she sounds, fully in control with everyone else moving to her whims. "Okay. We have our judges for today's challenge—Gigi, Josette, Margaret, Isobel, and Yuki. Names were literally drawn from a hat so if you have a problem with any of them, I really don't care. They will score us out of ten. For the sake of simplicity, they will each just score us out of ten based on how good they thought our dive was. I know, I know—" She holds her hands up as irritated chatter rumbles. "Yeah, we said we'd have different categories, but that was last night. Today we decided simple is best. There are five judges, so that means five different sets of eyes, five different opinions, five different scores. Everyone has the same chance here. We're throwing out the existing scores and starting clean. Whoever gets the most overall points today will be our Cup champion."

"Aren't we going to get in trouble for this?" It's Corey Cohen, her hand stuck high in the air. "How are the competitors going to get back to school without being seen?"

"How are *any* of us going to get back without being seen?"

Freya says, the mocking evident in her tone. "Get a clue, Corey. We're going to get in trouble. That's the entire fucking point."

Laughter carries on the wind and Corey's cheeks burn red. Teddy turns, something in her chest catching as she spots Nora's blond curls blowing. *Just think,* a little voice in her head says. *If you'd stayed away from her in the beginning, none of this would be happening. If you hadn't been so stupid as to think dating her would be enough to make the black hole happy, she wouldn't be about to dive off a cliff.*

Up in front Max is finishing up. "It's not that much farther from here," she says. "Once we get up there—well. Then the games will begin, I guess."

46

NORA

THEY REACH THE ceremony place as the sky begins to shift, darkness giving way to light.

Nora's breath catches as she takes it in: the water stretching out beyond the cliff to a flat, deep blue horizon, the grass beneath their feet giving way to crumbling stone at the actual cliff edge. From here the buildings that make up Gardner look so small, insignificant really. *No backing down now,* Nora thinks.

But as soon as she turns her back on the water, she can see that the others are not feeling the same as her. There's a hesitance in their steps, the way they've all slowed to an almost stop, like they're so fucking afraid. All the color has drained from Manuela's face; Jordan looks like she might vomit. Max, though—

"Okay," Max says, her voice loud and clear. "I guess judges, pick your spot, and the rest of us—get ready." She takes off her coat, revealing the wet suit underneath, and she keeps her chin up, like she wants them all to see how unafraid she is.

Nora yanks down the zipper on her own coat. "What?" she hears Max say, and there's no mistaking the irritation in her voice. Nora looks up and Max is standing there, arms folded, glaring at the others. "Hurry up," Max says. "We don't have all day."

And something passes between the others, the way they all shift slightly, a rolling of their shoulders, fingers twisting together, teeth biting at nails. The rest of their class stays back, like they know something has changed and they might have to take cover soon.

"Hurry the fuck up," Max snaps again.

And it's Saf who finally steps forward. "No," she says, shaking her head. "No, it's not happening, Max. No fucking way."

Max smiles a wicked little smile. "Oh, so you're forfeiting?" she says. "Fine. Easier for me." She raises her voice. "Does anyone *else* want to forfeit?"

"Stop it, Max." Saf steps closer. "No one's doing it. Including you. This is fucking insane, look at it. *Look* at the drop, Max, Jesus, it's *suicide*."

Nora folds her coat and lays it in the long grass, neat. She slips out of her sneakers, bare feet instantly bathed in morning dew.

"You agreed to it last night," Max says, and she points at the rest of them, accusatory. "You *all* agreed last night. And now you want to back down?"

"Last night was one thing," Abigail says, and Nora can hear how her voice shakes. "This is different. I'm out. I don't care, claim the win for yourself if you want, whatever. This is crazy."

"Come on, Max." This from Saf, again. "Let's just—we'll stop it right here. We'll go back to school. It's still a good story."

No, Nora thinks. They can't stop. It's not a good story, not if they quit now. Not if Max gets to walk away the winner, which she technically would be, because she was in first place when the Cup was suspended. There's only one way to beat her now. Nora cannot back down.

She stands there in bare feet, not even feeling the chill air, too overwhelmed by adrenaline. "Hey," she calls out. "If you're all too scared, that's fine. But I'm still in. So set up your little judging table or what the fuck ever and let's do this."

Saf's head drops and when she looks up again, her eyes are pleading with Nora. "Don't encourage her," she says. "Don't you do this, too. Look, whatever shit has gone down between you two this year is not important enough to risk your fucking lives."

"Isn't it?" Nora says, and cuts Saf off before she can begin protesting again. "I mean, why are we here? Why do we come to Gardner? Isn't it to learn how to survive? Aren't we supposed to be *different* from all the other girls out in the world? The way I see it, we're paying homage to our founders. This is what they would want from us. And I didn't enter the Cup to lose on a technicality. We agreed to this plan, and I'm not backing out."

Out of the corner of her eye, she sees Max nod, and Saf throws her hands up. "You," Saf says, spinning to pin her focus on Teddy. "Do something."

Hasn't she done enough? Nora thinks.

And it's like Teddy can read her mind, because she shakes her head hopelessly. "I don't know if you heard," she says, acid dripping, "but I don't really have a part to play in this anymore."

"Leave her out of this," Nora says. "I'm my own fucking person, you know. I make my own decisions. And I've *decided* to do the cliff dive."

Saf turns back to Max again. "Come the fuck on," she says. "Max, be serious. You can't possibly—"

Nora tunes it out. Saf arguing with Max, Max arguing with Jordan, the unsettled rising chatter of the rest of their class— she lets it all fall into the background. Out over the water the sky continues to lighten, the occasional weak ray of sunlight burning through cloud cover. Nora begins the walk over to the edge, grass becoming dirt, sharp little stones piercing the soft soles of her feet as she reaches the very limits of the earth and stands there. On the edge of the world, it feels like.

She peers over and immediately wishes she hadn't. The drop seems impossibly far, the black churning water below impossibly distant. On instinct she steps backward, even just that little distance enough room for relief to flood in. But no. She can't feel relief, she can't crave the idea of not doing this, of giving in. If she doesn't jump, then Max wins. Then Teddy wins. This is her last chance to prove herself, and maybe it's fucking stupid and maybe it's dangerous but if she backs down now, she'll be no better than the rest of them. If she backs down now, then everything that happened this year will be how she's remembered—the girl who was little more than a pawn, batted around like a toy by the two girls who get to walk away from this clean. Cleaner than her, at least, and if she doesn't do this then it's like she's saying she gives in, like she's letting them win and actually no, that's not right, that's not fair—that puts all the weight on them again, like it always has been. Like every action Nora takes is at the behest of one girl or another, like she's not capable of doing anything just because *she* wants it. And she does want this.

She steps toward the edge again. Lifts her arms over her head. It's a sheer drop, the cliff wall curving back in away from the water, a clean forty or so feet down into the ocean. The little island they swam around in the first challenge sits over to the left, in the cove that hides the beach. All she has to do is swim back once she surfaces, come up out onto the beach, and wait to be crowned.

Easy.

Nora looks straight ahead. The air is cold and she takes a deep breath, then exhales slowly, controlled.

One.

She eases her feet forward until her toes are hanging over the edge.

Two.

"Nora!"

She startles, her arms dropping, body suddenly loose. "What the fuck?" she says, and Teddy's right there, grabbing on to her.

"I think Saf has a point," Teddy says. She looks wired, a muscle in her cheek jumping. "I don't think you should do this."

Nora squirms, Teddy's fingers digging into her flesh. "Yeah, well, you lost the right to have an opinion when you stuck your fingers inside my best friend," she says.

Teddy flinches, and her big fucking doe eyes fill with hurt and Nora could cry right now but she won't because that's weakness and she is not weak, she's the strongest of them all, and she likes that she can hurt Teddy because Jesus fucking Christ isn't that the least of what she deserves? "Back off and let me do this," she says now, or yells, really, and she tries to wrench free of Teddy's grip.

"Nora, *please*," Teddy says, and for a second it's like she's holding on even harder but then Nora pulls free and Teddy's hands aren't on her anymore. Nothing to hold her back from the edge. Nothing to catch her as she realizes she's off-balance and she has one foot on the ground and one touching nothing but air and she gasps as she falls, throws her hands out and says, "Teddy—"

Then she goes.

Backward.

Weightless.

Falling.

47

MAX

MAX JABS A finger into Saf's chest. "If you want to leave, then leave! No one's fucking stopping you!"

"*You're* stopping me because I can't just *leave* you and Nora up here so you can do something so *stupid*—"

"It's not *stupid*, it's about legacy—"

"*Nora!*"

It's a scream, enough to shut Max up instantly, enough to make Saf's eyes widen. Max whips around in the direction of the noise and there's Teddy, standing right at the cliff edge, a statue. "What the fuck," Max says, and everyone else is silent now. She blinks. Wait. Wasn't Nora right there, too? Where's Nora?

Dread pours into her. "Where's Nora?" she asks, but of course Saf isn't the one she's talking to.

"Max," Saf says and she's scared, and it's unnerving. Max

has never heard Saf sound so scared before. "What's going on—"

Max takes off then, leaving the rest behind, covering the distance between them and where Teddy stands in panicked long strides. "Teddy," she says once she's there, and then again, louder, shaking her now. *"Teddy!* Where's Nora?" Even though she already knows, even though it's clear.

Teddy speaks slowly, as if she's in a dream. "She . . . she tripped, and . . . she went over the edge, she fell, I . . ."

Max drops to her hands and knees, stretching out over the edge as far as she can manage. Way, way down below she sees it: the ripple, white frothing lace spinning out from where something—someone—entered. "No," she breathes. "No, no—" No, this wasn't what she meant to happen, and looking at it now she can only see what Saf saw—the suicide of it all, the sheer arrogance of believing any of them could dive from there and really make it except—

She scrambles to her feet. Except that she has to, now, doesn't she? Because Nora's down there and she didn't go on purpose, it wasn't controlled or decisive, she just fell—*how the fuck did she fall, what the fuck was Teddy doing*—and Nora's a strong swimmer, sure, but this is a whole different fucking thing. Saf's words echo in her head: *Look at it, it's suicide.* But Nora can't die, she can't, she's not supposed to—they're supposed to graduate here together, and make fun of each other's senior portraits, and go off to college and meet new roommates who won't stand a chance because that sacred best friend spot is already taken—

Max can't catch her breath. No, all of that's wrong, isn't it?

Because Nora hates her now, and Max did something so horrible to her, and Nora can't die because then she'll hate Max forever and worse, she wouldn't know that every single thing she said about Max on that horrible day was true and of course Max loves her, of course of course of course—

She straightens, forcing herself to breathe more. Inches closer to the edge and stops, raising her arms above her head.

"What are you doing?" Teddy asks, and she sounds genuinely confused, like maybe she's in shock.

"Going after her," Max says, and then she yells: "Saf! *Saf!* Go get help, okay?"

And before she can even hear Saf's response, she pushes off the edge and dives.

48

NORA

NORA'S NOT SURE how long she's been in the water.

It's freezing, winter ocean tossing her. She's drifting in the grip of the current and she should fight back, she thinks, but she can't remember how to. Swim with the current, or away from it? *With,* she thinks—parallel to the shore, right? No; that's a riptide. Swim, then, anywhere.

Salt stings her eyes as she searches for light. Any sign of light means surface, light means air. *Air, air,* she thinks, and her lungs ache, her chest on fire.

She remembers feeling weightless. In the air, now down here. She remembers—falling. An argument. Teddy, *Teddy*—hands reaching out for her, Teddy's hands on her but too late, already gone, already over the edge—

No. *Look for the light, remember?*

She's looking but everything around her is darkness. When

she tries to move her arms only one does as she wants, the other hanging limp, floating. *It's no good,* she thinks as the cold seeps into her bones, her marrow. *I'm going to die,* she realizes.

And she gives herself over to the thought for a second, only a second. She's going to die down here and for what? A fake title in a pointless tournament that nobody in the outside world cares about? Because she had to prove to each of the girls who broke her heart that she's better than them? Nora laughs, the last gasp of air left in her lungs transforming into soft spheres, a cloud of bubbles erupting in front of her face. *I'm going to die.*

But then the bubbles dissipate and Nora sees something coming toward her. A shape moving in the dark and it can't be possible, she thinks, but it's in the shape of a person and they're swimming down to her and then Nora looks with the clearest eyes and there's Max. Max, come to rescue her, come to save her.

Nora begins to cry. "What are you doing down here?"

Max reaches out. Her fingers graze Nora's cheeks, drift over her lips. "What, I was just supposed to let you win?" she says, and then she shakes her head, her braids winding back and forth through the water. "I'm kidding. I came to bring you back. I couldn't let you die. I love you, remember?"

"You love me," Nora says, and it feels right but also like a lie, or a story she's telling the wrong way. She frowns, trying to remember like Max told her to, but then Max is shaking her.

"Don't fall asleep," she says sharply. "We have to swim to the surface."

"I can't," Nora says. "I think my arm is broken. Or dislocated, maybe. I think a lot of parts of me are broken."

"It's okay," Max says. "I got you."

She loops one arm around Nora, then, and with the other begins to stroke through the frigid water, legs kicking. And they begin to move upward, rising through the dark, and there's a speck of light. Like a tiny candle burning, or the flare of sunlight captured in a photograph, or the first star to appear in an ink night sky. "Max," Nora says. "Max! I see it!"

"I know," Max says, and she sounds tired but determined, and she keeps on swimming as the light expands, spreads to cover the whole surface above them. "Almost there—almost there—"

And the light is dazzling now and they break through, up out of the water into the clean air and Nora sucks in a huge, hungry breath, the relief of oxygen in her lungs after so long submerged.

The water slaps at her face as she twists to look at Max, to find those dark eyes gleaming with all the things she never said. But she's not there.

Nora blinks, and the Max she had imagined—hallucinated, conjured—vanishes, and it's just Nora all alone out there.

Stay alive. It's a hiss in her ear, and she knows it wasn't real but it's enough to catch her attention. To think *yes, yes, okay, I can stay alive. I can do that.*

It takes so much effort to make her body do what she wants again, and she grits her teeth as what's left inside her shoulder socket grinds together as she turns onto her back. But then it's done, it's over, and she's looking up at the sky and she can stay like this, Nora decides. Yes. Until somebody comes to rescue her. All she has to do is hold on, as waves break over her. As she slips under and surfaces again and again. As the sky shifts from light to dark. All she has to do is hold on.

49

TEDDY

THEY'RE NOT SUPPOSED to be down here, on the beach, but where else were they going to go? Who was going to listen, now, to Dr. Thompson ordering them back up the cliff, back to school? As if they could safely tuck themselves away and forget what they were in the midst of. What they had set in motion.

Teddy can't keep track of the time, doesn't know how long they've been down here, except that it was just getting light when they set out this morning—only this morning? God, it feels like weeks ago, months ago, that she met Saf at the athletic center and walked up to their doom.

She closes her eyes. Except it's not *her* doom, is it? It's Nora, out there in the water. It's Max, going in to save her.

After the alarm was raised, after whoever it was who ran back to school got there and screamed, half sobbing, that there had been an accident, they had descended. Saf and Jordan Riggs and all the others, moving as one, Teddy swept up with them in a way that was good because left to her own devices, she isn't sure she'd have been able to move. But they carried her with them, down the steep path to the bottom of the cove where they watched the coast guard appear on the horizon and commence the search.

Teddy is aware of things happening around her, to her. The arrival of Dr. Thompson, Dr. Kessel, Ms. Bell; a foil blanket draped over her shoulders; paramedics arriving, checking over every girl on the beach even though they protest, say they're not the ones in trouble—they're not the ones in the water, after all.

One of them says Teddy's name until she snaps to attention. "Follow my light," the person in uniform says, and it takes so much effort but Teddy manages eventually, her pupils tracking the light up and down, left to right. She lets the blanket be peeled back for a moment, cold caressing her limbs even through the wet suit, before the paramedic nods, satisfied that she has no bumps or bruises, that she's good to go.

In the beginning there is so much noise, some girls crying, the teachers huddled together making calls that should probably be done in private but again—the girls refuse to go, refuse to retreat. They have to watch, it feels like, they have to *keep* watch, their eyes on the ocean keeping Nora and Max in their sights, maybe. Like as long as they are looking, there's every chance they will be found.

And then it gets quieter, exhaustion setting in, and how long will it take, Teddy wonders, before they call off the boats?

How long will they drag this out, this charade—because that's what it is, isn't it? Even if she wanted to believe the opposite, it's impossible that either of them could have survived that drop, that distance. That was why she had gone over to Nora in the first place, wasn't it? To stop her. To coax her back from the edge, back from certain doom.

Wasn't it?

There's a shout, and Teddy snaps back into the moment again, confused by the darkening sky. Hours have passed, she realizes. Hours have passed with Nora out there somewhere and there's no way she's still alive, Teddy knows, except—the paramedic shouted, and one of the boats has turned toward the shore. One of the boats is making its way in and the whispers rip through those waiting. "A body—they found a body—"

Teddy digs her toes into the sand. She's numb, and when she looks around she sees Brooke on one side of Isobel and Saf on the other, the three of them leaning into each other as they sit on the sand. Beyond them Abigail Brody wraps her coat around Jordan Riggs; Freya and Josette cling to each other, staring out at the incoming boat. Keeping each other warm, keeping each other hopeful, maybe.

For what? Teddy thinks. *She's dead. We all know it. They're both dead.*

Except the boat is closer now, and then they're out of the boat and on the beach, and there's a moment when all sound drops out—like something sucked all the air and life away and there's just this pressure so heavy Teddy expects her eardrums to burst—and then it explodes. The rush of not whispers but shouts, this time, ripping up and down the beach, and girls on their feet suddenly, the teachers throwing their hands up like they've given over control of this entirely—

"*She's alive, she's alive!*"

Teddy, frozen on the ground still, her mouth moving but unable to say the words in her head: Who? *Who* is alive? Nora, or Max?

She looks up, casts around for someone, anyone, to tell her what she wants to know, the answer to the question she can't bring herself to voice, but then it reaches her—

"*Nora—it's Nora—*"

Everything moves so fast then. Later on Teddy will only remember pieces of it: Dr. Thompson ordering the girls back and them listening, finally, and the paramedics hunched over the rag doll form on the sand, and a sudden rush of wind that made Teddy look up, unsure if she was hallucinating or if there really was a helicopter there.

But it was—is—real, and one second Nora is there on the sand and then she's gone, whisked away so fast and far and Teddy can feel Nora slipping out of her grip once again.

Alive, is all she can think, repeating over and over in her head. *Alive. Nora is . . . alive?*

"Teddy?"

It's the hand on her shoulder that brings her back to her body, and it's sudden, a shock like falling and she opens her eyes to find herself still on the beach. Still sitting there, whole body like ice, and when she looks over it's Dr. Kessel whose hand is on her, gently shaking her, like she has been trying to wake Teddy up for hours. "Oh," Teddy says. "Hi."

Dr. Kessel smiles at her, gently. The way you'd smile at a cornered animal, trying to let it know you don't want to cause any harm. "It's okay," she says. "Come on. Can you stand up? Can you come with me?"

Teddy nods but doesn't move. It's only now that she realizes the beach is empty. Only she and Dr. Kessel on the sand where a second ago—what felt like a second ago—girls were swarming. The paramedics, the coast guard—

She snaps her head around, staring at Dr. Kessel now with wide eyes. "Is Nora—"

"Alive," Dr. Kessel says, and her eyes are red-rimmed. "They've taken her to the hospital, and they're—they're working on her. She is alive, but I don't know. . . ." She takes a deep breath and seems to gather herself, as if she's remembered that she's a teacher and Teddy is her student. "She's in critical condition. That's all we really know."

Teddy nods again. She has to ask the other question, doesn't she?

Her voice is tiny when she does. "What about Max?"

For a moment Dr. Kessel says nothing. Her lips part, her gaze fixed on the ocean. And she takes a deep breath again before she says, "The coast guard didn't find her yet. They had to suspend the search. They'll start again in the morning."

Teddy watches the waves, turned shiny and black under the evening light. *Start again?* she thinks. *Why? Max is gone.*

"I wish I knew what the hell they were thinking," Dr. Kessel says, so quietly Teddy's not sure if she was supposed to hear it or not.

But she did, and she can't stop herself from letting words slip out: "It's my fault."

The second it's out she regrets it, but Dr. Kessel is already shaking her head, moving so her arm wraps around Teddy's shoulders. "It was an accident, Teddy," Dr. Kessel says. "We know what happened. We heard from the other girls. You can't blame yourself. You were the one who tried to *stop* Nora from jumping. Right?"

Teddy feels her throat constricting. She coughs, like that will help, and tries again. "I . . . it was a bad idea," she says, her words syrupy. "We all knew once we got up there it was a bad idea. But Max wouldn't back down, and so Nora wouldn't, either, and I wanted to . . . I tried to . . ." She pauses, half expecting Dr. Kessel to jump in and finish speaking for her. But the teacher doesn't, is just watching and waiting, like what Teddy has to say is suddenly going to make it all make sense. "I tried to get her back but she pulled away from me and I think it sent her off-balance and then—she just fell. Right over the edge, into the water."

"And Max?" Dr. Kessel breathes.

"She went . . . after her," Teddy says. "To save her, I guess."

"Jesus," Dr. Kessel says. "Why in god's name would they—" And then again, like she remembers who she is suddenly, what her role is, she stops and breaks away from Teddy. "Hold on one second," she says. "We need to get you back up to school, but I don't think you can walk."

She stands and moves a few paces away, the absence of her letting the cold rush back over Teddy. Dr. Kessel puts her phone to her ear. "Frank? It's Dr. Kessel. I need you to bring a cart down to the cove. Yes, now. I have a student who needs . . ."

She keeps on talking, but Teddy can't hear it for the ringing in her ears, suddenly so loud. She stares at her hands in her lap, palms facing up. An accident. A terrible, horrible accident, no one to blame.

Except—

That moment. Holding on to Nora on the edge of the cliff, trying to convince her to come back, not to do it. That moment when she thought it didn't matter how much Nora hated her or the bad things she'd done, she had to try to talk her out of it, or force her away from the edge, if that's what it took. But then—the black hole. Calling to her, like *imagine the chaos, if she fell. Imagine the thrill, if you pushed her.*

Teddy traces the lines across her palms, the swirls on her fingertips. But she hadn't, had she. Had she? *Did I?* she wonders. *Did I push her? I don't think I did. But I wanted to. That's what the black hole inside me wanted.* Push her now, it said. *Imagine the thrill of that—pushing someone to almost certain death. Imagine.* And Teddy's hands had itched but she hadn't done it, had she? They had argued, and sure Teddy had grabbed Nora, but then Nora pulled away and that was what sent her off-balance, just like she'd said. That was what had done it. Nothing to do with the extra burst of energy Teddy had used in that split second, a moment to shift her restraint to a shove. But no, no, she hadn't done that. She had just thought about it. She had just wondered. Right? It wasn't her fault that Nora fell. She'd wanted to go over the edge, anyway. She was going to dive in, willingly make the jump and fall all that way down. Wasn't she? That made it okay, didn't it. If Teddy had pushed her. *But I didn't,* she thinks now. *I didn't.*

Did I?

PART FIVE

"*In lieu of flowers, the family requests donations be made to the Gardner-Bahnsen School for Girls Scholarship Fund.*"

—Obituary of Maeve Tierney, 2001

50

TEDDY

THE AFTERMATH IS both slow and fast, hard and easy.

Immediately after, exams are canceled, classes called off. Counselors are brought in for any girl to talk to, if she wishes, when she wishes, except many of the girls take the option Dr. Thompson offered and leave for winter break early. The dorms half empty, those staying behind rattling around the corridors, the cafeteria.

At first they wait with bated breath for news on Nora's condition, and at first they are rewarded: she survived the fall, survived the injuries sustained, survived those hours drifting out in the freezing ocean. But *survived* does not necessarily equal *okay*. She has several long and involved surgeries to repair the broken parts of her, and for a moment it seems like she might in fact be *okay*, but over one night something happens—a bleed, a swelling, a terrible something the details of which the girls can't keep straight—and she is rushed back into surgery, her skull cracked open. And afterward she is placed in a medically induced coma, and the doctors say they will try to bring her out of it at the right time, but whether she will actually wake up—

No one knows.

Dr. Thompson delivers this news to the final year girls a week after the terrible events of the cliff dive, those of them left seated in a ring around her in the common room. Teddy keeps her hands over her mouth, as if there's some great anguished sound she wants to make but can't let out. Nora, in a *coma*? Nora, alive but not awake?

She feels a hand on her shoulder, like she had on the beach that day, except when Teddy glances up this time it's Saf right there instead of Dr. Kessel. And Teddy snaps back to several days prior, when police had descended on Gardner, before anyone had been allowed to leave campus. Teddy had been wondering what the police response would look like when it arrived—because they had to arrive, didn't they? At a school like this, filled with rich girls paid for by powerful parents, when an accident happened of this magnitude, there had to be an investigation.

But Teddy hadn't quite been able to contain her surprise, when it was her turn to be questioned. No—that wasn't the right word, because they barely questioned her, barely pressed her on anything, the two detectives sent up there. They were both white, both nondescript, a man and a woman in dark suits and white shirts, and only the woman spoke, and Teddy thought they must have discussed it on their way up and decided that a school full of girls would respond better to her. "It's okay," the woman—Detective Ambrose—said, crossing her legs. "We just want to hear what happened, from your perspective."

Teddy watched the detective's shoe tapping at the air—a sensible low-heeled pump, a flush of red visible where the leather must rub above her toes. "It was a bad idea," she says, starting exactly as she did on the beach with Dr. Kessel. "We all knew once we got up there it was a bad idea," she says, and right now it's the second time she's said it this way but she will go on to repeat this story in these exact words again and again in the coming months, her voice cracking at the right part every time, the whole thing becoming more and more solid with every word.

When she's finished the detective looks at her colleague, who looks at Dr. Thompson, standing in the corner, and then back at Teddy. For a moment Teddy thinks this is it—she didn't say the right thing, she didn't sell it enough, and then she thinks of *course* she didn't sell it enough, how could they believe her when she says she didn't push Nora if she can't even convince herself of that fact?

But then Detective Ambrose nods, her eyes on Teddy's, a small, somewhat resigned smile on her face, like she's reassuring Teddy. "Thank you," she says. "That's all."

And then Teddy gets up, hands smoothing her skirt automatically, and she glances at Dr. Thompson like she can't leave until she has *real* permission, and once Dr. Thompson nods, too, she moves toward the door and slips out.

For a second she thinks about relaxing, but then she notices the next girl waiting her turn: Saf, sitting painfully upright in a chair across from Dr. Thompson's office. She's wiping her nose with the sleeve of her sweater, her eyes bloodshot as they meet Teddy's. They stare at each other, wordless, until the door opens and Saf is called in and Teddy just stands there, wondering how much more of this they can all bear.

When she finally walks away, she passes right by the board that still bears their Cup scores, their names so clear and bold.

51

TEDDY

AND MAX?

"Max wouldn't back down," Teddy says, over and over, and that's the truth, isn't it? Everyone saw it, and everyone tells the same story, when it comes to Max: she was the one who came up with the cliff dive idea in the first place. She was the one who wouldn't give it up, when they all got up there and saw the insanity for what it was. She was arguing with Saf, while Teddy was trying to save Nora.

If Max had just backed down, then none of them would be in this situation. Then Nora wouldn't be in a coma.

Then Max wouldn't be lost to the sea.

They never found her body. The boats did go out again, to Teddy's disbelief, but they returned hours later with nothing to show for their efforts, and by that point everyone was focused on the one girl still alive, focused on Nora and the miracle of her survival. When the detectives came and interviewed everyone, that was when it started to crystallize, Teddy thinks. Everyone repeating what they'd seen and beginning to recast things in their minds. Because yes, it *had* been Max's idea, and she was the reason that the Cup had been suspended in the first place. Well, *part* of the reason, and sure Nora and Teddy had their own parts to play, but Max was the one who had hooked up with Nora's girlfriend.

Those are the whispers Teddy hears, at least, in the immediate after. And people start looking at her differently—Saf puts her hand on Teddy's shoulder when Dr. Thompson tells them about Nora. Isobel picks up the fork Teddy drops in line in the cafeteria and hands it back to her. Brooke lets her go ahead in the showers. Abigail Brody, rolling a suitcase along the hall, stops to say, "I hope you're doing okay, Teddy." When she's sitting alone in the half-empty cafeteria, Freya and Josette set their trays down and smile at her.

By the time winter break arrives for real, Teddy has figured it out. In the telling of the story, somehow things have gotten twisted around: she's not the girl who might have pushed Nora in, and Max isn't the one who was brave enough to dive in after and try to save Nora. No, now it is Teddy who's the hero—the one who tried to talk Nora off the ledge, who physically tried to pull her back—and Max is the villain, the one who set the whole terrible thing in motion, who only went in after Nora to try to save her own reputation.

And even if it doesn't quite make sense, even if it's way too black-and-white for a situation that was anything but, it's also easier this way. Teddy can sense the comfort everyone

THE TOURNAMENT

else feels, as they fit Max into this new role that she slips so neatly into. After all, she was never really *one of them*, was she? A *true* Gardner girl. They try to be open-minded, they try to not be the privileged, stuck-up bitches rich girls like them get labeled as but sometimes they have to be that way. If Max hadn't been so desperate in her attempts to fit in with them, then Nora would still be alive. All those little uncomfortable things that they let slide over the years—pretending not to notice Max's fake labels, or how her parents never showed up for anything, or how she acted like Nora's family's homes belonged equally to her—well, now they see them for the warning signs they were. "It's not that she was a scholarship student, I don't care, it's just, like . . . why did she have to act like she *wasn't* one, you know?" Teddy hears Gigi Westin-De la Cour whisper in the library. "You know she only hooked up with Teddy because she wanted everything Nora ever had," Margaret Sim says late one night in the common room, not noticing Teddy in the corner. "It's really creepy, when you think about it."

It's almost shocking to Teddy, how quickly everyone switches. They went to school with Max, day in and day out, for years. They grew up alongside her. They've known Teddy less than six months, and yet—it doesn't matter, in the end, she thinks. All that matters is what those left-behind girls can deal with, and all that matters is that Teddy belongs with them in all the ways Max never did, never could, no matter how hard she tried or what school she went to or what connections she made. Teddy was born into it, and she's still alive. *I'm still here*, she thinks, *and they'd rather hate a dead girl than risk believing the real villain is still walking among them.*

On the last official school day before winter break, when everyone who remained is now leaving, too, Teddy drags her cases along the hall. It's empty now, echoing, the thrum of beating hearts and loud laughs gone. She's the last one left, she thinks, and if you had told her that fact at the beginning of the school year, she would have rolled her eyes. *Yeah, yeah, as if I'm going to last that long here.*

She runs her tongue along the sharp edge of her teeth. *But I did,* she thinks. No explanation for it, but she did.

Teddy is almost gone before she stops and doubles back. She doesn't know what calls her to do it but she walks up to Max's room, where the door has stayed closed, no one daring to even go near it. But now Teddy tries the handle and it turns, and the door opens.

Her lips part, a soft noise of surprise escaping her. Evidently *someone* has dared to go near, because the room has been stripped almost bare. The sheets are off, a naked mattress lying on the frame. On the floor are three cardboard boxes, and when Teddy slips one of the flaps back, she sees Max's things piled inside. She folds the flap back over and sees a piece of paper taped to the other side.

Note to the caretaking team—these boxes contain the belongings of Wren Maxwell. Mr. and Mrs. Maxwell have not responded to requests to collect their daughter's possessions. Please move these boxes to storage.

Teddy smooths her fingers over the note before backing out of Max's room, grabbing her cases, and finally leaving.

PART SIX

"If you have to ask if you're a real Gardner girl, you've already answered the question."

—ANONYMOUS,
Gardner: An Unofficial History

52

TEDDY

TEDDY PRESSES HERSELF flat against the bricks, breathing heavy. She clamps a hand over her mouth, like that will help. She *has* to keep quiet. If the others find her, they'll—

It hits her in the ribs, a sudden cold shock from the right. She whips around, temper flaring. "Fuck you, asshole!"

Isobel laughs and spins around in a tight circle, the neon-pink water pistol held proudly above her head. "It's called payback, asshole."

Freya comes sprinting around the corner. "Teddy, watch—oh." She stops short as Isobel blasts her with a jet of water, too, adding to her already dripping wet polo. "Well, fuck you," she says, and Isobel's already laughing again even as Freya takes aim at her, because who shoots first, who wins or loses, doesn't matter anymore. It's just a game.

The sun is high in the clear blue sky, and Teddy tips her

head back to soak it in as they make their way back to the spot they've staked out on the lawn today, ready to refill their water pistols from the bottles they filled and lugged down earlier. Technically they should be in Activity right now, but this close to the end of the year, no one seems to care about all that. The lawn is dotted with girls who probably should be somewhere else—three faraway girls practicing their ballet routine for tomorrow's Arts showcase, Noelle Winters and Corey Cohen tanning with shirts rolled up and skirts pushed down, Gigi Westin-De la Cour and Jordan Riggs surrounded by textbooks under the shade of a tall tree. Studying for one of the last finals they have left, Teddy assumes, and even with as well-behaved as she has been over the last five months, she can't bring herself to follow their example. It doesn't really matter, anyway—the time for worrying about grades and recommendations and college applications is way over. Everybody got their acceptances months ago; half the girls in their class have been walking around in sweatshirts emblazoned with *Brown* and *UPenn* and *Oxford* since then.

When they reach their spot, Teddy pulls her shirt over her head and wrings it out over Saf, lying with her eyes closed on the blanket. "Stop!" Saf says, opening her eyes and throwing her hands up. "Oh my god, I told you I wasn't playing!"

"That doesn't count," Teddy says, and she pulls the shirt back on over her sports bra, smoothing her hands over the letters stamped across her chest: *UCLA*.

She meant it, about being good. At home over winter break, unable to stop thinking about Nora and in desperate need of something to do, she'd found herself writing. By hand, at first, because her mother had put intense restrictions on all electronics, on the advice of the trauma counselor they'd arranged for Teddy to see three times a week. And then, after saying the magic words—"It's for my college essay"—on her laptop, typing it all up and editing as she went, fixing a sentence here and there, carving out an appropriately introspective missive about peer pressure and self-determination. After a couple of rounds with a private admissions advisor—and sure, a few strings pulled, connections worked, favors called in—she'd sent off half a dozen applications, and gotten accepted to four schools. Theodora Swanson was headed to college.

She slumps down on the blanket and cracks open a soda. "Hey," a voice calls, and when they all look over it's Margaret Sim. "Movie in the common room tonight?"

"Sure," Teddy calls back.

"Under three hours this time," Saf yells. ""I mean it!'

Margaret just laughs as she walks away, waving to Gigi as she goes. Since last winter, things have changed—in the big, obvious ways, of course, but in smaller ways like this, too. Walls came down, factions dissolved; now they all call each other friends, and not in the fake, school-spirit way they used to. Now you can walk into the cafeteria and sit at whatever table you like. If you're reading in the library alone, anyone might pull up to work silently across from you. They all went through something, that morning on the cliffs, that day on the beach.

The school managed to keep media attention to a minimum, somehow. *Somehow,* Teddy thinks with a wry smile. Yeah, like having a couple of dozen powerful media professionals among the parents of the school didn't have a whole fucking lot to do with it. Teddy has filters set up so nothing mentioning *accident* or *tragedy* or *Nora McQueen* can get through to her, and her father has threatened lawsuits to enough people that most have backed off. There's rumors of other lawsuits, too—Nora's parents suing the school, for one—but no one knows how true these things are, or what the outcome will be. Teddy never met Nora's parents, but she imagines they are handling things exactly as her own parents would: quietly, mercilessly, in pursuit of a fat check. Of course that won't change things, will it? It won't bring Nora back.

Not that she's gone, exactly. In a coma. A *coma*, and every time Teddy thinks about it, every time somebody mentions it, she wants to burst into hysterical laughter because comas are for soap opera storylines, not people she knows. But that's where Nora is, still: in the hospital, plugged into a bunch of machines, hovering somewhere between here and gone. In the beginning it made more sense, in some way—she had just gone through something horrific, and there'd been all those surgeries she needed, and it seemed logical that her body and brain would need a time-out in order to recover. But when the doctors tried waking her up, she just . . . didn't. And so that's where she's been ever since, lying in a hospital bed while the doctors say they can't explain it, that she should be able to wake up and breathe on her own, live on her own. And yet she doesn't.

Freya's pouring water into her pistol, the tip of her tongue sticking out of her mouth with concentration. "I can't believe we haven't gotten in trouble for this yet," she says when she's done, aiming a few test shots at the grass.

THE TOURNAMENT

"After this year, I think they're just happy for us to be doing things that won't, you know, lead to actual death," Isobel says.

For a moment they're all quiet, as if Isobel breached some convention by saying that word. But then Saf says, "Yeah, our parents can't sue them for letting us shoot water at each other," and everyone cracks up at once, even though it wasn't that funny.

Teddy laughs along, too. See, she can be normal now. What black hole? Ever since that day she's managed to keep it mostly quiet, docile. And sometimes she thinks it might be finished with her—finally satiated, perhaps, by the chaos on the cliff. The good-girl promise she made to her mother at the beginning of the year has been mostly fulfilled: good grades, nice friends, a college acceptance from a reputable school. At every point along the way that Teddy thought the old her might rear her head, she just . . . didn't. Sometimes she wonders if it's all because of Nora. Whenever a paper felt too challenging, or a reading too boring, class simply too mind-numbing, she would think of Nora, trapped in that bed, trapped somewhere between alive and dead, and think *I'll do it for her, I'll do it for both of us.*

Of course she feels terrible for Nora. So vibrant, so beautiful, so full of everything. It's not fair that she should end up in the position she's in. But.

It's safest. In a way. Not just for Teddy, for both of them. Okay, maybe *mostly* for Teddy, but still—as long as she's unconscious, Nora doesn't have to know that Max is dead. She won't experience that pain, that agonizing loss that Teddy knows will surely devastate her. As long as she's unconscious, there isn't a hole in the world where Nora once was—she still is, she still will be, and that helps Teddy sleep at night, because the idea of a world without Nora is also agonizing. And of course, as long as Nora's unconscious, she can't interfere with the truth that everybody has accepted now. She can't counteract the story that everybody has told over and over. Even if she wanted to, even if Nora's truth did end up being different from Teddy's truth—it doesn't matter. So as long as Nora stays that way, Teddy gets to be the hero, and poor dead Max the villain forevermore.

Teddy brushes her fingers over the letters spread across her chest again. She has more to lose now than ever before. In the old days, getting in trouble and expelled simply meant another school, another chance. Now high school is almost over, and the real world is not as forgiving, she knows. The things that protected her in the boarding school world—money, legacy, power—well, of course they'll still play a role out there, but the stakes will be so much higher. Teddy feels like she might have a real future now, instead of the amorphous blank space she used to picture when people asked her about her plans. College in California, and new roommates, and professors to impress. Maybe grad school after—a master's in something obscure, or law school, perhaps. Dinners in hot restaurants and drinks with hot girls and a million new wardrobe opportunities.

She's got a lot riding on herself.

Isobel gets to her feet, brushing grass from her knees. "One more round?" she says.

"We need more players," Teddy says, shaking her head,

clearing out all the thoughts she doesn't want or need right now. Look, she's with her *friends*, they're having *fun*, isn't this what everyone always wanted her to do? Be *normal*?

She spins her pistol around her index finger, then holds it up and squints down the barrel, scanning the lawns. Noelle and Corey would be easy to convince, and they do have a couple of extra water guns in their bags. She lowers her pistol and raises her hand to wave, only to be distracted by a figure running in a zigzag right past the sunbathers.

Saf props herself up on her elbows. "Is that—"

Teddy shields her eyes as she tracks the figure running toward them now. "Josette," she says. "What the fuck is she in such a rush for?"

Josette's ponytail whips around her face as she comes sprinting over, and stops, hands on her knees and panting. "Oh my god," she says. "I was just—and I heard—"

Isobel pats Josette on the back. "Jesus, catch your breath," she says. "What are you even—"

"Shut up." Josette holds a hand up, takes one deep breath, and then straightens. "I was returning some books to Mr. Gordon's classroom," she says, and she takes a shallow breath every couple of words, like this is so important she just has to get it out. "And as I was leaving—Mr. Gordon was across the hall—in Ms. Wright's room—and they were talking about a meeting—with Dr. Thompson—and all the teachers—"

Teddy snaps her fingers, impatient, although after the fact she thinks that she already knew what was coming, what news Josette had run to deliver. "Get to the point."

Josette gulps in air, and then she says it: "Nora's awake."

53

NORA

"**NORA, NORA,** it's okay, you're okay, stop fighting—"

What hits her first is the brightness. As if the world is on fire but she can't smell smoke, only a sharpness that makes her think of vodka slipping down her throat and warm fingers sliding around her wrist. It's only after that thought that she realizes she is thrashing, limbs jerking beneath thin sheets and then there's a figure looming large over her, two figures, more, and everything is so loud it's as if they are screaming inside her skull.

And then finally there is a familiar face—*Mom,* she thinks, desperate and relieved, and she goes still, calming as her mother rests a hand on her forehead. "Hi, my love," her mom says, and there are tears in her eyes, dripping off her chin. "Oh, it's so good to see you."

◆◆◆

Five months. That's how long she's been in the hospital, Nora learns not long after she wakes up, once she is calm and the doctors are sure none of the various needles and tubes connecting her to the quietly beeping machines were disconnected. Five months spent unconscious, everyone waiting for her to wake up.

Five fucking months? Nora wants to say. *How the fuck is that even possible? Five months went by and I have no memory of them? Five months of me not being there, the world moving on without me?*

It's what she wants to say, but she can't—after they pull the tube out of her throat Nora finds she can't even speak, nothing but air breezing past her lips whenever she tries, and a dull, deep-rooted ache at the back of her throat. She can't even make a sound when she cries, which she does on and off for the first few days—at her mom's and dad's faces, their steady presence at her bedside, and the way her mom just keeps saying, "Oh sweetheart. There you are," whenever Nora wakes up from the short spells of sleep that keep on taking her. As if she hasn't rested enough, she keeps thinking, and she laughs without any noise, thinking for a second that she wishes Max were here, because she'd find it funny. But then she remembers that she and Max aren't friends anymore—obviously. That's why Max is nowhere to be found, isn't it?

She tries to ignore the part of her surprised by Max's absence. If things were different, Nora would be at Max's bedside, no matter the past distance between them. If their roles were reversed and Max was the one lying in a hospital bed, Nora would spend every second next to her—fuck the fights and fuck the past, right? This shit puts everything in perspective. She regrets every second she wasted fighting with Max, not talking to her, every second of silence. But obviously Max doesn't feel the same. *So I guess we really are through,* Nora thinks, and she curls into herself in the bed, holding on to her stomach, where a gnawing hole has opened up.

As for what put her in this bed? "You were in an accident," one of her doctors tells her on that first day that she's awake, and Nora can't press for details without a voice, so she just listens as the doctor continues. "A very serious accident that left you in a very dangerous medical position. When you were brought in, your heart had stopped beating. My colleagues and I resuscitated you, but we quickly saw there were many other injuries we needed to attend to. We first . . ."

She takes in the long and complicated list of injuries and surgeries and treatments she's received and does not really know what to do with it all. It feels as if it happened to a stranger, or maybe like Nora is nothing more than a life-size, fully posable doll, the kind with an ad that proclaims *Comes with scars and a shaved head!* Of course the side of her head they had to shave in order to cut through her skull isn't completely shorn now, a patch of her ashy-blond curls growing back in soft and gentle, but Nora can't stop her hand from wandering to it every few minutes. Like that's the worst of all of it, even though she knows her body itself looks like a battlefield.

"Any questions today?" the doctor asks when Nora has been awake for three days—she counts them, and even if she didn't or couldn't remember, someone marks it every day on the whiteboard on one wall of her room.

THE TOURNAMENT

Nora picks up a pencil and writes on the notepad a nurse gave her. It takes an agonizing and embarrassingly long time to make her hand move the way she needs it to, to carve out the correct letters, and when she holds it up there's only one word there: *Outside?*

The doctor smiles and tucks her impossibly shiny straight hair behind her ears, revealing tasteful diamond studs. "Soon," she promises, and then from some other room an alarm sounds and she rushes off, heels clicking on the cold floor.

Soon, Nora thinks, and she imagines sitting at a bench outside with Saf and Brooke and Isobel, how nice that would be, even if only for a few minutes. Even if they haven't come to visit her yet. She's sure there must be an explanation for that, because sure things had been weird between them before Nora's accident but not the way they had been between her and Max, and she *knows* Saf would be here if she could. Wouldn't she?

She frowns, wincing at how it pulls on her stitches. Feels like there's something she's forgetting. Or . . . someone, maybe.

She winces again, a hot, throbbing pain suddenly taking up residence in her skull. "What's wrong?" her mom asks, rocketing out of the chair against the wall. "Are you in pain? Is it your leg? Your shoulder? Your head?"

Nora lifts her hand when she says *head.*

"Should I call a nurse? Or the doctor? Do you need pain relief?"

Nora tries to shake her head but it only makes the pounding worse. She puts a finger to her lips instead, and closes her eyes.

"Quiet? You want quiet? Okay. Let me straighten this blanket out for you . . . get some rest and then . . ."

Of course Nora can tell that something is going on.

Of course she's tired, and sometimes she wakes up and it takes a minute to remember everything—the hospital room, the coma, the accident—but she's still herself. So she notices the whispered conversations that take place just outside her door, out of earshot. She notices the nervous look in her mother's eyes, the way her dad clears his throat just to break the silence. She notices how everyone is very careful when they mention *the accident*, the details of which Nora is unclear on and can't remember at all.

But on the fifth day she's awake, a different doctor comes into the room. She's tall, dark skinned, intimidatingly beautiful, but when she pulls up a chair and sits at her bedside she becomes gentle, her voice when she finally speaks soft and clear. "Hi, Nora," she says. "I'm Dr. Greenwood. Dr. Park and your parents asked that I come and speak with you."

She pauses when Nora picks up the pencil and the stupid little notepad. When she holds up what she's written, the doctor almost smiles. "Yes. I am a psychiatrist," she says, and then with no preamble, no warning: "I'm afraid I have to tell you some bad news. Your friend Wren Maxwell died five months ago."

If she could make a sound, Nora is sure the noise she would let out would reverberate through the entire hospital floor. Maybe she'd shatter some windows with the pitch of her keening wail.

As it is, she can do nothing but weep silently and so, as if to make up for the quiet, she begins throwing whatever's in reach. The pencil and the notepad landing quietly, the plastic cup leaving a spray of water as she knocks it, the vase pitched at the wall finally emitting a satisfying crash and then she jabs a finger in the direction of the door, her face screwed into a pained, ferocious silent snarl. She watches her parents scurry out, Dr. Greenwood behind them, and she watches the shocked faces beyond the glass panels that separate Nora from the rest of the world, and if Max were here she'd think—

But Max is dead.

Max is dead, Nora thinks, over and over and over. And not freshly gone, but five months. All that time Nora was unconscious, Max was gone, and the world moved on without her but Nora can't wrap her head around it. She can't be dead. She can't have *been* dead, it doesn't make any sense—

At least she had a good reason not to visit, she wants to say—or write, rather, for someone to read back and laugh at it with her, but the only person who would find it funny no longer exists and what the fuck is she supposed to do in a world that her best friend, the girl she loved the most, no longer exists?

She is numb after that. They poke and prod at her, take her for more scans, make her follow lights and nod or shake her head at simple questions and when that's all over she's left by herself, all alone. Even when her parents are at her side, she is alone.

She stops asking questions, even the ones she knows must

be answered. Like *How did she die?* and *Why is no one telling me how I got hurt?* and the worst one, *Was it me? Am I the reason Max is dead?*

She keeps them all in her head, flicking to them in the moments she isn't berating herself, feeling sick at how angry at Max she has been, how wrong she was for thinking Max wouldn't come to see her because of some stupid fucking fight. During the small hours of the night, when the lights aren't quite so bright and the doctors keep their voices lower, she imagines the shit Max would say to her now. *What, you think just because you told me you loved me, like, a year ago, that I wouldn't be here? I'd have to really hate you to abandon you like that.*

When Nora thinks these things, she knows it's not quite right, but she can't pinpoint what exactly it is that's wrong. But she can feel the edges of her thoughts, her memories, blurry and unfinished. Feels like she could pick at the corner for long enough that the rest of the image would be revealed, the haze covering it peeled away.

And then, two days after Dr. Greenwood tells her Max is dead, she returns.

This time when Nora sees her, she doesn't even try to fight. Has no energy, and no vase to smash this time. Her parents aren't here, and she sits in the chair on Nora's right and says, "I'd like to tell you what happened to you, Nora. But you don't have to hear it, if you're not ready. I think it would be good for you, though. Fill in some gaps I suspect you might have in your memory. Does that sound right? Would you like me to tell you?"

Nora closes her eyes for a second. Behind her lids there is cool darkness, a peaceful black that feels familiar.

Then she opens her eyes and nods, once.

Dr. Greenwood clears her throat. "On the morning of December twelfth last year, you fell from the cliff edge on the grounds of your school. You fell quite a distance and landed in the water below. According to witnesses, Wren Maxwell jumped in after you."

Max, she wants to say. *It's not Wren, it's Max.*

"Your classmates raised the alarm and the coast guard was called. They searched and retrieved you from the water, but could not locate Wren Maxwell. According to those same witnesses, a classmate of yours named Theodora Swanson tried to save you before you went over the cliff edge, but she did not succeed."

Nora flinches.

Theodora.

Teddy.

"This was all apparently part of a 'challenge' thought up by Ms. Maxwell. Is any of this sounding familiar? Nora?"

A sour taste fills her mouth like she's going to vomit but nothing comes up as Nora pushes her hands into her stomach and folds forward, pummeled by the rush of memories like the waves pummeled her that day. And she knows, really, that it was all there in her head this whole time but some part of her brain—bruised and battered as it is—has been holding it all back, keeping her safe, but that time is over now and it's all coming back, not in pieces but in one shocking flood of remembering:

The knife flying out of her blood-slick hand, and the truth of what Teddy and Max had done, and the white-hot hatred she had felt for both of them.

The note sliding under her door, and the meeting in the laundry room, and one final chance to be the best, make their mark on Gardner.

Walking up to the cliff through early-morning dew, and Saf and Max arguing, and Nora wanting nothing more than to prove to everyone, to Teddy, to Max, to her own fucking self, that she was worth something all by herself.

Her feet on the edge of the world, and Teddy—Teddy pulling at her trying to reason with her, and then—

Nora squeezes her eyes shut again, but there's no dark relief behind her eyelids this time, only the memories so vivid as if she's right back there—

And Teddy's hands are on her but the look on her face changes, a flash of something cold and gleeful, and then comes the push. Teddy's fingers digging into her shoulders and suddenly shoving her, a split-second force that sends Nora flying backward—

When Nora opens her eyes this time, hot tears drip down into her open, gasping mouth. That was it. That last look at Teddy, alone at the edge as Nora stared up at her, tumbling down, a scream ripping out of her. The last sound she'd made.

She's aware, then, of Dr. Greenwood on her feet, her hand hovering over the call button, and she shakes her head, throwing her own hand out to stop her. *No. I don't need anything. I don't need anyone. I know. I know.*

Dr. Greenwood steps back and then sinks into the chair

slowly, like she read her mind. "Do you remember it happening, Nora?"

She swallows the sourness in her mouth and eases back a little. Nods.

"Okay," Dr. Greenwood says. "I'm sorry for what happened. I know it must feel overwhelming right now. If you'd like me to stay and talk more, I can—"

Nora's vehement head shake cuts her off. *Please leave.*

The doctor stands and gestures somewhere beyond Nora's room. "Your parents are just out there. I'll send them in, if you want. Or perhaps I'll take them to get coffee," she says, preempting Nora's objection, and then she rubs a hand over her face. "A couple of detectives are going to come to see you tomorrow. I've kept them off as long as I can. You're not in any trouble. They just want to get your account of the accident. It's really nothing to worry about. Okay, Nora?"

She turns on her side and pulls the covers up over her shoulders, hoping the doctor gets the hint. It doesn't take more than a few seconds before she hears the doctor's footsteps retreating, and then she repeats her words in her head: *It's really nothing to worry about.*

Oh, but it is, Nora thinks. Because she knows what they're going to ask her, and she knows the answer they're expecting—Dr. Greenwood let it slip, didn't she? *According to those same witnesses, a classmate of yours named Theodora Swanson tried to save you before you went over the cliff edge.* They think Teddy's the hero, and that's what they're going to want to hear Nora say—that yes, everyone is right, Teddy tried to pull her back and it was all just a tragic accident, a stupid game that went way too far. But she can't say that. Not only because it isn't the truth, but because of everything. All the chaos Teddy caused—Jesus, Max is *dead*, because she went in after Nora, to try to save her, and Nora only went in because Teddy pushed her—but before that, too: the fight, the hookup, all the bullshit Teddy fed her and Nora ate right up because sure, maybe Teddy had done some bad things before she came to Gardner but she wasn't a bad *person*, right? And she'd been trying to be better, and she'd become one of them, hadn't she, a real Gardner girl, and most importantly, most embarrassingly—she had wanted Nora when all Nora needed was to be desired. Seen, heard. But all of that had been a lie, too, another game for her to play, Nora just something for Teddy to toy with. And all the other shit she'd done at other schools to other people—that pales in comparison to this. *Max is dead,* Nora thinks, and it still doesn't sound real but it is. *Max is dead, and I almost died, and I'm supposed to pretend she's the hero?*

No. When the cops come tomorrow, Nora already knows what she has to do.

Teddy has to pay.

54

TEDDY

NORA'S AWAKE.

It's all anyone can talk about at dinner, whispers flying across the room. Teddy can see it, almost—the way everyone looks electrified, this new and exciting rumor lighting them up. Nora McQueen is awake. What an exciting and delicious development, so close to the end of the year, coming in just under the wire!

The tray in Teddy hands shakes, the china rattling. She pretends it's fine, that her hands are completely steady, just like her nerves, as she makes her way over to a table and takes a seat between Josette and Isobel. Isobel's in the middle of speaking but Brooke interrupts her, staring at Teddy. "Oh my god," she says. "You have to hear this."

"Hear what?" Teddy cracks the top off a bottle of water and lifts it carefully to her lips. She wants to gulp it down greedily, but she won't. *Play it cool. Everything is normal, you are normal, remember?*

Isobel flips her hair as she turns, angling her body toward Teddy, and the others follow, leaning in and circling close. "Okay, so you know how Yara has been dating that townie all year? Well, his mom is on the board of the hospital where Nora is, and according to her Nora didn't just wake up today. It's been, like, a *week*."

There's a moment of stunned silence, and then everyone begins talking at once.

"A week? She's been awake for a whole *week* and no one told us?"

"What does that mean? Is something else going on? Why wouldn't they tell us?"

"Wait—is it the hospital holding back, or Gardner? Do you think Dr. Thompson found out right away, or did all the teachers just find out today, too?"

"So if she's been awake for a whole week, that means no one's visited her. That's *crazy*, imagine waking up from a five-month-long *coma* and then none of your friends even show up! They're making us look terrible."

"Oh my god, wait—do you think she knows about Max?"

"Do you think she knows *anything*? She might not remember what happened at all."

"But even if she doesn't remember, they can't not tell her that Max is . . . dead. Like. Come on. Right?"

"Is it fucked up if I hope she doesn't remember? I mean—if I were her, I think I wouldn't want to remember. It's bad enough having to remember it from *our* perspective, and we weren't in the water. *We* didn't almost die, and I still have nightmares, sometimes."

This last one comes from Saf, so quiet Teddy isn't sure anyone else hears. When she looks over, Saf is looking down, scraping a nail along the edge of the table, and for a second Teddy thinks about blurting out *No, it's not fucked up. I hope she doesn't remember, either.* Except that's way too dangerous.

It's true, sure: Teddy hopes that Nora doesn't remember what happened that day. But Saf wants that out of kindness. She doesn't want Nora to have to relive the trauma and pain of that day ever again. She doesn't want Nora to wake up screaming.

Teddy wants it for self-preservation.

She almost laughs. Wow. Imagine the old her, hearing the new version of her talk about *self-preservation*. The old Teddy didn't give a shit about that. But that's the thing: that was the *old* Teddy, and now she has too much to lose. As long as Nora was unconscious, things were good, right? That's what she kept telling herself these past months, at least. But now Nora is awake, finally, and Teddy should be happy about it, she should be relieved that her former girlfriend is *alive* and *breathing* and safe, except that she can't be. Because if Nora is awake, then that means she might speak. She might tell somebody her version of that day's events, and if they don't match up with the story everyone else has told? If Nora's version of the truth includes Teddy trying to kill her? Then everything is going to come crashing down around Teddy.

She lets out a long, slow breath, and she's glad the others are so busy throwing out question after question and gossip after gossip that they don't even notice her sitting there, silently thinking. If they knew what she was thinking about—what's in her head right now—

Because I did it. Under the table Teddy digs her nails into her thighs, a pleasant kind of pain. Fuck. There it is. *I did it. I pushed Nora.*

It's some kind of a relief to finally have it laid bare, even if only in her own mind. For months she has tiptoed around the thought, allowed the version of events proffered by her friends and classmates to become her truth, too. But now she can't pretend anymore. She has to get ahead of this, and she can't get ahead of it if she can't even admit to herself what she did.

Even if I didn't really mean *to do it,* Teddy thinks now. *I didn't plan it, I didn't* decide *to do it, it was just . . . she was right there, and the black hole put the thought in my mind, and my mind put it into my hands before I could even know what I was doing, and then—*

Then she was gone. Falling. And of course Teddy has known all along what she did, but it was okay. She could hide it. Forget about it. As long as Nora stayed put. She could tell herself she would never do something like that, that it was too far even for her, of course it was. And everyone was so eager to help her do that, weren't they? They made her into a hero, and Teddy hadn't asked for that, which only made it all the sweeter. A hero couldn't push a girl off a cliff. Teddy couldn't have pushed Nora—she tried to save her, because she'd loved her, hadn't she, or at least felt something big and deep for her, and yeah. It all made sense, when Teddy saw it from their perspective, watched herself through their eyes.

But now there are new moving pieces. Nora is awake—has *been* awake, apparently, an entire week passing during which she might have already ruined everything. She might have already told.

Or.

Maybe she hasn't said anything at all, Teddy thinks. Maybe it's like Saf said, and she can't remember anything. Wouldn't that be best? Not just for Teddy, but for Nora, too. She wouldn't have to relive the pain, and Teddy would get away with it. Win-win. Right?

"Teddy? Hello, Earth to Teddy?"

She snaps to attention, finding everyone watching her. "What?"

Brooke rolls her eyes, impatient. "I was saying we should figure out a time to go see her, if we're allowed. This weekend, maybe. Before school finishes and we all leave, at least. You think they'll let us visit?"

Teddy has to swallow before she can answer, her throat dry. "I don't see why not," she says. "We can call and find out, at least. Right?"

Freya nods. "What if we speak to her parents first? At least they might tell us what's really going on. Like, if she's still too sick for visitors and that's why no one's told us yet, they could tell us."

"I could call them," Saf says, twisting a piece of hair around her finger. "My parents sometimes go for dinner with them if they're in the same city."

"Sounds like a plan," Teddy says, and she smiles, big and reassuring, like they've got this, like things are going to be okay.

And then, while they continue talking through what they should do, Teddy puts the finishing touches on her own plan. Because she can't wait until the weekend, and she certainly can't risk having other people around to hear what might come out of Nora's mouth.

She sits back. Tomorrow afternoon is the Arts showcase. The entire school will be busy: crammed into the assembly hall in the audience, or preparing for their piece, or lending a hand backstage getting things ready and making sure the whole show runs smoothly. That's what Teddy is supposed to be doing, which means she should have enough cover to slip out. If anyone notices she's not where she's supposed to be, they'll just think she's off running an errand—picking up someone's forgotten sheet music, or finding a needle and thread to do a last-minute costume repair. And so no one will really notice if she leaves campus. She won't have long, but she won't need long, she figures. She just has to see Nora for herself and find out what she remembers. And maybe it'll be perfect—maybe she'll walk in and Nora will smile, just so happy to see her again and ready to forget everything that came before. Sure, Max is dead, and she almost died, but what does any of that old shit matter anymore, in the grand scheme of things? At least she's alive, and at least Teddy's there for her.

Maybe.

She might not remember any details of that day; maybe all she'll have is the night before, waking up to an alarm at an obnoxious hour, and then blackness.

Or maybe she'll see Teddy and panic, press a button to call

a nurse, start shouting *It's her, it's her, she tried to kill me, she's going to do it again!*

Teddy picks up her fork and stabs it into the congealed pasta on her plate. There's only one way she's going to find out. Tomorrow, she'll go to the hospital, find Nora, and finally know the truth.

55

TEDDY

TEDDY STEPS OUT of the cab and shields her eyes as she stares up at the glass-and-metal structure before her.

It was as easy as she had hoped to get away from Gardner without anyone noticing. As she had expected, everyone behind the scenes of the showcase was so busy worrying about their act or prepping last-minute sets or running through tech that it meant nothing to them when Teddy set down her clipboard and simply walked out. The grounds were quiet and no one was there to notice a lone student walking all the way down to the entrance, where a cab was idling, waiting to whisk her away.

She glances over her shoulder, making sure the cab is still there. She's promised the driver an extremely generous tip if he waits; she can't spend any longer here than she absolutely has to. She doesn't expect anyone to notice her absence at school, but she also doesn't want to take unnecessary risks, and every minute she's not there increases the odds of someone realizing.

Besides, this really doesn't have to take long. She'll know, she thinks, as soon as she sees Nora's face. What happens after that . . . well. She hasn't planned that yet. There's too much unknown right now.

Teddy takes a deep breath before striding into the building. It wasn't hard to find out what floor Nora's on, thanks to Yara Klein's townie boyfriend, and she has several different stories ready to go in case she's questioned, which she assumes she will be. Or at least, she kind of *hopes* she will be, because what kind of hospital would let anyone just walk in and right up to a patient's room?

Inside the elevator she holds her breath, waiting as it slides up and up, pausing occasionally to let people in and out, nurses in wrinkled scrubs and people holding flowers and crying, maybe from joy but maybe grief. Eventually it reaches her level and Teddy steps out into an unexpected stillness. The corridors are almost empty, and although Teddy can hear the noises of a hospital that she'd been expecting—machines beeping, the gentle hiss of air—it's all at a fraction of the noise of the other floors.

She steps into the corridor and turns left, looking down toward the nurses' station. Nora is in room 108, according to her intel. She'll have to pass the nurses' station in order to get there, and there are two nurses there right now, making quiet conversation as they tap-tap-tap on keyboards. Teddy smooths the waistband of her uniform skirt. If they spot her, if they stop her and ask where she's going and who she is, she probably won't even have to lie. She can just say she's a friend from school, visiting, and they'll see her uniform and know she's telling the truth and maybe they'll even let her continue on her way, even if they aren't supposed to, because what harm could a visit from a boarding school girl do? But the problem isn't whether they'll believe her or not, it's that Teddy doesn't want to be seen at all.

She takes a deep breath. *Wait, wait—*

Someone in a white coat approaches the nurses' station from the opposite side, and just as one of the nurses begins talking to who Teddy assumes is a doctor, the other nurse stands and crosses the corridor, disappearing into a patient room. Teddy doesn't think before she moves, her soft leather flats making barely a noise as she makes it past the nurses' station and then she tucks herself into an alcove, back pressed flat against the wall. There's another elevator here, to her right, and diagonally across from her hiding spot another corridor stretches out, a neat row of glass panels and doors on either side.

Teddy squeezes her hands into fists as she scans the numbers etched on the wall beside each door. There's room 106, 107—

She stops breathing. 108. She doesn't have to read the numbers. She can see Nora from here, sitting up in bed with her eyes fixed on something, and Teddy's insides twist at the sight of her. It's Nora, *her* Nora, alive and beautiful, and for a moment Teddy forgets what she's here for, forgets every single thing that brought the two of them to this place, right now, and she wants to run over and burst through the door and wrap Nora up so tight in her arms that she'll never escape, they'll never be parted again. *I'm sorry,* she'll say, *I'm so sorry for everything,* and Nora will smile up at her and say *There's nothing to be sorry for* and that'll be it, and life will move on and—

"Excuse me." The woman's voice carries clear through the quiet floor. "I'm looking for a patient. Nora McQueen."

Teddy leans out slightly, trying to glimpse whoever is on their way to see Nora. Another doctor, perhaps, or maybe family, some relative of Nora's whom Teddy might have gotten to know one day down the line, if things had gone differently. But she can't see, not without giving herself away entirely, and then Teddy hears the click of heels and presses herself back against the wall. It feels like forever until the footsteps are close, and then the woman rounds the corner and turns away from Teddy, walking down the corridor on her way to Nora's room, and when Teddy sees her face she has to bite her tongue *hard* to stop herself from swearing loudly.

Her mouth fills with a metallic taste. It's the detective who interviewed her, back when it all happened. The one with the weary smile and the sensible pumps, who'd said Teddy wasn't in trouble, who Teddy hadn't ever seen again after that day, except in a clip from the local news where she spoke for maybe ten seconds, before fading out of everyone's consciousness.

But she's here, now. To talk to Nora. *To find out what she knows,* Teddy realizes.

She watches the detective knock on the door, then open it wide.

56

NORA

"NORA MCQUEEN? Hi." The woman steps inside and closes the door behind her. "I'm Detective Ambrose. It's great to see you up."

Nora takes in the detective standing in front of her: white, dark hair pulled into a low bun, dark jeans and a blazer. Her eyes catch Nora off guard: they're a crystal-clear blue, and already watching Nora so intently that she feels a warmth rise in her cheeks.

"Detective." Nora's mom rises from her chair in the corner and holds a hand out for the other woman to shake. "It's been a while."

Nora looks between them, surprised, and then not. Of course her parents have spoken to this detective already. All these things that happened while Nora was gone, all these things she has to catch up on, this blank time when the world moved on without her.

"Detective Wells sends his best," the detective says to her mom. "He was supposed to join us here today, but he was called to an emergency."

"Okay," Nora's mom says, and maybe the detective can't tell but Nora can hear the stress in her mom's voice, higher pitched than normal and shaking. "So it'll just be you talking to Nora?"

"Look, we just want to get a basic statement from Nora about the accident," Detective Ambrose says. "It's more of a formality than anything else. We have a pretty solid idea of the events of that day and—" She stops, looking back over at Nora. "I'm sorry, Nora, I'm talking about you as if you aren't even here. I apologize. But like I was saying, we already have a solid account of that day, based on the statements given by everyone else who was present at the time. We only want to hear in your own words what *you* experienced that day—"

"She can't talk," her mom interrupts. "I thought they would have told you that. She has some damage to her vocal cords. They say it'll heal eventually, but for now she can't talk, only write. I could have sworn I told them to make *sure* you knew that."

Detective Ambrose aims a mild smile in Nora's mom's direction. "I'm aware," she says. "It was more a figure of speech."

She looks back at Nora. "I'll just ask you a couple of questions, and you can write down your answers or anything else you want to say, and then I'll have you write out your account. It doesn't have to be exceptionally detailed. Just, what you can remember, as best you can. Okay?"

Nora swallows. She barely slept last night, and her stomach is in knots. All morning she waited for the knock on the door, waited for this detective who in her mind she'd built into a near mythical figure to arrive, unable to focus on the exercises she'd been given or the news her mom had been reading off her phone or really anything but the prospect of what she knew she had to say today. What she has to do. And now Detective Ambrose is here and waiting and once she does this there will be no undoing it, Nora knows. No going back.

Nora picks up the pencil and a fresh notepad, pressed into her hand earlier today by the nurse Nora likes the most, as if she knew today was monumental. Of course Nora had simply run out of pages in the other notepad, but it felt good to imagine someone doing that for her because they knew she needed it, like there were people on her side. But before she sits back she glances at her mother, and then at Detective Ambrose. She can't do this with her mom in the room.

Detective Ambrose gives Nora a slight nod, and then says, "Mrs. McQueen, would you mind waiting outside?"

Nora's mom looks at her, eyebrows furrowed in concern. When Nora looks at her lately, she can see the lines on her face that weren't there before, and she wonders how many sessions under a laser it'll take to erase the stress she's etched on her mother's skin. "Is that okay?" her mom asks. "Do you want me to go, or stay?"

Nora mouths the word in silence. *Go.* She smiles, so her mom will know it's okay.

Like things will ever be okay after this.

But her mom returns Nora's smile. "I think I'll go get a coffee," she says. "That'll give you a little bit of time. But I'll be right downstairs, Nora, okay? I'll be right there."

"This shouldn't take too long," Detective Ambrose says, and then her mom is gone, the door closing behind her.

Detective Ambrose looks closely at Nora now. "It's just us," she says. "Is there something you wanted to tell me? Something you don't want your parents to know—" She's interrupted by a ringing, and Nora watches the detective pull her phone out and frown at the screen before hitting ignore. "Sorry," she says. "Okay. If there's something you want me to know, just write it—"

The phone rings again, shrill and insistent, and Detective Ambrose sighs as she glances at the screen again. "Damn," she says under her breath, and then takes a step back. "Look, Nora, I have to take this call quickly. But I think whatever it is you want to say might be easier to get out without me hovering over you. Yeah?"

Wait, you're just going to leave me? is what Nora would say if she could get the words out. But instead she nods. Like she has a choice.

"Good. Good," Detective Ambrose says. "I'll be as quick as I can. Whatever you want to tell me, whatever it is you want to say, Nora—I don't want you to worry. We've heard it all from everyone else who was with you that day. You won't be in any trouble. So write it out, and when I get back we'll go over it together. Okay?"

Nora nods again, and Detective Ambrose opens her mouth but then that ringing comes again and she throws her hands up.

"Two minutes," she says as she backs out of the room, and then she's gone, and Nora is alone.

She takes a deep breath as she looks at the blank page in

front of her. *Just write it out.* As easy as that. Like what she has to say isn't going to change everything. What had the detective said? They already have a *solid idea* of what happened that day, based on everyone else's accounts. So that means no one else knows the truth, either, and once Nora does this, it's going to turn everything upside down for everyone.

Not everyone, a voice in her head says, and Nora sits up a little straighter, her shoulders back. No, not everyone. Max is already dead. Max is dead, because of what Teddy did that day, and it doesn't matter how this changes things for everyone else, does it? It only matters that Nora does this for the one person who isn't here anymore, for the one person who loved her enough to dive in after her and try to rescue her. If she doesn't tell the truth, then Teddy will get away with what she did to Nora and to Max, just like she's gotten away with every other shitty thing she's ever done.

Nora exhales, her fingers gripping the pencil tight. Her hands work better now, but it still takes her a painfully long time to carve out the letters. The sharp scratch of the *T,* the loop of the *p.* A defiant jab to end the short sentence.

Nora stares at the words she has finally written. *Teddy pushed me.*

She hears the door open again and relief floods her. Detective Ambrose is back, and the hardest part is over. Now things will—

"Nora?"

Her head snaps up. It's not Detective Ambrose.

No. Standing at the foot of the bed is Teddy.

57

TEDDY

SHE DOESN'T HAVE long, she knows. Teddy saw Nora's mom leave the room, and then only a minute or so after, the detective, phone up to her ear, mouth moving. Teddy had watched from the alcove as a panic gripped her—who was the detective talking to? What had Nora said? Was the detective calling for backup now, sending someone out to Gardner to pick Teddy up, bring her in for questioning? Or had Nora said nothing, was it just a call she'd had to take, some other urgent police business, or maybe a home emergency—childcare, her kids' school calling because one of the little darlings fell and bumped their head?

She hadn't even figured out what she wanted to say to Nora but she had no choice, she had to move—who knew how long Nora would be left alone?

And so she pushed off the wall and hurried over and now

she's here. In Nora's room, face-to-face with Nora finally.

"Nora?" she says again, wonder in her voice. "Oh my god. It's so good to see you. It's so . . ." Her voice fades and Nora doesn't say anything, is just staring at Teddy with wide eyes, like she can't quite believe the place they've found themselves in. Or like she's looking at the girl who tried to kill her. Could be either and there's no way for Teddy to know unless and until Nora speaks, but Teddy wants to have her say first. Maybe if she talks, Nora will understand why she's there, maybe if she says she's sorry enough then Nora will know Teddy didn't mean to do it, or—or—or if Nora doesn't know, if she can't remember at all, then it'll just be like Teddy's saying sorry that Max is gone. Which she is, she really is, and—and *fuck*, she doesn't have enough time to be thinking like this, she has to start talking—

"I'm so sorry," she says, "I'm so sorry everything got so out of control and you got so hurt. I never meant for that to happen, none of us ever meant for things to go this far, did we? We were just being stupid and I wish we could go back and stop ourselves before we even walked up to that cliff. Then you wouldn't be in this bed and Max would . . ." She swallows hard. *Come on, come on, keep going, convince her.* "Then Max would still be alive. I know I fucked up, what I did with her, what we did to you, but it all feels so small and stupid in comparison now, doesn't it? I'd give anything to bring her back for you. It was all so fucked up and god, waiting on the beach while they looked for you for hours—we all thought you were gone but then they pulled you out of the water still alive and this will sound so fucking stupid but it really was like a miracle. And I wish I had come to see you before but I guess I didn't know if anyone would want me around before, and then when we heard you were awake—we only found out yesterday, I don't think they even wanted us to know, but you know how it is at school. Can't keep a secret from all those bitches! So I came as soon as I could, because I wanted to see it was real. I wanted to see you were awake for myself, and I know it all must feel so weird for you right now, after being in a *coma*, I mean—" Teddy laughs, the noise ricocheting around the small room. "It's *insane*, right? A coma! What the fuck! And I guess I just wanted to make sure you know how sorry I am, for everything. But I did try to stop it. I did try to pull you back, and if I'd tried harder maybe I would have done it and you wouldn't have fallen, and Max wouldn't have gone after you, and everything would be different now. I wish things were different, Nora, I really do. Do you believe me? Do you trust me?"

Teddy takes a breath finally, and now it's Nora's turn to speak, and Teddy has made it so easy for her, hasn't she? All she has to do is say yes. *Yes, I believe you, Teddy. Yes, I trust you, Teddy.* Even if it's not true, wouldn't it just be easier for everybody if she said it?

But Nora isn't saying anything, and Teddy searches her face for a sign. Something, anything, that says Nora is on her side. That the story everyone else has called the truth is the same story Nora tells, the same version of events that Nora remembers.

All she can see is Nora's dark eyes, wide and afraid, staring at Teddy as if she's a complete stranger. Like she doesn't know the girl standing there in front of her.

It throws her off for a second. What if Nora really *doesn't* recognize her? What if the reason nobody has told them that Nora woke up is because she's awake, but not really back? What if it's not only the events on the cliff that Nora can't remember, but all that came before it, too? *Including me,* Teddy realizes.

She takes a step toward the bed, her hand reaching out in Nora's direction. "Hey," Teddy says, softer now. "It's me. Teddy. You remember me, right? It's okay if you don't. But just—say something. Anything. Please."

Nora's mouth opens but nothing comes out.

Teddy's close now, close enough to hear Nora's rattled breathing, and she reaches out again, to put her hand on Nora's arm—

But Nora jerks backward before Teddy can touch her, and it's then that Teddy notices that she's holding something in her right hand. Her fingers clutching it so tight that her knuckles are white.

She looks up at Nora, and now she can see the recognition there in Nora's eyes. She knows exactly who Teddy is. And she knows exactly what Teddy did.

A strange kind of calm settles over Teddy. "Nora," she says, eyes darting to her hand. It's a notepad—small, rectangular, and clearly of great importance to Nora. "Show me that."

She doesn't know what may or may not be written in there, or who it was intended for, but Teddy knows she must have it.

Nora's still staring, wide-eyed, and her nostrils flare.

She doesn't say anything. She simply shakes her head.

Teddy glances over her shoulder at the door. How long has

she been in here? How much time has passed since the detective stepped out? How much longer does she have to fix the fucking mess she made?

She looks back at Nora. "Fine," Teddy says, and then she lunges for the notepad.

58

NORA

THERE'S A LONG MOMENT, a silent moment, where everything is suspended and Teddy's lunging at her but hasn't reached her yet, and Nora thinks that if she can move, right now this very second, while everything is slowed, that she might be able to get away. To end this before it begins.

But then Teddy's on her and it's too late. Nora opens her mouth but no sound comes out, of course, and so instead she focuses all her energy on keeping her grip on the notepad. Teddy's hands are on hers, though, grappling with her fingers, trying to find her own hold on the notepad, and then she finds it and a tug-of-war commences. Nora on one side, weakened from so many months in this bed, and Teddy on the other, fueled by the only thing Teddy is ever fueled by, Nora has finally come to understand. She'd known it as soon as she'd seen Teddy there at the foot of the bed, that she wasn't

THE TOURNAMENT

there to see Nora for herself, to make sure she was okay or to say sorry for any of the terrible things she'd done. That's not how Teddy operates, it never has been, and maybe it's Nora's own fault for wanting to believe the best of Teddy, choosing to be on her side back in the beginning, when everybody else believed the rumors that followed her, the stories about the bad things she'd done. Maybe if Nora hadn't been so determined to prove to Max that she didn't need her, she wouldn't have gotten so caught up in Teddy's web, and none of the shit that led to this point would have happened. Teddy wouldn't have gotten bored of Nora, she wouldn't have gone after Max—

Tears sting at her eyes. Max, yes, Max—stubborn, infuriating, doomed Max. The only girl Nora has ever truly loved. That's who she's fighting for now, because no one else will. Nora is the only one who knows what Teddy did. What Teddy *is*. Nora looks up at her and it's like she's seeing the real Teddy for the first time, the mask fully off now, her eyes bright with anger as she yanks at the notepad but Nora goes with it, holding on so desperately, and then Teddy spits out, "Fucking let *go*, Nora, I *need* this," but Nora can't. She makes herself think of Max again but this time it isn't the girl Nora called her best friend, fell in love with. This time it's a bloated body, eyes milky white and skin bruised and blackened. That's Max now, isn't it? Somewhere out in the ocean, or maybe there is no body now, maybe she's completely disintegrated, pulled apart by the waves. But she's only down there because of Teddy, isn't she, and Nora's only too weak to fight back the way she wants because of Teddy, and if she doesn't tell the world who Teddy really is, there's nobody left to do it.

And she summons every ounce of strength she has and pulls back, teeth gritted as she feels paper slicing into her fingers, and for a moment she thinks she might win. She locks eyes with Teddy and a wild, triumphant grin spreads across her face, their strained, panting breaths a soundtrack to their grappling, and she might be weak but she won't let Teddy get away with this.

But then a sudden, sharp pain explodes above her left eye, as if someone took a pickax and stabbed it right through her skull, and Nora feels the smile slip from her mouth a split second before everything blooms to black.

59

TEDDY

TEDDY STUMBLES BACKWARD, the notepad finally in her hands, the absence of Nora's fight leaving Teddy the winner. But that victorious moment is sweet and all too brief, because then Teddy looks at Nora and watches in horror as Nora's eyes glaze over, her pupils blown out wide and black, bottomless pits, and an alarm starts to blare.

"No—shit, shit—*nonono*, Nora—" Teddy floats a hand out in her direction but does nothing more. Her other hand clasps the notepad tight and she doesn't even know what's in there but she had to get it, didn't she? If Nora would have just handed it over, this could have been easy. But now—

Teddy's heart thrums, a relentless pounding, her breath coming fast. "Nora?" she says, as though her words might reach through the blankness on Nora's face and wake her up, somehow. "Can you hear me?"

Nora's body begins to jerk, an uncontrolled, uneven shaking that rattles the bed and all the machines she's still connected to. Teddy's breath catches now, watching the seizure take hold, and fuck *fuck* she didn't mean for this to happen, she didn't mean any of it, she'd only wanted the notebook—

She looks down at the little thing in her hand. Looks at the door. When she stepped into this room she'd known she only had a couple of minutes, and now that time's up. Another alarm starts to chime. Any second now a team of doctors and nurses is going to run in, and if they find Teddy standing there they'll start asking questions, and she's not supposed to be here. No one was ever supposed to know she was here, and so it's time to go, it's time to run.

Teddy risks one more look at Nora. "I'm sorry," she whispers, inaudible over the machines going wild. "I'm really sorry, Nora, I swear I am."

She makes it to the door in two steps, slips out and closes it behind herself, and then walks as fast as she can without running to that same hiding spot from before. In the alcove she presses herself against the wall again as the doctors she had predicted run into Nora's room. From her position she can just about see Nora lying in the bed, but then she's gone, doctors blocking the view as they crowd around the bed and even from here she can feel the frenetic energy, the panic coursing through them and back out into the hall, floating on the air all the way to Teddy.

Everything happens in flashes then. Teddy watches the doctors working on Nora, hears snippets of instructions shouted. She sees the detective walking, then running, hands on her head as she stops outside the room. A blink and Nora's mom is there; another blink and the detective is steering her away, pressing her backward and there's a new alarm wailing, which Teddy quickly understands is not an alarm but the sound of Nora's mother fracturing. She watches the doctors work and work, the rhythmic pumping of shoulders pressing hard toward the bed, the sheen of silver paddles in the air. She watches as they slow, slow, step back, the last figure holding their hands up in the air as the machines hum a still, steady noise. And then the noise is gone. Ended. And she can read the doctor's lips from here.

Time of death.

There's a ringing in Teddy's ears, and for a moment she doesn't quite know what to do with herself.

She feels the notepad in her hand and looks down at it. Looks back up, to the room where Nora is, or was.

Then she turns toward the elevators, slipping away as quietly as she came.

60

TEDDY

WHEN TEDDY WALKS out of the hospital doors, she's surprised by the sun. The heat of it, the brightness making her eyes narrow as she searches for the cab that brought her here, the one she hopes is still waiting. She has to get out of here. Nora is dead and Teddy has to get back to school, back to the world in which she is the hero and nobody yet knows that Nora's gone, just like Max. Although this time was not Teddy's fault, not entirely. *I didn't push her,* she tells herself. *Not this time. I didn't touch her. I just wanted—*

Teddy looks down, at her left hand, almost surprised to see the notepad there firmly in her grasp. Oh. Yes. This is what she wanted. Wanted it so bad she was prepared to fight Nora for it, even though she has no idea what it contains.

She allows her grip to relax, fingers uncurling and blood

flow restoring. Maybe she doesn't need to look inside. There's a trash can fifteen feet away. *I could toss it in there,* Teddy thinks. *Let it go. What does it matter now? Nora can't say anything anymore. Whatever version of that day she remembered doesn't matter anymore. She can't tell anyone that I pushed her, or that I saved her. There's only one version of the truth now. So whatever she wrote in here—it's irrelevant. I don't need to know. It's over.*

Teddy inhales sharply. It *is* over. Nora is dead. Teddy watched her die, she saw her eyes, the way her pupils exploded and she could swear she saw the moment Nora left her body. Like everything that animated her, everything that made her the girl Teddy couldn't help but be magnetized to in the beginning, dissolved into thin air. But in a strange, unnerving way, it doesn't feel that different from before. It's not like Teddy's going to go back to school and miss Nora in the halls. She's gotten used to her absence already, they've all gotten used to Nora not being there with them. Because really, she hasn't been with them, and it's not like she was expelled and sent away to some other school, where they could still call her up and text her and send her pictures they took in the common room, blowing kisses, telling her how much they missed her, hearing her voice in a recorded message back to them. She was in a coma. Unconscious, oblivious to the world changing around her. Oblivious to all her friends and classmates moving on without her.

Teddy looks at the notepad again. She could toss it, *should* toss it maybe, but there might be answers to her questions in there and if she doesn't look, she'll always wonder.

Teddy brings it closer and flips to the first page. There, in shaky but determined letters, is her answer.

Teddy pushed me.

She expects her heart to skip a beat, her breath to catch, the black hole to wake the fuck up and sing for her attention. She expects her body to react in some way but all she feels is numb, a quiet kind of empty that's less painful than it is peaceful. There it is. Nora remembered everything, and—

And she had been about to tell the cops, Teddy realizes. If the detective hadn't stepped out, then she would have read Nora's message. And if Teddy hadn't slipped in when she got the chance, if she'd hung back and simply watched the detective walk back into the room, she'd have read Nora's message, and it would be game over for Teddy. Now she does feel her body react, a shiver running through her at the knowledge she came so close to being caught. But now she has the note, and Nora's dead, and this is where the story ends.

A beeping cuts through her thoughts, and Teddy looks up to see the cab driver gesturing. Right, right—it's time to leave, time to run back to school where she'll pretend like she never left, and pretend like she doesn't know Nora's gone now. She'll pretend, whenever the news reaches them, to be as shocked as the others, and she will really be sad, because it is sad—Nora didn't deserve to die. Neither did Max, but what happened can't be undone, and if Teddy's the last one left standing, then she isn't about to throw her life away.

She runs her thumb over the letters, feeling them there, knowing that Nora must have put all her weight into writing them. The trash can is right there, but something doesn't feel right—it isn't safe enough. If she puts it in there, what's to say someone doesn't dig it out? A slim chance, but a chance nonetheless, and one Teddy cannot take.

She takes a few steps to the side of the entrance. There; she knew she could smell it. A girl, early twenties maybe, with long pink nails and matching hair, stands tucked on the other side of the entrance, a cigarette burning between her lips.

Teddy loosens her limbs as she approaches, shaking her hair over her shoulders. "Hey," she says as she closes in on her target. "Can I bum one?"

The girl exhales a plume of smoke into Teddy's face, looking her up and down for long enough that it starts to become uncomfortable. Teddy's about to say, *Never mind, bitch,* when the girl nods and dips her hand into her pocket. "You know what?" she says. "Take 'em all."

And she presses a half-empty pack and a neon-green lighter into Teddy's outstretched hand. "Wait, are you sure?" Teddy says, even though she's already pulled her hand back, bounty secured. "I don't want to—"

"My doctor's been trying to get me to quit for months," the girl says, and it's only then that Teddy notices the tubes hanging over the V of her shirt, the hospital-issue slippers on her feet. "Someone should get to have fun. Smoke one for me, yeah?"

The girl takes one last deep drag on her cig and then drops it to the ground, leaving it smoldering there as she walks off and back into the hospital.

Alone, Teddy tucks the cigarettes into her waistband and

turns the lighter over. That it was so easy feels like this is what she's meant to do.

She flips the notepad open again and tears out the page with Nora's writing on it. Two, three flicks of the lighter and the flame bursts to life, shimmering. Teddy brings it to the edge of the paper and watches as it catches instantly, the flame eating up the page, the red-hot line swallowing the words until only Teddy's name remains and then that is gone in an instant, too, Nora's accusation turned to ashes. And as it burns, it's like she's burning away her own knowledge of the act. With Nora dead and this note gone, there's no one but herself to say what really happened that day on the cliff. And she long ago decided that she liked the other truth more, the story all the other girls told. So why not make that the truth, for good? It won't be pretending, like it was before, when Teddy knew deep down what she'd done but let the part of her that wanted to protect herself from that knowledge rule. Now she can forget what she did entirely. If she's the only one left, then she should be out there living her life, making the most of everything that Nora and Max won't get to. They both had such plans, and no, it isn't fair that they don't get to follow through, to go out into the wide world beyond Gardner and make good choices and bad ones, too, break hearts and have theirs broken, live so much that one day they think back on Gardner and laugh at how important that small period of time seemed in the moment—it isn't fair at all. But the tournament was never about fighting fair, was it?

Teddy lets go at the last second, hissing as the flame kisses her skin, and the remaining corner floats up before it disappears. She watches the air for a second, then tips her face up to the sun and closes her eyes, the light searing red on the insides of her eyelids. It's a beautiful day.

She opens her eyes and walks over to the cab. Gets in, and when they start to move, she doesn't look back.

ACKNOWLEDGMENTS

This was a tough one! Oh my god! But we made it!

Thank you to Kate Prosswimmer, Andrenae Jones, and everyone at McElderry Books.

Thank you to Suzie Townsend, Sophia Ramos, and Olivia Coleman at New Leaf.

Thank you to *Law and Order,* because knowing I could watch an episode at the end of a drafting session was honestly the only thing getting me through that long winter.

Thank you to my family.

Thank you to Janet McNally for all the podcast episodes.

Thank you to Maggie Horne and Rory Power. Sometimes I just say "I'm going to send 10k and I don't need you to actually read it, I just need you to reply with 'Yes it's good, I think it's A Book' so that I can keep going" and they do exactly that.

Thank you to every mean girl in media, and in real life, too.